UNION STATION

Books by David Downing

The John Russell Series
Zoo Station
Silesian Station
Stettin Station
Potsdam Station
Lehrter Station
Masaryk Station
Wedding Station

The Jack McColl Series
Jack of Spies
One Man's Flag
Lenin's Roller Coaster
The Dark Clouds Shining

Other Books
The Red Eagles
Diary of a Dead Man on Leave

UNION STATION

DAVID DOWNING

Soho Press, Inc.
227 W 17th Street
New York, NY 10011

Library of Congress Cataloging-in-Publication Data

Names: Downing, David, author.
Title: Union station / David Downing.
Description: New York, NY : Soho Crime, [2024] | Series: The John Russell
WWII spy thrillers ; 8
Identifiers: LCCN 2023025096

ISBN 978-1-64129-357-0
eISBN 978-1-64129-358-7

Subjects: LCSH: Russell, John (Fictitious character)—Fiction. |
Los Angeles (Calif.)—History—20th century—Fiction. | LCGFT: Thrillers
(Fiction) | Spy fiction. | Historical fiction. | Novels.
Classification: LCC PR6054.O868 U55 2024 | DDC 823'.914—dc23/eng/20230526
LC record available at https://lccn.loc.gov/2023025096

Printed in the United States of America

10 9 8 7 6 5 4 3 2 1

For the father, mother and brother with whom I grew up, in what now seems a far kinder Britain

UNION
STATION

Abbreviations

BOB: The Berlin Operations (or Operating) Base of US intelligence, which by 1953 was a wholly CIA concern

CPSU: The Communist Party of the Soviet Union

DDR: Deutsche Demokratische Republik, known in the West as East Germany

DEFA: Deutsche Film-Aktiengesellschaft–East German film studio sponsored by the Soviets in the first few years after the war

GRU: Soviet military intelligence

MfS: East German security police, aka the Stasi

MGB: The Soviet Ministry of Security from 1946 to '53, successor to the NKD and precursor of the KGB

RIAS: "Radio in the American Sector" radio station

SED: Sozialistische Einheitspartei Deutschlands (Socialist Unity Party), formed in 1946 by a merging of the communist KPD and socialist SPD in the Soviet sector of occupied Germany. After 1950 East Germany's ruling party

Prelude

March 10, 1953

"So which magazine are *you* from?" Stephen Brabason asked.
Not, John Russell thought, that the actor really cared. He just wanted to emphasise how many other interviewers were paying court to him that day.

"I work for a couple of newspapers," Russell told him. "One in England, one in Germany."

"Oh," the actor said, sounding almost interested. "Do you speak German?"

"I do. I lived there for a time. Immediately after the war," he added, because letting on that he'd also been there for most of the inter-war years rarely elicited a positive response. "And I know you have a lot of fans in that country," he said ingratiatingly.

Brabason let slip the smile which had launched quite a clutch of B movies, and, of late, a smattering of As. Russell was at a loss as to how or why. Having watched the latest, a sub-Hitchcock murder mystery in which Brabason played the second male lead and heroine's saviour, Russell knew the man was only capable of playing one character, albeit in a stunning variety of costumes. And having now met the man, it was the clear that the character in question was Brabason's idealised version of himself.

The actor was finishing work on a romantic weepie called *Her Decision*, which centred on a couple taking in the heroine's dead sister's children after she and her husband have both been struck by the same bolt of lightning. Russell, invited to a prerelease screening, had followed Effi's advice and kept an eye out for the decision in the title, and been suitably impressed by the accuracy of her prediction that he would wait in vain. "So what drew you to *Her Decision*?" he asked Brabason. Apart from the money and the fact that his agent had urged him to do so.

The actor thought about his reply, which said something for his professionalism, if not the film.

"Was it the chance to work with Meredith Kissing?" Russell asked. Any on-screen chemistry between the two was notable by its absence, but that, according to Russell's actress wife, Effi, was because both leads were more interested in partners of their own gender. A common enough Hollywood occurrence, but not one that received much of an airing in the press.

"Well, she's an absolute sweetheart, of course. And we do work well together."

"Would you say the story is about redemption?" Russell asked. "Risible redemption" had been Effi's verdict when he outlined the film's plot to her.

"Well, yes, I can see that," Brabason agreed, reaching for his cigarettes and offering the packet.

Russell declined. "Your character feels partly responsible," he suggested helpfully.

"For his nephew's death, yes. And it forces him to go the extra mile." The actor offered up his smile again, this time through a suggestive cloud of smoke.

Russell remembered Effi and their adoptive daughter, Rosa, imagining the conversation in the writers' room as they came up with the ludicrous denouement, and stifled a laugh. Get a grip, he told himself, not for the first time in his short career as a Hollywood reporter. "What was your own childhood like?" he asked.

The actor had a two-drag think. "Fine," he said tentatively. "Normal," he added with rather more enthusiasm. "We weren't poor, but we certainly weren't rich. Just average Joes in an average town. To answer your earlier question, I think that's why I'm drawn to characters like Martin in *Her Decision*. They're the back-bone of America."

Russell wondered how many average American Joes became the pirates, trapeze artists, and brain surgeons Brabason had played, but saw no point in asking. How could he get anything that his readers might find interesting out of this man? "How did you get to Hollywood?" he asked, for want of anything better.

"By bus," Brabason said, with what actually looked like a genuine smile. He tapped ash into the ashtray. "I'd done some acting in high school, and the drama teacher knew someone who knew someone out here and I was invited to come for a screen test. So I sat on a Greyhound for two days, and when I got here I passed the audition."

The man was good-looking, Russell conceded, though less so in the flesh than on screen. And older.

"The parts were small to start with, but they got bigger and bigger. And I like to think I improved as an actor."

"And do you think your films have got better?" Russell asked, knowing it was a loaded question. The man hadn't yet made one that anyone would remember. His entire output ranged between poor and mediocre.

"In what way?" Brabason asked.

"Well, the better an actor gets, the more he needs the scope that complex characters and psychological themes provide."

"More complex than *Her Decision*, you mean," the actor said, surprising Russell. "We can't all be Laurence Olivier. Or, God help us, Marlon Brando. And lots of people like simple stories with straightforward characters who just get on with the job."

"They do," Russell agreed. "So can I ask you about some of your other films and characters?"

He did so, and the actor's answers and anecdotes, though rarely enlightening, were soon copious enough to fill out a thousand-word piece. "And the future?" Russell asked in conclusion. "Any new projects your fans would like to hear about?"

There was one, a war movie about a bunch of GIs island-hopping their way across the Pacific. It was an ensemble piece, according to Brabason, and less gung ho than the usual fare. "It's actually a damn good script," the actor said, as if he couldn't quite believe it.

Russell thanked him for his time, and made his way out through the Culver Studios complex. "Nice, isn't he?" the blonde receptionist said as he handed in his pass.

Walking across the car lot, Russell had to admit that Brabason had been hard to dislike. If his physical and mental attributes were hardly exceptional, his luck certainly had been, and who could blame him for that? Effi might not agree, but making bad movies wasn't a crime.

The sun was still losing out to the clouds, the temperature noticeably higher than it had been an hour ago, but still cool by LA standards. For Russell, who'd lived all but the last three years of his life in more temperate climates, it felt extremely comfortable. Rain was expected later that day but would probably be over before he had time to raise his convertible's roof.

He let himself into the blue Frazer and worked his way out of the lot and onto Washington Boulevard, thinking ahead to lunch. His favourite diner was out on the coastal highway, a drive that would have felt long in Berlin but here seemed almost inconsequential. A walk on the beach before he ate would make the food taste even better.

He drove west on Washington, then north through Venice and Santa Monica and onto the road that followed the coast. The beaches to his left were sparsely populated, and it was hard to pick out a horizon between the dull grey sea and sky. He passed the Casa del Mar Hotel, outside which some hopeful starlet in a shiny dress was having her picture taken by a posse of cameramen, and was soon on the open highway, joining a two-way procession of huge gleaming trucks spewing out dark exhaust. The traffic thinned out a little after the intersection with Sunset, and a few minutes later he was pulling into the diner's lot. The smell of bacon almost sucked him in, but three years in Los Angeles had taught him that lengthy walks were the only way for his body to survive a way of life built around motoring.

He crossed the highway and walked down through an area of shaded picnic tables to the sandy beach. The tide was neither in nor out; the only people in sight were around two hundred yards away, walking eastward with a couple of dogs. Russell started off in the other direction. Even under such a dull sky, it felt like a beautiful spot: on one side the ocean stretching into the distance, on the other the wooded mountains rising behind the highway and its narrow strip of houses and small businesses.

As he walked, he went back over the interview. It would make for an adequate article, but nothing more—he would never win acclaim as a film critic. During his life in Germany he had always liked the cinema, but—as he now realised—the films on offer in Berlin had covered a much broader spectrum than those on show in LA. He had grown up with everything from art films to escapist trash and had learned that any genre could be handled badly or well. Here in Hollywood the palette seemed much more restricted, much more focused on appealing to the lowest common denominator. And according to Effi, things were getting worse rather than better: actresses who'd flourished with noir were being returned to their prewar boxes; more and more writers were relying on self-censorship to avoid falling foul of the dreaded McCarthy.

And then there was the context. Russell and his son, Paul, had often enjoyed a Western in prewar Berlin, but watching them here in LA it was harder to get past the role they seemed to play in American life, reinforcing myths and outright lies about the country's history.

When Effi and he had decided three years earlier that she should accept a film offer from a Hollywood studio, they and their adopted daughter had come out to LA for what they assumed was only a few weeks' well-paid work for his wife and an extended vacation for himself and Rosa. But one film had led to another, and a school was found for a reluctant Rosa, which brought on her English in leaps and bounds. Not wanting to sit around all day admiring the newly refurbished Hollywood sign, and thinking it might be fun to interview Hollywood stars and attend lavish receptions, Russell had asked Solly Bernstein—his long-term agent in London, and the man for whom his son and daughter-in-law now worked—to find him work as a Hollywood/California correspondent. Solly had duly obliged, fixing Russell up with the two papers he'd mentioned to Brabason.

It had been fun for a while, but after six months or so the vacuousness at the heart of it all had begun to wear on him. After more than thirty years of wars, revolutions, and other horrors, he found it impossible to take Hollywood seriously. A job was a job, but he wasn't learning anything useful, and that, he realised, was important to him. It wasn't as if they needed the paltry money he was making—Effi was earning more than enough for all of them, and then some.

Early in 1952 she had stepped into the part of the housekeeper in *Please, Dad*, a popular radio show about a widower and his two children and had quickly become an audience favourite. There were already rumours that the show was destined for television in the season starting that fall, and Effi, unlike the current children and neighbours, looked the right age for the part. By the end of that year the TV version had been running for three months, and she was fast becoming a household name among the increasing number of US citizens who owned a TV set.

Rosa meanwhile had grown more accustomed to American life and discovered more than a few things she liked about it: the sunshine, the food, the sea, new friends. If she was missing Europe she was hiding it well.

And all of them, Russell knew, felt safer here. Five years had passed since his showdown with Stalin's enforcer Lavrenti Beria, but it still felt like dangerously unfinished business. Barring a life on the moon, he, Effi, and Rosa were about as far away from Moscow and Beria as they could get, and that was how he liked it.

He should count his blessings, Russell thought, because there were certainly plenty of them. Probably more than he deserved.

A particularly noisy truck rumbled past, making him realise how accustomed he'd grown to the steady stream of traffic a hundred yards to his right. Above it, skimming the mountain slope, two large birds were soaring and swooping in search of prey. To his left, a couple of small white boats were sailing close to shore, and out beyond them what looked like a sizable freighter was heading out into the Pacific. Way up ahead, someone was walking towards him. Behind him there were only empty sands.

Someone on one of the white boats was shouting something to someone in the other, barely audible above the wash of the incoming tide. The trucks were still lumbering by. He was surrounded by people, but only as extras, as part of the scenery. Out of reach.

"In a lonely place," Russell murmured to himself. A film he and Effi had seen and loved during their first few months in LA. Bogie at his best. And the wonderful Gloria Grahame.

The approaching walker was now about three hundred yards away. A man, it looked like, and one wearing a longish coat. A raincoat perhaps—they were not uncommon. It seemed too bulky for that, though, and overcoats really were unusual, even in LA's so-called winter. There was something about the figure that made Russell think of Russia.

He resisted the sudden urge to turn and run. He'd been thinking about Beria, and here he was imagining that this might be the Soviet leader's agent, when there was no reason on earth why his enemy should have decided, after five long years, that killing his blackmailer had become a safe thing to do.

Almost in spite of himself, Russell was still walking, and the gap between him and the now-obvious overcoat had reduced to fifty yards. He could make out the man's face under his hat; the Latin colouring and thin lips brought Jacques Mornard to mind, but Trotsky's assassin was still in a Mexican prison. Or was he?

Twenty yards. The man had both hands in his overcoat pockets, and there was a faint smile on his face, a sheen of moisture above the upper lip. He wasn't Hispanic, Russell realised, as the right hand emerged from its pocket with something shiny, and his own stomach dropped through the floor.

The "something shiny" was a long-stemmed pipe. "Good morning," the stranger said cheerily with an English accent.

"Good morning," Russell echoed, feeling the cold sweat on his back.

The man was already past him.

Turning his head, Russell saw the pipe slipped back into its pocket. Had his imaginary Soviet agent been as anxious as he had? Had pulling the pipe out been a nervous reaction?

And only a Brit would wear a thick overcoat on a day like this.

Once his non-assassin was a decent distance away, Russell turned back in his wake towards the diner. He felt decidedly shaky, and more than a little foolish, but was inclined to forgive himself. This particular apparition had not been sent to kill him, but the enemy was real and certainly had no shortage of agents, as Russell knew only too well.

His own decade-long career in espionage had begun on the first day of 1939, when Soviet agent Yevgeny Shchepkin had recruited him to write articles for the Soviet press extolling the plusses of Nazism. It had, he hoped, ended in late 1948, when he and Shchepkin had secured their release from their perilous roles as double-double-agents for both the Soviets and the Americans with the help of a film showing Stalin's enforcer Lavrenti Beria engaged in rape and murder. After hiding their copies of the film, they had threatened Beria with exposure if anyone close to them died a suspicious death. His acceptance of the deal had cut their ties with the Soviets, and shorn of these, they were no use to the Americans. Russell was free, and Shchepkin would have been, too, if he hadn't already been terminally ill.

And so far the deal had held. Russell had destroyed his copy of the film at Shchepkin's suggestion, but the Russian's copy was still presumably wherever he had left it. Russell could see no reason why Beria would take the risk of reneging on their bargain. But people made mistakes, let emotion override reason. People went mad, got terminally ill. Such a possibility, and the fear that went with it, might seem fainter with each passing year, but it was still there at the back of Russell's mind, as the last fifteen minutes had made abundantly clear. And maybe Stalin's death the previous week would shake things up in ways that Russell couldn't anticipate. Beria might be stepping into Stalin's shoes at this very moment and imagining himself beyond accountability for even the worst of crimes.

Only Beria's death would truly free them, Russell thought, as he patiently waited for a gap in the traffic to re-cross the highway. Though perhaps they'd need to ram a stake through his heart as well.

The diner's lot had thinned out a little in the lull between breakfast and lunch. One reason Russell liked the place was the shelf of newspapers just inside the door, which reminded him of Berlin coffee houses and provided, on this occasion, a choice between the *LA Times* and *Examiner*. He took the *Times*, not because he preferred its right-wing opinions, but because it reflected the views of the current city establishment, and thereby offered a surer indicator of the way things were going, at least in business and politics.

There were a couple of empty booths on the city side, which sometimes boasted a distant view of downtown, but today only offered a highway and beach fading into greyness. The menu was happily unchanged, and as he pondered the choice between meat loaf, turkey club, and the all-day breakfast, the waitress arrived with the first instalment of his bottomless coffee. She looked like a teenager, and probably was one. "The club sandwich," he decided.

"Chips or fries?"

"Fries."

She almost skipped back towards the kitchen, stopping to top up a couple of coffees en route.

Russell skimmed his way through the paper, finding as usual that violence in varying forms haunted most of the stories. The numbing procession of traffic deaths felt like a minor war, and few days passed without several people succumbing to a knife or a gun. The Korean War carried on exacting its daily toll of deaths, though the respective numbers—thousands on the communist side for every ten in the United Nations—seemed more like propaganda than reporting. More unusually, but well in tune with the times, a schoolteacher suspended for hitting a pupil who "refused to look him in the eye" had just been reinstated.

The anti-communist theme was not restricted to the Korean War coverage. On the contrary, it turned up all over the place, from the latest doings of Senator McCarthy and the House Un-American Activities Committee to a city scheme for putting school textbooks on public display before they were board-approved. This would allow Brabason's "Average Joes" to decide whether the tomes in question were subversive. One of the books involved was *The Robin Hood Stories*, and Russell found himself wondering whether it was possible to conceive of Errol Flynn as a socialist.

Rather like McCarthy, the latest rabies scare was also refusing to disappear. Three dogs and one cat had joined the ten other pets who had tested positive and were presumably now on death row. Or more likely already ashes. Russell congratulated himself and Effi on resisting Rosa's plea for a dog.

In what he supposed was better news, "a noted nutrition expert" at the Harvard University School of Public Health had urged all Americans to eat steaks and ice cream for breakfast, and tiny but frequent meals through the rest of the day. Russell thought that a few hours off-campus might rid the "expert" of his delusion that everyone could afford to eat steak, at breakfast or any other time.

His own meal arrived, the piled-high sandwich held together by toothpicks. Even jettisoning the third layer of bread it was enormous, but he ploughed bravely on, pleasure holding the guilt at bay.

Over a refilled coffee he reluctantly went back to the paper, and the news that might actually affect him. Yesterday had seen Stalin's funeral in Moscow. There was a lengthy article describing the ceremony, one unusually free of ideological insults, as if even the *LA Times* recognised that someone of real significance had passed away. A psychopathic shit to be sure, but no one could doubt his influence. He had played a not insignificant role in making and then defending the most thoroughgoing revolution of the century, and then played a pivotal role in betraying most of what it stood for. He had caused or decreed the death of millions of innocent Soviet citizens, and after a shockingly incompetent start had efficiently deployed his own implacable brutality to save the world from the Nazis.

Of late Stalin had reportedly become less predictable, and Russell guessed that the Politburo colleagues he'd left behind were probably wetting themselves with relief. They weren't saying so, of course. According to the *Times*, Georgi Malenkov, now first among equals if the order of speaking was anything to go by, was still hailing "our teacher and leader, the greatest genius of human-ity." He was also suggesting a meeting with Eisenhower, which Stalin had neglected to do, and saying he considered it his "sacred duty" to continue a "peace policy" that the genius had apparently been keen on. Beria had spoken next, which felt ominous to Russell, and had also stressed how devoted he was to peace. So, surprise surprise, was third-placed Molotov.

On the very next page they were all there in photographs, carrying the coffin, lining the tomb, saying their pieces. Russell stared long and hard at Beria, now looking considerably fatter but every bit as vicious as he had when projected onto their Berlin apartment wall four years earlier. It wasn't over, he thought, without knowing why.

Looking up he saw sundry Americans sat in the booths and at the counter, talking, eating, and drinking, going about their lives. Moscow was closer than they thought, and not in the way Joe McCarthy meant. Russell didn't think Beria would have any more time for Robin Hoods than the senator did.

GERHARD STRÖHM WOKE UP IN his Moscow hotel bed feeling decidedly hungover. He had never been much of a drinker, and hadn't imbibed a great deal the previous evening, but was still willing to bet that he felt worse than his fellow German delegates, all of whom had happily kept pace with their Soviet hosts. Party leader Walter Ulbricht and state president Otto Grotwöhl had been knocking them back like there was no tomorrow, and *Neues Deutschland* editor Rudolf Herrnstadt hadn't been far behind. At the end of the evening only Ströhm and Wilhelm Zaisser, the Minister of State Security, had managed to navigate their way through the elevator doors at the first attempt.

He rubbed his eyes and lay there listening to the sounds of vehicles down on Gorky Street. It was almost eight, but he felt reluctant to get up.

His mind went back to the previous day. The funeral, the huge crowds, a city close to bursting with incoherent emotions.

Ströhm was still trying to make sense of his own feelings. Like almost everyone else he had found himself weeping when the coffin was lowered into the mausoleum. The sense of loss was immense, overpowering, and the fact that it also seemed ludicrous made no difference at all. Like the old Bolsheviks brought to trial in the thirties, despite all they knew and guessed, they all shared a mad yearning to believe. They knew the size of the hole Stalin had left, and maybe they'd been weeping because deep down they knew that neither filling that hole nor failing to do so would make things any better. For both better and worse, Stalin was irreplaceable.

And here they all were, stuck on this tragic ship, which had sailed with such great intentions, but which now, despite all denials, was not only utterly lost but lacking any compass or map. In circumstances such as these, what could even the best–intentioned new helmsman do?

He shook his head, hoping to shake out the pessimism, and went to run a bath. At least the water was hot at the National—a Greek comrade he had spoken to the previous day had lamented the lack of such at the Metropol. And the shortage of pillows.

Ten minutes later Ströhm was on his way down to breakfast. Sequestered in one corner of the ornate dining room like a gang busy planning a robbery, the leaders of the SED—the East German Socialist Unity Party—were already well into breakfast, sifting through the slices of dubious cold meat. Herrnstadt and Zaisser nodded welcomes, but Ulbricht and Grotwöhl ignored him. As expected, all his colleagues looked fresher than he did, which, considering their levels of consumption the night before, said a lot about what they were used to. People said that living in Karlshorst—the Berlin suburb where the Soviets had planted their conqueror's colony—was just like living in Russia, and its privileged German occupants had certainly adopted the drinking culture.

Ströhm spread some toast with Georgian cherry jam and looked around the room. Though undoubtedly elegant, it reeked of the past. There was nothing modern about Moscow, the only things pointing you towards the future were the idealised workers on their huge billboards. The Revolution was living in the past. Literally so.

He found himself wishing he was back in his Friedrichshain apartment with Annaliese, Markus, and Insa. Then again, if it hadn't been for them, he probably wouldn't have been here in Moscow, because over the last five years his wife and children had been his only persistent source of hope. Just by being there, they had provided the strength and reasons he needed to keep on trying; left to his own devices he might have just given up.

It was 7:30 A.M. in Berlin, and he could picture the scene there, Annaliese fussing around as she made sure that Markus and Insa had all they needed for their day at the Party crèche, before dropping them off and walking across to the State Hospital and her job as a ward sister.

"What are *you* smiling at?" Ulbricht asked him out of the blue, as if the buried Stalin was still quite capable of detecting one man's lack of respect.

"I was thinking how enormous the crowds were yesterday," Ströhm said innocently. "Few leaders could expect such an out-pouring of love when they die."

"True," Ulbricht said curtly, and Ströhm saw Herrnstadt repress a smile. All of them knew there'd be dancing in the street if Ulbricht dropped dead.

Half an hour later they were all on a bus, heading out through the city to visit a collective farm. Ströhm suspected that the trip had been arranged to keep them occupied ahead of the Soviet-satellite meetings that afternoon, and in such a way that the different delegations were kept apart, allowing them no chance to gang up on their mutual masters. With the Bolshoi shut until evening, a collective farm or model factory were the only obvious options.

If the view from the window was any guide, the route had not been chosen with a desire to impress—Moscow's suburbs and the surrounding countryside still looked desperately poor. Ströhm suspected that the "tourists"—those foreign delegations who were not yet in power—would be seeing Russia's better side, and why not? Why not let them keep their illusions if it made them more determined to succeed at home? So few in the West had any idea how much the Soviet Union had lost in the war, so why gift them a true picture of how long the recovery was taking?

Despite being under several inches of snow, the collective farm did look clean, efficient, and well-organised. Tractors gleamed and peasants smiled, the latter keen to explain how their life had been transformed. There was a table replete with snacks, and, God forbid, tumblers of vodka. Ströhm hadn't yet seen one of the new collective farms back home, but those who had were given to sadly shaking their heads.

The return drive through a picturesque snow shower was pleasant, but for Ulbricht's snoring in the front seat, which gave the bus's groaning engine a run for its money. Ströhm fantasised about enlisting the others to carry their leader off the bus and dump him in a snowdrift.

Back in the city, another meal was waiting, and that was barely finished when the limousine arrived to carry four of them—Herrnstadt, as the editor of the Party's paper *Neues Deutschland*, was meeting with his Soviet counterparts—the short distance to the Kremlin. Once inside they found themselves in a queue of delegations, each parked in a room off a long corridor, and periodically shuffled forward like a game of musical chairs. Their own appointment was for 2:30 P.M., but it soon became apparent that the wait would last several hours.

They went through their briefing notes, but not with any sense that they needed to. The four of them were there to listen, not to put forward ideas of their own. Any speaking would be purely reactive and would probably involve explaining why last time's instructions had not been followed with either more rigour or more flexibility.

Ströhm set about putting himself in a positive frame of mind. He told himself that was the least he could do, given that his country's future was at stake. He told himself that he needed to give the Soviets more credit, to recognise their real achievements made over the last eight years, despite the devastation wrought by his own countrymen in the war. Almost everywhere west of the Volga they'd more or less had to start from scratch, rebuilding the factories, the dams, the cities they'd raised with such titanic effort before the war. Economically, they'd had an impossible job, and yet they'd somehow made a fist of it. Credit where credit was due.

Politically . . . well, that was a different matter. He could see that there'd been no real alternative to "the Party knows best"— a planned economy was bound to inhibit free discussion. And the Party often had known best. What democratic government would or could have taken a snap decision to move industries employing thousands of people five hundred miles to the east, out of reach of Hitler's tanks? And it was not as if the Party was trampling on a democratic tradition. It was still, in Ströhm's most wishful thoughts, trying to make one possible.

But he was not a Russian. The CPSU might know best when it came to the Soviet Union, but he had never believed it knew best when it came to Germany. For almost a decade Moscow's stooges—himself included—had wielded some sort of power in eastern Germany, but only at the discretion of the Soviets. And in that time things had slowly gone from bad to worse. Bringing communism to eastern Germany had always been a near-impossible task after the Red Army had raped its way through Berlin, and that was the start. It wasn't long before looting the country for reparations and creating "necessary sacrifices" like the lethal Wismut uranium facility had turned widespread resentment into utter loathing.

The easiest option was to tell yourself there was nothing you could really do, and just enjoy the not inconsiderable perks. Many had taken that path, but not all. There were still those like himself, at all levels of the Party, who were prepared to try to make the best of what would probably be a once-in-a-lifetime shot at fulfilling their political dreams. But there weren't that many of them anymore, and with each new shortage, each new stink of corruption, there were fewer people prepared to give them a hearing.

Maybe Stalin's death would loosen things up and give the different national parties the chance to try different ways. Ströhm wasn't privy to what went on in the minds of the Soviet leaders, but the noises they were making seemed encouraging, and he would love to believe that over the next few months some transformative vision would emerge from a new collective leadership.

Or not. For the moment, here they all were, queuing up to receive their marks for recent performance. A gold star for some, black marks for others. A grudging "could do better" for the Poles, an acerbic "last chance to pull up your socks" for the Hungarians.

Ströhm sighed and stared at the obligatory portraits of Lenin and Stalin. Lenin had made mistakes, but Ströhm still liked to think he'd been a decent man. It was hard to think that about Stalin. A necessary one, perhaps, but necessary to whom? And for what?

It was almost five before they were finally ushered into the seat of power, a nondescript committee room almost entirely filled by a long table and its dozen chairs. The air was full of smoke, and it took Ströhm a few seconds to identify Georgy Malenkov, Lavrenti Beria, Nikolai Bulganin, and Nikita Khrushchev sitting in a row on the far side of the table. Molotov, they were told, was ill. Ströhm had met Malenkov and Bulganin on several occasions, Beria on only a few, which had suited him just fine. The man gave him the creeps. He had never met Khrushchev but had heard he was blunt to the point of rudeness, and a good deal smarter than he liked to appear.

There was no sign of a stenographer, but the room was presumably equipped with hidden recording devices.

The DDR delegation took up the facing seats, Ulbricht and Grötewohl flanked by Zaisser and Ströhm, who, as the SED Central Committee's liaison with its CPSU equivalent, was the most junior member of the delegation.

The "discussion" lasted about twenty-five minutes, which seemed rather short when the future of German socialism was at stake, but at least it offered some hope. Malenkov did most of the talking, occasionally deferring to Nikolai Bulganin on matters of detail. Khrushchev looked vaguely belligerent, Beria slightly amused, but neither said much. The gist of the CPSU's general "advice," as gradually became apparent, was for the SED to take its foot off the accelerator pedal. "Across the board," Beria insisted, mixing metaphors.

Whether this "advice" constituted a real change of direction on the new Soviet leadership's part, or just a pause to consider the alternatives to the current orthodoxy, was not clear to Ströhm. Or, he suspected, to the Soviets themselves.

There was one specific instruction. The previous year, the principal border between West Germany and the DDR had been hardened, making it almost impossible for would-be emigrants to cross. This had predictably funnelled those who wanted out towards the only border left open, the one between the Soviet and Allied sectors in Berlin. So Ulbricht had asked the Soviets if they could close that border too, and a couple of months before Stalin's death they had given their provisional approval. Which they were now rescinding. The outflow of skills and talent would continue.

The Germans had their orders.

The limousine was gone, leaving the four of them to trudge back across Red Square and down the slope to the National. Nobody said a word, but Ulbricht and Grötewohl looked the most unhappy, which probably had to be good news.

There were still four hours before their night train left from the Belorussian Station, and Ströhm was pleased to find his Soviet counterpart Oleg Mironov waiting in the lobby. Mironov spent most of his time in Karlshorst, ostensibly attached to one of the Soviet intelligence apparats, and the two of them had met regularly since Ströhm had secured his current position. A guarded friendship had gradually formed as the two men discovered they harboured not dissimilar hopes for the future.

"Let's take a walk," Mironov suggested, and Ströhm readily accepted. "The river, I think," the Russian decided, once they were back on the sidewalk. "My father used to say that times of change were times to take shelter," Mironov remarked, "but the open air seems safer to me. Not that I'm planning to reveal any secrets," he added with a smile.

"And is this a time of change?" Ströhm asked, staring up at the Kremlin wall to his right.

"Oh I think so. It has to be. I mean some things are going well—everyone knows we'll soon have a hydrogen bomb—but the problems are mounting, particularly in the satellites. I rather suspect that Rudolf Slánský will be the first of many."

The Czech party leader, having lost favour with both the Soviets and his own Politburo, had been tortured into making a transparently false confession and hanged the previous December. "Ulbricht?" Ströhm asked.

"I'd say he's on borrowed time. He's too rigid, too stuck in the past. He learnt all his tricks under Stalin, and I doubt he could learn any new ones."

Saint Basil's Cathedral was behind them now, the river a hundred yards ahead. "How is your father?" Ströhm asked, thinking it politic to change the subject.

"Mmm. I went to see him a few days ago. He's cantankerous as ever, and getting a bit funny in the head, I think. He is almost eighty, so it's not surprising, but if he does go completely gaga, I'm a bit apprehensive about what he might come out with."

"Orlaya didn't make the trip?"

"No. My wife prefers Karlhorst." Mironov grimaced. "I can never wait to get back home myself," he added. "I'll miss you, of course," he added with a grin. "But there's something corrosive about lording it up in someone else's country. No matter how well-intentioned you might be."

Ströhm let that go. "Do you think your new leadership will solve a few problems?" he asked.

"Who knows? I wouldn't be in their shoes. I mean, it's all so devilishly difficult. Our economy is almost sclerotic—the heart keeps pumping, but there's too many blocked arteries. We can't get rid of them because they're intrinsic to any integrated planning system, but if we don't find a way to get around or through them the blood will just stop flowing. It already has in some sectors. We've done wonders with steel and construction and power, but agriculture is a total mess. And people have more sophisticated wants than they used to. Our soldiers in Berlin— forgive me for bringing them up, but while they were doing terrible things to your women they were inside thousands of houses, and they saw how Germans lived, all the things they had. It was like a storybook to them, and when they came home they spread the story. We're proud that we can match the West in technology and culture, but until we can get rid of food queues and turn out a decent washing machine for every Soviet family, we'll never get people to believe that the future is ours."

Remembering how pleased Annaliese had been with hers, Ströhm could hardly disagree.

"This year's going to be a real rollercoaster ride," Mironov went on, with almost indecent enthusiasm. He looked around, making sure their stretch of towpath was empty. "Stalin's gone. And yes, there are feelings of sadness and loss. But there's also a sense of relief—haven't you felt it?"

"I have."

"And relief comes with expectations. The new leadership is going to have to do something different. They can't shut the doors any tighter, so they'll have to open them up. The tricky part is knowing by how much—open them too wide and everything will fall apart. Another thing my dad once said to me: the hardest thing to do in a heavy wind is keep a door half-open." He looked at Ströhm. "And that's exactly what we have to do."

THE MEETING BROKE UP, THE final *final* changes having been inserted in the script. They would run through it on the sound stage next morning, whereupon the star Eddie Franklin would doubtless insist on those few last-minute revisions he always dubbed "the final nails."

If, unlike some of her fellow cast-members, Effi Koenen had experienced little difficulty in making the leap from radio to TV, that was probably because her experience as an actor in pre- and postwar Germany had been so wide. She had done everything from burlesque to movies, from live theatre to musicals. When she had worked on the radio incarnation of *Please, Dad*, she'd been known for acting at the mike rather than simply speaking her lines, not because she wanted to impress anyone, but because that was what live theatre had taught her to do. Having also made twenty-plus films, she understood why actors who'd only worked in that medium found it hard to get things right in the very limited number of takes a live studio recording allowed.

Effi knew she was good in the part, but whether the part was making the best of her talents wasn't so clear. Housekeeper Anna—"Mrs. Luddwitz"—with her no-nonsense willingness to say what she felt in any given situation, was a role she could probably play in her sleep. But working on the show was enjoyable, and though she found its star somewhat lacking as a human being, she had to admit he made a good comedy foil. And the two children they'd brought in for the TV series were an absolute delight. Effi had expected a pair of spoilt Hollywood brats, like the two who'd been in the radio show, and who, much to everyone's relief, had been deemed to look too old when the television version was first considered.

"You happy with it?" Beth Sharman asked, falling into step beside her.

The thirty-ish writer had joined the two who worked on the radio version when the TV series was given the go-ahead and was now Effi's best friend on the set. "One of your best, I think."

"We'll be up there with Lucy yet." *I Love Lucy*, which was made in the same studio, had conquered America over the past eighteen months. Lucy herself had even sent McCarthy packing the previous September.

"Sorry to burst your bubble," Effi said, pleased with her use of the English phrase. After three years in America she was virtually fluent, and her normal slight German accent was less noticeable than the one she put on for Mrs. Luddwitz, but there were always stray new phrases to learn. "Lucy and Desi are timeless," she told Beth. "You've heard of Everyman? Well, they're Every-Marriage. They could spin it out forever. Whereas our little set-up is too specific for global conquest."

"You're probably right. We're doing okay, though."

They had reached the outside world, which looked as grey as it had that morning.

"Are you going straight home?" Beth asked.

"I'm picking Rosa up from school in an hour or so. Would you like to get a coffee somewhere? Or even a drink."

"Now you're talking."

Effi's car was fortuitously placed on the end of a row—getting in and out of parking spaces had never been a forte. She'd been driving on and off for more than a decade but still didn't like it that much. LA was better than Berlin—the streets were wider, the drivers mostly slower, and her car had automatic transmission—but she only drove when she needed to, never for pleasure. "Where shall we go?" she asked, once they were side by side on the Buick's bench seat.

"How about the Blue Angel?"

"Good choice."

The mile drive passed without incident. Effi liked the bar on Fairfax for two reasons. One was the palm-filled garden at the back, which today lacked the sunlight it needed; the other was an unusually wide selection of German wines, which a then-doting patron had introduced when Von Stroheim and Dietrich teamed up in Hollywood more than twenty years before.

The bar was almost empty ahead of the post-work rush. "A glass of Riesling, please," Effi answered Beth's query. The writer ordered herself a Manhattan, and the two of them took a table overlooking the garden of sun-hungry palms, their fronds swaying in the breeze.

"You ever smoke?" Beth asked, lighting one of their sponsor's products.

"Only in movies. The first time I was asked to, I coughed so much the audience would have thought I had consumption. I was playing a woman with two sons in the *Hitlerjugend*—the

Hitler Youth—and they thought I should have habits the boys could disapprove of. Standard Goebbels fare."

Beth laughed, but then grew serious. "I've been wanting to ask. Didn't that bother you? Tell me to mind my own business if you want to."

Effi took a sip of wine to consider. "At the time? Not really. Not at first, anyway. The films were such obvious propaganda that few of us were able to take them seriously. Later, yes, some regrets. When I agreed to take one role, John and I had one of our few real falling-outs. He was right—I should have turned it down—but then he was making the same compromises as a journalist that I was as an actor. They were difficult times, and we quickly got over it. I don't say this as an excuse, but I think it's hard for Americans to imagine what it was like in Germany then. You dared to put up a fight, and that was the last your friends might see of you. People just disappeared, and the next thing you knew they'd died in a camp. Always of pneumonia, though by the time they told you that the body was already burnt or buried." She looked out of the window. "Seems unreal here, doesn't it. And of course it is. It wasn't like HUAC putting you on a blacklist and stopping you from working. I know that's terrible, but at least no one dies. Or hardly anyone," she added, thinking of Mady Christians, the Austrian actress whose early death from a cerebral haemorrhage had followed relentless Committee harassment.

Beth made a face. "You're right that few people die, but any sense of national sanity might. HUAC often feels like a bad joke—I mean, I keep asking myself who could actually believe this shit. But they do, and it keeps getting closer to home."

"Laura?" Effi asked. Laura Fullagar played the housekeeper next door, whose over-the-fence conversations with Mrs. Luddwitz produced some of the show's better moments.

Beth sighed. "There are rumours. Believable ones. She makes no secret of what she thinks of McCarthy."

"Neither do you. Neither do I."

"But I was never a party member and couldn't give them a single name of anyone who was. I'm assuming—hoping—that you could say the same."

"I was never in a party, full stop. I wasn't interested in politics. John was in the KPD—the German communist party—in the twenties, but he left long before I met him. I certainly couldn't tell HUAC anything, but then I wouldn't if I could."

"Easy to say."

"I suppose so," Effi conceded. And easier if you were forty-four and other things were now more important than your career, she thought. "Are you certain that Laura was in the Party?"

"No, but I'd be surprised if she wasn't. Before the war she was very close to Dick Moran, and he was named in the *Red Channels* pamphlet."

"Hell."

Beth drained her glass. "It's like some terrible disease," she said. "You know it's around, and you know that some people are going to catch it, and you just hope it won't be you or one of your friends."

"And on that note," Effi said, checking her watch, "I'd better be going. Can I drop you anywhere?"

"No, thanks. I think I'll walk over to Crossroads of the World and buy some new clothes while I still have a salary. I'll see you tomorrow," she said, as they reached the car.

Effi drove up Fairfax and took a right onto Santa Monica Boulevard. Rosa's school was about two miles from their rented house on Melrose, and often she chose to walk, but Effi was pleased when she didn't. Almost seventeen, her adoptive daughter would soon be of an age to strike out on her own, and Effi was keen to make every moment count.

Driving alone she found it easier to concentrate, which according to John was proof of an open heart. When they'd first come to

LA, expecting only to stay a few months, she and John had hired a governess-type woman to keep up Rosa's education, but once it was clear that they'd be there for at least a year, a place had been found for the girl in one of the Hollywood schools which mostly catered for the children of the town's entertainment industry. Serving such a rich clientele, these schools all had good teachers and facilities, but this particular institution came with the added attraction of an enthusiastic arts mistress. Given Rosa's proclivity for turning the world into drawings, this was more or less essential.

Effi was early—these days she almost always was. After decades of others complaining about her lack of punctuality, she seemed to have gone to the other extreme. As everyone said, there was nothing like children for turning your life upside-down.

Rosa had found school a bit difficult at first, but then adapted faster than Effi had dared to hope for. Her English had improved dramatically, and was now as good, if not better, than Effi's— Russell sometimes joked she spoke his own language better than he did after thirty years in Germany. She made a few friends, and if most of them seemed to be fellow outsiders, then that was probably not unusual for a school in Tinseltown. Her artistic talents, already formidable, only grew more extraordinary, and when the art teacher left to have a family, Rosa discovered an evening class which seemed, unusually for LA, to welcome people from all parts of the city's diverse population. Perhaps living under Hitler had made Effi more sensitive to racial prejudice than most, but LA left a lot to be desired in that department, and in odd moments Effi had found herself reminded of Berlin during the Nazis' first few years in power. Rosa's instincts, she thought, were much the same—her latest interest was Negro music, which white Americans called "race music," as if they'd been spared the burden of belonging to one themselves.

Rosa, Effi thought, was all right. Despite a personal history distressing enough to break most children, she had exceeded all her parents' expectations. She was kind and clever and immensely talented. She had always seemed at ease with herself and was increasingly at ease with others. Rosa was fine, Effi told herself again. It was John she should be worrying about.

He had enjoyed the novelty of their first year in Hollywood, and endured the second because he thought it would be the last. But then both she and Rosa had prospered, Effi professionally and their daughter as a person, and John had put their interests above his own. She had loved him for that but was enough of a realist to know that there might be a price. These last few months she'd been reminded of the last winter before the war, when he'd been reduced to writing about pets and postage stamps as Europe slowly caught fire.

That hadn't ended well. Ten years of ad hoc espionage, of playing Russian Roulette with Nazis, Brits, Americans and, of course, the Soviets. He needed to be reporting on—or at least writing about—things that interested and concerned him. Something he could get his teeth into. Given that the conditions of his residency forbade him from taking paid employment here in the US, that wouldn't be easy. But surely not impossible. She should be encouraging him to get on with the book he'd already been commissioned to write, before some young disciple of Shchepkin's waylaid him in a bar with a new siren song he couldn't resist.

A bell was ringing inside the school, and only a few seconds had passed when the kids began flooding out. Rosa appeared after several minutes, walking alone, looking out for the car. She waved and smiled when she saw it, and patiently waited for a gap in the traffic to cross the street.

Several friends had remarked how much Rosa resembled Effi, some of them knowing the girl was adopted, others not. It was true that they shared a similar mouth and colouring and were both raven-haired and slimly built. But Rosa's eyes were darker, and her movements less graceful than Effi's—it was as if, in John's words, a lack of physical fluidity was the price she was still paying for her survival.

"Hi, Mom," she said in an exaggerated American accent as she climbed into the car.

"Oh, pulleeez!" Effi retorted with a grin.

"Are we going straight home?" Rosa asked in her normal voice.

"That was the plan. I was actually going to cook."

Rosa made a face. "Cook what? Couldn't we go out for Chinese?"

The idea was not unwelcome. And John would be happy. "I suppose so," she said. "But we can't eat out all the time."

"Why not? If we can't afford it, who can?"

"It's not good for us?" Effi said automatically. She was sure it wasn't, though she wasn't sure why. She remembered John's ex-brother-in-law, Thomas, telling his daughter, Charlotte, that people should learn how to look after themselves before they let others do it for them. It had been over a Sunday lunch in Dahlem before the war, and Lotte was well into her twenties by now. Effi wondered if she enjoyed cooking.

They found John already at home, making the most of a late emerging sun on their back porch. Like half of Hollywood he was reading John Steinbeck's *East of Eden*, but unlike most he was less than impressed. "All the characters are either pure evil or close to perfect," he had said when Effi asked him how he was finding it. "Does that sound realistic? And after three hundred pages I still haven't met anyone with a black face. Does that sound like America?"

"It sounds like Melrose Avenue," Rosa said pointedly.

"*Touché*," Russell conceded with a grin. "How was school?"

"Mostly boring."

"We were thinking Chinese," Effi interjected.

"Never a bad idea," Russell agreed. "Are we driving to Chinatown or walking round to Wong's?"

"A walk will do us good."

"Okay."

It was getting dark by the time they arrived at the restaurant, streaks of orange in a still-cloudy western sky. The food at Wong's was not the best, but it was good enough, and the staff were friendly. They ordered most of their usual dishes, plus the obligatory new one that Rosa insisted on. The eggplant concoction she picked that evening was better than many previous choices.

"So how was Stephen Brabason?" Effi asked as they walked slowly back. Rosa as usual was walking slightly ahead of them, looking this way and that like a reconnaissance scout.

"Nicer than I expected," Russell said. "Pity he's such a hopeless actor."

"Eddie Franklin's opposite," Effi remarked.

"Is he giving you trouble?"

"No, not really. But we—the show—may have a problem." Switching into German, she repeated what Beth had told her about Laura Fullagar.

"That's a shame," Russell said, following her lead. "For her and the show. She's good."

"Yes. And she has a child to support on her own. Her husband was killed in the war."

Rosa had dropped back alongside them. "I really don't get it," she said. "What are they all so upset about? Do they think there's some dark plot to destroy the American way of life? Or are they expecting the Russians to sweep across the ocean and turn them into slaves? I mean, really. How stupid can they be?"

"They are," Effi said.

"What they're upset about—the people funding and running this scare campaign—is the prospect of losing markets in Europe and Asia," Russell said. "Which they will rightly see as a curb on their freedom, and wrongly claim is a curb on everyone else's."

"That does make more sense," Rosa said thoughtfully.

But not something you should say in school, Effi stopped herself from saying. Rosa was usually as uninterested in politics as her own younger self had been, and Effi was pleased to see this wasn't from lack of caring.

"The land of the free," Russell noted wryly. "It's probably a good thing I can't work here. At least they can't take my job away."

Effi squeezed his arm. "Speaking of work, how is your book research going?"

EIGHT WEEKS LATER

Several Dead in Plovdiv

The breeze blowing in through the streetcar top-lights was taking the edge off the heat, but it was only nine in the morning and Russell's shirt was already clinging to his back. According to his paper it was going to be hotter than yesterday, which even the locals had considered outrageous for early May.

He was on his way downtown, having decided that the parking problems associated with driving were better avoided. For one thing, finding a space was often absurdly difficult; for another, he had no idea how long his appointment at US Immigration would be. The wait would probably be horrendous, and who knew how picky Uncle Sam's minions would be feeling in weather like this?

As an added bonus, the streetcars reminded him of Berlin.

He got off at the final stop, and after a couple of wrong turns found the offices he'd visited three years before just off Broadway. Ten minutes early for his appointment at 10 A.M., he had time to go through the important stuff in his paper: the Stars had beaten the Beavers twice in Portland the previous day, and his horoscope advised him to "disregard" the "topsy-turvy conditions" which surrounded him. Rather like the "diminutive brunette model" in Santa Monica, who had spent seven hours ignoring pleas to come down from her perch atop a 140-foot water tower.

His name was called earlier than he expected, and the lesser tidings of politics, wars, and individual catastrophes would have to wait. The delightfully air-conditioned eighth-floor office he was ushered into had a north-facing view of distant hills and mountains but was only otherwise distinguished by the number of filing cabinets on display, each no doubt crammed with records.

His was most likely the one on the desk, which a forty-ish man in a crisp beige suit was busy sifting through. "Please sit down, Mr. Russell," the official said without lifting his eyes. These were hidden by wire-framed glasses, the upper lip by a thin brown moustache. His last barber had been either a sadist or criminally incompetent.

The name on the desk was Clarence D. McClellan.

"You arrived in the United States on May thirty-first, 1950," the official announced, a hint of surprise in his tone. "You were designated a special case and given three years probationary residence. Which expires"—he glanced at his desk calendar—"exactly four weeks from today."

"I'm aware of that," Russell said, in as friendly a tone as he could manage. He realised he was still seething over the casual confiscation three years ago of the American passport he had risked life and limb to secure in 1939, on grounds that they hadn't even bothered to fully explain. He had considered a legal challenge to the decision, but friends' advice and his own sober realisation of just how big a can of worms he might be opening had dissuaded him. That, and his belief that the three years on offer would be more than enough. He hadn't counted on Effi's success or Rosa adapting so well.

"Are you also aware that your visa was conditional on your not taking paid employment during your stay?" McClellan asked.

"Stay" sounded ominously temporary. Maybe it was the similarity of situation, but McClellan reminded him of a certain Herr Mechnig, who had called Russell in to his Berlin office for an almost identical interview in early 1933. "I am," he answered the

American's question. "And presumably you know that I made one mistake. I was invited—begged, almost—to write a piece for the *Examiner* about conditions in Germany after the airlift—the editor was worried that his readers lacked any understanding of the true situation in Europe. I foolishly accepted. The moment I realised I'd made a mistake, I donated my earnings to charity."

"Which one?"

"The Orphans' Trust," Russell told him. That had been Effi's suggestion: "Who would deport someone who gave money to orphans?" she'd said.

"Mmm. Eschewing all political activity was another condition of your continued residence."

"And I have done so."

"Yes? Do you recognise the names Brad Selowski, Barbara Havering, and Dennis Palermo?"

"I do."

"They're friends of yours, yes?"

"Acquaintances would be more accurate. Ones I haven't seen for a more than a year."

"Because they've all been blacklisted?"

"That might well be why they're not as socially gregarious as they used to be, but as far as I know none of them has been charged with a criminal offence. Like I said, they were no more than acquaintances, and I certainly never joined any of them in anything which could reasonably be described as political activity."

"Are you an acquaintance of Laura Fullagar?"

"I think I've met her once or twice. As I'm sure you know, she works on the same television show as my wife."

"She's never been to your house?"

"Not to my knowledge."

"According to our information, you and your wife accompanied Barbara Havering and her husband to a Weavers concert in

January 1952," McLellan went on, before pursing his lips in disapproval.

Russell repressed the desire to laugh. "We did. I like Pete
Seeger's songs. I like him, come to that, but then I've always been
a sucker for people who stand up for what they believe in."

"You like his politics."

"That's not what I said, but even if I did, going to hear him
sing would hardly be engaging in political activity."

"Perhaps not, but you can see why we might be concerned."

"Not really. I watch John Wayne movies and Groucho Marx's
TV show. But I'd lay odds their politics are different."

"I expect you're going to tell me you're fond of apple pie."

"I wasn't, but I am." Though the Germans do it better, he
thought but didn't say.

"You're not in touch with any of your old Intelligence buddies?"

Buddies? Russell thought, inwardly shaking his head. He
assumed McClellan was talking about American "buddies." The
Germans would all be dead, and probably most of the Soviets.
"No," he said.

"You don't miss it?" McClellan asked almost wistfully.

Perhaps the man had been in the OSS during the war or had
just got excited reading Russell's file. "Not in the slightest," he
answered.

McClellan shrugged. "Personally, I'd find living the life we
allow you less than inspiring," he said provocatively.

"Then set me free," Russell said wryly.

"The only way I can do that is by cancelling your visa," McClellan retorted. He sat back, as if considering that option.

Surely they wouldn't kick him out, Russell thought. Not with
the fan mail Effi was getting. And the man had nothing to justify such a punitive step, not unless Congress had decreed that
going to see the Weavers was akin to crapping on the American

flag. It would just be spite. Then again, McCarthy was spiteful-ness incarnate.

"Why would you do that, when the only real victims would be my wife and daughter?" Russell asked with rather more force than was probably wise.

"It wouldn't upset you on your own account then?" McClellan responded.

"I would miss the baseball," Russell conceded, hoping it would be taken as a peace offering.

"Really?"

"And the take-out food."

McClellan shook his head, a ghost of a smile hovering on his lips. "I'll give you another two years" was his verdict, which Russell supposed might have been worse. "You don't come across as someone who belongs here," was the official's surprisingly nuanced parting shot. "But neither do you feel like a threat to national security, so for now I'm giving you the benefit of the doubt. The same conditions still apply, and we will of course be monitoring your compliance." He rose to offer a hand, which proved as cold as his eyes. Russell shook it briefly and headed for the elevator.

Back out in the heat, Russell wiped the fresh sweat from his brow and took the short walk to an Italian deli he knew on Main. This lacked air conditioning but boasted enough fans to propel the *Hindenburg*. Russell picked a spot underneath one and took off the jacket he'd worn to look smart for his inquisition. His coffee arrived, brought by a waitress who looked like a slum child from Naples but spoke like a born Angeleno.

Russell reran the interview in his head. He knew he shouldn't have been surprised by how much McClellan had known about his life, but he was nevertheless. The blacklisted names really were only acquaintances—he and Effi hadn't met any of them more than three or four times, yet those meetings had ended up in someone's records. Whose? The Immigration department's? The FBI's? The CIA's? Had he been followed, or just been seen with others who had? And how were they intending to monitor his compliance? Should he be checking their house for listening devices and hidden cameras, listening for a tell-tale click when he picked up the telephone?

True, McClellan had not known everything. He hadn't mentioned the deal Russell had signed the previous year with a New York publisher, probably thanks to the ruse the latter had suggested, that the actual contract should be with the firm's British subsidiary, and the advance paid into a London bank account. The subject matter—American firms who had continued doing business with their German partners once the two countries were at war—would have certainly sounded alarm bells in McClellan's brain. While it was possible he had simply chosen not to mention this, Russell couldn't think of a reason why.

McClellan hadn't brought up Russell's new job either. The German newspaper he worked for had suggested a series of articles on how American democracy works, and his English paper had also liked the idea. The LA mayoral campaign was already underway, and looked likely to be interesting, but after some thought Russell had decided that the fight for a Congressional seat would mean more to European readers, and as luck had it, a special election was due that fall in the San Fernando Valley's 29th District. He had interviews booked that week with all four candidates.

Given what McClellan did know, it was hard to believe his sources had missed out on this journalistic assignment. Perhaps he was waiting to see what Russell wrote.

He would worry about that later. For the moment it felt good to be working on something that interested and stretched him. Even reading the newspaper seemed less depressing when you felt involved—no matter how tangentially—in what was going on.

But only slightly less depressing. The war in Korea was all over today's edition: a new round of intense fighting, reports of Communist atrocities, an article about brainwashing. The only thing missing was proof that Fu Manchu was behind it all.

The local stories were also full of violence: the LAPD had killed another man in custody, a prison warden had been beaten up, a youth had been knifed. A man was on trial for poisoning his wife, and the carnage on the highways continued. At least the brunette on the water tower hadn't jumped.

Was this the topsy-turvy world he was supposed to be disregarding? Easier said than done.

Of more immediate concern to Russell, there was a long and thoughtful article by a UCLA professor on the political situation in Moscow. The author was not expecting "personal rivalries" in the new Soviet leadership to go beyond "bureaucratic infighting," and didn't think there would be a "repetition of the nearly ruinous struggle for power that followed Lenin's death."

Thoughtful didn't mean right. The notion that an era of harmony would ensue as the Soviets picked up the pieces of Stalin's legacy seemed far-fetched to Russell. And if, as he expected, a life-and-death struggle was already underway, he needed to know how Beria would come out of it. Dead would be best, some inescapable hellhole in the frozen north just about sufficient.

Russell sighed, moved on to the sports pages, and read the game reports from Portland. The Hollywood Stars—the Twinks to their fans—seemed to be getting better as the season progressed, and he was looking forward to attending a game at Gilmore Field when the team came home. Russell had liked cricket as a boy, and baseball seemed like a sped-up version, with most of the virtues and few of the defects. It was the one American obsession he had really taken to, one of the few things that made him think that he could, in McClellan's phrase, "belong here."

Which brought him back to his eighth-floor interview. The entire proceedings had been based on the notion that McClellan had this great bounty to either offer or refuse—life in America. But if it wasn't for Effi and Rosa, would he even consider that as a permanent prospect?

It was true he felt safer thousands of miles from Moscow than he had in Berlin. And where else would he—they—go? England was the obvious candidate. He missed his son, and a grandchild was on the way. True, the Labour government he had so admired had now been booted out, but its Conservative successor was showing no signs of rushing to turn the clock back. If he wanted to live where people were treated in a civilised manner, what would be better than a country with a free national health service?

But he also missed Thomas, who still lived in Berlin, and if they did leave LA, then Effi would miss her sister, Zarah, who had only recently moved there, after several less-than-ecstatic years in Iowa. The war had certainly spread his family far and wide. Wherever they were, they'd be missing someone.

JOHN HAD TOLD HER THAT Laura Fullagar's name had come up at his immigration interview on Monday, but two days later Effi still hadn't passed that information on to the woman in question. The rumours about her castmate's communist past had been circulating for a couple of months, but nothing had happened, and she and the others who worked with Laura had begun daring to hope that it was only a false alarm. "Was the man just fishing?" Effi had asked Russell, and he had agreed that this was more than possible. "If they really have something on her, you'd think the committee would have called her in by now."

Which had sounded reassuring.

"On the other hand," he'd added, "maybe they're still busy getting their ducks in a row."

Which had not.

Yesterday there had been no obvious opportunity to have the conversation, or so she had told herself. Dress rehearsal day was always hectic, but she could have found a moment. The trouble was, she was still undecided. Being warned might help Laura, but it was hard to see how. It was not as if she could leap aboard a time machine and change her past. The news might just scare her into doing something unwise.

But saying nothing also felt wrong, partly because Effi didn't trust her reasons for doing so. Was she more concerned about her own situation than Laura's? Was it just a fearful reluctance to get involved, to keep her head down until the problem went away?

Another echo of the Nazis, Effi thought. Lately there seemed a lot of them.

She could ask for Beth's opinion, but that would just be passing the buck. No, she thought, climbing out of her Buick in the studio lot, today she would find the time to take Laura somewhere private and tell her.

The best-laid plans. The members of the cast and the crew she found drinking coffee in the cafeteria all looked like they'd had a shock, and many were casting surreptitious glances at the table in the corner where a tearful Laura was talking to Beth.

Effi joined them. "What's happened?" she asked.

"The producer and sponsor have called Laura in for a meeting at noon," Beth told her.

Two hours before we record the show, was Effi's first thought. One which, she immediately realised with more than a little shame, was more professional than sympathetic. "Did they give any reason?"

"No."

"They didn't need to," Laura said. "Everyone knows what they want."

"Names," Effi murmured.

"Eventually, yes," Laura said, suddenly getting to her feet. "Look, I need some time to think. By myself. Don't worry," she said, managing a smile. "I won't run off and leave you short-handed."

It felt as if the whole cafeteria watched her hurry out.

"Should we . . ." Beth asked.

"No," Effi decided. "The producers must be mad, setting up a meeting just before we record. Surely they're not thinking of taking her off the show at two hours' notice?"

"But if they tell her they're pulling the plug right after, will she feel able to do the show?" Beth completed the thought.

A copy of yesterday's *LA Times* was on the table, open at the page which carried the report of bandleader Artie Shaw's testimony before HUAC in New York City. Effi had read it at John's suggestion and been appalled by the way Shaw, an intelligent man by any standards, had abased himself before the committee, crying his eyes out as he admitted to being a dupe of the communists. As a result, he would work again, but whether he'd ever get past the humiliation was another matter.

"She was reading that when I joined her," Beth said.

"No wonder she was crying."

"WELL, I THINK WE'RE DONE here," Oleg Mironov said. "Do you feel like a walk?"

"Why not?" Gerhard Ströhm agreed. Every couple of weeks for more than a year, he and Mironov had spent an hour or so in the latter's Karlshorst office sharing the information that their respective parties wanted shared, but lately, under the guise of a stroll, they had gone on to exchange their more personal opinions where no one could overhear them. Both men had sought and received official permission to do this from their superiors after arguing that the other man would probably be more forthcoming in such circumstances.

Outside the sky was grey, and the leafy suburb where most of Ströhm's senior SED colleagues lived cheek-by-jowl with the Soviet MGB looked even more depressing than usual. It was strange, Ströhm thought, how houses built for the privileged few looked so much uglier when occupied by those who claimed to speak for the people.

It was a ten-minute drive to their usual walk in the Plänterwald, and, given that the driver and Mironov's security guard were almost certainly MGB, the two of them always spent the journey staring out of their respective back seat windows.

Ströhm was hoping for good news from his Soviet colleague, albeit without being sure anymore what such tidings might look like. March and April had been strange months, offering up hopes and new difficulties in bewildering profusion, and bringing forth political behaviours that often seemed perilously schizophrenic. Sometimes it seemed as if the Soviet leadership had decided on being nice to everyone, releasing prisoners, purging police, trying to placate the West with a "peace offensive." With, moreover, Stalin's éminence grise Lavrenti Beria leading the charge. At other times, it was hard to tell the new bosses from the old one.

Meanwhile, in Ströhm's own country things were going from bad to worse. The serious food shortages in March had accelerated the human haemorrhage to the West, creating further problems for its already malfunctioning economy, and though the Soviets had responded positively to Ulbricht's desperate pleas for assistance, the German leader had more or less ignored the conditions attached, pressing on with the hard-left policies which was causing most of their difficulties.

The problem, Ströhm thought as they drove across the Spree, was that nothing seemed clear or certain. If the Soviets couldn't decide what they were doing, how could the satellites? The leadership in Moscow was presumably split, with some favouring the old way, some a more moderate approach. But which would come out on top? There was no way of knowing, particularly when the ones you expected to go one way went another. Ströhm found it confusing enough; for men like Walter Ulbricht, who had spent their whole careers sucking up to the person in charge, not knowing who that was had to be the ultimate nightmare. No wonder his political course was veering all over the place.

Ströhm's reluctant conclusion was that he and his moderate colleagues badly needed Moscow's help. The Kremlin had to either bring Ulbricht firmly to heel, or, better still, get rid of him and Grotewöhl, and put the more liberal Zaisser and Herrnstadt in their places.

The car was approaching its usual parking place where the road left the riverbank. The Planterwald's square kilometre of forest had been a popular spot in prewar days, but its current position on the western edge of the Soviet sector had left it out on a geopolitical limb. Even on the sunniest days the number of walkers was low, and today the place seemed virtually uninhabited.

With the sky looking even darker, both took a furled umbrella before starting down their customary path, Mironov's security guard a discreet thirty meters behind them.

"Have you heard about Plovdiv?" Mironov asked.

"The town in Bulgaria?"

"The tobacco workers came out on strike. On Saturday. They confronted the local militia and forced them to retreat."

"Why did they come out?"

Mironov shook his head. "Who knows? Lousy conditions, I expect. I'm sure they had their reasons, but it's not important. What's important is that they did. Since Stalin died the Party has been afraid that something like this might happen, and now it has. All those who favour keeping things tightly controlled will feel justified."

Ströhm wanted to know what had happened in Plovdiv since Saturday.

"The situation was resolved," Mironov said. "I don't have details, but there were deaths. Stones were thrown at Party leaders, and the militia had to open fire. Which of course was unfortunate, but . . ." He sighed noisily. "And now it's here they're most worried about."

"Here," Ströhm echoed, though he wasn't exactly surprised.

"Beria has received another lengthy report on the situation here, and it makes terrible reading."

"Have you seen it?"

"Not the final draft, but I was asked for my opinion on inter-Party relations."

"Which could be better."

"Indeed, but how?

They turned onto another path while Ströhm was wondering how to say what he wanted to. "Let me be frank," he began almost apologetically. "You often make us feel like children. Which is fair enough—you are the senior Party, the one with the experience, the parents. And children should listen to their parents. But . . ."

"But?"

Ströhm hesitated. He knew this conversation would be reported, and that it might get back to Ulbricht. "But when parents are distracted," he said slowly, "and the children are given no guidance, they tend to act up."

"You think Ulbricht will ignore our instructions."

"You have to be clear that you're not merely offering comradely advice."

"Or he'll do something rash."

"Not overtly. He'll push at limits, occasionally glancing back over his shoulder at mummy and daddy."

"Who are too distracted to notice," Mironov said dryly. "So, assuming they'll be that way for a while, what can be done?"

"Someone has to tell them that something really bad is going to happen if they let things go on the way they are. Something that won't be in either the children's or the parents' interest. Of course, if Beria's report is as bad as you think it is, they may have already realised as much."

"And the trouble in Plovdiv should be another wake-up call," Mironov said hopefully.

As they reached the path beside the Spree it started to rain, and after unfurling their umbrellas, they began walking south back to the car, looking, Ströhm imagined, like two middle-aged businessmen who'd met in the forest to cut an illicit deal.

"We're just messengers," Mironov said, almost smugly. "The people who used to get shot when they brought bad news."

"I like the past tense," Ströhm told him.

On the ride back towards Karlshorst, he asked to be dropped off at the S-Bahn station.

"Why aren't you using your car?" Mironov asked him.

"Because these days a Party official riding down Stalinallee in a rich man's car looks almost like a provocation," Ströhm told him.

"Take another route."

"I like trains," Ströhm retorted as he reached for the door handle. "And I'll talk to you soon."

There was a fifteen-minute wait for an inbound train, but the journey itself took less than ten, and the No.4 tram ride up Warschauer and Bersarin not many more. There was no one at home when he reached their spacious apartment on Tilsiter Strasse, but Annaliese's shift at the nearby Friedrichshain Hospital had ended a while ago, and picking up the children at the crèche never took very long.

When they all arrived a few minutes later his wife looked exhausted, his children far too awake, but he felt his heart lift just the same. Which was of course wonderful, even if it did remind him how much it needed lifting lately. "Bad day?" he asked.

She forced a smile, but it didn't last long. "I lost a couple of patients I liked. One was the lovely old man I told you about.

Eberhard. A political dinosaur, of course—the way he talked about Comrade Walter—well, I was afraid someone would report him. But he had a wonderful heart, and he never complained, despite all the pain he was in. He was so looking forward to joining his wife in heaven. I shall miss him."

It was Ströhm's turn to smile. Sometimes he thought people should all be given religion when they reached seventy. By then they were too old to do much damage, and their final years would be less depressing.

"How was your meeting with Mironov?" Annaliese asked.

Ströhm shrugged. "We agree about the risks, but there's not a lot we can do. Beria's as likely to listen to Mironov as Ulbricht is to me." He found himself recalling Mironov's father's quip about half-open doors. The SED would either have to throw theirs open or slam it shut, and if it was going to be the latter, he wanted no part of it.

"You looked exhausted," he said. "Let me cook."

She shook her head. "Putting the kids to bed will be more tiring," she said. "Why don't you do that? Read them a chapter of *Anne auf Green Gables*."

He did so. They had borrowed the book from Thomas Schade's house a few months before—his daughter, Lotte, had loved it as a child. It was too old for Insa, and probably Markus as well, but either his voice or Anne's infectious good nature usually succeeded in lulling them off to sleep. As he sat there beside them for a few more minutes, Ströhm tried to imagine living in a time and place like that and found that the leap was beyond him.

After he and Annaliese had eaten they listened to the wireless: a classical concert on the local Russian station and then a news programme on the American RIAS. The latter, not surprisingly, was full of people explaining why they had chosen to abandon their work and homes in the East.

He went back to the music.

"My patients have a lot of time to think," Annaliese said. "And today one of them worked out that if there's no change in the current emigration rate, the last person will leave sometime in November 1962."

"That's not funny."

"No, it's tragic."

He looked at her, but she didn't say anymore. His wife had always been refreshingly combative, but these days she seemed more inclined to keep herself in check.

Until recently, he had always thought she felt as conflicted as he did. Her experiences in the brutal, US-run Rheinberg POW camp directly after the war had left her with an enduring distrust of Americans, which had in turn made her more inclined to give the Soviets the benefit of any available doubt. He knew that she had always felt as uncomfortable with Party perks and privileges as he had, but they had struck a bargain between them. Until things got appreciably better, they would accept rewards whose refusal would look like rebellion, but only in exchange for lives committed to the service of others, in her case her patients, in his the East German people.

Had she lost faith in that bargain? Everyone knew that things were not getting better, but had she decided that they never would?

If she wanted them to leave, would she say so?

He looked across at her, eyes closed as she listened to the music, and felt the familiar tug of love.

Was he scared to ask because he feared the answer?

AS HE DROVE WEST ON Wilshire that Wednesday, Russell thought about the interviews in prospect and Los Angeles politics in general, which were currently dominated by the imminent mayoral election. This was only three weeks away, the choice between incumbent Fletcher Bowron and challenger Norris Poulson, both Republicans, but from different wings of the party. Bowron had been in office for fifteen years, and as the overseer of the city's dramatic growth during that time, had done a passable job without overly endearing himself. Poulson had been a US congressman for most of the last decade, backing McCarthy's anti-communist crusade and generally supporting the causes of the Republican right.

The most prominent bone of contention in this election was public housing, and one project in particular, which Bowron and his cohorts at City Hall had set in motion in a rundown area just north of downtown called Chavez Ravine. As far as Russell could see, Bowron's consideration for the less well-off was real enough, but compromised by being highly paternalistic. The new public housing in Chavez Ravine would only be built once the homes of even poorer people had been bulldozed. Poulson had no problem with the latter but had much grander plans for the confiscated land than homes for the less well-off.

The housing row was symptomatic of the wider difference between the ideological views of the two candidates, both here in LA and across the country. On the one side was the New Deal point of view, which believed in city, state, or federal intervention to offer help to those who needed it. On the other was the Big Business point of view, which wanted everything left to the market. Somewhere like Chavez Ravine, in Poulson's opinion, should be gifted to the city's private developers, and the only thing City Hall needed to do was get out of the way.

Poulson was clearly winning this particular race, which probably explained Bowron's dramatic outburst on TV the previous evening. Russell hadn't seen it, but the *LA Times* had printed the mayor's speech verbatim over three pages. Which was quite remarkable, given that most of Bowron's invective had been aimed at the newspaper itself. The *Times* and its owner, he had said, were "the mouthpiece of a small group of people who control a vast commercial, financial, agricultural, and industrial empire." This "immensely wealthy, incredibly powerful group" were helping Poulson to victory because he would represent *their* interests, not those of the public.

This was extraordinary stuff, Russell had thought as he read it. Bowron sounded more like a Marxist than a Republican. And what he was saying sounded perilously close to the truth, which had to be a high-risk strategy for a politician who'd held the same office for fifteen years. If one took Bowron at his word, these "special interests" must have been there all the time, so why was he only now attacking them? Because he was losing, of course, and because the compromises he'd made with them were no longer sufficient. They wanted more, an end to New Deal thinking, to things like public housing, which reeked of socialism and cut into their profits. They wanted Poulson, and Bowron was desperate.

And the *Times* had not even deigned to offer an editorial response, as if the charges were too ridiculous for words, and they hated to hit a man when he was down. "If you have no defence, pretend you don't need one," one of Russell's old editors had told him.

He turned right off Wilshire and went in search of his first interviewee's Westwood address. This was a further ten minutes away, a grand white house on a gently winding street, with a distant backdrop of the Santa Monica Mountains. Rather to Russell's surprise, Morton Fitzgerald answered the door himself, before leading the way to a leather-chaired study at the rear of the house. He was tall, with a full head of grey hair and rather weather-beaten face. As Russell knew from his research, the man had spent thirty years in the military, retiring as a Major General, having commanded a division in North Africa and Italy. For a fifty-three-year-old he looked in pretty good condition, the consequence perhaps of almost daily rounds of golf at the Brentwood Country Club. He also belonged to local hunting and shooting associations and was a pillar of the city's Republican establishment.

Where would he find the time for any future Congressional duties? Russell wondered. And why did he want to?

"General . . ." he began and was immediately interrupted.

"Please, don't call me that. In my book, the army's the place for generals, and my soldiering days are in the past. I'm just Morton Fitzgerald now."

"Understood." Over the next half-hour Russell came to believe that Fitzgerald was a basically decent man with a sense of fair play that many of his Republican colleagues might well find indulgent. His hero was Abe Lincoln, though he also had a soft spot for his fellow soldier Teddy Roosevelt, choosing to regard the latter's quasi-socialist phase as a mistake arising from an over-generous spirit. Fitzgerald had two grown-up children, and surprisingly seemed prouder of the one who'd become a doctor than the one who'd followed him into the army. His wife, occasionally visible through the window wearing a wide straw hat, was a keen gardener and chairwoman of the local chapter of the Daughters of the American Revolution.

His politics apart, Russell found little to dislike about the man. In office he would probably be what the press called a "safe pair of hands," but Russell thought the voters would find him too bland. His political motivation was hard to pin down—he wasn't in it for money or power, so it was either an addiction to service or some unconscious need to find a new challenge. Maybe his friends were urging him on.

When Russell questioned him about Poulson, Fitzgerald made it clear that he had no time for the man. There was nothing specific, no criticism of his policies, just a tell-tale grimace. Which suggested to Russell that the man had an uphill struggle on his hands. If the *Times* thought Poulson was the right choice for mayor, they weren't going to champion Fitzgerald for Congress.

Which, Russell thought, once back in his car, might be a pity.

Morton Fitzgerald was far from inspiring, but the Republicans could do a lot worse.

THE *PLEASE, DAD* EPISODE THEY were recording that day was built around Dad's upsetting realisation that he was getting older. This was brought into focus by the older child noticing wrinkles on his forehead and asking what they were. Eddie Franklin had a great solo turn trying to straighten them out in front of a mirror, and when his latest shot at a girlfriend, the pretty but raucous redhead Marjorie, tried to reassure him, she predictably made things worse. Not for the first time, Effi wondered whether Marjorie was the writers' idea of a sly dig at Lucy.

Her chat over the garden fence with Laura's character had the latter saying "They're all just boys in men's bodies, aren't they?" allowing Mrs. Luddwitz to observe how unfortunate that was, given that most men wanted the opposite.

Beth thought that being fired at noon was bound to affect Laura's performance when they came to record the show two hours later—"and who could blame her?"—but Effi doubted it. "She's a good enough actor to turn herself off. She'll be fine until she comes offstage."

And she was. The paleness in Laura's face when she eventually emerged from the meeting suggested things had not gone well, but makeup were on hand to put things like that right, and when the time came to record, no one in the studio audience would have noticed that anything was wrong. Laura was, as usual, word-and character-perfect.

After the recording Effi tried in vain to find her, and it was a furious Beth who passed along the bad news, the writers' team having been alerted to the likelihood that Laura's character would be replaced. "Someone from HUAC will be taking her testimony on the twenty-eighth—that's the day after we record the last episode of the season. Until then, at least, she's still on the show, and our bastard sponsors win both ways. No sudden burst of bad publicity to spoil the next few weeks, and then the audience get a whole summer to forget she existed."

"Have you seen her?" Effi asked.

"Only briefly. She just wanted to get home. She said she'd call if she needed to talk."

Effi shook her head. "I don't suppose there's any other way we can help her."

"Shooting Joe McCarthy comes to mind, but when all's said and done, he's just a symptom."

RUSSELL'S SECOND APPOINTMENT WASN'T UNTIL 2 P.M., so he stopped for lunch at a diner on Wilshire before continuing east to the junction with Normandie Avenue. Driving north along that road between two lines of towering palms, he could see Griffith Park up ahead in the distance, its higher slopes shrouded in heat haze.

The second candidate's house was as impressive as the first's, albeit set on a mere city plot; both cars in the short driveway looked new and expensive. Russell's ring on the sonorous bell was answered by a good-looking man in his thirties, who introduced himself as "Nick Hayden, Greer's campaign manager." He barely glanced at Russell's credentials before passing him on to a hovering maid and setting off for another appointment. Where local elections were concerned, making a good impression in Britain and Germany was probably not a high priority.

The maid took him through to a large lounge at the back of the house, where Greer Holleman was waiting. This candidate was forty-three years old and had a more interesting personal history than Morton Fitzgerald. Originally from Arkansas, where he'd trained as a lawyer, Holleman had met his future wife, Gwen, the daughter of prominent LA businessman Beckett Lettson, on a prewar transatlantic crossing, and had soon become head of the company's legal department. Gwen had only outlived her father by a couple of months, dying early in 1936 while giving birth to a Mongoloid son, and Holleman had inherited everything.

The sixteen-year-old boy was here in the room, standing over a large model railroad. Holleman introduced him: "This is Luke."

"These are my trains," the boy said, giving Russell a wonderful smile.

"And that's the *Super Chief,*" Russell replied as the silver coaches rattled past. The cynic in him thought the boy might be there to make the father look good, but there was genuine affection in Holleman's eyes.

"Of course," Luke agreed.

"We can talk outside," Holleman said. "I'll just get someone to be with Luke."

After the maid-companion had been summoned, the two of them went out into the garden, a glade of grass surrounded by trees. The two canvas chairs might have been borrowed from a Hollywood studio. "On a clear day you can see the observatory," Holleman said, gesturing towards a gap in the trees. "Not that we have enough of those these days. One of the things I want to do in Washington is sound the alarm about the smog we're creating. Not just here, but all over the country."

"And how do we get rid of it?" Russell asked.

"We incentivise business to make that happen. Mostly carrots, but I wouldn't rule out an occasional stick."

"Well, I wish you luck with that. Can we start with a bit of background? Do you still have family in Arkansas?"

He had none, and stressed how glad he was that he'd moved to California. For an American civilian he'd seen quite a lot of the world. He and Gwen had spent their honeymoon in Rio; with and without her he'd spent time in England and several parts of the Continent. When Russell asked how he envisioned America's place in the world, Holleman thought about it for a while. "As a teacher bringing freedom and progress," he decided. "One good at keeping order," he added with a smile.

Stripped down, Russell recognised the usual agenda. Holleman's was slicker and more enthusiastic than Fitzgerald's, but just as right wing, just as wedded to business-friendly laissez-faire.

Yet when Russell asked him about race in America, there were none of the usual hints and prevarication. "I know that many people who share my views on the economy have—how should I put it?—old-fashioned ideas about race," Holleman said. "I don't. I believe capitalism, our free enterprise system, is essentially colour-blind. A worker is a worker, an investor is an investor. The system doesn't care where they come from or what colour they are. It cares how well they do their jobs."

Russell asked him about the mayoral election.

"Poulson is solid. He'll get the job done. He believes what I believe, that politicians just need to let the market have its way, and everyone will prosper. And he's going to win." A sad shake of the head. "After watching Mr. Bowron on the TV last night, I'd say he's been in the job a little too long. He looks like he needs a rest."

Holleman was earnest, and Russell saw no reason to doubt that he believed his own spiel. Russell wasn't sure how clever the man was, but he was bright enough for this. And he was certainly personable. Likable, even, for a right-wing Republican.

On their way back through the house they found Luke still engrossed in his trains, the maid watching over him from a seat by the door. "Say goodbye, Luke," Holleman told his son, and Russell was blessed again with that all-consuming smile.

Out in the hall he turned to Holleman. "I have to ask. As a single parent with a child who needs so much care and attention, how will you cope with all the travelling that a congressman has to do?

"Luke goes where I go," was the straightforward answer.

Murals

Russell had a lazy morning on Thursday. Once Effi had left for the hairdressers, he settled himself in the room that served as his study, but after staring out of the window for ten minutes he went out to the garden, where a Mexican hammock was hung in the shade between two palms. It was a little cooler than yesterday, but still ferociously hot, and he would have liked to put his idleness down to that, rather than the lingering sense that the work he was doing didn't much matter, to himself or anyone else.

He had arranged to meet a friend for an early lunch that day, and Effi still wasn't back when he left in the Frazer for Greenblatt's Deli. Theodore Cullen was there before him, ensconced in his customary booth in the still mostly empty establishment. Cullen was a history professor at UCLA, and his willingness to drive seven miles there and back for lunch owed everything to the deli's legendary turkey sandwiches.

A tall man with a slight stoop, Cullen was slightly older than Russell, which put him at around fifty-five. Like Russell, he had fought in the First War and been too old for the Second. He was married with grown-up children, had been a tenured professor since the midthirties, and was writing a book on how individuals and groups in earlier centuries had financially profited from wars.

Cullen had initiated their relationship after hearing of Russell's prewar experiences as a journalist from his own wife, who had read about them in an interview Effi had given to one of the film magazines. They had met for a drink and enjoyed each other's company enough to meet for another. Cullen was what Americans called a liberal, what Europeans would see as a moderate social democrat. He was a staunch, if not uncritical, fan of FDR, and these days worried that the great man's legacy, never much more than skin deep, was being slowly peeled away to reveal an earlier, uglier nation.

"Did you hear about the mural committee?" was the professor's first question.

"No."

"Some pea-brain has decided that two particular murals in one of our public buildings are examples of left-wing propaganda, intentionally designed to stir up race and class hatred. So his fellow pea-brains have set themselves up as a committee to check all the other public buildings." He shook his head. "The people of this city get crazier every day."

"What was in these murals?"

"That wasn't mentioned, but I'm assuming scurrilous portraits of poor folks and coloured folks mistakenly blaming white fat cats for all those troubles that they've really brought on themselves. What else could it be?"

"Mmm. You're probably right, but it might just be that they're murals. I mean, art for everyone, free to everyone. Sounds pretty damn socialistic to me."

Cullen laughed. "Like your British NHS!"

"Indeed."

The turkey sandwiches arrived and were given due reverence for the next ten minutes. "Still, the news isn't all bad," Cullen decided over coffee. "I think our current war is coming to an end."

"Yes? I guess I've gotten used to it. Like background noise."

"What is there to gain anymore? Neither we nor the Chinese

can afford the loss of face a defeat would represent, so instead of hurling expensive artillery shells across an artificial border we might as well just stare at each other. No more coffins coming ashore at Long Beach."

He was probably right, Russell thought. He told Cullen about his "Democracy in the US" articles.

"The mayoral election?" Cullen asked.

"No, the special congressional. I decided the mayoral was a foregone conclusion."

"It certainly looks that way."

Russell gestured towards the professor's copy of the *Times* and asked if the paper had rebutted Bowron's accusations.

"Sort of. You might say a classic response of its kind. The editor mocks Bowron, condescends to him, feels aggrieved by him—he does everything but answer the specific charges."

"Because they're true?"

Cullen sighed. "In essence, yes, but that won't matter. He's sounding like a loser, and American voters like winners."

"What about my guys in the congressional race?"

"I haven't been paying much attention, to be honest. Fitzgerald is old school, Holleman a bit of a blank slate, but I wouldn't expect too much. On the Democrat side Spinetti is a know-nothing blowhard, and Fairley's way too left-field to stand a chance. The first three are all business as usual; none of them plan to rock any boats or kill any golden calves, which is good news for the haves, and leaves the have-nots with the consolation of knowing their lives aren't about to be turned upside-down."

They talked about the book Cullen was working on, and Russell asked whether he'd considered bringing the story up to the present. "Or would that make it harder to find a publisher? I imagine most of the people who made a killing out of the last war are still in business and wouldn't take too kindly to someone raking through their grubby deals."

Cullen was more cynical. "I doubt they'd be that worried. You and I might find profiteering in time of war immoral, but it's rarely been illegal. And these days, if laws have been broken, the people concerned have enough money to string out the legal process until kingdom come." He shook his head. "And when all's said and done, it's only an academic tome; these people only worry when stories like this reach the general public, and their name gets sullied. If the newspapers pick stuff up, they'll go after them, not some academic they can dismiss as a deluded commie." Cullen looked up. "I guess in Hitler's time you'd have gotten a visit from someone."

"And it wouldn't have been a lawyer."

"Every cloud. It hasn't gotten that bad here yet, and I doubt it ever will. But maybe I'm being naive."

"Perhaps," Russell said. "But you'd know better than me. I'm still trying to make sense of this place."

"Good luck with that."

After Cullen's Oldsmobile had driven off down Sunset, Russell sat in the Frazer for several minutes, wondering what to do with his afternoon. He knew he should go home and work, but the morning's reluctance persisted, and he decided to go for a drive instead. After filling up with gas, he drove the other way on Sunset, turning left onto Highland and heading up and over the Cahuenga Pass. The traffic was unusually light on Ventura, the sun beating down on his hat and shoulders in the open convertible as he crossed the southern rim of the San Fernando valley. The world around him, which always seemed so thrilling in the neon-lit nights, seemed seedy and faded by day, as if it knew it had already suffered one drought too many.

The long and winding Topanga Canyon Boulevard took him back across the mountains and down to the sea near his favourite diner, but he stopped for neither food nor beach walk—March's imaginary assassin still gave him the shivers. Instead he followed the coast road back into Santa Monica, where he walked to the end of the crowded pier and drank in the ocean and sky.

Effi's show went out that evening, and watching it was a family ritual. His other favourite, Groucho Marx's quiz show, *You Bet Your Life*, was also on, and staring out to sea, Russell realised for the first time how sinister the name of that show could sound.

WITH THE RECORDED SHOW GOING out that evening, all concerned had the day off. After returning from having her hair done, Effi made herself a tuna sandwich and took the new script out to the hammock. It wasn't bad now, and would doubtless get better, but she wondered how Laura's trials would affect morale. Star-turn Eddie excepted, the show had always felt like a family endeavour.

After reading it through she decided on impulse to call Laura. Her son answered, then put his mother on.

"Just checking that you're okay," Effi said.

"I am. Thank you. Beth already called, and it's not the end of the world, is it?"

"No, it isn't. But it's a pain in the backside. And suffering for other people's stupidity is always so annoying. Anyway, I just wanted you to know that we're behind you. That I'm behind you."

"I thank you for that," she said, sounding close to tears. "I really do, but I must go."

"Okay, I'll see you tomorrow."

"Yes, of course."

Feeling disheartened, Effi went into the kitchen and heated up some spätzle from the fridge. Comfort food, she thought. She was in a strange land at what seemed a very strange time. She had a sudden memory of her nana's spätzle, her and her sister, Zarah, on either side of the table in her grandparent's Brandenburg house. They must have been six and eight, something like that.

She was having her usual Thursday tea with Zarah at the Bullocks Wilshire that afternoon, and until it was time to go she pottered about the house. The studio-supplied cleaner came twice a week, so there was nothing much to do, and she had to restrain herself from leaving too early.

When she reached the famous top-floor tearoom, her sister was already there. Zarah seemed to look more American with every passing week, which made Effi wonder whether she did too. And what in fact she meant by "looking American." Maybe it was all about context—LA's brightness against Berlin's greyness, and the tendency to wear more vivid colours which the former induced. Or maybe just good health and makeup—both had been in short supply during their last few years in Berlin.

"You're on time," was the first thing Zarah said, sounding almost affronted at this deviation from usual practice.

"I'll go out and come back in half an hour if you like," Effi said, sitting down.

The arrival of a waitress interrupted them. "Something different?" Zarah asked her sister, ordering the usual Earl Grey tea and coconut cream pies when Effi shook her head. "So how are things?" she asked, once the waitress had gone.

Effi realised she had no desire to talk about Laura Fullagar. "I'm fine," she said. "Watch the show tonight. It's a good one."

"You're always good," Zarah said, ever the supportive sister.

Effi hoped that she had been one too. Excepting the three years she'd spent alone and undercover in wartime Berlin, her life had been much easier than Zarah's. Her sister had married a man who ended up a war criminal, had been gang-raped repeatedly by a quartet of Red Army soldiers, and eventually spent two years in Iowa having a baby at the age of forty-three in the house of her vindictive new mother-in-law. Fortunately for Zarah, her new American husband, who had returned home with an eye to running the family business, had eventually realised his mistake, and managed to secure a high-salary consultancy with one of the burgeoning LA defence industries out in the San Fernando valley. The family—which also included the other light of Zarah's life, her eighteen-year-old son, Lothar—now had a large house in Van Nuys, less than a half-hour drive from Effi's.

"Are you happy here?" Effi heard herself ask, as if the question had come from someone else. "In America, I mean?"

Zarah's face was suddenly full of concern. "Are you asking me that because you aren't?"

"No, not really. But are you?"

Zarah gave her another questioning look. "Yes, I am," she said, as if she had trouble believing it. "I'm with a man I love, we have enough money, a lovely house, a new child to raise. And Lothar seems to be finding his feet. What's not to like?" she added wryly. It was one of Mrs. Luddwitz's favourite expressions.

Effi smiled.

"Though my sister moving somewhere else would put a dent in things," Zarah added.

The coconut cream pies arrived with their accompanying pot of tea. Effi did the pouring while Zarah savoured a first forkful of pie and wiped her lips with the embroidered napkin. "Wonderful," was all she said.

"We have no plans to leave," Effi promised, which was something of a politician's answer.

Zarah knew her too well. "John's not happy here, is he?"

"Some days he is, some days he isn't." She didn't want to discuss her husband's state of mind, because she knew Zarah would be unsympathetic.

"When you're doing so well, and Rosa the same, I'm sure he won't want to upset the applecart," Zarah added pointedly.

"He won't. But he does have a son on the other side of the world," Effi noted, knowing that Zarah would empathise.

"I know he does. But you can afford visits to England and to pay for him and his family to visit you here. Once the baby is old enough. I know the two of them enjoyed it here when they came that Christmas, so maybe they'll move here eventually."

"Yes, maybe. Who knows? So how's Lothar doing?" she asked, keen to change the subject. "Has he decided on a university?" To say that Lothar had always been troubled was perhaps an exaggeration, but effectively losing his father at the age of ten had done him no favours. He still regularly wrote to the imprisoned Jens and received the occasional reply full of misery and self-justification, which did the boy no good at all. Lothar's one abiding interest was astronomy, a solitary hobby if ever there was one.

"He's applied to Caltech," Zarah was saying, "and I'm sure he'll get in. He's got the brains, though God knows where from. Not from his mother or father."

"Jens is emotionally dense, not stupid," Effi responded.

Zarah almost threw her last spoonful of pie at her sister. "And I am?"

"No more than me. And we both get by. I think that sort of intelligence may be overrated."

The spoon went into her sister's mouth. "Mmm, so good. And you may be right. I assume we're still on for Sunday?" The two families were meeting up for Mother's Day in Griffith Park: an observatory visit followed by a picnic.

"Absolutely. Bill's coming, I hope."

"Of course."

They discussed who was bringing what food for the picnic, Zarah cooking one half, Effi buying the other, and then the two of them browsed their way through Women's Clothing until Zarah checked her watch and exclaimed that she needed to go: "The babysitter has to be home by five."

They parted with a sisterly hug in the car lot, and Effi drove back to the house on Melrose, where she found Rosa already ensconced in the hammock, reading a book with the title *Invisible Man*. "Is that one of your new science fiction novels?" she asked.

Rosa gave her the sort of pitying look that only a teenager could. "It's about black people in America," she said.

"What about them?"

"How they live, how they're treated. Like the Jews in Germany before Hitler decided to kill us all."

Effi opened her mouth and shut it again. There was really no answer to that.

Later that evening the three of them sat and watched the show, and, rather to her own surprise, Effi found herself wondering if this was what she really wanted to do, if this was where she truly wanted to be.

ON FRIDAY THE TEMPERATURE WAS almost down to seventy, about right as far as Russell was concerned. He had the two Democrat candidates to see that day, which would probably be more interesting than working on his book. The first interview was scheduled for eleven, with the only candidate who actually lived in the 29th District, and for the second time in consecutive days Russell took the highway north and west into the San Fernando valley.

Fifty-five-year-old Lou Spinetti had a ranch-style house in Sherman Oaks near the Encino Reservoir. Driving up to it, Russell noted the row of magnificent trees behind the parched-looking acre of grass but saw no evidence of gardening. Spinetti himself was little better groomed; he had thick wavy hair which he couldn't stop stroking, a burly figure and pugnacious face. If the name suggested Italian ancestry, neither features nor colouring confirmed it.

After a long career in state politics, he was eager to take the step up, but what he might offer the nation was harder to fathom. Spinetti was a fan of both FDR and Poulson, which seemed to stretch bipartisanship a touch too far. He was happiest discussing foreign affairs, and the need for a resolute stand against Chinese and Russian aggression. The US had to be ready to fight both at once if that proved necessary, which in Spinetti's opinion it probably would.

Despite some obvious coaxing, he had nothing to say about education, race, health care, or the economy. In fact his only domestic suggestion was that wider highways might be needed for transferring troops from coast to coast. As far as Russell could see a Congressional seat for this Democrat would just be a pulpit for attacking communists, so he asked about Spinetti's Republican foe Joe McCarthy. "An enemy of my enemy is my friend," the candidate said earnestly, adding, for no reason that Russell could discern, a murmured "the sermon on the mount." When innocently asked if Jesus had actually used the "enemy of my enemy" phrase, the would-be congressman admitted that the messiah might not have used those exact words, but insisted "that's what he meant."

Russell was shaking his head all the way back to his car. What had California's Democrats come to, putting such an idiot forward?

He drove back towards town, stopping for lunch at the intersection between Ventura and Laurel Canyon, and then following the latter south before turning east onto Mulholland Drive. Cullen's "no-hoper" lived near the Hollywood end of LA's most picturesque road, in an old wooden house with a fine view of the city and a garden boasting some spectacular giant plants and a Chinese moon gate.

At sixty-two Clement Fairley was the oldest of the four hopefuls, but he looked in pretty good shape. Grey-haired with piercing blue eyes, attired in checked shirt and jeans, he looked more like an aging cowboy hero than a candidate for Congress. But this was America, Russell reminded himself.

Like Spinetti he had long been active in politics, but his were more about fighting for local good causes. His day jobs had been many and various, mostly because he had no need of a wage, having inherited a fortune from an oil-striking father. Hence the beautiful house.

Fairley's wife sat in on their chat. An attractive woman in her fifties, confined to a wheelchair for reasons that were not explained, she smiled throughout the interview, occasionally nodding agreement with her husband's arguments.

He had been an FDR fan at the beginning but had eventually found him too timid when it came to confronting big business. Confronting was Fairley's watchword. Regulating businesses more strictly was the only way to make them treat their workers like human beings, and only strong government could introduce and enforce such a programme. The health insurance firms needed confronting too, as did the arms manufacturers, and the racists who still ran the South like they'd won the Civil War.

Fairley's ideas of how to make use of a seat in Congress reminded Russell of the prewar movie *Mr. Smith Goes to Washington* and the Jimmy Stewart character, who had sought to cure all social ills with nothing more than infinite energy and the irrepressible rightness of his own convictions. It might have worked in the movie—Russell couldn't remember how that had actually ended—but he couldn't see it happening in reality.

He liked Fairley on a personal level, and even shared most of the man's convictions, but strongly suspected that both of them were whistling in the dark.

NOW THAT EVERYONE HAD READ next week's script it was time to discuss it. This time Dad was off on a business trip with his middle-aged secretary, worrying about how they'd all cope without him at home, oblivious to the secretary's lovelorn looks and sighs. Needless to say, the children and Mrs. Luddwitz were having a ball, and when Eddie came home he started worrying that they hadn't missed him at all. But then the children produced the large and extremely messy chocolate cake they had made in his honour, and all was sweetness and light. Which, as Mrs. Luddwitz observed, was "better than sourness and dark."

It was all a bit cheesy, but as Beth was fond of pointing out, creating forty new storylines each year was bound to generate some duds. This one wasn't that bad, and sensible changes were already being suggested, not least by Eddie, who for all his vanity never stopped searching for improvements.

Laura looked better that day, Effi thought. The shock was fading, and now there was the waiting. If a few of the team were keeping their distance, they were taking care not to be obvious about it, and most of the cast and crew were clearly intent on being supportive.

In the canteen over lunch everyone was talking about the director Robert Rossen's appearance in front of HUAC the day before. It was Rossen's second bite at the cherry. Having got himself blacklisted for refusing to name names in 1951, he had now chosen to resurrect his career by offering up more than fifty. The more prominent among them had already been named by others, but Rossen had also named a lot of film and TV writers whom most of the public had never heard of.

"Writers like me," as Beth noted. "Makes you wonder about people, doesn't it? About to be bitten by a rabid dog? Just offer up someone else for the dog to sink his teeth into."

"I think I'd shoot the dog's owner."

"Er, that would be Uncle Sam."

"God bless him," Effi murmured. The show's producer, having spotted her, was walking towards their table.

"There's someone here to see you," he explained.

Effi's initial thought was that now they'd come for her, but nothing in the producer's face supported that possibility. She might be kidding herself, but surely the prospect of losing Mrs. Luddwitz would have him more worried.

"He's in my office. You can talk to him there."

"Who is 'he'?"

The producer shrugged. "He told me something, but his English isn't very good. I think he's German."

He was. A man in his thirties with slicked-back fair hair and rather Slavic features who began by asking in execrable English whether she preferred to speak that or German.

"German," she said gratefully.

"*Das is gut*," he said with a smile. "I am Otto Neubert, and I represent the Berlinale organising committee. You are aware of the Berlinale?"

"The film festival? Of course. We left Berlin before the first one, but I know about it."

"Well, the third annual festival is in five weeks' time—it runs June eighteenth to June twenty-eighth. I understand that your season will be over by then, and we would like to have you as a guest of the festival. We envisage a long afternoon, with excerpts from films you made before and after the war—and of course your current television show—followed by a moderated question and answer session with the audience. I'm sure people will be fascinated by your experiences of working in such a melange of genres and media. But of course we are open to other suggestions."

Effi stared at him, feeling somewhat stunned. "I'm honoured," she eventually said. She really was.

"But?"

"There are no buts. I must discuss this with my husband, of course, though I can't imagine he'd have any objection."

"We would pay your travel and hotel expenses. Yours and your husband's. I imagine a train to New York, a ship to Hamburg, and probably a flight to Berlin, rather than risk the train through the Soviet sector."

"That's very generous," Effi said. She thought of asking if Rosa could be included but decided that would be greedy. They could pay for her themselves, if she wanted to come. Effi somehow doubted she would.

"I have people to see about next year's festival, so I'm here until Tuesday," Neubert said. He handed her a printed business card on which he had scribbled *Beverly Wilshire, Room 141.* "If you could let me know before Tuesday, we can set things in motion, and put you in touch with the organisers in Berlin."

"I'll call you," Effi told him. "Probably tomorrow."

Neubert smiled and got up. "I have to say that pleases me. I loved your work with DEFA right after the war," he added. "Particularly *The Man I Must Kill.* There were some wonderful films made in those few years, before the Soviets turned it into a propaganda factory. Anyway, I look forward to hearing from you."

"I'll walk you out," Effi offered. She was still trying to take it all in, and on her way back from seeing the German to his taxi, realised she was almost skipping along. Why did she feel so pleased? Because, like most people—and every actor she'd ever met—she liked being recognised for her work. Because the idea of drawing her career together in the way that Neubert had suggested was both exciting and flattering. And they'd be going home, if only for a few weeks. John would get to see Thomas and Paul and Marisa—they could stop off in London at their own expense. And Rosa . . . would she want to go?

She found out when she got home later that afternoon.

Rosa looked thoughtful when Effi told her about the invitation. "I'll think about it," she said, "but will you be upset if I say no?"

"Of course not. We'll miss you of course, but . . ."

"I do want to go back one day. To see where I lived with my first mother and Frau Borchers, and where you and I and Dad lived. But not yet. I'm not ready yet."

Effi gathered Rosa into her arms. "Will you feel deserted if we go?"

"No, no. You must."

"You can stay with Zarah and Bill."

"I know. That would be fine. But could I stay with Aunt Ali and Uncle Fritz in New York? If they'll have me." Her eyes lit up. "I could go on the train with you and Dad, and you could pick me up on your way back. I so want to spend some time in New York. Hear the music, go to the galleries. It's so much more *alive* than anywhere else."

RUSSELL NEEDED A DRINK AFTER interviewing Clement Fairley—there were few things more depressing than hearing your own opinions expressed by a wealthy dreamer. Noticing a bar on Sunset he'd never been in, he thought he'd give it a try—sometimes the most unprepossessing exteriors hid a magic kingdom within.

Not this one. It was dark, dismal, and smelled of damp, which was quite a feat given how hot and dry the last few days had been. Russell decided the place suited his mood and ordered a beer from the half-asleep barman.

Seated at the bar, he could hear Frank Sinatra's voice coming from outside; "Fools Rush In" was the song. Music neither loud enough to hear nor quiet enough to ignore was one of Russell's pet peeves. And he'd never much liked Sinatra.

The beer was cold and insipid, but still managed to hit the spot. He started mentally sifting through the four interviews he'd taken that week. Ted Cullen had been right about the two Democrats, Spinetti was indeed a blow-hard, Fairley a classic no-hoper. The two Republicans he'd met on Wednesday had at least been coherent, though perhaps that wasn't so hard if your main proposal was to sit back and let things rip. None of the three with a chance of winning had struck him as people he'd want to vote for, but then he wasn't your average Angeleno. Far from it.

In any case, he was supposed to be explaining the process to a foreign readership, not marking the candidates out of ten. What they believed or said they believed was one thing, but the context in which they operated was probably more important. Who was paying for their six-month campaigns, and for all the favourable media coverage they couldn't do without?

The beer was dreadful, but it did slip down. He ordered another.

As the candidates had offered four different views on the Chavez Ravine controversy, he decided that would make a good case study for the first article. Fitzgerald only had a vague idea where it was, Holleman had thought the cleared land should be handed over to private developers, and Spinetti wanted luxury homes for the very rich. Fairley believed the land should be given back to the people who'd been evicted and would probably like to see all developers horse-whipped.

It was time to go home. Russell gulped down the last of his beer and headed out into the light. The music he'd heard was coming from a second-floor window, and was louder outside. A woman with a thick Southern accent was now insisting "it wasn't God who made honky-tonk angels."

"Who then?" Russell wondered out loud, as he pulled out into the early evening traffic.

Effi's car was in the drive when he finally got home, and his first glimpse of her face told him something good had happened.

"I've been invited to the Berlinale," she almost shouted. "*We* have," she corrected herself.

"That's . . . wonderful. Tell me more." He could see how happy she was, and did his best to appear so himself, but his initial emotional reaction was more ambivalent. He was excited at the prospect of seeing Paul and Thomas and their respective families, but more than slightly anxious about putting his and Effi's heads in such proximity to the Soviet bear. He told himself he was being stupid, that the MGB could have killed them here in LA if that was what they wanted to do.

Effi filled him in on everything Neubert had said, and he quite understood how pleased she was at the honour they were paying her. Which of course she richly deserved.

The news that Rosa probably wasn't coming was something of a relief, though he knew how much he'd miss her.

And as the evening went by he found himself noting further positives to set against the negative. He could use the opportunity to do research for his book; he could enjoy a week of idle luxury on an ocean liner; he would be back in the city where he'd spent so much of his life.

As he and Effi laughed their way through *Our Miss Brooks* and *The Life of Riley* he told himself that he and Shchepkin really had managed to walk away, and that threats to life and limb— "revoltin' developments" as Riley would say—were something they'd left behind.

Driving Lessons

By coincidence, a letter from Thomas arrived for Russell in the Saturday post. It was full of all sorts of news, from the flourishing winter squash in Hanna's garden to the East's parlous economy, all delivered in his ex-brother-in-law's usual sardonic style. The woes of Hertha, the football team they had both supported since the 1920s, showed no signs of abating, but Thomas was enjoying his semiretirement, doing part-time stints at a migrant reception centre and helping to run the secondhand bookshop in Schmargendorf he and two friends had set up two years before.

He and his wife, Hanna, were still living on the same street in Dahlem. They admitted the house was too big for the two of them, but Hanna didn't want a smaller garden, and Thomas had no desire to move. Their daughter, Lotte, was now in her midtwenties, and was living in the eastern sector. She worked for the ruling SED party newspaper and was, as far as Russell knew, still an enthusiastic believer in the DDR. But then she always had been one for lurching to extremes. While her late brother, Joachim, had usually gone off to Hitlerjugend meetings with a "must I, really?" look on his face, Lotte had donned her Bund Deutscher Mädel uniform at every opportunity, even wearing it to bed on several occasions.

But despite her current allegiance to the East German regime, she and her parents were still close, and as long as the intracity border remained essentially open, Thomas saw no reason to worry that the family would be permanently separated.

He and Hanna had visited LA at the start of the previous spring for a three-week stay, and Russell had been taken aback by the amount of grey in Thomas's hair and new beard. His friend was getting close to sixty now, but then they all were entering that stage of life when growing older became real. Even Effi, whose forty-fifth birthday was only a fortnight away.

Thomas closed his letter with the news that he'd heard from Russell's twenty-six-year-old son, which was more than Russell had done. Paul was a terrible correspondent and hadn't written a word since announcing more than a month ago that Marisa was pregnant and that his boss, Solly Bernstein—Russell's agent for almost two decades—was seriously ill. Two letters from his father requesting an update had elicited zero response.

But as far as Russell knew, Paul was flourishing. A child of a so-called broken home, a teenager scarred by a year on the Russian Front, his son was successfully running a well-respected literary agency in his father's homeland, and could be forgiven for not writing more letters than he did.

Russell left Thomas's on the kitchen counter for Effi to read and retired to his study for two hours of fairly aimless pottering, before setting out for Gilmore Field and the afternoon game. There was plenty of parking at the stadium, but getting a car out afterwards took forever, so as usual he settled for the two-mile walk. His British actor friend Alex Sugden, whom he'd met at a Hollywood party two years before, was waiting at the ticket booth, dressed in the sort of gaily-striped blazer that their countrymen wore to the Henley Regatta.

Russell wasn't convinced that Alex missed Old Blighty as much as he claimed—his Hollywood career was effectively over, and though he'd certainly made enough money to go home if he wished, he showed no signs of doing so. He just enjoyed remembering the old country, and Russell enjoyed it with him—between innings they talked about Stanley Matthews's miraculous performance in last week's Cup Final, and the imminent Coronation of Britain's new young queen. Both were more interesting than the game, which was effectively over by the middle of the third, when the San Francisco Seals put up a nine-run lead. The two of them should have left then, but like sports fans the world over preferred waiting for a miracle that was never going to come.

NEXT DAY THE WEATHER WAS picnic perfect. Effi's and Zarah's families met in the Observatory/Planetarium car lot before spending an hour inside. Both had been there several times before, but the exhibits were beautifully done and, for the children at least, bore repeated visiting. As usual, Lothar had to be almost physically dragged away from the huge model of the moon.

There were a lot of people around but driving a mile and walking a few hundred yards in the world's largest city park was enough to find them a secluded spot with a panoramic view. So far, so good, Effi thought, as she helped Zarah unload the hampers.

But the rest of their Mother's Day outing seemed disinclined to celebrate motherhood. Having been warned by Effi that Rosa preferred a month in New York City to a month in the Valley, Zarah was trying, somewhat unsuccessfully, to hide how hurt she was. And Effi herself was not immune. When she and her daughter had started looking at LA art schools, Effi had assumed they still had years in close proximity, but what if the girl found one in New York she really loved?

Rosa was sitting on a tree stump, pencil and sketch pad in hand. Predictably, she had eschewed the magnificent view of the city, and was drawing another lonely stump, from which fresh green tendrils of growth were already reaching out. The girl had been eight when she came to Effi, and the succeeding nine years of motherhood seemed to have passed in a flash. Had she put herself second often enough? Effi wondered. Had she made the most of those years, or too often allowed her work to take her away, as was about to happen again? John always said not, but then he would, wouldn't he?

He was talking to Lothar a few yards away. Both looked serious, and Effi hoped John had remembered that Zarah didn't want them contacting her jailed ex-husband on her son's behalf.

Bill and three-year-old Casey, by contrast, didn't seem to have a care in the world. Bill always looked like a perfect father, but according to Zarah he was late home so often on workdays that he hardly saw his son between weekends.

Which might—who knew?—even be good for the boy. Effi remembered Russell recalling how little he'd seen of his own dad, without expressing any regret about it. Maybe fatherhood was best served in small helpings.

ON MONDAY MORNING RUSSELL TOOK the streetcar downtown to sort out the travel arrangements for their European trip. After Effi had spoken to Ali and Neubert on Saturday evening, and he had exchanged telegraphs with Thomas and Paul on Sunday morning, they had been able to settle on an itinerary, and now all that remained was purchasing the various tickets and invoicing the festival organisers. They had decided to take the train across country, stay a night with Ali and Fritz in Brooklyn, then take the *Queen Mary* across the Atlantic. After four days in London with Paul and Marisa they would fly on to Berlin, arriving four days ahead of the festival. The organisers had booked them into a hotel on Ku'damm, but Russell assumed they'd be staying with Thomas and Hanna.

It took an hour and a half to sort it all out, and it was almost noon by the time he had the sheaf of tickets in an inside pocket.

Feeling hungry, he stopped at an inviting diner on Broadway, and had just placed his order when a group of youths decided they needed music and started feeding their coins into the over-loud jukebox. Russell sat there nursing his mug of coffee, thinking that in a few weeks' time he would be sitting in a proper café on Ku'damm, drinking a cup of real coffee, listening to nothing louder than the murmur of conversation.

He was beginning to sound like his father, he thought.

The newspapers would be just as depressing in Berlin, but probably not as infantile. Today's was blaming Mexico for a huge influx of heroin into California, and conveniently ignoring the fact that sellers went where sales could be made. The *Times* was also anticipating an invasion of mobsters from other states, as if unaware that such people were already running half their city. Meanwhile, a nationwide poll had revealed that three-quarters of Americans favoured inserting "under God" after "one nation" in the Pledge of Allegiance. Which Russell supposed was no more ridiculous than singing "God Save the Queen."

Of most personal interest, there was an opinion piece intriguingly entitled "Exorcising Marxists." After admitting that Marx had been right to point out capitalism's record of instability, the writer went on to lambast all those who didn't realise how easy it would be to stabilise the system, if only people stopped feeling ashamed of "good Americanisms" like "big business, corporation, tax write-offs, merger, profits and private wealth." If anyone was still in any doubt as to who he represented, the writer ended with a wonderfully tell-tale list of measures the country should avoid. These included subsidies, give-away foreign policies, price controls, excess profit taxation, and government intervention in the economy. Russell was beginning to think that the Americans could teach the Soviets a thing or two about propaganda.

And then there was the heartbreaking story he really didn't want to read but felt inexorably drawn to. A ten-year-old boy had gone missing in the San Bernadino Mountains. The family had driven up from Glendale with a picnic lunch, and no more than ten minutes had elapsed between his parents knowing he was there and noticing he wasn't. In the week since an extensive search had failed to yield a single sighting—who or whatever had taken the boy had somehow managed to do so without leaving a trace.

Russell had his own sad story of a boy last seen on a mountain. Hirth's son must have been about ten in late 1945 when Russell and the band of Palestine-bound Jews he was crossing the Alps with had left the boy to fend for himself. They'd had their reasons at the time, but the abandonment of a child to almost certain death had haunted Russell ever since, and a story like this brought it all back.

A sin to set against his good deeds. If anyone else was counting, he could only hope that the latter outnumbered the former.

He gulped down the last of the dreadful coffee and headed for the streetcar. At home he spent most of the afternoon going through the research he'd already done for his prospective book and found it depressingly thin. The publisher's advance was long spent—it hadn't been much more than Effi earned in a week—and he had little to show for the money. Most ex-employees of those American companies who had traded with the Nazis after Pearl Harbor had simply refused to talk to him, either because they feared self-incrimination or because they had signed away their right to do so. When Thomas had tried, on Russell's behalf, to speak to a couple of the Germans involved, he'd only elicited threats, and Russell had made it crystal-clear that his friend wasn't to put himself and Hanna at risk by pursuing the matter. Maybe Russell could do so himself when he and Effi were in Berlin. Such a stated intention would at least be something to offer his increasingly impatient publisher.

At four he put his papers away and went to pick up Rosa. After school on Mondays and sometimes Wednesdays, Russell gave his daughter driving lessons. When they had started a couple of months before, he'd been worried the experience might strain their relationship, but it had, if anything, made it stronger. From day one she had proved a competent driver, and the "lessons" were now more like motoring trips they took together, in which stops for refreshments, views, and conversation were just as important.

Today began with them driving west on Sunset and taking occasional detours through the residential areas on either side. After passing UCLA they stopped at an ice cream parlour where the jukebox was turned even louder than the one from lunchtime. Rosa looked through the disks and came back to their booth without inserting a coin. "It's all white music," she complained, much to Russell's astonishment. He suddenly remembered what Effi had told him about the book Rosa was reading, and how she'd compared the Nazi treatment of Jews like herself to the American treatment of Negroes. "Aren't all the jukeboxes the same?" he asked, in lieu of anything more perceptive.

"No," she said simply. "There are some places downtown that put rhythm and blues and gospel music in theirs. But it's almost impossible to buy the records in white areas. Dad, I would love to go to Dolphin's in South Central. That's the most famous record store for that kind of music. It's so much better than anything you'll hear in here," she added, just as Patti Page started singing "(How Much Is) That Doggie in the Window?" "Would you believe that this has been top of the white charts for months?" Rosa asked contemptuously.

"There are different music charts for different races," Russell said, a sentence that began as a question and ended as a statement. "So where do you hear black music?"

"Lots of places. At some friends' houses. There are a few good jukeboxes downtown, and sometimes I can pick up South Central radio stations."

"Would there be singers I've heard of?"

"I doubt it."

"Who do you like?"

She thought about that. "Billy Ward, the "5" Royales, Fats Domino. There's so many. You could buy me some records for my birthday," she added with a smile.

Back on the road, they headed north across the hills on Sepulveda, before turning east onto Mulholland for the ten-mile drive back to Hollywood. While Rosa concentrated on the twisting road, Russell sat and contemplated the new things he was learning about his daughter. And there was more to come. When they reached the Universal City Overlook, with its view of the Valley and San Gabriel Mountains, Rosa pulled the Frazer into one of the empty parking spaces and switched off the ignition. "There's something I want to ask you," she began. "I have a friend. His name is Juan Morales, and he's in my evening class. A really good painter. You wouldn't believe his colours. But that's not . . ." She turned towards Russell. "I saw him in the lunchtime break today. He walked over from his school to mine," she added in explanation. "His Uncle Cesar has disappeared."

"Disappeared?" Russell echoed, still inwardly processing this sudden appearance of a boy in his daughter's life.

"No one has seen him since last Wednesday. Dad, what do you know about Chavez Ravine?"

"I've read some stuff. It's an area just north of downtown that City Hall's been clearing for a public housing project."

"They've been trying to clear it. Some people have refused to go, and are still there, living in trailers and outhouses or just outdoors. Juan's father moved his family out early last year, but his brother—Juan's uncle—wouldn't leave his home. And he's still there. Or was. As I said, none of the neighbours have seen him since Wednesday, and when Juan's father went down to Union Station—which is where Cesar works—they told him Cesar hadn't come to work since then. So Juan's father went to the police, who told him it was way too early to file a missing persons report, and that he shouldn't come back for a couple of weeks."

"Could the uncle have just gone away?"

"Not without saying anything. The family is really close."

"So what do they think may have happened?

"That he's been arrested. Cesar has had a few run-ins with people who want him to leave, and some threats from others who won't even say who they're working for." She mistook Russell's look of weary outrage for scepticism. "Juan and his family wouldn't make something like this up. I know, I've met them. Though not the uncle. They just want to know he's alive and okay, and I thought maybe . . . well, you're a journalist, and you look into things, don't you?"

"And I'm white," Russell said. "Or what Americans think of as white."

"So the police wouldn't just ignore you, would they?"

He wasn't a white whose views they'd share, but they didn't know that. "I'll see what I can do," he promised. "Cesar Morales—does he still have a house with a number?"

"I'll ask Juan what it is. Everyone says they had a real community in Chavez Ravine, before City Hall decided to improve things."

Everyone? Russell wondered. His daughter's world seemed to have grown a lot bigger without his noticing. "I'll look into it," he said, as much to himself as her. The question was how. "Tell your friend to let you know if the family hears anything," he added.

"TELL ME ABOUT CHAVEZ RAVINE," he said to Ted Cullen over lunch the next day.

"The home of our first major league team," his friend said hopefully. "If the city can only persuade one to move out here."

"What? I know the public housing project is dead in the water, but a baseball stadium? Are you serious?"

"Not completely. There's a few people pushing for it, but it's probably a pipe dream. Once Poulson comes in the developers will pounce, and we'll see private housing for mid-income families. They won't want to wait for their profits."

"Okay. So, going back, when were the original residents told they'd have to leave?"

"It was early in '51 when the letters went out. The homeowners were offered below-market prices, but also told that the longer they tried to hold out, the less they'd get. So most sold up and left." Cullen sighed. "And then City Hall changed its mind. After a couple of Bowron's supporters deserted him—bought off, by all accounts—he no longer had a majority for pushing on with the public housing scheme, and his enemies engineered a city-wide referendum to get the whole thing cancelled. A group called CASH—the Campaign Against Socialist Housing—weighed in with lots of money, and Bowron and his friends were all tarred with the Communist brush by the *Times* and others. And given the choice between money for the poor and money for themselves, the good citizens of Los Angeles did what you'd expect, and voted the project down. Now we're just waiting for Poulson and the coup de grace."

"Right. But some of the original residents are still there."

"A few holdouts, yes, but whoever gets hold of the land will move them out as soon as they need to."

Russell didn't doubt it.

"Is this professional interest, or just curiosity?" Cullen asked him.

"Strictly professional at first. I told you about the series on US democracy—well, I was already thinking the Ravine dispute would make a good case study for my European editors. Then yesterday my daughter told me one of her friends used to live there." Russell went through what Rosa had told him about Uncle Cesar's disappearance. "I said I'd investigate, but after thinking that through, I realised I don't have the contacts here, and wondered if you could recommend a local journalist who does. I mean, there might not be anything here, but for someone who knows who to call, it won't be that much work, and he might find himself with a decent story."

"I do know someone. Not well, but for quite a long time. His name's Cal Tierney, and he's been a fixture in LA newspaper circles for twenty years or more, mostly on City desks. I think he's even older than I am. These days he's semiretired, but several papers still like to use him as a guest columnist. And if there is something sinister behind your man's disappearance then that would be the kind of story he loves. Give him a call anyway, say I recommended him."

RUSSELL TOOK THE DOWNTOWN STREETCAR again on Thursday morning, this time en route to the Los Angeles Public Library. It was a cloudy morning, spits of rain dotting the sidewalk as he walked from the terminus to the entrance on Grand.

He spent the next two hours in the newspaper archive, confirming and adding detail to what Cullen had told him about the saga of Chavez Ravine. He had arranged to meet the professor's journalist friend Cal Tierney at the *Examiner* building on Monday morning and wanted to learn as much as he could by then. As he skimmed his way through the more recent newspapers, he also kept a lookout for any salient news from Berlin and Germany that might have passed him by. Thomas had kept him broadly up to date in his monthly letters, but with their upcoming trip in view, Russell thought it wise to take no chances.

Not surprisingly, news from Germany was of only occasional concern to the local press. The general impression given was that the new West Germany was doing well, the new East Germany very badly. The most obvious proof of the latter's dire situation was the number of people opting to leave, which by the end of April had risen to over twelve hundred a day. Farmers were being driven out by collectivisation, small businessmen by crippling rules, the young by a lack of education opportunities.

How, Russell wondered, were Ulbricht and his Soviet masters going to stop this exodus? There was as yet no sign that they planned on ratcheting up tensions with the West and then using the resultant crisis to justify a crackdown—quite the opposite, in fact: the new regime in Moscow was sending out apparent peace feelers on a regular basis. So West Berlin was unlikely to be affected, and neither he nor Effi had any intention of crossing into the Soviet sector.

There was one story that did catch Russell's eye. Two hundred skeletons had just been discovered under the ruins of a Berlin department store, victims of a wartime British or American bombing raid. The house where Rosa had spent several years in hiding had suffered a similar fate, but the body of the woman— Frau Borchers—who had cared for the girl after her mother's death had never been found, and Russell found himself feeling relieved that his daughter had chosen not to travel with them.

He packed up his notes, headed out onto Fifth Street and stood there on the sidewalk, wondering where to have lunch. The Harvey restaurant at Union Station, he decided. The food was good, the decor gorgeous, and the mile-or-so walk would do him good.

The station itself was also a thing of beauty, both inside and out. Constructed less than twenty years earlier, designed as a blend of Spanish mission and art deco styles, it was Russell's favourite building in LA, and he dropped in on a regular basis, sometimes to eat, sometimes just to wander through its precincts and platforms.

He used the west entrance, and stopped at the newsstand to buy a copy of that week's *Time* magazine before walking down the arcade to join the queue in the restaurant lobby. As he'd hoped, the tables inside were rapidly emptying as passengers on the soon-to-depart *El Capitan* made their exits, and a few minutes later he was crossing the famous Navajo rug–style floor. When the waitress came to his table he ordered the broiled whitefish with mashed potatoes, cherry pie à la mode, and a pot of coffee to follow. Maybe the man at Immigration would decide he belonged here after all.

Waiting for his food, he cast his eye round the room, taking in the parrot motif wall tiles and the high vaulted ceiling. A couple arguing caught his attention, and then, beyond them, a lone diner on the far side of the room. He was probably still in his thirties and wearing a worn pale grey suit, and the way he was staring into space somehow seemed odd. He also looked familiar, but it took Russell a while to remember from where: the man had been loitering outside the library when Russell was wondering where to eat.

A coincidence, perhaps—he couldn't be the only library user who liked to eat here. The man was probably a would-be actor, the strange stare part of his preparation for an upcoming audition. Wherever you went in LA you saw people pretending they were someone else.

The fish plate arrived, demanding his whole attention, and by the time the coffee was brought the man was gone. His *Time* magazine had a lengthy article on "The U.S. Negro, 1953"—at least five thousand words, Russell reckoned—which, in light of Rosa's recent interest in Negro music and literature, he thought he should read. But not now.

Instead he skimmed through a few of the shorter articles. The news that the French were using napalm in Indochina was a lot less surprising than the fact that the hideous stuff had first been tried out on the Harvard Business School football field. Presumably not while a game was underway. A piece on how Guatemala and its "picturesque Indians" were becoming a problem for Uncle Sam came complete with a map showing New Orleans a mere 1,080 miles away. Almost within canoeing distance.

More sobering, there was a whole page devoted to the newest USAF jet fighter, which flew faster and higher and carried a heavier payload than anyone else's. Russell remembered how Paul had collected models of Luftwaffe planes, and all the portraits of flying aces on his bedroom wall. His son had found out the hard way what war was really like, and Russell could only hope that all the young American boys drooling over pictures like these would spend the rest of their lives in blissful ignorance.

Full of coffee, he paid the check and made his way to the men's room. He was on his way back to the west entrance when he saw a pale suit reflected in the glass wall of the information kiosk.

Another coincidence? There was only one way to find out. He left the building and slowly made his way back down Main to Fifth Street and the nearest No.3 streetcar stop. He hadn't looked back on the walk, but once at the stop he took a good look round. The fact that Pale Suit was nowhere to be seen should have been reassuring, but it wasn't.

When the streetcar arrived Russell took a seat at the back, and sure enough, there was a cab about four cars back. He couldn't see who was in it, but as the streetcar worked its way west and eventually turned north into Hollywood the cab kept its position. When Russell got off at the Melrose terminus, it continued on north up Larchmont, but he no longer had any doubts. He was being followed.

By whom was the question, but there wasn't an obvious answer. As he walked up Melrose to home, he went through the possibilities, which proved depressingly more numerous than he had expected. He gave the Soviets top billing, closely followed by US Immigration. McClellan had actually told him they'd be monitoring his compliance with the visa conditions. Then there were other US authorities—McCarthy's lot and Hoover's FBI might have rediscovered his past and thought they'd dug up political gold, though he couldn't imagine his old CIA employers taking much interest. And then there was the book he was supposed to be writing—he supposed he might have somehow struck a nerve with his desultory enquiries, but if so he had no idea how or with whom. Ditto the special election candidates, who seemed even more unlikely.

Possibilities but no probabilities. As far he knew, he was no threat to anyone, which might not say much for his work but did wonders for his peace of mind. He liked the fact that five years had now passed without anyone trying to kill him.

If they, whoever they were, were professionals, there'd be another watcher parked close to his home. When he finally got there he noted three possible candidates, and mentally noted the license plate numbers of the pair he had to pass.

Once inside, he sat for a while by the window, willing the cars to leave, but none of them obliged. He knew he would have to tell Effi—in the past when he'd thought it better not to worry her, she'd always put him right in no uncertain terms—but he wasn't looking forward to doing so. She had enough to worry about with HUAC breathing down her and her colleagues' necks.

They were having dinner with friends that evening, and when she and Rosa came home together, he decided to wait until they were on their own, preferably after the dinner. Soon after dark they left Rosa at home with *I Married Joan* and some heated-up meat loaf, and Russell drove them out to the Little Gypsy in West Hollywood, watching the mirror for the same pair of lights. At the intersection with Highland he managed to lose the cars between them and recognise the number.

The Hungarian restaurant on Sunset was going through a fashionable phase and was crowded. Their friends, a couple whom Effi had met when making her best-forgotten first Hollywood

movie, were already on their second gin and tonic, which probably made it hard for them to realise that Russell's mind was mostly
elsewhere. As was Effi's, he thought, but he doubted anyone else
would notice—unsurprisingly, she was a much better actor than
he was.

He had assumed that the problems at work were distracting
her, but on their way home found out otherwise. When he told
he'd been followed all day, and that they were being followed now,
she just said, "I know. I thought I was followed home from work,
but I hoped I was just imagining it, the way I used to in the war.
Apparently I wasn't." She suddenly sat up straight. "What about
Rosa?"

"I'm sure she's okay," Russell replied automatically, speeding
up as he did so. Ten nerve-wracking minutes later he was pulling
the Frazer into their drive and noting the blue TV light flickering
on their living room ceiling. Inside they found Rosa stretched
out on the couch, as the news camera panned across the devastation tornadoes had wrought on a Texan town called Waco.

In the kitchen, Effi asked him if they should tell her. "She feels
so safe here compared to . . ."

"I know, but we have to. She has to be on her guard, at least
until we find out who it is."

Effi agreed. "We'll tell her at breakfast. Play it down, but . . ."

"Play it up?"

"You know what I mean."

"I do."

"Okay, so what do *we* do?"

"Find out who's behind it, I guess."

"I know it sounds silly, but could we just ask?"

Russell shook his head. "They wouldn't tell us. So all we'd do is
make them aware we know."

"How about asking them at gunpoint?" Effi asked, surprising
herself as much as him. "We do have the guns we bought when

we first got here, in case Beria decided he had nothing to lose. Mine's upstairs."

"Mine's in my car. But I think they're a last resort. If I pull a gun on an Immigration investigator, I don't think I'll be here much longer. And it may be something as simple as that—Immigration checking up on me."

"Then why follow me as well?"

"Good question. I don't know."

"Maybe it's HUAC investigating me because of Laura, and you because of me."

"That also sounds feasible."

"You don't think it's the Soviets?"

"They're usually more direct," he said wryly. "And if they wanted to know where we were, they would have found out years ago."

"But maybe Beria's situation has changed. Got suddenly stronger or suddenly weaker. Or something. I don't know. People lash out."

Russell shook his head. "I'm not sure why, but I really doubt it."

"I don't suppose there's any point in going to the police?" Effi asked.

"It would be like taking a complaint about the stormtroopers to the local *Kripo* station. A shrug would be the best you could hope for."

"Wonderful. I suppose we'll just have to wait and see. If it's Immigration or HUAC I expect they'll soon be in touch."

"Well, I did nothing un-American all day," Russell told her. "And I'm sure you didn't either. So our report cards are bound to be good."

"In your dreams," Effi said.

Later in bed, lying awake next to his sleeping wife, Russell sought a way forward in vain. He supposed that even here in LA, most people would probably seek help from the police. But then most people weren't carrying his and Effi's political baggage. Once the LAPD found out that she was consorting with HUAC victims, and that he was accusing some of the city's best-known businesses of collaborating with the Nazis, the two of them would probably be arrested.

A month ago he'd been bored. He wasn't anymore.

UNLIKE THE ACTORS, THE WRITERS worked on Thursdays, so Effi drove by the studio to pick up Beth for their lunch date. She found her friend alone in the script room, searching drawers in vain for something to pin back her hair. Glancing round the room as she waited, Effi noticed that the final board on the episode wall seemed to have been scrubbed clean. "I thought the last two episodes were written," she told Beth.

"They were," Beth said unhappily. "And I'll tell you all about it once we're out of here."

They walked out through empty sound stages to the sunlit lot.

"Zach told us this morning," Beth continued, as they walked towards the car. "He and the sponsors weren't happy with the script."

"The Good Samaritan one? Why not?"

"Well, he trotted out all the standard excuses—not enough laughs, not enough focus on the family, not 'punchy enough' for a season finale. And when we wouldn't buy any of that, he said that the sponsors might find it provocative. Which meant that they hadn't even read it, and that he was second-guessing our wretched paymasters. Maybe rightly, but who knows?"

Beth had given her a précis of this script a few weeks earlier, and Effi had no memory of anything provocative. "Remind me of the storyline," she said.

"The kids are playing out in the yard when they see an elderly Mexican man pulling a cart full of cast-offs trip and fall on the sidewalk outside. They rush out to see if he's all right, and though he's getting back to his feet, he looks far from well. So they persuade him to come and sit on the porch, and when it starts raining, they invite him inside."

"Where's Mrs. Luddwitz all this time?"

"She's doing the beds upstairs, and it's quite a while before she becomes aware of what's going on. When she does hear this strange voice downstairs, she comes rushing down, banging into Eddie as he comes in through the front door, and the two of you find the children in the kitchen, playing Candy Land with this strange Mexican man.

"I should add that before all this happens, Eddie has been lecturing the kids on how important it is to help people in need. Anyway, both of you lose your heads a bit, shouting at the children and the poor Mexican. When the kids finally get to explain what has happened, and remind their dad what he'd said that morning, you and he both feel a little shamefaced. The Mexican gets a piece of cake, and Eddie waits for the street to be clear, so he can surreptitiously take the man back out to his cart. It's all going well until a hydrant goes off, spilling all the neighbours out of their front doors, and leaving Eddie and the Mexican caught like startled rabbits on the sidewalk. After listening to the bigot across the street accuse him of letting down the neighbourhood, Eddie calmly asks the man if he's heard of the Good Samaritan and says how proud he is that his children have followed his Biblical example. Meanwhile the kids and the Mexican are happily waving each other farewell. The end."

"And that is provocative?"

"Apparently it sends the wrong message."

"A Christian message?"

"A message some might find socialistic."

Effi was speechless for a moment. "Let's go to lunch before I go and give Zach a piece of my mind," she said, starting the engine.

"The sad thing is," Beth noted as they left the lot, "he really does think he's saving the show."

"What from—integrity? This is all about Laura, isn't it? They're trying not to attract attention until she's safely gone." Effi couldn't remember feeling more furious. And that morning she'd been feeling so good about what she was doing. She'd had a letter from a Czech director about a possible movie, and though she couldn't take such work behind the Iron Curtain without committing Hollywood suicide, it was really nice to be asked. She'd even half-decided to sign on for another season, as long as John and Rosa had no objections. You couldn't argue with the money, and some-one had to pay for Rosa's college and their old age.

But this. Was stupidity like this something she wanted to be part of? Hadn't she sold herself short enough times under the Nazis?

They reached the farmers market and walked through the stalls to the outside café they often frequented. Once they were seated Beth leaned forward. "I'm sorry. I didn't realise you would be so upset."

"I'm okay," Effi said. Explaining her reaction would involve explaining her whole life as an actor. First for the Nazis, then for the Soviets, now for the Americans. All so intent on dumbing things down.

White Cops, Black Lists

Rosa might have been joking—these days Russell sometimes couldn't tell—but buying his daughter some records for her birthday seemed like a great idea, and having looked up the address in the telephone directory he was now on his way to Dolphin's, the record store she had mentioned. He had chosen to drive rather than take buses—whichever he used he'd stick out like a sore white thumb, but you couldn't roll up the window in a bus.

Before setting off he'd done an inventory of the cars parked nearby, and when he turned right onto Western checked to see which was behind him. It was the beige Hudson.

As he motored the five miles south to Vernon, the faces on the sidewalk remained white. In his three years in LA, Russell had never had reason to visit the Negro district south of downtown, and he wasn't sure what to expect. Which, he knew all too well, was somewhat shameful for someone who had always taken pride in his social awareness. As a resident in Hitler's Nazi Germany for eight years, he had thought himself reasonably sensitive to racial prejudice, but apparently this wasn't the case. As far as his daughter was concerned, Negroes were as "invisible" to him as they were to most of his fellow Caucasians.

She had a point, one easier to explain than excuse. The area they lived in, and those in which they dined or sought entertainment, were white areas. He used his car for most journeys, and the work he did was not only solitary, but thanks to US Immigration also devoid of involvement with any Americans. So his acquaintanceship with Negroes had been little more than the occasional glimpse of a brown face doing a menial job in someone else's home or business. Those with whom he'd shared more than a word or two could probably be counted on his fingers.

By contrast, he had known many Jews in Germany—as fellow members of the Party, as journalistic colleagues, and, after the Nazis took over, as old friends and acquaintances who were now suffering persecution. So it wasn't just him—the situations were different. Before Hitler, many German Jews had occupied prominent positions in business and the professions, but as far as he could see, that was not the case in America. Here, slavery's Jim Crow shadow still kept the vast majority of Negroes in what whites considered their rightful place, as an economic underclass doing physical labour of one kind or another. Away from work, physical segregation was still seen as the natural order of things, and any nominal political rights were contingent on these not being used to upset the status quo.

There had been some changes lately. Segregation in sports and the military had been successfully challenged, but when it came to housing and neighbourhoods, the old order was still clinging on, as tenaciously here in Los Angeles as anywhere in the South. The Supreme Court had recently ruled that racial zoning and the restrictive mortgage covenants that allowed them were illegal, but that hadn't stopped white areas greeting Negro incomers with violence, nor encouraged the LAPD to offer the latter any protection. Police Chief Parker, whom the *Times* admired so much, refused to hire any new Negro officers, and wouldn't let those already employed partner with whites. Its borders might be growing slightly more porous, but what many whites still called Darktown was as much of a ghetto as those that the Nazis had surrounded with walls and wire.

After turning east onto Vernon, he checked that the Hudson was still behind him, and wondered what his shadow was thinking about possible destinations. Was the suspect en route to a secret place of illicit work? Was he meeting fellow communists in some seedy back room? Russell doubted whether visiting a record shop was high on his list of guesses.

Shortly after crossing Broadway and Main, he had the sense of entering another country. Just like that, all the faces on the sidewalks were brown, and the only visible white ones were up on billboards, encouraging their brown countrymen to buy white products. And he himself was drawing looks. Nothing hostile as far as he could tell, and maybe it was more the car inviting attention—it looked a lot newer than most of the others now sharing the road.

Dolphin's, as he'd discovered from the telephone directory, was at 1065 East Vernon, and that, his *Renié Atlas* had suggested, was a block this side of Central Avenue. He heard it before he saw it—even at eleven in the morning, music was pouring out through the open door. The store had a huge picture window full of record sleeves and, extending out onto the sidewalk, a currently empty glassed-in booth complete with gramophone.

In front of which, a young white man was shouting at two white uniformed cops.

Rather than step into something that might prove problematic—LA cops, it was frequently said, were best not approached with anything other than bribes—Russell kept on going. The lights were red at the Central Avenue intersection, and he watched the threesome in his wing mirror as he waited for green. An arm shot up, and he caught a glint of what was probably steel handcuffs before someone hooted their impatience behind him. Reasoning that the cops would be taking their victim somewhere else, he turned left onto Central and then left twice more, before parking the car on a side street a few yards from Vernon.

Approaching the latter on foot he poked his head round the corner. The cops were gone, the store only a short walk away.

Russell walked up to the entrance and sauntered in, causing three pairs of eyes to glance his way, each with the same look of surprise. "Hi," he said to the young man behind the counter. "There was a bit of trouble outside," he added, mostly to break the silence.

"You could say," the young man said. He shrugged. "Same every day." He had slicked black hair and a thin moustache and was wearing an exquisite dark red suit. "What's that accent you have?"

"An English one, I guess."

"Ah, that explains it."

"Explains what?"

"How you think you can walk in here like you did, this being such a dangerous neighbourhood and all. That trouble outside you saw—that was another white man trying to shop here. The police put him right, told him what a risk he was taking, being so far from where he should be."

"Will they come back?"

"As sure as the sun goes down."

It was Russell's turn to shrug. "If they do, they do. It's my daughter's birthday next week and she likes the music you sell here, so I'm hoping to buy her some records."

"What do you have in mind?"

"She told me she likes Billy Ward, Fats Domino, and the '5' Royales—have I got the names right?"

"Just about."

"So I thought a record or two by each of them. Can you do that?"

"I can. Now Billy Ward's best is 'Sixty Minute Man' . . ."

There were guffaws from the other two customers.

"But as I was going to say, maybe not—how old is this daughter of yours?"

"Almost seventeen."

"Then maybe not. He has a hit right now with 'Pedal Pushin' Papa,' which sounds kind of appropriate, no?"

"Yeah."

"Fats Domino 'Going to the River'—that's good. And the '5' Royales . . ."

"'Baby Don't Do It,'" one of the customers suggested.

"Yeah, she'll like that. And you could add the best record of the year by a country mile—and that's 'Hound Dog' by Big Mama Thornton."

"Okay. Sounds great."

The young man began collecting the 78s from their boxes. "You want to listen before you buy?"

Russell shook his head. "I think I'll get out of here before the cops come back."

"Wise move. Most days we have to sweep up the records they've accidentally dropped." He handed Russell the four disks in a brown paper bag, and was giving him change for the five-dollar bill when the cop car drew up against the opposite curb. "Do you have a ride?" the young man asked.

"My car's just round the corner."

"I can let you out the back."

Russell was tempted, but the need to know triumphed. Would they really take him to task just for being in a Negro district?

They would. They were out of the car so fast that the fat one dropped his nightstick.

Russell tried just walking away, but the thin one was quick enough to block his path.

"Mister, what do you think you're doing here? This is a very dangerous area."

"I realise that, officer," Russell said with a friendly smile. "And I wouldn't come here at night. But in the morning they're mostly sleeping."

"Who are?"

"You know. Them."

"Okay. But what are you *doing* here?" the fat one asked.

"Oh, I needed some records. I work for a television company, and they're making a programme about race music and where it comes from. Jungle rhythms, devil worship, that sort of thing. You can't buy music like this in Hollywood."

The look on the fat one's face was priceless.

"Hey, lookie," the thin one said, his eyes on the street beyond Russell.

Turning to follow his gaze, the fat one and Russell saw two people getting out of a shiny new Cadillac. The man was brown, the woman a blonde. "Get yourself back to Tinseltown!" the thin one shouted over his shoulder as he and his partner hurried off to greet these new arrivals.

Never a dull moment, Russell thought.

"They love their job," the young man from Dolphin's observed, appearing at his side.

The cops had both man and woman face up against the side of the car, and were searching them for weapons, roughly in the man's case, lovingly in the woman's. Then the handcuffs were out.

"What are they arresting them for?" Russell asked.

"What do you think?"

The handcuffed twosome had been shoved into their own back seat, and the fat one was squeezing himself in behind the wheel. As his partner pulled away in the cop car, he pulled out behind in the Cadillac.

"Now you've got no protection," Russell wryly observed.

"I may break down and cry."

"So what'll they do with them?"

"They'll be taken to the Newton station. If he's not carrying drugs or a weapon he'll probably just get roughed up a bit. If he's not unlucky, that is, and the cops are already upset about something or other. Then it's God's call. The girl'll just get a talk-ing-to, once they've all had a feel. Her parents'll get called to come and get her, and they'll get lectured too. Chief Parker don't like mixing. We might subvert his people, turn them all into commu-nists or sex perverts. Hell, our music might even bring them back to life." He glanced at Russell. "No offence."

"None taken. Must be bad for business."

"In the daytime, yeah. At night there's too many white faces for them to handle. Some of them famous too. We had Ava Gard-ner in the other night. She was dancing at the Dunbar Hotel and came in to buy some records. I'd like to see them try and arrest that lady. Hmm."

Russell smiled. "Well I'll try and bring my daughter down some evening. She'd love it."

"If she likes our music she's welcome anytime. We're open twenty-four hours a day, you know."

Russell offered a hand, and after the briefest of hesitations, the young man took it.

Walking back to the Frazer, Russell could hear a siren rapidly growing louder. He got himself quickly behind the wheel, and after turning right onto Vernon took a look in the rearview mirror. A cop car was pulling up opposite the store. The protec-tion was back, and so, of course, was the beige Hudson, which pulled out behind him as he started out for home.

Waiting at the first red light he realised when he'd last seen white cops stopping white civilians from entering shops—in Nazi Berlin in '33. There the stores had been owned by Jews, but the rationale had been the same.

AFTER DROPPING ROSA OFF AT school that morning Effi sat behind the wheel for a while, thinking about what differ-ent childhoods they had had. Her own had been privileged, albeit not as emotionally full as some she'd heard described. She couldn't say she'd been close to her mother and father—they'd always seemed more interested in each other than their children—but she and her sister had been wonderfully close. Materially, they had never really wanted for anything, and their parents' benign neglect had offered her and Zarah a degree of freedom that few girls their age had been granted back then. If her parents hadn't encouraged her acting, they certainly hadn't stood in her way. And they'd always been financially supportive—the flat she still owned in Berlin had been their twenty-fifth birthday present to her.

By contrast, Rosa had been four when her mother chose life in a Christian woman's garden shed over death somewhere in the east, seven when her mother had been killed by a British or American bomb, eight when the Swedish diplomat Erik Aslund brought her to Effi's flat in the final weeks of the war. Since then Rosa had spent six months in postwar London, four years in broken Berlin, and now three at the end of Hollywood's rainbow. So much trauma, so many moves. So different from Effi's own experience.

The one thing they shared was a talent for self-expression—Effi as an actor, Rosa as a visual artist. Effi was quite aware that Rosa's talent was more special than hers, almost, she sometimes thought, to the point of proving a burden. She had a sudden memory of the teacher at Rosa's previous school, who clearly fancied herself as an artist, looking almost resentful when she first saw the girl's drawings. A gift like that could make you feel alone, Effi thought. She was glad that Rosa would be spending the month with Ali, another Jew who'd been orphaned and hunted and somehow survived.

Effi looked at her watch and realised the meeting at the studio would be starting without her if she didn't get a move on. As far as she could tell, no one had followed them to the school, and no one pulled out after her now. Whoever they were, it seemed they'd lost interest, at least in her.

She hadn't yet thought of anything useful to say at the meeting, but loyalty to Beth, who had begged all the cast and writers to attend, encouraged her to shave a minute off the five she usually needed to reach the studio entrance on Highland. A swift walk through the stages brought her to the costume room, where Beth had decided the meeting was least likely to be noticed.

It had already started, and with a reasonable attendance—as far as Effi could see, the only missing adults were Eddie and Laura. The two children had presumably not been invited.

Bruce Manning, who played one of the elderly neighbours who'd moved in next door early in the season, was sounding philosophical: "Ten years ago the Communists were our allies, and it was fine to be one. Now they're not, and it isn't. That's just the reality."

Beth was shaking her head. "That's not the point. I think everyone read that script before the copies all went mysteriously missing. The storyline is a straight lift from the Bible with a few comic twists. It's about giving help to people who need it. Are we really saying that charity is un-American? That the Good Samaritan was a communist? That's absurd."

"No more absurd than the *Times* saying public housing is a communist plot," Manning replied. "Like it or not, that's the kind of world we're living in."

"The land of the free," Beth's writing colleague John said wryly.

"Well, it is," Clark Newman insisted. Playing the show's patriotic mailman was obviously a labour of love. "And sometimes freedom needs protecting."

"This is all just politics," Carol Berkman chipped in. She was Bruce's wife in the show.

"You better believe it," Beth said with a laugh.

"But we're entertainers," Carol persisted. "We try to make people happy or sad, make them laugh or cry. To get them out of themselves for half an hour, give them a break from their problems. We're not supposed to be delivering political messages, no matter how right they might seem. Not communist ones, not anti-communist ones."

"That's not . . ." Beth began, then stopped.

"Our primary obligation is to the show," Bruce interjected. "To the people who pay for it and the people who make it and the people who watch it."

"Don't we have one to ourselves?" Effi asked.

"Not to mention our families," Mary Thurman said, misunderstanding Effi's point. She played Eddie's latest girlfriend. "I need to keep working to feed mine, and the way I see it we have three choices—quit, kick up a fuss, or accept that it's their decision. Well, I can't afford to quit. And if we kick up a fuss HUAC will be all over us like a rash, and half of us will end up on the blacklist whether we deserve it or not. So I vote for swallowing our pride or our principles or whatever they are and letting them have their way. But maybe some of you fancy playing Joan of Arc?"

Silence greeted this last remark, and looking round the faces Effi realised that no one did.

"I don't think we need to be that dramatic," Beth's other writer colleague interjected. Tim Beasley and his crumpled white suit had been a Hollywood fixture for almost a quarter century. "I don't like what's happened here anymore than Beth," he began. "That script was good, and the reason they pulled it was not. But I think we're missing one salient point. We're not being asked to write a show that mocks kindness and compassion; we're just being told that we can't write one that pushes those values in a way those idiots upstairs consider provocative. So what we can do is get the same damn story past those same damn idiots by writing it in a different way. We just have to be a little more subtle about it. And we can do that. Because we're the creative ones, right?" he concluded, looking at Beth as he did so.

"I guess it's worth a shot," Beth agreed reluctantly, inviting what felt like a collective sigh of relief. She stayed in her seat while the room emptied out, the anger in her eyes slowly morphing into sadness. "Where did my country go?" she asked Effi.

"A question I remember asking myself," Effi remarked. "In 1933 most likely, though the thought seemed to linger for years. But that's probably not what you want to hear."

Beth grimaced. "God, I hate them."

Having lived with Russell long enough to know who she meant, Effi changed tack. "Has Eddie voiced an opinion? It is *his* show."

"I doubt the sponsors would agree with you. But no, he hasn't, which probably tells you all you need to know."

"I suppose it does. Do you know why Laura didn't come?" Effi asked, already half-knowing the answer.

"Because she thinks everyone's blaming her for the current crisis."

"But that's ridiculous. She's just a victim. The only one here, so far."

"That might be obvious to you and me, but it isn't to some of our colleagues, and they *have* been mouthing off. Laura's not imagining it."

RUSSELL DROVE HOME FROM DOLPHIN'S thinking about what he'd just experienced. The words "tip" and "iceberg" came to mind, and driving the final mile down Melrose he couldn't help noticing how peaceful and prosperous everything seemed. Not to mention white, though he did spot one young black woman waiting in line at the streetcar terminal. For a two-hour journey home, he guessed.

A note informing him that Cal Tierney had called was on the stand in the hall, left by their cleaner, a middle-aged Hispanic woman named Ximena whom the studio had provided, and whom Effi had persuaded with no little difficulty to answer the phone when both she and Russell were out. Looking at the note, Russell realised he had no idea where Ximena lived. He had the impression LA's Hispanics were less ghettoised than the city's Negroes, but an impression, he realised, was all it was.

He called the number she had neatly printed out.

Tierney picked up, the familiar hum of a newsroom behind him. "I found your man," he said. "The uncle, Cesar Morales. I actually found about ten of them—it's not an uncommon name—but your man is in the Chino prison hospital."

"Where the hell is that?"

"Out in San Bernardino County. Its actual name is the California Institution for Men. It's the only state prison in southern California."

"How did he get there? Is he okay?"

"No one will tell me what's wrong with him, and no visits are allowed in the first two weeks of a sentence. Or so I've been told. Sounds like crap to me. As to how he got there—he was arrested on the sixth for assaulting a police officer and, believe it or not, charged, convicted, sentenced, and jailed by the afternoon of the seventh."

"That sounds remarkably fast."

"Unbelievably so. But until someone talks or I manage to access a written record, I can't be sure. I do believe that he's spent the last week in the Chino hospital wing."

"So what's next?"

"Nothing till Monday I'm afraid. I'm out of town for the weekend—family business I can't put off. But Monday morning I'm going to talk to Cesar's neighbours up in Chavez Ravine, see what they can tell me about his arrest."

"Mind if I come with you?"

"Not at all. And if you can get your daughter's friend to come too, the locals may be more inclined to open up."

"I'll get Rosa to ask him."

After they'd arranged a meeting place and time, Russell made a sandwich with what he could find in the fridge, poured himself a coke, and took them both out to the patio, where his *Time* magazine was waiting. He'd started on "The U.S. Negro, 1953" earlier that morning, and after his visit to Dolphin's felt duty-bound to wade through the rest.

It made for curious reading. Five thousand words was a lot for what could have been said in less than five hundred, and the general tone was that of a teacher let down by a promising pupil. Yes, Negroes had been given a raw deal in the past, but now America was willing to give them a real chance. If they worked hard, and seized all those opportunities that were now on offer, then the good life could also be theirs. And of course, by implication, if they failed to rise to the challenge, then sadly they would have no one to blame but themselves.

There was nothing about ending segregation, or about securing fair and equal treatment from the police and other authorities. There was no indication of how a group denied decent standards of education, health care, and housing for several centuries were supposed to compete with a white majority which had enjoyed those benefits. The author might be well-meaning or utterly cynical—it was hard to tell—but his picture of America bore about as much relation to reality as the most saccharine Hollywood movie. Russell knew how the young man behind the counter at Dolphin's would respond to a piece like this: "You're joking, right?"

He lay in the hammock for a while, watching the palm fronds gently waving to and fro against the pure blue sky, then went back inside to work on his opening article for the series on US Democracy. He'd been writing for about an hour when the telephone rang.

The voice on the other end was not one he recognised. "Am I speaking to John Russell?" the woman asked.

"You are."

"My name is Janice Sullivan."

It rang no bells. "What can I do for you?"

"You sound English."

"I am. English."

"Oh," she said, before pausing for a mental recalibration. "But you are the John Russell who is writing a book about American companies that did business with Germany. During the war."

Russell was suddenly interested. "I am."

"You spoke to my husband, Milo, a few weeks ago."

"I remember." The man's aggressive denials had been less than convincing.

"I think he hung up on you."

"He was not the only one," Russell conceded, wondering where this was going.

"He worked for Dreverel."

"I know he did."

"Well, he died," she said flatly. "A few days after you called him. Not because of that, though. A climbing accident, up in the mountains. He loved to climb."

She sounded less than devastated by the loss, but Russell felt obliged to offer condolences.

She ignored them. "About his hanging up on you. It wasn't that he didn't *want* to talk to you—he just wasn't allowed. Way back in the war, the company offered him $500 if he signed these papers promising not to talk about what had happened, and like a fool, he did. And once he'd put pen to paper they told him they'd sue our house out from under us if he ever broke his promise. So that's why he hung up on you."

"Nice of you to let me know," Russell told her.

"You're welcome. But that's not why I'm calling."

"Oh?"

"He signed the papers. I didn't."

"Ah. But do you have access to the information your husband was prevented from sharing?"

"I know what he told me. Which, before you say it, I know is just hearsay. But he also kept records. There's a work diary which covers the years you care about. Dreverel's dealings with a firm called Schauflegen."

Russell seriously doubted whether disapproval of Dreverel's treasonable wartime activities was the woman's prime motivation. "You're looking to sell the diary?"

"I am. When Milo was in the hospital he told me he'd rather sell it to you than the company, because he really did feel bad about what they did in the war. And that's why I'm giving you first dibs. But I don't have his guilty conscience, so I want a decent offer, or I will go back to the company."

"Do they know about the diary?"

"Not yet."

"I'd have to see it to make an offer. As you said," Russell added disingenuously, "the information's just hearsay. It's the diary that's worth something, not knowing what's in it. So you're not giving anything away by letting me see it."

"I already worked that out."

"Okay. So where is the diary? And where do you live?"

"In the Valley, but I don't want you coming to my house. The diary's in a safety deposit box, and I'll bring it to you somewhere public. Do you know the coffee shop–restaurant at Clybourn and Sherman?"

"No, but I can find it."

"Is Monday morning okay?"

"I've already got an appointment then. How about the afternoon?"

"I can do that. Three o'clock?"

"Three o'clock."

She abruptly hung up, leaving Russell holding the phone to his ear. He was taking it away when he heard the tell-tale click.

Had someone really been listening in to their conversation? And if so, which phone were they tapping, his or hers? Or was the click something perfectly normal that he just hadn't noticed before?

There was an easy way to find out. He called Ted Cullen's secretary and asked that Ted call him back as soon as he could. There was no click after the outgoing call, and none after the later incoming call from Cullen, which Russell used to set a lunch date. If there was a problem, it was Janice Sullivan's, and he would mention it when he saw her on Monday. But maybe not until he had his hands on the diary.

Back in the garden, the *Time* magazine article still lay open on the table. On a sudden impulse, Russell reached for that day's *LA Times*, and carefully leafed his way through all sixty-four pages. There had to be at least a hundred faces pictured, and every one of them was white.

Cars Full of Shadows

Taking the U-Bahn under the sector border always felt a little strange to Gerhard Ströhm, as if those who ran the railway were the only people unaware that Berlin had been split into two. It was still a simple process, though: their papers were checked at Potsdamer Strasse, but no questions were asked. For all the security policeman knew, he could have been leaving for good.

Perhaps his Party card eased the way—Ströhm didn't know. And he *should* know, he thought, regressing, as he did these days with increasing frequency, into the person he once had been, a calculating threat to the bastards in power rather than one of them.

When they reached Zoo Station there were no checks at all, just a posse of bored-looking British soldiers more interested in vulnerable female migrants than members of the SED Central Committee.

He and Annaliese crossed Hardenbergstrasse and walked arm in arm down Joachimsthaler Strasse to the bustling Kurfürstendamm. Every time he came to the Western Sector, it felt a little more estranged from its eastern brother, a livelier, noisier, even happier place, though doubtless the last depended on who you were. There were also more beggars, more groups of furtive children— happiness for some was penury for others. Ströhm had never wavered in his hatred of capitalism, only in believing that there was currently a better alternative.

Being early, they took their time looking in Ku'damm's shop windows. The prices seemed outrageous to Ströhm, but the amount of choice was extraordinary, and business seemed to be brisk.

Thomas and Hanna Schade were waiting outside the Film-bühne Wien. Gerhard and Annaliese had first met each other at a family picnic in the Schades' Dahlem garden, Ströhm invited by Thomas's ex-brother-in-law, John Russell, Annaliese by Russell's wife, Effi, whom she'd met during the war. When the Russells had moved to America in 1950, the Schades and the Ströhms had kept in fairly regular contact, despite—and perhaps in unspoken defiance of—the ossifying border between their halves of the city.

The film they were here to see was *The Rose of Stamboul.* Neither man liked musicals, but both the women did, and it had been their turn to choose. Annaliese was particularly fond of the female star, Inge Egger, who had once spent a week in her hospital ward, and never refused a request to sing.

The Rose of Stamboul lived down to Ströhm's expectations. The plot, taken from a thirty-five-year-old operetta, was suitably ludicrous: a young political reformer in Turkey adopts a literary alias to protect his politician father, and after his writings win him an adulatory following among women, he ends up with an arranged wife who can't love him because she's already given her heart to his literary alter ego. As the story unfolded the film's characters would occasionally burst into song, shattering even the faintest hope of credibility. Ströhm had trouble staying awake in the non-musical scenes and felt the point of Annaliese's elbow more than once. She, at least, was enjoying it.

Once it was over, they walked to the nearby Café Kranzler and took one of several empty tables outside the temporary building—the original structure had been mostly wrecked in the war. Letting his gaze wander, Ströhm thought he detected several fellow citizens of the DDR enjoying an after-show hour or two sampling the delights of the Western sector. Those westerners who still flocked in numbers to theatre and concert performances in the Eastern sector usually emerged onto streets already half-asleep and headed straight for the U-Bahn.

"We have news," Thomas announced once their coffee and strudels had arrived. "Effi's been invited to the Berlinale next month, and John's coming with her. They'll be here about three weeks, staying with us, I hope."

"Oh, that's wonderful," Annaliese exclaimed. "I was only thinking the other day that it's been ten years since Effi started coming to the Elisabeth to cheer up the wounded."

And the same amount of time since he and John Russell had skulked in blacked-out railway yards watching Jewish transports departing for the east, Ströhm thought, but didn't say. It would be good to see him.

"Does she have a film in the festival?" Annaliese was asking.

"Not a new one, I don't think." Thomas said. "They seem to be doing a career retrospective, with a question-and-answer session tagged on the end."

"That'll be fun," Annaliese said. "She's not one for taking prisoners."

"No," Thomas agreed. "And I'm looking forward to the whole thing. With so many people coming over from the east it'll feel a bit like the old Berlin."

"There are quite a lot coming already," Ströhm said drily.

"Yes, of course. And I was going to ask you about that. Aren't your people getting worried?"

"Yes is the short answer. But doing something about it is another matter." He took a quick look around to make sure that no one was listening. "The Soviets have more or less told us—I say more or less because the level of insistence keeps changing—they've told us—told Ulbricht—that we have to slow down, give people something *today*, something more than promises of a golden future."

"And are you?"

"Not so you'd notice. Ulbricht and Grotewöhl are not resisting openly, but they're not really changing course either. Today the Central Committee announced it was going ahead with raising the norms for all the Stalinallee construction workers."

"Less pay for more work."

"Right. I'm praying that Moscow insists on a rethink. Because I think they're playing with fire. Did you hear about what happened in Plovdiv?"

"The tobacco workers, yes I did. They killed quite a few, I think, though these days our papers always sound like they're exaggerating."

"I would love to tell you that they were," Ströhm said wryly.

"But they weren't."

Ströhm shook his head.

"Lotte came to see us last weekend," Thomas said, lowering his voice and glancing at Hanna. She and Annaliese, presumably bored by the politics, had started their own conversation.

"How is she?" Ströhm asked, suspecting that Thomas wasn't changing the subject. He occasionally ran into Lotte at party functions, but only really to say hello. He wouldn't say he knew her.

"She was evasive."

Seeing that Thomas was hesitant to continue, Ströhm quietly reassured his friend that anything he said would be in confidence.

"Thank you, but all I really have is a feeling of unease. Lotte has always thrown herself into things. She worshipped Hitler as a young adolescent, then fell head over heels with your party."

"And you think she might be doing it again?"

"I'm afraid she doesn't realise how dangerous that could be."

"Ah."

"She has this new boyfriend, Werner something or other. He also works at *Neues Deutschland*, as a printer I think. The things she says about him sets all my alarm bell ringing. He's so committed, so fearless. He has so much belief in the people, so much integrity. Forgive me for saying this, Gerhard, but these don't seem qualities that your current leadership puts much stock in."

Ströhm nodded. "I know what you mean. In the long run young people like him and your Lotte are our best hope, but it's true that these days we seem to be either making them angry or demoralising them completely." He sighed. "And yes, in our current situation anger can get someone in a lot of trouble . . ."

Thomas looked even more worried. "Gerhard, I realise this is an imposition, and please don't hesitate to say no, but I was wondering if you could make a few discreet enquiries about this boy. Believe me," he added, seeing the look on Ströhm's face, "I don't relish the thought of having my grown-up daughter spied on. But Hanna and I, we're both afraid of what might happen."

Ströhm took a quick look round. "Well, I hope your fears are unfounded, but I'll see what I can find out. And if Lotte says anything more to alarm you, just call me, and I'll call you back on a public phone as quickly as I can."

Thomas looked surprised.

"You wouldn't believe how many lines in this city are tapped," Ströhm told him. "The Soviets, the Americans, the British, they're all at it. Someone told me the French would join in if they could, but all their engineers are out in Indochina."

SATURDAY WAS ROSA'S BIRTHDAY, AND, keen that nothing should spoil it, Russell and Effi had come to a tacit agreement the previous evening, that discussing their various problems could wait until after the day was done. Zarah, Bill, Lothar, and Casey were expected that afternoon, along with a trio of Rosa's friends that included Juan Morales.

By two everyone was there, and Russell was busy grilling hamburgers and hot dogs in the kitchen. Out in the garden, watching Rosa and her friends, Effi decided that they all had one thing in common—like Rosa herself, they were misfits of one kind or another. One of the girls was a short-sighted piano prodigy, the other a mixed-race Anglo-Indian whose parents were divorced, and whose father was an Oscar-nominated camera-man. The boy from school, according to Rosa, was a mathematical genius who much preferred playing baseball. And then there was Juan, who seemed like a sweet normal boy, but no doubt felt like a fish out of water in Rosa's Hollywood evening class. He had already promised Russell that, school or no school, he would accompany him and Cal Tierney on Monday.

They might all be misfits, Effi thought, but none seemed sad or depressed, and they were certainly an interesting bunch.

Russell's records had proved popular, probably too much so as far as the neighbours were concerned. Representatives of both families had cautiously emerged from their back doors, as if afraid they might find that their biggest nightmare had moved in next door. The relief when they saw a garden full of white folks was tangible, though they couldn't disguise their doubts about the music pouring out through the window. After hearing "Baby Don't Do It" for the fifth time, Effi could understand their disquiet.

She had bought the kids tickets for *Abbott and Costello Go to Mars*, which was showing nearby, and once they had left, and Zarah and her family had headed for home, she and Russell sat out on the bench in the debris-strewn garden, exhausted but happy.

"I think she had a good time," Russell said.

"Oh she did. You know, we've been so lucky with her."

"We have. But she's been lucky too, having you for a mother."

"You haven't done so badly yourself, Mr DJ. Though the ham-burgers were a touch overdone."

"You mean burnt."

"I was being kind." She turned to face him. "I forgot to ask—were you followed yesterday?"

"I was."

"I wasn't. And I was hoping that was because they'd learned whatever they wanted to learn."

"Apparently not," Russell said. "In my case, anyway. My guy tracked me all the way to Dolphin's and all the way back again. In a different car. Whoever they are, they have access to a lot of vehicles. I don't know." He smiled. "I've almost got used to a permanent tail—it feels a bit like having a dog. Once yesterday, on the way back up Western, I just made it through a light and he didn't, and my first thought was that I ought to slow down in case he lost me. How crazy is that?"

"Very. You're not saying we shouldn't be worried?"

"No, I'm sure we should. It just feels . . . I don't know . . . at first it felt sinister and now it doesn't. It feels like we're just being checked on, that someone wants to find out where we go, who we know, what we do, that someone's been asked to compile a report for God knows what reason. My money's still on Immigration."

"Which would explain why they've stopped following me," Effi observed.

"It might. And if it is Immigration we've got nothing to worry about, because I've been a very good boy."

She gave him a sceptical look. "I think the English phrase is 'Pull the other one, buster.'"

DESPITE WHAT HE'D THOUGHT AND said the day before, Russell couldn't help feeling angry that Sunday's outing to Venice Beach also involved his seemingly permanent shadow. Threatening or not, the intrusion was most unwelcome.

Assuming Effi had noticed and Rosa hadn't, he managed to

put the matter out of his mind once they'd left the car in the vast amusement park lot. Doubtless the driver was still somewhere behind them, but at least he was out of sight.

The park was clearly popular, but looked decidedly anti-quated for a project that was only two years old. Perhaps the whole idea was outdated, because walking through the stalls and rides reminded him of prewar days, when this sort of entertainment still seemed fresh and exciting. He remembered how Paul had always been begging for a day at the funfair on Potsdamer Strasse. And then there was that evening at Luna Park soon after the Reichstag Fire, looking for the missing rent boy Timo.

Glancing at Rosa, he was pleased to see her wide-eyed and happy. Effi also seemed to be enjoying herself, despite being occasionally recognised and stopped by fans. Russell watched her deal with them in her usual charming way and knew that it was something he could never do. He had once asked if she enjoyed such attention, and she had told him "mostly, yes." A few people were obnoxious, but most were not, and who didn't like being appreciated? "If I ever start snapping at people, and telling them to go away, I'll know it's time to quit."

After a late brunch in a gleaming silver diner, they left the park for a walk round the original town, whose makers had tried to recreate its Italian namesake. Whatever success they'd had, the craze for oil had destroyed it, with canals and bridges either over-grown or buried amid a forest of clanking derricks.

"Remember our trip to the one in Italy?" Effi asked the two of them, and both smiled at the memory. Russell had been dumped in far-off Trieste by American intelligence and had threatened to quit if Effi and Rosa weren't flown down for a weekend in Venice. Those had been three days of love and happiness in a summer littered with broken bodies. He had a sudden memory of his thirteen-year-old daughter's enraptured face as she stared at the wall mosaics in Torcello's seventh-century cathedral.

By midafternoon they were back in the car and travelling north, having agreed to take the long way home. They had just turned onto Sunset when Rosa announced in a noticeably brittle voice that she thought they were being followed. "I was looking back at the ocean," she explained, "and I noticed the man in the green car behind us. I kept seeing him at the amusement park, but I thought we were just going the same way."

In the rearview mirror Russell watched the man let a couple of other cars pass him. He'd obviously ended up right behind them at the lights.

Effi looked at Russell, who nodded his agreement.

"You're not mistaken," Effi told, turning round to face her daughter. "But we don't think there's any reason to worry. They've been following your dad and me for a few days . . ."

"So why didn't you tell me?" Rosa asked, leaning forward. "And who are 'they'?"

"We don't know. And we didn't want to worry you for no good reason."

"I think being followed is a pretty good reason."

"You may be right," Russell agreed.

"So who could it be?" Rosa asked. She seemed more angry than frightened, which was probably a good sign.

Russell went through the possibilities, and said that his money was on the US Immigration service. Which might have once been true, but not anymore—over the previous week he had seen so many different cars and drivers, and he very much doubted that the LA Immigration office employed that many. If by some strange chance they did, they surely wouldn't be using them all on a single case for weeks on end.

"If you really want to know," Rosa cut into his thoughts, "why don't you hire a private detective like Boston Blackie?"

Russell couldn't help smiling. Over the last few years PI Blackie and his fearless female secretary had been putting the world to rights, first on radio and then TV. The show was one of the family's favourites, and the recent announcement that the current series would be the last had disappointed them all. "It would have to be a one-man operation," Russell mused out loud, taking the idea seriously. "If we go to an agency, it might turn out to be the one watching us. But I suppose there must be some real-life Boston Blackies out there with only a feisty secretary to keep them company. I'll start looking tomorrow."

"DO YOU KNOW OF A private investigator you could recommend?" Russell asked Tierney the next morning as they walked out into the lot behind the *Examiner* building. He had taken the trolley downtown, thinking that his tail could spend a couple of hours watching the front entrance for his reemergence.

"For this?" Tierney asked, surprised.

"No, for something else. I'm being followed," he added, seeing no reason to keep it from the journalist. "I was followed here—when we come out onto Main you'll see a green Buick parked on the other side of the street. I'll be hunkered down so the man doesn't see me."

"Okay," Tierney said, looking amused.

They climbed into his black Pontiac.

"Effi's being followed as well. It's been going on for a week, and we'd like to know who's behind it."

"Time to hide your face," Tierney said, as they neared the mouth of the entrance road.

A minute later he announced the all clear. "Your friend was there," he confirmed. "And yes, I know of a few PIs. None well, I'm afraid."

They were about to turn left onto Sunset. "We need someone discreet," Russell. "Effi's a celebrity these days, and I don't want the story ending up in Hedda Hopper's column. She'd probably imply it was HUAC investigators."

"Might it be?"

"Conceivably. But for a week? They don't give the impression of being that thorough."

Tierney grinned. "I've never met him, but I've heard good things about a guy named Jessup. Frank Jessup. He works alone, as far as I know. Has an office in Santa Monica, and he'll be in the book."

Russell registered the name. "I'll give him a try." They were driving down Lilac Terrace now, and entering the area slated for development. A mile or so later, when they reached the bottom of Paducah Street, they'd seen only three human beings, and received a hostile stare from each.

Many houses had been demolished, though no apparent effort had been made to move the debris. Others just looked abandoned.

"I'm not expecting to learn very much," Tierney said. "I spoke to Cesar's brother, and he'd already asked around for anyone who'd seen anything. No one had, and he says they wouldn't lie. But I'd like to see the place. I always find that makes it more real."

They didn't have to seek out Cesar's house—Juan was sitting outside the address with a friend he introduced as Vicente. The house behind them had been razed by a bulldozer, but according to Juan, Cesar had rebuilt the ramshackle shed in which he kept his seeds and garden tools and now lived in that. The vegetable plot, needless to say, was utterly wrecked.

Inside the shed was an army cot, a kettle, and a few hanging clothes.

"I tidied up a bit in case he comes home," Juan said.

Outside, in a fire pit that Cesar had dug out, the burnt remains of several books could be just about distinguished.

"He kept a diary," Juan said. "Ever since the letters came."

Another one, Russell thought. Narratives of rich men's greed. No doubt Dreverel would pay to see Milo Sullivan's diary reduced to ashes.

"And no one saw anything," Tierney muttered to himself.

"Vicente heard them arrive," Juan said unexpectedly.

"You did?" Tierney exclaimed, turning to the other youth. "How? Where were you?"

"Up there," Vicente said, pointing up at the low ridge which ran behind the property. Among the trees which lined the crest a couple of tents were just about visible.

Vicente had been having a piss when the two cars had pulled up on the darkened street below. It was probably around midnight, but he had no watch. It was a cloudy night, so all he could really see were the car-lights and shadows moving across the beams they threw. Four, maybe five men, Vicente thought, but all he'd really seen was moving shadows. "There was a sound of something falling. Or someone, I don't know. I stood there for a few minutes, but nothing else happened, so I went back to bed. I should have gone down to see if Cesar needed help, but I had my sister to take care of, and . . ."

"Where is she?" Russell asked.

"At school."

"You did the right thing," Russell told him.

"I thought so then. Anyway, I lay there listening, but heard nothing more until the cars left about fifteen minutes later. Maybe twenty. I went down in the morning to check, and Cesar was gone, and his things were everywhere. But I couldn't see any blood. Still, I felt really bad."

"You didn't see the fire when they burned his books?" Tierney asked.

"That was later. Someone must have come back the next day when I was at school."

"You've been a great help," Russell told both boys, thinking that the last place he'd seen a heap of charred books was outside a Berlin university in the spring of 1933.

"But will you be able to get my uncle out of prison?" Juan wanted to know.

"We'll try," Tierney promised. "Now how would you like a lift to school?"

Not much, the faces said, but they acquiesced. After dropping them off Russell asked Tierney what he thought.

"It all sounds too cloak-and-dagger for regular police. More like hired hands—which doesn't preclude a few cops of course. In fact, there had to be at least one cop involved in getting Cesar into Chino—you can't just drop by as a civilian with someone you want imprisoned. But with a cop who knows someone on the inside . . . who knows?"

"But the cops downtown are claiming Cesar was tried and sentenced."

"Yeah, but until I find some paperwork we only have their word for any of that."

Despite himself, Russell was astonished. "Why would they make it up?"

"For dollars, of course."

"And none of the cops who aren't corrupt will notice? I assume there must be some."

"A few. But it's always easier to look the other way. And if someone with any sort of clout manages to kick up a fuss, the corrupt ones will just claim the whole thing was a tragic mix-up. If Cesar dies, they won't even have to do that."

"Jesus!"

"He doesn't work for the LAPD."

Russell laughed, but not with amusement.

AFTER TIERNEY HAD DROPPED HIM off in the *Examiner* car lot, Russell walked back through the building and out the front entrance. The green Buick was still there, the driver discarding his cigarette as he quickly looked away. As Russell slowly strolled the half-mile to Pershing Square and the Biltmore Hotel, he imagined the man walking along behind him, wondering whether he'd regret leaving his car.

Almost half an hour early for his appointment with the publisher's envoy, he found himself an empty seat near the statue of Beethoven on the square's perimeter path and settled down to wait. Did he really want to write this book? Or was he just upset at the thought that the decision might be taken away from him? If so, he was being ridiculous.

It was a mild, cloudy morning, but sunshine was promised for his trip to the Valley that afternoon. Three benches to his left, his tail was reading what looked like a comic book.

He'd felt obliged to discuss how much he should offer Janice Sullivan with Effi—she, after all, had earned most of the money in their joint account—but she had just shrugged and told him "whatever you think it's worth." Quite a lot to a blackmailer had been his first thought, to him maybe not so much, and then only if the book got written.

At two minutes to, he walked across Olive, through the enormous entrance lobby and down the Champs Élysée–wide inner promenade to the first-floor coffee shop, where the publisher's rep Calvin Petersen was supposed to be awaiting him. As Russell surveyed the tables for a likely candidate someone tapped him on the shoulder. "John Russell?"

Petersen's table was already half-covered in books and papers, suggesting a long residency. The young man's suit was lightweight enough for LA, but the dark shade was more suggestive of the north, as was its wearer's pale skin. "I've ordered you a coffee," he told Russell, as the cup was placed before him. "I only have thirty minutes for each author," he explained, "so time is precious."

"So I see."

Petersen was looking at his notes. "Your book was due for delivery on March thirty-first. You asked for an extension on April twenty-eighth. We acquiesced, of course, but . . ."

"Not completely," Russell interjected. "I asked for six months, you gave me three."

"Which are up on August first," Petersen said placidly. "Are you confident of delivering the manuscript by that date?"

"Confident would be pushing it. It's possible, of course," he added brazenly, "but I wouldn't feel comfortable making a promise I couldn't keep."

"I thought you . . ."

"Let me explain. You know who my wife is?"

"An actor in a family television TV show, I believe."

"She's one of the principals, yes. She also has a long and distinguished career in German cinema and theatre."

"I didn't know that."

"No reason you should. But because of that, she's been invited to the Berlin International Film Festival this summer. She's honoured, of course, but as you can imagine, returning to Germany after all that's happened will be a difficult experience. So I shall have to accompany her. Which means, of course, that I'll be unable to devote as much time to my writing as I could if I was here. But, and here's the silver lining, I will be able to interview more Germans for the book, and thus make it increasingly lawyer-proof."

"Yes, but . . ."

"That's one problem," Russell ploughed on, "and there's another. But this is also more of a positive than a negative. You see, the book is getting *bigger*, more sensational. I'm now in contact with a woman whose husband worked for"—Russell glanced round the room for effect—"Dreverel Chemicals. He was paid to keep silent, but now he's dead and she has the records he left behind. I'm seeing her this afternoon, and if the evidence is as good as I think it'll be, it may open up a whole new area of research. Which will of course take time, but will also make the finished book so much better."

"So what are you suggesting?" Petersen asked wearily.

"The end of the year. Provisionally. You really can't hurry this kind of stuff," he insisted.

Petersen sighed. "It has been impressed on me that the company believes your book could be important. They still want it. But they're also aware that with each passing year the war becomes less of a publisher's goldmine. So they want your book on World War II before World War III breaks out." He gave Russell a wintry smile. "I'll tell them the end of the year."

ISAAC ARENBERG HAD BEEN EFFI'S US agent for several years. An immigrant from pre-Hitler days, he was now in his late fifties, with a clientele that included several actors much more famous than she was. On several occasions Effi had literally bumped into one of these as she climbed the narrow staircase to his fourth-floor Hollywood Boulevard office.

Izzy, as he was universally known, had been good for her. After the failure of her first Hollywood movie, he had managed to get her decent roles in two more before announcing that radio and TV might now be a better bet. "The forties were great for actresses," he had told her. "All those noir films with women driving the plots. Lead roles, supporting roles, there for the taking. But then the men came home, and they wanted the world back the way it was. Movies included. The women's parts got younger and dumber, and you, *mein bubele*, are neither young nor dumb. Producers these days—they want a girl who looks like she's just been hatched. Skin that hasn't even settled on the flesh, not a wrinkle in sight, no character in the eyes. You know what I mean. I look at you and I see it all—the war and the Nazis, a loving family, cares and sorrow—you've had a full life and it shows. But they want innocence, and by that I don't mean a lack of guilt. I mean a lack of experience."

He had delivered that speech more than two years ago, and at the time she had known he was right. Now, sitting at the same table—the one he reserved for all his lunches in the deli across from his office—she feared he was right again. "But I'm not a communist," she insisted. "I've never been one."

Izzy waved a fork at her. "You know that and I know that, but we don't matter. It's what the senator and his cretinous supporters think they know that matters. Look, as your friend, I'll say this—if you want to tell Hollywood and America to go fuck themselves, I wouldn't blame you. But as your agent I have to say something different—if you want to work, and keep earning money like there's no tomorrow, then you can't afford to be seen defending Laura Fullagar."

"She's my friend," Effi said. Which was a bit of an exaggeration. And also, she knew, beside the point.

"I know she is. And she was also a member of the American Communist Party. Here, now, that means you don't work in Hollywood unless you give up former comrades. Yes, it's stupid, unfair, despicable—all those things—but that's the way things are."

"I hate that phrase. It's just another way of saying 'I give up.'"

"Yeah, I know. But maybe you're just giving up *for now*."

"Nice try. Izzy, do you really think they'll come for Mrs. Luddwitz if I speak out in Laura's defence?"

"HUAC won't have to. The word'll just go out."

Effi played with her food. "You know, before the war I couldn't stand up for actor friends who were Jews or Reds or homosexuals or anything else that Goebbels disliked. Here the Jews are safe, but the others are just as threatened. The only other difference is that they don't send you off to a camp."

"A big difference."

"Yes, it is. But still . . ."

"But still. And if you've been dealing with these dilemmas for twenty years you should be getting good at it."

Effi sighed. "I know I've often managed not to notice things that I should have, but once I do notice them, I don't find it easy to look away."

"This I know about you," Izzy said. "Now eat your lunch."

BUOYED BY HIS SUCCESS WITH Petersen, Russell took a cab up to Chinatown for his lunch. Of course he still had to write the book, but six months should be enough, provided he could dig out enough damning evidence. It was worth doing. There were few things more disgusting than making profits from strengthening the enemy while your fellow countrymen died trying to defeat him.

When he emerged from the Chinese diner the Buick was gone, but another car had doubtless appeared in its place. He didn't spot it until after he'd picked up at the Frazer at home and left for his appointment with Janice Sullivan. Crossing the Cahuenga Pass he thought he recognised a silver Pontiac from earlier in the week, and sure enough, when he turned off Ventura the Pontiac followed.

The "coffee-shop restaurant" at Clybourn and Sherman was a very large diner with a very loud jukebox, which Janice had probably decided would suit a clandestine conversation. Most of the customers looked to be late shift workers from the nearby Lockheed complex, enjoying their afternoon breakfasts to the sounds of Perry Como and Eddie Fisher.

Russell ordered a coffee and kept watch on the door. Rosa was right, he thought—this music was dead.

Through the window he could see Sherman Avenue stretching out to the west, flanked by rows of stucco creations that were almost but not quite identical. Most of the morning's clouds had been drawn aside like a magician's cloak to reveal the usual perfect day, leaving only a couple of renegades clinging to the Santa Monica mountains.

Another quarter-hour went by with no sign of Janice Sullivan, and Russell grew ever more certain she wasn't coming. The click on the telephone line, he thought. If Dreverel had been keeping tabs on her, maybe someone had been sent to change her mind? Russell hadn't noticed Janice's name in the *Times* among the city's latest murder victims.

He exited the restaurant, and stood by his car for several moments, relishing the lack of a soundtrack. Once behind the wheel he drove out of the lot and south on Clybourn. She might not have wanted Russell at her home, but her Van Nuys address was listed in the telephone book.

Ten minutes later he was looking at the house. It sat among trees on the edge of a luxury development, with a well-tended garden and distant view of the reservoir. The maid who answered the door told him Mrs. Sullivan had gone out for a drive and might not be home for several hours.

It sounded rehearsed. Janice had anticipated his visit and was either hiding inside or lurking somewhere close by until she saw him leave. The open garage and lack of a car on the driveway suggested the latter, so Russell took his leave and spent ten minutes touring the neighbourhood before he returned. This time the car was there.

The Hispanic maid insisted her mistress was still out but couldn't explain the car in the drive or refute Russell's mendacious insistence that he'd seen the woman in question drive up a few minutes before.

"What do you want?" Janice asked, suddenly appearing in the hall beyond.

"What you were offering me last Friday." Russell told her. "Or at least an explanation of why you changed your mind."

"I just did." She took a deep breath. "I'm sorry I didn't cancel our meeting. Now, can we just leave it at that?"

"Do you know that there's a wiretap on your telephone?"

She looked astonished. "No, I don't. What would make you think there is?"

"How else could they know you had the diary?" Russell guessed.

The maid had vanished, and they were now only standing a few feet apart. Janice shook her head. "They run the world, don't they?"

"You sold it to them."

"I wish. Two guys came from head office—at least that's where they said they were from—and they told me Milo's diary had been part of the deal he signed. They waved some paper in front of my face, and then hustled me out to the car to go and collect it. I guess they knew about the safety deposit box from the wiretap."

"Yep."

"When we got to the bank the manager could see something was wrong—he took me aside and asked me if everything was all right with my 'friends.' But what could I say? Call the police? Guys like these would have friends in the police. And they had scared me. They still do, even though they've got what they wanted."

"Would you still talk to me about what you know of Milo's dealings?"

She looked at him. "No. It doesn't feel safe. I'm sorry, but I won't. Whatever Milo did, whatever the company did, the war is over, and they can't be doing it now. So why would I?"

For truth, Russell thought, for justice. But he didn't say so. He could see there was no point.

THAT EVENING, WHILE ROSA WATCHED *Burns and Allen*, he and Effi recounted their respective days. The abduction by night at Chavez Ravine, the heavies at Janice Sullivan's door, the heartfelt advice from a friend that now was not the time to stick your neck out . . .

"It sounds like one of Rosa's science fiction novels," Effi said, "in which a horrible past keeps sticking its head through the floor of the present."

Russell smiled. "She's reading a new one in which everyone's blinded by a meteor shower and perambulating plants called triffids take over the world."

"That seems almost preferable," was Effi's response.

Anderson, Anderson & Davies

The coffin was lighter than Ströhm expected—Harald had obviously lost weight since the last time he'd seen him. As they carried it towards the freshly dug grave in a shaded corner of the Dorotheenstadt Cemetery, he was surprised and gratified by the number of mourners in attendance.

A stand was waiting for the flag-draped coffin, and as they carefully set it down Ströhm couldn't help thinking that Harald would have preferred the old KPD banner to the new DDR design. Or perhaps the skull and crossbones—"Pirate Jenny" had always been his favourite song.

Looking round, Ströhm was pleased to see several Central Committee members, but disappointed by the lack of anyone from the Politburo. Most would have known him in pre-Nazi days, before they left the real servants of the people in their careerist wake.

Harald Gebauer had been Ströhm's oldest friend in the Party. They had known each other since the twenties, worked together in the underground resistance before and during the war. After Hitler's downfall Harald had gone back to his native Wedding in the French sector, where he knew every street and almost every-one, but when the Soviet occupation sector hardened into a separate state the Party decided they needed every efficient and industrious administrator it had to run the new domain. Harald was sent to Weissensee, where he knew virtually no one, and spent more time dealing with the Soviets than his fellow Germans.

Ströhm had visited from time to time, and often got the impression that Harald was pulling himself together for his old friend's benefit. He had drunk no more than usual at their get-togethers, but the word on the party grapevine was that his solitary drinking at home had gone from bad to worse, and the swiftness of his death from cirrhosis of the liver had not surprised his doctor.

The eulogy delivered by his young deputy on the Weissensee committee mentioned none of this. It was long, well-written, and no doubt appealed to the young apparatchiks who made up most of the audience, and who might actually believe that Harald's guiding star had been the absent Walter Ulbricht. Ströhm heard only the gross hypocrisy of claiming collective credit for the goodness of a man they had neither liked nor understood.

"A good time for him to die," he overheard someone say once the coffin had been lowered into the ground. "The Party no longer needs do-gooders like him."

Ströhm picked out the culprit, and once the ceremony was over walked over to confront him. Helmut Breitner was a fellow member of the Central Committee, and one of the men charged with organising the new security police. "I heard what you said about Harald," Ströhm told the man to his face. "You should show some fucking respect. He was worth a hundred of you."

"How dare . . ." Breitner started to say, but Ströhm was already walking away, knowing how close he'd come to hitting a man at a funeral.

Ten minutes later he was sitting in a strange bar on Anklamer Strasse. With two stiff drinks inside him, and about to order a third, he felt Harald's ghost at his shoulder and waved the barman back.

Looking into his empty glass, he murmured "Harald, that shit Breitner was right to call you a do-gooder. You did more fucking good in your life than anyone I ever met."

EARLY ON TUESDAY, RUSSELL DROVE himself and Effi down to Miracle Mile, and parked the Frazer in the Bullocks lot. After they'd both gone in through the rear entrance, Russell made a beeline for the doors at the front and walked the few yards to the nearest bus stop. In the ten minutes that passed before one arrived only women emerged from the store, and all of them walked off in the opposite direction.

He had shaken off his tail, hopefully without arousing suspicion. When Effi returned to the Frazer alone, after a leisurely coffee upstairs, their watcher would know they'd gone their separate ways, but would have no way of knowing that they'd done so with him in mind.

The ten-mile ride to Santa Monica would probably take about forty minutes. Russell just stared through the window for a while, getting used to the motion before he opened his paper to read. The hunt for communists was still in full cry: undercover agents were being employed on all major Californian campuses to weed out "subversive educators" and employees of the city's Public Housing Authority were being investigated for communist tendencies. With the mayoral election only a week away, every attempt was being made to sully Bowron's name, which perhaps explained why his rival Poulson was loudly predicting a smear campaign against himself.

In other news, a British team was on its way up Mount Everest, and the Soviet newspapers were promising their readers a better standard of living. Russell's money was on the Brits.

The bus was in Westwood now, about halfway to its destination, and his mind went back to a conversation with Effi the previous evening. He hadn't seen her so quietly determined since the day in the mountains the year the war started, when they'd calmly agreed that despite the obvious risks they couldn't just sit on their hands until Hitler was beaten. When he's said as much, she'd agreed: "It does feel like it did back then. But the situation's almost the opposite. Then it was all about secret resistance, now it's all about going public. I could make the grand gesture and speak out on Laura's behalf, but it wouldn't help her or anyone else. People will just say: Oh, her too. Laura's seeing HUAC on the twenty-eighth, and when we leave for Berlin two days later they'll all say I'm running away."

Russell had held her but offered no advice. As a Berlin journalist in 1933 he'd faced a similar moral dilemma and come up with nothing better than lengthy procrastination. Eventually the decision had been taken for him, when the Nazis closed his newspaper down.

It was almost 11 A.M. when he got off the bus on Second Street and started walking north in search of Idaho Street. Frank Jessup's office was three floors above a realtor's, and Russell was raising a hand to rap on his door when a woman emerged with angry eyes and sternly pursed lips, looking like a character from a Raymond Chandler book.

Frank Jessup, however, bore no resemblance to Russell's mental picture of Philip Marlowe. He had curly light brown hair and a pugnacious Irish face, but his voice, as Russell was about to discover, lacked any hint of a brogue. At that moment the detective was still shaking his head in bewilderment at what his last client had said or done, but he quickly recovered. "Mr. Russell, yes. Have a seat. Have a cigarette."

Russell took the one but not the other.

"So what can I do for you? You didn't tell me much on the phone."

"I did not," Russell admitted, and decided not to say that his line might be bugged—he didn't want Jessup thinking him paranoid. "I've been followed for the last couple of weeks—my wife has too—and we want to know who's responsible. She's a television actress," he added, "but this is not some crazy fan. We've identified six different cars doing the tailing, and several different drivers—obviously they've been harder to see. It feels like an agency, private or government."

"Why would a government agency be interested in the two of you?"

Russell explained his situation with Immigration, and that HUAC seemed to have Effi's show in its sights.

Jessup scratched a sideburn. "I'd be surprised," he said. "It sounds more like one of the big private agencies. Have you been upsetting anyone else?"

Russell smiled. "My life's work." He explained about the book he was writing, and who might not want to see it in print. "But I've had the contract for months, and hardly got anywhere, so why start following me now?" He also told Jessup about the democracy articles, none of which had yet been published. The only other possibility was his interest in Chavez Ravine, but he was pretty certain that the tails had appeared before he'd even talked to Cal Tierney.

"Mmm. And you haven't been involved in any altercations—with a neighbour, perhaps. Or even a perfect stranger."

"Nope."

"Okay. Well, your book seems the most likely culprit. But we'll see. You just want to know who's following you?"

"And who hired them."

"Okay. The first'll be easy, the second may take a little time. Agencies tend to be very tight-lipped about their clients."

"But there are ways?"

"Usually."

"So any guess as to how long you'll need? The reason I ask is we're leaving on the thirtieth for a month in Europe."

"That should be enough."

They discussed fees. Jessup's daily rate seemed exorbitant, but Russell wasn't about to haggle—this didn't feel like something to economise on. He stressed the need for discretion given that Effi was in the public eye, and Jessup was happy to promise it. After Russell had handed over a suitable retainer, along with the photos of Effi and Rosa he'd brought with him, he wrote out their car licence numbers and address.

"Great," Jessup said, shovelling the notes into a drawer. "I'll call you when I know something."

Outside, the morning clouds had done their usual disappearing act, and the sun was shining down out of a clear blue sky. Russell walked to the seafront, found a stand selling coffee with a few rusty metal tables and chairs, and sat there enjoying the view for fifteen minutes. He had liked Frank Jessup, and, probably more to the point, had gained an impression of competence. Now they just had to wait.

A few days earlier he had read in the paper that the fifty-year-old Pacific Electric Railway between Santa Monica and West Hollywood was running its last train on the weekend he and Effi left for Europe, and it occurred to him that this might be the day to sample its delights. So he made his way to the downtown terminal, where a large and almost empty red railcar was about to depart. Inside it felt more like a tram than a train, but the ride was pleasant enough, first following the Santa Monica Boulevard as it arced north and west towards Hollywood, then cutting diagonally through the grid of streets in its own shady back alleys. The sights weren't particularly interesting but the sense of old-world charm was balm to Russell's psyche. He was, he realised, beginning to find the past more attractive than the future.

A regular bus and a walk brought him home from the West Hollywood terminal. Effi had left the Frazer parked in their drive and taken her own car to the studio; the car that had tailed them that morning was parked a short way down the avenue, having probably followed her to the studio before resuming its vigil.

Of more immediate concern, two men had climbed out of another parked car and were now walking towards him. They were wearing blue suits, one slightly paler than the other, and what looked like identical fedoras. At best they were here to sell him insurance. At worst . . .

He waited for them key in hand outside the front door.

"John Russell?" the bulky one barked.

"Who wants to know?"

"We need to talk to you," the man said, ignoring the question.

"Then talk."

"Inside would be better."

The street was as usual devoid of pedestrians, but there was no shortage of passing cars. "I don't think so," Russell said, guessing that these were Janice Sullivan's visitors.

The man's eyes were on the key, his mind probably weighing the pros and cons of forcing Russell inside. If so, he decided against it, because his hand emerged from an inside pocket with nothing more lethal than papers. "We're here to serve these," he said, holding them out.

"These" were four crumpled sheets of legal-looking documentation, which were purportedly created by a firm named Anderson, Anderson & Davies Associates. "Legal-looking" because anyone could have an impressive masthead printed on their stationery. The gist of the content was an order to "cease and desist" from (a) "further harassment" of Mrs. Janice Sullivan, et cetera, and (b) "harassment of any past, present, or future employee of the Dreverel Corporation."

"When am I supposed to have harassed Janice Sullivan?" Russell asked, not expecting an answer.

"Yesterday. At her house," the other man said. It was the first time he had spoken, and his partner's look suggested he should wait a while before doing so again.

"Whom do you represent?" Russell asked them.

"The firm on the letter. We're legal assistants."

"And I'm Ike's batman. You work for Dreverel."

The man didn't have a very pleasant smile. "You have to sign your copy," he insisted.

"No," Russell told him, offering the sheets back. "I don't believe they're genuine." And if by some weird chance they were, putting his name to the "further" would amount to an admission that he had indeed harassed Janice.

The two men shook their heads in unison, like puppets attached to the same strings. "You'll regret it if you don't," the talker said.

"Why? What exactly are you threatening me with?"

"That's for us to know," the partner said, moving a step closer.

"You must have learned that line in law school," Russell told him. "Well, if you don't want these back . . ." He held up the papers, then carefully ripped them in half.

They both clearly wanted to hit him, but the talker had the sense to realise that this was neither the time nor place. So he smiled his nasty smile instead. "We'll be meeting again," he said, before turning abruptly on his heel and marching away, followed by his sidekick.

Russell watched them go, feeling more than a little shaky. If they'd knocked on the door when he was already home, forcing their way inside would not have been hard, and things might have turned a lot uglier. How, he wondered, had they gotten his address? And how had they known he had been out to Janice Sullivan's house?

Of course, if they worked for the same people as those tailing him did, then that would explain it. And confirm Jessup's opinion that someone was seriously upset at the thought of what he might put in his book and prepared to act accordingly. If so, the joke was on them, as he hadn't yet uncovered anything really incriminating.

NEXT MORNING HE WAS ABOUT to leave for the library when Cal Tierney called. "I'm at the LA General," the reporter said. "I take it you know where that is."

"Boyle Heights."

"That's the one. The lawyer I found got Cesar Morales out of Chino, and they've moved him here."

"That's great."

"I guess. He's in pretty awful shape. The nurse I spoke to said he's been unconscious most of the time, and not making much sense when he isn't. I obviously need to talk to him, but I can't wait around here all day—I've got others to see."

"I'm on my way," Russell said. "Half an hour?"

"I can wait that long."

It took a little less. LA General Hospital had been built in the thirties, and designed by someone with Stalin's sense of style. It occupied a vast chunk of land on the far side of the Los Angeles River, about two miles east of Union Station, and was the place of last resort for the city's poor. Russell had recently read that Marilyn Monroe had been born in one of its charity wards.

The walk to Cesar's wing seemed to take almost as long as the ride. "Have you talked to a doctor yet?" was Russell's first question for Tierney.

"No, but according to the sister—who's a real sweetheart, by the way—he should be here around ten-thirty. And I haven't let Juan or his father know, because I don't know how to reach them during the day."

"I'll do that once I've seen a doctor."

"Okay. Then I'll go and talk to the police. Before they have time to agree on their story."

"Good luck with that."

The young doctor who showed up an hour or so later introduced himself as Richard Hunter. After Russell had given a brief resumé of the circumstances and explained his connection to the patient, the medic said he'd examined Cesar on admission and would fill Russell in once he'd seen him again. He was at the bedside for almost fifteen minutes and watching from a distance Russell saw a face growing graver and graver.

"He has a large oval-shaped indentation on the side of his head," the doctor reported. "Whether from being hit or falling and hitting himself is impossible to say. The surprise—and the only good news—is that whatever it was didn't kill him. Yet."

"He's still in danger."

"I should think so, but I'm no specialist."

"Should he be seeing one?"

The doctor grimaced. "Half the people in here should be, but that's not the way our system works. Your accent is British, isn't it? What do you think of your new National Health Service?"

"I haven't lived there for years, but it seems like a good idea."

"It sounds like paradise compared to what we have here."

"Maybe. But here is where we are. If I'm willing to pay for a specialist would you make the arrangements?"

"I will, but it won't be cheap. We're talking four figures."

Russell managed not to wince. "I guess that's better than five."

The doctor took down Russell's number and hurried off, leaving Russell to tell Tierney's "sweetheart" that Cesar's family would probably come to see him after work. He gave her his number too, and she promised to call with any news.

His next stop was Union Station, where he eventually managed to track down Cesar's brother and bring him up to date. Driving back to Melrose in the Frazer, pursued as ever by his shadow, he thought about the large amount of money—money Effi had earned—that he had just spent. He knew she wouldn't mind. If anything it would get her thinking about all those people they weren't helping who needed it just as much as Cesar.

Which was one of the reasons he loved her. One of the many.

"GERHARD, I'VE ASKED TO SEE you because I'm concerned," Rudolf Herrnstadt told Ströhm. They had left the *Neues Deutschland* editor's office for "a breath of fresh air," a phrase which these days usually meant somewhere without microphones. They were now sitting in Herrnstadt's official car almost underneath the Brandenburg Gate, staring through the windscreen at the renascent Tiergarten.

"As we're both all too aware," Herrnstadt continued, "things are not going well. Since Comrade Stalin's death a struggle has been underway in our Party between those who, rightly or wrongly, believe in pushing for a rapid transition to socialism, and those who fear that doing so can only lead to disaster. And I believe you and I are in the second camp," he concluded, turning to Ströhm for confirmation.

"I would say so."

"I'm glad to hear it, because we're going to need all the help we can get."

Two hundred yards in front of them a group of British soldiers were putting down sweaters for goalposts. "May I ask who the 'we' is?" Ströhm said.

Herrnstadt didn't evade the question. "Our Politburo contains three roughly equal groups: those I call 'we,' those around Walter, and those who are waiting to see who comes out on top. You know who's in each group as well as I do."

"Probably. Rudolf, are you just making sure we're on the same page or do you have some sort of proposal in mind?"

"Neither, really. I half-assumed the former, and it's early for the latter. No, the concern I mentioned is about you. We will be needing you in the weeks ahead, and I want you to bear that in mind, and be a lot more careful."

Ströhm was surprised, if only momentarily. "Careful?"

"A week ago you and your wife went to a cinema in the western sector, where you met another couple. The husband was a prominent businessman in Nazi times, and then served as a city councillor for the SPD. Not the most suitable companions for a Central Committee member."

Ströhm shook his head in frustration. "They're family friends. As a businessmen Thomas Schade did more to obstruct the Nazis than most, and our own Party merged with the SPD!"

"Of course. But in the current climate such connections can easily be made to look suspicious. A few days ago you went to Harald Gebauer's funeral and lost your temper with one of Ulbricht's favourites." Herrnstadt held up a hand to ward off a response. "I'm sure the man deserved it—he *is* a complete shit— but you're just giving them ammunition for the future. Another thing, why is your wife not a member of the Party?"

"She's never been interested in politics."

"Well, if she doesn't have any strong opinions, why not join? She doesn't have to go to meetings."

Annaliese would have a strong opinion about that, Ströhm thought, but that wasn't what Herrnstadt wanted to hear. "Okay, I'll talk to her."

"Good. One more thing: refusing to live out in Karlshorst might be seen as anti-Soviet."

Or anti-corruption, Ströhm thought. "We live where we live because it's only a short walk from Annaliese's work," he explained.

Herrnstadt said equably: "An excellent reason, like all your others, but you see the point I'm making."

"I do."

"I can protect you up to a point, but if anything happens to me . . ."

"I understand."

"I hope you do. We're playing for high stakes here. Remember what happened to Slánský."

Ströhm did. "But Stalin has gone since then," he murmured.

"Beria hasn't."

In the distance one of the British soldiers had scored a goal and was dancing with delight.

THURSDAY MORNING, RUSSELL MET UP with Tierney and his lawyer friend at a coffee shop on Broadway. Don Cheveley was a casually dressed, soft-spoken Angeleno in his early thirties. He had wavy dark hair, warm brown eyes, and a permanent air of injured innocence. The latter, Tierney had already told Russell, served to mask a ferocious tenacity.

Cheveley had spent much of the last three days cajoling and threatening the LAPD. Cesar had been released, but if the police thought that was the end of the matter, they clearly had another thing coming. The lawyer wanted notes, log entries, and witness statements before he would even consider ruling out a suit for wrongful arrest and injuries received. "I'm looking for substantial damages," he told Russell. "Enough to pay for Cesar's specialist care at least. Hopefully more."

"What exactly do you think happened?" Russell asked.

"Best guess—the people interested in developing Chavez Ravine have hired some extralegal helpers to drive out the few remaining residents. Cesar was one of the most outspoken, and he slept alone. They probably just wanted to give him a scary night down at the station; I mean, if they wanted to kill the man, there was nothing to stop them doing that where they found him. But something went wrong, and rather than try and explain away injuries in custody, they came up with the ludicrous idea of hiding him in a prison hospital. But then the LAPD's not exactly famous for the wit and wisdom of its employees. Thank God."

Tierney's smile was grim. "A couple of my contacts are asking around, and they usually manage to find someone who'll talk off the record. Once we know what actually happened, it should be easier to prove it, or at least give us enough ammo to make them think we can." He grinned suddenly. "I mean, I can't believe even the LAPD thinks they can get away with something as outrageous as this."

Someone might actually pay, Russell thought, but whether that would help Cesar was another matter.

After draining his coffee and eyeing his watch Tierney set off for another appointment, and Russell seized the opportunity to ask Cheveley about the legal document he'd received from Anderson, Anderson & Davies. After the alleged firm's emissaries had departed the previous day, Russell had first confirmed its existence in the telephone book, and then taped back together the pages he'd torn asunder.

"Do you know this firm?" he asked Cheveley after passing them over.

"One of the biggest in LA," the lawyer told him.

"Oh. I was hoping it was the figment of someone's imagination."

"Far from it." There was distaste in his voice.

"Not the most reputable?" Russell asked.

"Let's just say their clientele is rich and ruthless and expect their lawyers to do whatever it takes."

"So I should take this seriously?"

"Not necessarily. They may just be trying it on. I'd have to know a lot more . . ."

"Maybe later," Russell said, seeing that Cheveley was eager to get going. "I'm off to Europe soon, but when I get back . . ."

"Give me a call."

"I will."

Back home an hour later, Russell made himself a sandwich and ate it with a beer on the patio. His usual tail aside, there'd been no suspicious characters lurking outside; if Jessup was out there following the follower, he was keeping himself well hidden.

As it wasn't one of the cleaner's mornings, there was no way of knowing if the doctor had rung, so after finishing lunch Russell called the hospital and had himself put through to the sister on Cesar's ward. She told him the specialist was coming to examine Cesar at ten the next morning, and that Doctor Hunter had already tried calling Russell to let him know that his presence might prove helpful.

In his workroom he thought about what Cheveley had said and decided not to do anything provocative until he got back from Germany. He wasn't getting anywhere in any case, and tickling the tiger's tail would simply enrage the beast to no purpose. Far better to encourage a false sense of security, until he actually had something. Something he might find in Germany. He already had a list of firms and people who merited investigation.

He would take the first democracy article with him, and hand it in personally for a late June publication. By the time he got back to LA the mayoral election would be over and the Congressional special election far enough into its stride to merit a second.

Having thus rationalised an afternoon of idleness, he grabbed the book that Rosa had just finished and took it out to the hammock. It was an easy read, if not exactly a comforting one; the author John Wyndham had a gift for making the outlandish feel real. The book worked as an adventure, but it soon became obvious to Russell that he was also reading something more. The mobile plants were interesting in themselves, but the book was an astute observation of what the sudden collapse of civilisation revealed about humans and the way they lived with themselves and each other. And this, Russell realised, was the point of the new science fiction.

He offered this idea to Rosa when he picked her up from

school and received a "well done" smile in return. She was also happy for another reason. Juan had turned up at lunchtime and told her that Cesar had seemed a bit more like himself the previous evening. A spark of hope, at least.

Russell told her the specialist was seeing the old man tomorrow, and that he'd arranged to be there.

"I'm so glad you're doing all this for him," Rosa told him.

"Thank Mrs. Luddwitz," Russell said. "She's paying."

Effi had indeed waved aside any worries about the money in exactly the way that Russell had predicted: "What's that famous line from Marx you were always coming out with?—'From each according to his ability, to each according to his needs.'"

"If you ever get called before HUAC, quoting that might get you a few headlines," Russell had suggested.

AS EFFI STARTED UP LAUREL Canyon Boulevard a glance in the rearview mirror confirmed that the silver Pontiac was still behind her. Today's driver was the one who always wore sunglasses but never sported a hat.

She was looking forward to the PI's report, and finding out who their stalkers were. They'd been tailed for more than a week, and what earthly reason could anyone have for following John and herself for such a length of time? They surely knew *her* schedule by now.

To hell with them, she thought; her life was an open book. This morning's visit might get someone excited, but so what? She knew she was doing exactly what Izzy had warned against, but she was damned if she was going to let the US government decide whom she could befriend.

Laura Fullagar lived about halfway up the Canyon, her small house clinging to a hillside on one of the tracks to the left. The parked car suggested she was in, so Effi climbed the wooden staircase and rapped on the door.

Laura was clearly surprised to see her, but not, Effi judged, unpleasantly so. Invited in, she found a large and beautifully decorated room in a state of some disarray. The style, Effi guessed, was the norm, the mess a reflection of Laura's current situation.

"So have you decided what to do?" Effi asked, once Laura had made them coffees.

"Oh, yes. I don't think I ever had a decision to make, to be honest. Not with a child to support. I shall admit to being a member of the Party—I could hardly deny it—but stress that I was only twenty-two when I left. I'll name a bunch of people whose names they already have. I've spoken to most of them in the last few days, and none have any objection. If the committee asks for more, I shall tell them I don't have any. Which happens to be true, but even if it wasn't . . . Anyway, they'll have their symbolic victory, another penitent to add to their list. I'll grovel like Artie Shaw if I have to, and play the poor helpless women misled by the Reds. I'll tell them America is special. The place God was hoping for, the best country on earth." She smiled wryly and looked straight at Effi. "As a child I used to believe that," she said. "Now I know it's only the richest."

Effi just nodded.

"I know I'll be dropped from the show—they've more or less told me as much. But I won't go to prison or be on a blacklist, and I'll be able to work."

"The show will be poorer without you," Effi told her, prioritising kindness.

Laura dismissed the compliment with an airy wave of the hand. "It's nice of you to say so, but the money was always better than the part. And who knows, maybe this will be a blessing in disguise. The theatre was always my first love—it just doesn't pay well enough."

"What does your son think?"

"He's too young to understand it all, so I haven't told him much.

But he knows that I've been unhappy—children always do—and I'll have to come up with something better before it all goes public next week, and his friends all find out. At least school will be out by then, and hopefully it'll all be old news by September."

Driving back down to Hollywood, Effi decided she'd been right, and the show would be poorer without Laura. A good actor might always be replaceable, but the show's reputation would be tarnished by its kowtowing to McCarthy. And the story of the spiked "Good Samaritan" episode would come out one way or another. If Beth left or was fired, Effi could see her friend spilling the beans; come to that, she might even spill them herself. John would certainly know how to find someone willing to put out the story.

ON FRIDAY MORNING RUSSELL WALKED up to Hollywood Boulevard and found a place to sit outside with his coffee, as he had throughout his years in Berlin. The *Times* was not a lot cheerier: incumbent Mayor Bowron had lost his temper in front of the Housing Committee, and the US Air Force was busy bombing dams in Korea, presumably in hope of drowning its enemies. The upcoming coronation in Britain was again heavily featured, but there was no fresh news from Everest. The Twinks' game in Portland had been rained out for the third day running.

It was a relief to get back to *The Day of The Triffids*, though he had to admit that people were not behaving much better in that. After reading a couple of chapters, he walked back home, picked up the car and drove down to Bullocks in search of a birthday present for his wife. Nothing grabbed his attention there, but he eventually found some beautiful red earrings at a Mexican shop on Olvera Street. He and Effi had never made a big deal out of gifts, preferring to celebrate their birthdays by doing something together, and he had already booked a table at Ciro's for the following night. Effi had always loved to dance, and since meeting her so had he.

With an hour to spare before the rendezvous with Dr. Hunter and his specialist, he picked up a sandwich at the usual deli on Main before driving out to City General. The consultant arrived before him, and was already examining Cesar when Russell arrived, Hunter hovering at his shoulder. "Dr. Baumann will see you after the patient," the head nurse told him. "You can wait in my office."

Around ten minutes had passed when the two doctors appeared. Baumann was considerably older, grey-haired and gaunt. He didn't waste time on pleasantries. "Mr. Russell. I understand you're picking up the bill for Mr. Morales."

"I am."

"I think it advisable to run some tests, purely as a precautionary measure. I doubt they'll tell us very much. I suspect the only thing that will is time."

"Is his life in danger?"

"Probably not, at least in the sense you mean. But there has been some damage to the brain, which may or may not be self-healing. The man he was may be gone. But as I said, only time will tell."

"I understand."

"The good news is—he doesn't seem to be in any pain, at least for now." He paused. "I'm sorry I can't be more precise in my diagnosis, but head injuries are notoriously difficult. As for treatment, rest and a good diet are all I can recommend at this moment, but the results of the tests may suggest something more proactive. He should remain here for the weekend, and provided there are no further complications, he should then be moved to a nursing home. I can recommend one in Pasadena, but you may wish to choose one yourself."

Pasadena wasn't exactly close. "Do you know of anything nearer?" Russell asked.

"I know of homes in Glendale and Highland Park, but I wouldn't recommend them."

"Then Pasadena it is." The family could always move Cesar if visiting was too difficult. "I don't suppose you could hazard a guess as to how long he might be in the nursing home?"

"Not really. But once the test results are in on Monday I should know more. If you give me your address I will send you a summary of my findings. Along with my invoice."

EFFI CAME HOME THAT EVENING feeling frazzled. The writers were having trouble with the season's last script—the one rendered necessary by the scrapping of "The Good Samaritan"—and the show's familiar route from A to Z had been thrown into confusion. The producers had been yelling about how important the season finale was, giving everyone else the chance to blame them for fucking it up. "I can't wait to get on that train," she told John and Rosa.

A large gin and tonic usually had her smiling, but not that night, and watching *The Adventures of Ozzie and Harriet* did nothing to improve her mood. The episode was all about elder son David getting his own front-door key. Father Ozzie disapproved, saying that David would probably lose it, then tried to blame his wife when he predictably mislaid his own. This was the future of shows like hers, Effi thought, all family foibles and no social context. Because including the latter was too damn threatening. Maybe they should change the national bird from the eagle to the ostrich.

They also had the last-ever episode of *Boston Blackie* to watch, and Effi spent most of it wondering whether they were currently making the last *Please, Dad.* And if they were, did she really care?

That the next day was her forty-fifth birthday was just the icing on the cake. John always said she looked ten years younger, but he would, wouldn't he?

SATURDAY TURNED OUT A WHOLE lot better. The weather was perfect, a clear blue sky and not too hot. They all went swimming out at Malibu and ate a late lunch at a beachside café before Rosa drove them all the way back along Sunset. Russell had included their daughter in the Ciro's reservation, but she insisted on their dancing the night away with just each other.

And so they did. What better way to spend a birthday, Effi thought, than dancing with the man you loved.

The German Connection

Russell was barely awake when his wife left for the studio on Sunday morning, but managed to register that she might not be back until late. There was no sign of Rosa either when he finally got up, so he made himself coffee, collected the paper, and took both out to the patio. Invisible children were making noise somewhere nearby, but the usual hum of traffic was conspicuous by its absence.

He turned to the dubious pleasure of Sunday's *Times*. With the mayoral election only two days away, the main editorial was a thorough hatchet job on the incumbent Bowron. Whoever controlled the newspaper, they could hardly wait for Poulson's new broom.

In Korea, the Reds had been routed again—after so many humbling defeats, Russell couldn't help wondering why the front line never seemed to move. He remembered sitting in a trench at Ypres all those years ago, watching a corpse bubble up to the surface of the churned-up field, just after reading in a week-old British paper that morale had never been higher.

Julius and Ethel Rosenberg were still alive, two years after receiving the death penalty for atomic espionage, and on Monday the Supreme Court was deciding whether to review their sentences. According to the *Times* reporter, they could still escape the electric chair if they agreed to name names, but neither had so far shown any willingness to adopt the new moral axiom that betrayal of friends was good, betrayal of country bad. Russell could imagine the pigs in *Animal Farm* singing something similar.

It was all extremely depressing.

He was saved from himself by his daughter, who plonked herself down on the seat beside him and suggested the movie star tour. "We haven't done it for ages," Rosa said. "And it's always fun."

"Why not?" Russell agreed. She was right—for God knows what reason they always did enjoy it. Ten minutes later they were on their way to Beverly Hills, Rosa clasping their frayed copy of Thom's guide to the homes of the stars, the usual tail a few cars back. Russell wondered what he'd make of the tour in prospect.

For the next hour or so they wound their way up and down the famous grid of palm-lined streets, hoping for glimpses of the famous. There was no sign of Groucho on Foothill Drive, nor Chico on nearby Elm, but Rosa was convinced she saw George and Gracie through their living room window on Maple. They parked for a while on Roxbury, but neither Jack Benny nor James Stewart put in an appearance.

They stopped again at the top of Tower Grove Drive for the stunning view of the city, then finally swung past the beautiful house on Benedict Canyon Road where Bacall was probably still teaching Bogie to whistle.

After that, where better to eat lunch than in a restaurant shaped like a hat? After having the good fortune to secure the Wilshire Brown Derby's last available booth, Russell sat there thinking that the one thing he loved about Hollywood was its utter absurdity.

"When are you taking me to Dolphin's?" Rosa asked out of the blue.

"Not today," Russell answered, wondering how much his life

would be worth if he did so without getting Effi's permission. "When we come back from Europe," he promised.

Rosa was not mollified. "There must be record stores in Harlem," she thought out loud.

"There must," Russell agreed, making a mental note to warn Ali and Fritz.

STRÖHM'S OFFICE WAS ON THE fourth floor of the SED Party headquarters, the optimistically named House of Unity on Wilhelm-Pieck Strasse. The building itself had a somewhat checkered history. A Jewish-owned department store in the 1920s, it had been Aryanised in the 1930s and used by the Hitler Youth organisation during the war. The Party had moved in soon after the Red Army's arrival, and a huge poster of Stalin had hung from the central façade for several years. Ströhm had not been involved in the debate over taking it down, but as the Soviet leader had still been alive at the time, he doubted the decision had been taken lightly.

His room was spacious, with windows overlooking Prenzlauer Tor's five-way intersection. The desk was large enough to lie on, or it would have been without the various stacks of paper. There were two framed photographs: one of Annaliese and the children, the other of old comrades, most of them long-deceased, on a Party picnic in 1929. Given his frequent meetings with Soviet officials, the drinks cabinet by the door was well stocked with bottles of vodka.

He had taken down the portrait of Stalin, intending to replace it with one of Rosa Luxemburg, but had eventually decided Lenin was a safer bet. On the opposite wall, above the three-person sofa, he had thrown caution to the wind and hung an anonymous expressionist work he'd come across in the building's basement among several piles of discarded paintings. One visitor had thought it an early, pre-abstract Kandinsky, but there was neither signature nor label. For all Ströhm knew, Goring had picked the work up on one of his wartime trawls of Europe's galleries, and it was worth a fortune. Ströhm just loved the deep dark colours.

Of course hanging such a painting on his office wall was exactly the sort of thing Herrnstadt had warned him against. The fact that there was nothing political about the painting seemed more than slightly odd in a building devoted to politics, especially when everyone else had aspirational posters brimming with positivity, but Ströhm was reluctant to take it down. He had thought long and hard about what Herrnstadt had said, and reached the conclusion that for now a little more caution would suffice. He wasn't actively plotting to get rid of Ulbricht—nor, as far as he knew, was Herrnstadt—and if or when he ever decided to do so, then that would be the time to keep his thoughts and feelings more firmly under wrap.

In the meantime he still had a job to do, and a difficult one at that. Anything problematic in the relations between the DDR and its Soviet sponsors was likely to end up on his desk, from policy differences at the highest level to a single Red Army soldier caught shoplifting. The two countries shared relationships in business, military, intelligence, and cultural matters, and none were frictionless. The fact that the basic relationship between fraternal parties was also one between national victors and losers only seemed to complicate matters, and Ströhm sometimes wondered whether things would have been a lot simpler if the DDR had no German progenitors.

He had two important matters to deal with that day, neither of which looked easy. The first concerned the rape and subsequent suicide of a thirteen-year-old girl in a mountain village south of Dresden. There was no doubt about the culprit—the Red Army lieutenant responsible had not only been identified by several witnesses but had freely confessed to the crime. His superiors' insistence in trying the man in a Soviet military court had created a problem, which had been compounded when the girl's father seriously injured the Soviet official who came to offer the family compensation. The girl's father was now the subject of an administrative tug-of-war between the local German and Soviet authorities.

If that was all, Ströhm would have sent a subordinate, but it now transpired that the wounded official's father had important friends in Moscow, so he would have to go himself. Which meant at least an overnight stay, just to eat Soviet humble pie and remind the locals who was really in charge.

The second matter was a lot less tragic, but harder to resolve. Over the last decade or so the Soviets—and presumably the Americans—had made rapid advances in the field of listening devices. Ströhm had no idea what the Yanks were doing with theirs, but the DDR's Soviet allies were concealing the damn things all over Berlin, regardless of sector. Senior SED functionaries were finding them in their homes and offices and complaining bitterly that someone had to talk to Moscow.

Ströhm had raised the subject with Mironov, who initially argued that allies should have nothing to hide from each other, and then complained that the Soviets were even being bugged by their own DDR disciples, the MfS. The latter, who had recently taken to calling themselves the "Stasi"—not, he hoped, because it rhymed with Nazi—were the last people Ströhm wanted to talk to. With his luck he'd probably end up in front of the man he'd almost punched at Harald's funeral.

He got up from his chair and walked across to the window. From the building's roof the Tiergarten treetops were visible above the houses opposite, but from here all he could see was grey sky. He thought about John Russell coming back from California and its sunshine and imagined the questions he'd be asked. Or maybe just the one: "Why can't you admit that it's over?" He smiled to himself. On the last occasion he'd sought out Russell for an ideological discussion the two of them had ended up torching a car with the corpses of two Soviet intelligence agents propped up in the front seats.

ON MONDAY RUSSELL HAD LUNCH with Ted Cullen at Greenblatt's Deli. Over the weekend all four of the special election hopefuls had weighed into the mayoral contest, none in support of Fletcher Bowron. Fitzgerald had strongly attacked the incumbent without even mentioning his challenger, while Holleman had lamented Bowron's record, more in sorrow than anger, and given Poulson a ringing endorsement. Spinetti had given Poulson a few grudging nods in a speech that was mostly about himself, while Clement Fairley had taken Bowron to task for not making the case for public housing and accused Norris Poulson of being a "developers' puppet."

As they waited for their food, Russell reminded Cullen of Bowron's infamous TV appearance, in which he had ranted about the "special interests" backing Poulson. "Apart from Norman Chandler and his *LA Times*, Bowron didn't exactly spell out who they were, but I assume he was mostly talking about big business—industry, commerce, the banks."

"In LA, you need to include oil and water."

"Okay, so Bowron was implying that all these interests were plotting together against him."

"And bankrolling Poulson. But in this case I doubt they needed to do much plotting—Bowron has just been around too long."

"But if they did need to. These people have no formal organisation pushing their interests . . ."

"Cartels are illegal."

"True. So is there some sort of shadow organisation?"

"I would be surprised, but maybe I'm being naive. As far as I can see it's mostly dinners at expensive restaurants, get-togethers on each other's yachts, weekends at hunting lodges. Trying to make sure the political process works in their favour, or at least doesn't work against them. Agreeing who to support with donations, who to back in their papers."

"So what about my special election? Who are Bowron's special interests backing? And why?"

Cullen considered. "I don't know, but my guess would be Greer Holleman."

Russell was surprised. "Why?"

"Because he's a perfect candidate. He's reliable, he's clever but not dangerously so. He talks well and he's good-looking, which is becoming important now that more and more people have TV. Coming from a poor background makes him look like a winner, and bringing up a kid with Mongolism on his own gets him the women's sympathy vote. He's very sellable."

"But he didn't even seem that interested in politics."

"He probably isn't in issues, but that's another plus—he'll be happy to do whatever the so-called special interests want. No idealism to ditch, no moral compass to hold him back." Cullen laughed. "You know, I've convinced myself—Holleman's their man. The others may be idiots, but they all believe in something, even if it's only themselves."

Which, Russell thought, was probably true.

Back home, Doctor Baumann's report was waiting in the mailbox. As he had predicted on Friday, the test results were inconclusive, and offered next to nothing when it came to assessing the extent or longevity of the damage to Cesar's brain. Four days' observation by Doctor Hunter and the nursing staff at LA General had shown marked variations in the patient's cognitive abilities, ranging from almost full lucidity to an almost total absence thereof. Either state might eventually become the norm, or the patient might continue to vacillate between them. The consultant recommended re-running the tests to check for any changes after Cesar had enjoyed a full month's rest.

Baumann had spoken to Palm Villas, the nursing home he'd mentioned in Pasadena. They currently had space, and were expecting to hear from Russell, who would of course be responsible for transporting the patient. Cesar was capable of walking with a little assistance, so a taxi would be appropriate. The consultant assumed Russell would be informing the family of the new arrangements.

An invoice was included. The amount seemed eye-wateringly high for a few inconclusive tests, but the American health system was a seller's market, and Russell supposed they'd have to pay it.

After looking up the number in the book, he called Palm Villas. The woman he spoke to seemed eager to help, which was hopefully true of the whole establishment. The prospective fees made Doctor Baumann's feel almost inconsequential, but he would worry about that later. Admission was set for 3 P.M. next day.

He could ask Juan to come, Russell thought. Cesar might need reassurance if a stranger came to drive him away.

HARALD GEBAUER'S FUNERAL HAD TAKEN place three days after the Ströhms' latest evening in West Berlin, and there, among the mourners, Gerhard had spotted an old KPD comrade. Bruno Koska had worked with Ströhm in the underground resistance before and during the war, which would in itself have been reason enough for a convivial catch-up session. Even more to the point, the last Ströhm had heard, his old comrade was working in the *Neues Deutschland* printing shop. Distracted by his altercation with Helmut Breitner, Ströhm had neglected to make contact that day, but one call to the newspaper office had confirmed that Koska still worked there, and a second had set up an evening drink at a bar in Weissensee they both knew.

As Ströhm had noticed at the funeral, Koska had put on a

good deal of weight since prewar days, but otherwise seemed remarkably unchanged. He was certainly willing as ever to speak his mind. "I heard what you said to Breitner at Harald's funeral" was the first thing he said once they'd sat down with their beers. "I doubt I'd have been as brave," he went on, adding with a grin that "I guess you have to be on the Central Committee to take a risk like that."

"Or be too angry to care," Ströhm replied. "How have you been?"

"Not so bad. Just the usual complaints. Both my children are doing well at school, and my daughter's becoming a champion athlete. You wouldn't believe the sports equipment they're getting these days."

Ströhm was pleased the DDR was doing something right.

"How about you?" Koska asked. "Do you have a family?"

"Yes. Five years now. Two children, a boy and a girl. My wife works at the State Hospital in Friedrichshain. Look, Bruno, it's great to see you, but I also have an ulterior motive. Tell me to fuck off if you want, and there'll be no hard feelings, but I'm looking for information about one of your colleagues. Not for the Party, I hasten to add. The father of the girl he's going with is a friend, and some of the things she's been saying about this potential son-in-law have got him worried."

"Who are we talking about?"

"His first name's Werner, we don't know the second. The girl is Charlotte Schade, who works upstairs."

"It's Werner Matern who's going out with Lotte. I don't know him that well—I'm not sure anyone does. He's likable enough, on the surface at least. He's a quiet lad, always reading on his own during breaks. I don't know, Gerhard. Back in the day, when our lives were all on the line, there was always someone you weren't quite sure you could rely on. Matern strikes me that way, but I couldn't really tell you why. Maybe it's that he gives so little of himself away. Then again, maybe he's more forthcoming with her. Who knows? I've nothing concrete against him."

"Does he wear his politics on his sleeve?"

"Not really. I'd guess he's pretty pissed off with the way things are going, but he's not alone there." Koska shrugged. "Sorry I can't be more help."

"No problem," Ströhm told him, wondering if there was anyone else he could turn to. He still had friends in the security services, but mentioning names to them wasn't something one did lightly. And Thomas had asked him not to approach Werner himself, knowing Lotte would find out and know who had put him up to it.

"Do you remember that night in '38?" Koska asked, sending the two of them off down a trail of reminiscence.

SCHOOL WAS OUT FOR THE summer, and Rosa was keen to come with them next day. After picking up Juan outside his flat, Russell drove to LA General and parked as close as he could to an entrance. The three of them found Cesar sitting in a wheelchair, dressed and ready to go. "You can leave the wheelchair in reception once you've got him to the car," the sweetheart nurse told them, and got a smile from Cesar in return.

But there was a worrying look on the man's face as they wheeled him out through the building. "Who are they?" he asked Juan, presumably referring to Russell and his daughter.

"Friends," Juan told him. "Her name is Rosa and he is another Juan."

When they reached the car the boy helped his uncle into the back seat, and then got in beside him. Rosa had gone to return the wheelchair, and while they waited Cesar seemed quite agitated, but once the car was in motion a smile seemed to spread across his face. He didn't ask where they were going.

The drive out to Pasadena took about twenty minutes, finding

Palm Villas another ten. It was a large and attractive establishment, with well-groomed gardens and enough healthy-looking
palms to justify the name. Inside, the communal spaces were
spotless and easy on the eye, as was the room which Cesar had
been given. The bed was comfortable, the cupboard spacious, not
that Cesar had anything to unpack.

"My dad will bring clothes this evening," Juan told his uncle,
"and what's left of your stuff from Chavez Ravine."

"Where are we?" Cesar asked him.

"This is your home for a few weeks," Juan told him. "A place
for you to rest and get better."

Cesar nodded, but his eyes were still awash with confusion.

The woman who'd admitted him had suggested tea in the
common room, so the four of them made their way there, Cesar
walking slowly but steadily.

Once John and Rosa had collected the teas, the four of them
sat, mostly in silence, examining the new world around them.
There were at least a dozen others in the large room, and most
were considerably older than Cesar. Seeing a familiar look on
Rosa's face, Russell knew she was itching to draw them. Over the
years, whenever he'd looked at his daughter's sketches, he'd feared
that her inner world would always be mired in pathos. He had that
feeling now, and the sudden pang of sadness almost took his
breath away.

When he suggested it might be time to leave, she said she'd
stay for a while, and help Juan get his uncle used to the place.
Russell wished Cesar goodbye and received a polite but uncompre-
hending smile in return. Out in the Frazer, Russell just sat behind
the wheel for several minutes, letting his own emotions sort themselves out. The car that had tailed them all day was on the other
side of the lot, its driver hiding behind the obligatory newspaper.

With Effi working late there was no reason to rush home, and
a drink seemed like a good idea. He drove back to Broadway,

where fate gifted him a parking spot right outside his favoured bar, and for the next twenty minutes he enjoyed sipping two Manhattans, his mind a grateful blank.

Then someone turned the television on and there were the Rosenbergs, or there were the Rosenbergs as they had been two years ago. God only knew what they looked like now.

According to the newsreader, the Supreme Court had rejected their petition for a sentence review, and they would probably be executed in the next few weeks. There were murmurs of approval in the bar, and several drinkers raised their glasses to the screen.

Russell found the Rosenbergs' treatment barbaric. If a nation employed spies, it was somewhat hypocritical to complain when other countries did the same, and he thought captured spies should simply be returned to their employers, not treated as if they'd done something abhorrent. Given that exposure had probably exhausted their usefulness, unemployment seemed punishment enough.

He supposed his opinion might be biased, particularly when it came to the Rosenbergs and handing over atomic secrets. He had, after all, done much the same himself in 1945, as payment to the Soviets for getting his family out of conquered Berlin. If the US government ever found out, he supposed he might still face the death penalty, but eight years on, with most if not all of the witnesses gone, any case would be hard to prove.

If life was mostly pathos, it was also a lottery. He'd got away with it, the Rosenbergs hadn't.

The next faces up on the screen belonged to Poulson and Bowron. It was of course election day, not that Russell had a vote. He drained his drink and left.

Out on the sidewalk he decided against going back to an empty house. But what to do instead? The sea was his first thought, baseball the second—the Twinks were playing the Angels again that evening, and he'd never been to Wrigley Field.

The Los Angeles Angels' home was only a few blocks from Dolphin's Record Store, straddling the border between white and black residential areas. Russell got there an hour early, parked in the enormous lot, and strolled right round the stadium. It was a more impressive affair than Gilmore Field, with a Spanish-style façade and two tiers of covered seats extending along the first and third base lines.

Once inside he found a row of phone booths and called home. Effi wasn't back yet, but Rosa was, and he told her he was at the game. "Leave a message for Effi if you go out," he told her. With all that was happening he didn't want her worrying unduly.

Rosa said she would. "Do you think he'll ever get better?" she asked.

"I hope so, but I've no idea. How was it after I left?"

"Just sad, really. I'll see you later, all right?"

Russell bought himself a couple of hot dogs and went to his seat in the lower tier, just a few yards beyond first base. The Twinks had won the previous evening's game 11 to 3, but there was to be no repeat. They did hit two home runs—the second of which was their starting pitcher's first-ever—but they also managed to walk in two Angels, and then concede the winning run in the bottom of the eighth. Russell's tail, sitting several rows back, looked as depressed as he was.

Effi and Rosa were both asleep by the time he got home, and he sat out in the garden for a while, watching the moon rise up behind the Downtown skyline, thinking about Cesar and the Rosenbergs and his own dices with death. There but for fortune . . .

VARIATIONS ON "POULSON WINS!" HEADLINED all the newspapers when Effi stopped the following morning to buy a packet of mints at the kiosk outside General Service Studios. The outcome was hardly a surprise, and probably not that important in the grand scheme of things. She hadn't liked what she'd seen of either Poulson or Bowron, but maybe living through the Weimar Republic and Hitler had soured her on all politicians.

The show had been recorded the previous afternoon and would be broadcast that day. It had turned out better than most had expected, the writers having finally emerged from their sulk with something worthy of a season finale. The producers had been smiling, the cast and crew happy as kids on the last day of school. The nearby bars had doubtless done good business.

This morning most of the actors and writers had come in to empty their lockers or desks and say goodbye for the summer. All but the children seemed in good spirits—they'd been enrolled in a special school to catch up with their education.

Effi was having lunch at home with Rosa, and on the point of leaving when a secretary intervened. There was someone to see her, "someone official."

This didn't sound like good news. The man was waiting in the office where she'd received her Berlinale invitation, but Effi suspected that was not a good omen.

"My name is Calvin Sikorsky," he introduced himself. He was probably into his thirties, with stubble for hair, horn-rimmed glasses and very white teeth. His suit trousers were too short for him, revealing bright blue socks. "I just want a quick chat."

Effi sighed and took a chair, obliging him to do the same. "Who do you work for?"

He thought about that for a moment, before settling on the State Department.

So, the CIA, Effi thought. She wasn't Russell's wife for nothing.

"We understand you're travelling to Berlin in the near future. For the film festival, correct?"

"Correct."

"Well, naturally this is a matter of interest to the US Government," Sikorsky said.

"Why? I'm not an American citizen."

"Ah. That is, of course, true. But you are an American celebrity, are you not? Your show—perhaps you don't know this—is watched in Berlin by our soldiers and administrators, and by many Germans as well. What you say and do in Berlin will reflect on the US of A. So, in a very real way, you will be representing us."

Effi could hardly believe what she was hearing. "I don't accept that for one minute. I don't *represent* anyone."

Sikorsky thought about that and decided to ignore it. "Having researched these festivals, we know that you will be giving interviews to the local press and wireless stations, and probably taking part in roundtable discussions . . ."

"I expect so."

"Well, we are concerned that you might voice opinions which won't be fully understood. In a Berlin context, that is."

Effi couldn't help smiling. "Are you saying that as long as I make sure that I'm 'fully understood' I can say whatever I like?"

He looked flustered. "No . . ."

"I don't want to be difficult," Effi said, taking a little pity on him. "Why don't you come clean and tell me exactly what it is you're afraid I might say? Then I can tell you whether I have any intention of saying it."

He ran a hand through the stubble. "We don't want any undue criticism of the HUAC investigations."

Effi decided to let the "undue" pass. "Why censor me?" she asked. "Americans are free to criticise them. And they do."

"What we do within our own borders is one thing, what we do in Berlin is another. Critics of the senator here at home are not offering a propaganda victory to our enemies, as you would be doing if you said the same things in Berlin. Surely you can see that?"

"Of course I can. Why would you think I would want to help the Soviets, or their regime in the Eastern Sector? Or are you suggesting that I'm stupid enough to do so by accident?"

"You did work for them for several years."

"No, I didn't. I worked for DEFA, a German film company that was backed by the Soviet occupation authorities, at a time when the American occupation authorities were much more interested in preserving Hollywood's share of the German market than supporting the local Berlin studios. And when the Soviets started pressuring DEFA into making propaganda films I stopped working for them, as I'm sure you know."

"Yes . . ."

"Let me say this: If I am asked about HUAC, which I accept is likely, then I will balance any criticism I make of its workings with criticism of the similar censorship in the East. Will that satisfy you?"

"Not really. Equivalence is not what . . ."

"Okay, then let me cut to the chase," Effi said. "You're asking me not to do something which I may—*may*—choose to do. What will be the consequences if I ignore your request? What exactly are you threatening me with?"

Sikorsky looked hurt. "Absolutely nothing. We just wanted to be sure that you're aware of the situation in Berlin—how precarious and difficult it is—and how a visitor like yourself could have more effect that you might realise."

"I lived there most of my life. I'm in frequent contact with friends and family who still live there. Believe me, I'm aware of the current situation. Probably more so than the US State Department." Effi paused. Was she being unreasonable? No. Was she being unwise? Possibly. There was certainly a lot they could do that would make life more difficult for herself, John, and Rosa. At worst, they could refuse to let her and John back into the country. "Look," she said, "I promise to bear what you've said in mind. I'll do my best to think before I speak—something I've not been famous for—and not to upset any applecarts without meaning to. As I've already said, I have no desire to be a propaganda tool for the Soviets. What more can I say?"

"Then that will have to suffice," he said resignedly. "But one last thing," he said, reaching for his pocket. Effi's heart sank, but all that emerged was an autograph book. "My daughter loves your show."

Driving home, Effi found herself wondering what awaited her in Berlin. Would there be someone from the American consulate constantly at her shoulder, noting down every word she said? If so, she'd give whoever it was a piece of her mind.

That afternoon Rosa had an interview at the Otis College of Art and Design. Effi let her daughter drive them both down to Wilshire, and when they arrived Rosa announced that that they hadn't been followed.

"Are you sure?" Effi asked.

"Sure as I can be," Rosa said as she pulled the car up by the kerb.

"Now you say that, I don't remember noticing anyone behind me this morning."

"So what do you think it means? If they've stopped, is that a good thing or a bad thing?"

"Good, I hope, but I really don't know." They looked at each other. "Let's wait and see if they've stopped following your dad," Effi suggested.

When it was established soon after the First War, the Otis College had been the first art school in Los Angeles. It occupied two large and elegant properties adjacent to MacArthur Park, one named "The Bivouac," which had been bequeathed to the County by its owner, Harrison Gray Otis, the other subsequently acquired for the school's enlargement.

The college had a high reputation, was close to their current home, and, as their interviewer made clear, its admission committee was impressed by the drawings which Rosa had submitted. More so, it turned out, than Rosa was by the college. "It felt so old-fashioned," she said, once they were back in the car. "It's a beautiful old house, and I liked the man who interviewed me, but all the paintings on the walls, all the art in the various studios—it was all so traditional."

"Maybe all the schools are like that," Effi said, fearing they wouldn't be. What were the odds that Rosa found something more to her taste in New York?

She supposed they could all move there. New York was the home of American theatre, after all. John had lived there for ten months in 1942, and the only thing she remembered him complaining about was the weather. He complained about that here.

THURSDAY AFTERNOON, EFFI AND BETH were sat in the spacious lobby of the Hollywood Roosevelt Hotel, wondering how much longer they would have to wait. Eleven floors above them, in Room 1117, Laura was testifying before an executive session of the House Un-American Activities Committee. These hearings were supposedly private, so Effi and Beth would probably have been refused entry, but in any case Laura had flatly refused to countenance their attending. "I'm really grateful you're here," she'd told them, "but for one thing I'd like to go through this humiliation alone, and for another I don't want your lost careers on my conscience."

That had been two hours ago, and Beth was expecting her down soon. "It's past four, and that bunch of low-lifes never did a full day's work in their lives—why should they start now?"

As usual, she was right. The Laura who emerged from the elevator looked a bit shaken, but she managed a smile for her two supporters. "Let's find a bar," she said. "Somewhere dark and quiet."

"I know the place," Beth said, and five minutes later they were ordering drinks in a down-at-heel place on Highland.

"So how did it go?" Effi asked.

Laura shook her head. "What can I say? It was chilling; it was ridiculous. You know, they didn't even want me to name names—they just wanted me to confirm ones they had. They had this list of the people in our discussion group back in forty-two, which I duly rubber-stamped. They suggested a few names which I didn't recognise, and which I guess they got from others in the group. They didn't seem upset when I denied any knowledge of these people. In fact the chairman praised me for agreeing to appear as a friendly witness. And that was that. I might have lost my job, but at least I've proved my patriotism."

"You were up there for two hours," Beth said disbelievingly.

"They like to hear themselves talk. And there was a problem with the camera, which took an age to fix."

"So you are on film?"

"Oh yes. For the record, I was told. They doubted the session would be broadcast, but they couldn't give me a guarantee."

"So you can work."

"If anyone wants to risk hiring me. I'm not on a blacklist. And there are enough friendly witnesses I know who are still getting work, so who knows . . ."

"It could be a lot worse," Beth said, as much to herself as Laura.

"It could," Laura conceded, but she was shaking her head as she said it.

WITH EFFI GIVING LAURA MORAL support, Rosa suggested that this might be the day for her and her father to see the latest science fiction film. *It Came from Outer Space* had been released earlier that week, and fresh from enjoying reading *The Day of the Triffids*, Russell announced himself willing to give the movie a try. He was far from the only one. The cinema on Hollywood Boulevard was surprisingly full for a matinee performance, mostly with people much younger than he was.

He had to admit, he was never bored. The film began with a big fuzzy ball crashing to earth in the Arizona desert. A meteor, the hero assumed, until he found out it was a spaceship full of aliens. It was an accident, not an invasion, and after making contact with the intruders—who had managed to simulate a human appearance by copying locals whom they'd temporarily abducted—the hero promised to buy them the time they needed to repair their ship. But this was 1950s America. The locals, having initially refused to believe in the aliens, now refused to believe in their innocence. Foreigners would be bad enough, aliens from outer space even worse. They formed a posse and went for their guns.

In the end the aliens' raid on the local hardware store provided them with all they needed to escape, and the big fuzzy ball headed back into space. The locals all looked a bit confused, like cats who'd suddenly had their prey whisked away from them. A violent confrontation had been avoided, but there was no sign that anyone had learned anything.

As they queued to get out of the auditorium Russell found himself pondering Effi's cinematic golden rule: "Were the women's roles significant to the filmmakers' purpose?" The answer, he realised, was a definite no. The heroine had been a mirror for the hero and had screamed a lot. Only two other women had put in brief appearances, the wife and girlfriend of two abductees, one old and worried, the other young and brassy. Three stereotypes.

There had also, he realised, been a complete dearth of black or brown faces.

"So what did you think of it?" he asked Rosa as they left the parking lot.

"I thought it would be better," she admitted. "Ray Bradbury usually writes really good stories, but this was . . . the hero wasn't much to begin with, and then he sort of staggers away when he sees how ugly the alien really is—I mean, how shallow is that?"

"You would have asked to draw him."

"You bet I would!"

"Anyway," Russell said. "I'm not sorry we went. It didn't feel like good science fiction, but it worked well enough in its way. The aliens had the shock value, but the film was about the locals' response to them, and how that reflected the world we live in. If the screenwriter didn't have McCarthy and HUAC lurking somewhere in his subconscious when he came up with the story, I'd be very surprised."

"That would never have occurred to me," Rosa said.

"Nor me when I was seventeen. But the older you get, the more you notice the way things work. Sometimes you wish they didn't."

His wife's car was in the drive when they got home, Effi herself in the garden.

"This is my third G and T," she told them. "Someone else will have to cook supper."

"Was it that bad?" he asked.

"No worse than expected—I'm just sick of self-important men and the damage they always manage to leave in their wake. How was the film?"

"Full of self-important men, but they didn't do any real damage. Not for want of trying, though."

"Ah. I have a message for you. Your journalist friend Cal Tierney called. He said the police have come up with a story, and he's going out to Pasadena tomorrow morning to check it with Cesar—apparently the old guy was quite lucid when his brother visited him last night. He's assuming you'll want to go with him, so if he doesn't hear to the contrary, he'll pick you up here around ten."

"I want to go too," Rosa said from the kitchen doorway. "And I'll ask Juan as well."

Russell opened his mouth and closed it again—the phrase "the more the merrier" felt sadly inappropriate. "Did Cal say what the police have told him?" he asked Effi.

"No, but it must be a doozy."

WHEN CAL TIERNEY TURNED UP early on Friday morning, they asked him in for a coffee. "You must be Mrs. Luddwitz," he said to Effi.

"For now," she answered with a smile.

"So what did the police tell you?" Rosa was eager to know, just as the doorbell signalled Juan's arrival.

"They told me he fell down the stairs at central. Accidentally, according to the logbook they couldn't find until yesterday."

"So why send him to Chino? Was he ever charged with anything?"

"No, he wasn't. They say he seemed fine after the fall, and the intention was just to keep him in for the night. Whereupon, as predicted by yours truly, we come to our old friend, the administrative mix-up. They say it was a busy night, and the holding cells were already full before midnight, so they made room by shipping out half the inmates to Chino, and somehow Cesar ended up in the wagon with them. He only collapsed when he got there, which is how he ended up in the prison hospital."

"Sounds like bullshit," Russell said mildly.

"Because that's what it is. They're all lying to protect each other, and that's what they'll keep on doing. If Cesar is *compos mentis* enough, we should find out what really happened, but proving anything will still be damn near impossible."

"My dad said Uncle Cesar was okay last night," Juan chipped in. "And he told my dad they threw him down the stairs."

Tierney's eyes lit up. "Then let's go get him on the record."

The drive took a little over half an hour, and after what Effi had told him, Russell took care to check for a tail. As far as he could tell, there was none. For reasons best known to themselves, their shadows had called it a day. But why? Had they found out whatever it was they wanted to know? More to the point, what was it they wanted to know? And if they now knew, were he and Effi less or more at risk? There were only thirty-six hours to go before their departure, and he still hadn't heard from Jessup.

Arriving at Palm Villas, they made their way to Cesar's room, where two shocks awaited them. One was the smile on Cesar's face, though on closer inspection this seemed more conciliatory than real. The other was the smart-suited young man sat beside the bed.

"This is Bob," Cesar said helpfully. "He's a lawyer."

"Robert Turnbull," the man agreed, without getting up or offering a hand. "I know who you are," he told Tierney. "You can tell your readers that Cesar here has just been given a check for seven thousand dollars."

"In exchange for what?"

"In exchange for his signature on an exculpatory letter concerning events on the sixth of this month."

"Exculpating the LAPD?"

"Precisely. The agreement also contains what people refer to—most unfortunately, in my view—as a gag order. If Mr. Morales speaks to anyone—and particularly the press—about the night in question, he will render the financial settlement null and void."

"And why would he sign something like that?" Tierney asked.

"Oh, he already has. Before witnesses, I might add. Two lovely young nurses."

"Can I see this letter?" Tierney asked.

Turnbull reached into his briefcase and pulled out a sheet of paper. "I have two other copies in case you're thinking of tearing that one up."

"Perish the thought," Tierney said dryly, glancing through the document before passing it on to Russell.

"I believe five thousand dollars was the 'unrepeatable offer' Mr. Morales declined for his property in 1951," Turnbull went on, "but to show our good will we have repeated it nevertheless. The extra two grand is in compensation for the unfortunate series of events which saw Mr. Morales spend several nights in prison."

Russell was looking at the document, and particularly the masthead. Anderson, Anderson & Davies were busy boys. He looked round at the others: Rosa and Juan both looking distraught, Tierney close to throwing a punch. Cesar was still wearing his smile, but the hint of bewilderment had grown a lot stronger.

"You must let me know where to send the check," Turnbull said, before gingerly placing his business card on the bed and taking his leave.

The others left half an hour later, and on their way out Russell stopped in the lobby to call Frank Jessup.

"I've just left a message with your wife," the PI told him. "I'm in Hollywood tomorrow morning, and I thought we could meet up."

"You have stuff to tell me?"

"Yes, but not over the telephone. There's a coffee shop on the corner of Gower and Sunset, not that far from you."

"I know it."

"Nine-thirty?"

"I'll see you then."

"SO WHO DO THEY WORK for?" Russell asked Jessup as a bus rumbled past the diner's window.

The private detective examined his plate to make sure he had eaten every last crumb of the cherry pie. "That was so good," he said, wiping his lips with a paper napkin and reaching for the sugar dispenser. "The name of the agency is G. J. Associates. Gregory Johnson, who started it up, died in the war. The family still owns it, but it's run by a man named Sandy Tregorren. It's a big firm, probably the biggest in the city. They employ at least a dozen operatives, and the only individual clients they'd consider

would be movie stars. Mostly they work for big business—oil
and water, the airplane people, pharmaceuticals, property developers . . ."

"Government agencies?"

"No," Jessup said, stirring the sugar into his coffee.

So not Immigration or HUAC, Russell thought. "So who
hired G. J. Associates to follow Effi and me?"

Jessup lowered his cup. "A legal firm named Anderson, Anderson & Davies. Who are also one of the city's biggest."

"I've heard of them," Russell said wryly. "So who hired them?"

"That's where it usually gets a little murkier. Everyone knows
there are informal links between business leaders, but most people
assume the big corporations respect the laws forbidding any closer
relationship. Well, they don't. Not in LA, anyway. There's a tight-
knit group of business and media concerns . . ."

"Bowron's 'special interests'?"

Jessup grimaced. "You could say that, though I don't remember Bowron having any problem with them when they were
supporting him." He took a sip of coffee. "Where was I?"

"A tight-knit group."

"Yes. Well, the knitting part is an unofficial liaison committee
which deals with any common problems, coordinates the group's
political responses. There's an agreed annual budget, for paying
lawyers and G. J. Associates and probably bribing people at City
Hall and the LAPD. The committee members hold monthly un-
minuted meetings at each other's houses and work out a common
strategy wherever they think one is needed. I imagine bringing
down Bowron was one of them."

"I take it you didn't discover all this in a week."

"Of course not. And I still couldn't prove it if I wanted to. But
you work in this city, you put two and two together. There's too
much stuff only makes sense if a group like this are pulling a lot
of the strings."

Which sounded convincing. "So Effi or I have upset a member of this club. Which one?"

"That was the difficult bit. But money talks, even when you're dealing with people like this. Perhaps even more so—you'd think they'd pay their minions well, if only to ensure their loyalty, but they don't. I guess penny-pinching is a habit the rich never lose."

"So who?"

"The Lettson Corporation. It was their man on the committee, Nick Hayden, who set up the surveillance operation. Presumably at the owner Greer Holleman's request. Have you had any dealings with him?"

Russell was shocked. "I interviewed him once, about three weeks ago. I'm writing an article for overseas papers about the special election."

"The timeline sounds about right. Did you give him any reason to feel aggrieved or threatened?"

"Not that I'm aware of. I actually thought we got on pretty well. Does Hayden work for anyone else?"

"Not as far as I know. Running the Lettson personnel department and Holleman's campaign must take all the hours God sends, and he still has to fit in his work on the liaison committee."

"So Holleman has to know."

"I would say so. And one thing I forgot—the checks paid in by AA&D were drawn on his campaign expenses account."

"But why?" Russell thought out loud.

"That's the question I haven't been able to answer. And my suspicion is that only Holleman or Hayden could tell you."

"How much would two weeks' surveillance have cost them?" Russell asked.

"At least four grand. You may not know what it is, but you must have something on him."

"Yeah. But I'm damned if I know what it could be. And speaking of money, what do we owe you?"

"Not as much as that," Jessup said with a smile, reaching into an inside pocket for the invoice.

It could have been worse, Russell thought when he saw the figure.

Effi and Rosa were both out when he got back home, so he went straight to his office and dug up his notes on the Holleman interview. As Jessup had said, the timing looked right—he had interviewed Holleman on Wednesday, May 6, and first noticed he was being followed eight days later. Was that a reasonable amount of time to arrange a surveillance operation? The lag suggested a lack of urgency, but perhaps it took that long to get the necessary agreement and funding through the big boys' liaison committee.

As he went through the interview, nothing leapt out at him. If Holleman had let something slip that he shouldn't have, Russell had no idea what it was. So had he said something to Holleman? If he had, he couldn't see what it might be.

And then he realised. The one thing that connected them was Germany. Holleman had been there in the thirties, and here was Russell saying he wrote for a German paper. Had that sounded an alarm in Holleman's mind? Or at least given him cause to check Russell out? Two weeks' surveillance would have thrown up a few things, not least that he was writing a book on American businesses which conducted illicit trade deals with the Nazis. But Russell had already confirmed that the Lettson Corporation had closed down its European operation in 1940, so why would Holleman worry about that? Unless, of course, Russell had missed something, and there was still some dirt to dig up.

The other thing the surveillance would have shown up was his and Effi's impending visit to Germany. Perhaps Holleman was afraid that Russell might uncover some dreadful secret on the trip.

Of course, if Russell had spooked him, Holleman would have sought information in any number of ways. He and his friends would have access to informants in all sorts of places—in local government and law enforcement, and probably in the federal government and its intelligence services. By this time the man would have a dossier on him that would almost match Beria's. And if its compiler had come to a conclusion, it surely had to be that Russell was not privy to any information that might endanger Holleman's candidacy.

Then again, did spending $4,000 on investigating a journalist he'd only met once seem like the act of an innocent man?

THEIR CAB REACHED UNION STATION around half-past six, and Russell dealt with their baggage while Effi and Rosa went through to the high-ceilinged waiting room. With trains, ships, and aeroplanes to deal with, the two adults had done their best to limit what they were taking, but as he watched the red caps haul the pile away Russell couldn't help wishing they'd tried a bit harder.

He had planned on seeking out Juan's father for news of Cesar, but Juan himself had turned up that morning with a letter from his dad. The family were deeply grateful to him and Effi for paying for a month's stay at the nursing home but could not possibly accept any further financial assistance. The doctor was optimistic that Cesar would be fit enough to leave by then, and if he wasn't the family would find a way to manage. Whenever he was fit enough to leave, his brother and sister-in-law intended he stay with them, at least for a while.

"As it is, Juan has to sleep on the living room couch," Rosa had said. "But they will find a way to manage. They shouldn't have to, but they will."

Russell found her and Effi camped out in the waiting room, waiting with their carry-on cases for the boarding call. His own case was full of notes for his book, which he already suspected would receive little attention. As for Holleman, Russell intended to ask his old journalist friend Jack Slaney to make some enquiries when they met between trains in Chicago. Having not seen Slaney for several years, Russell had set up the rendezvous as soon as he knew they were spending several hours at Chicago's Union Station and was now really pleased that he had.

Soon after seven the boarding call went up, and everyone reached for their bags. As the waiting passengers surged out onto the train concourse Effi and Rosa scanned them for celebrities and came up empty—"You're the only one," Rosa complained to her mother.

"Maybe Bogie and Bacall are late," Effi teased her. Bogart had been Rosa's first Hollywood crush. There was "something so sad about him."

They were booked into *Pine Arroyo*, one of the sleeper coaches which had ten single person roomettes and six double bedrooms. Russell had thought a drawing room sleeping three in one of the *Regal* coaches made more sense, but Rosa had been adamant in demanding a room of her own.

Pine Arroyo was near the front of the train, a couple of baggage cars back from the quartet of diesels which headed the *Super Chief*. Rosa's roomette was two down from their double, on the side of the train which would generally face north and west, where the light would be better for drawing. Their double, which had a private toilet, had its window on the same side.

The three of them were in the Pleasure Dome Observation Lounge when the whistles blew for departure, having already reserved their seats in the dining car next door. Russell could feel the rumbling of the diesels through the floor as the train clanked into motion, and as their coach reached the end of the low platform, he had a swiftly passing view of Greer Holleman and his son Luke standing in a cone of light, the boy with rapt eyes and his wonderful smile, the father fondly watching his son. The tableau vanished from view almost as soon as it had appeared, and

Russell might have thought it a trick of the imagination if he hadn't remembered Holleman saying, as the two of them had watched his son's *Super Chief* circling its oval of track, that he and Luke often came to watch the real thing arrive and depart.

As the train rounded the curve and ventured out across the huge concrete drain that carried the Los Angeles River, Russell again found himself wondering how and why he had worried the man so much.

"What are you thinking about?" Effi asked, seeing the look on his face.

"Cesar," he lied, not wanting to worry Rosa. "That's LA General," he added in explanation, pointing out the brightly lit monolith a few hundred yards to the south.

A steward loomed over Effi's shoulder and told them their table was ready.

An hour or so later, with Rosa in her own room and the lights of suburbia finally thinning out, he told Effi what he'd seen.

"Like the universe is trying to tell you something," she suggested.

"Perhaps, but what? Maybe Herr Furslanger is still working in Berlin."

Bodi Furslanger was an astrologer Effi had occasionally consulted before the war, more for the man's emotional insights than any belief in his power to predict. His canvas tent had remained a feature of Leipziger Strasse throughout the thirties, mostly because many of his clients were senior Nazis.

"He was killed in the bombing," Effi said.

"Something else he didn't see coming," Russell said unkindly.

Effi ignored him. "It was when you were living it up in England. The summer of 1943, I think. There were hundreds went to his funeral."

"Which is probably more than'll come to mine," Russell conceded.

"Oh I wouldn't say that. Think of all the intelligence people who'll turn up just for confirmation."

Russell laughed. "You should be on the stage."

She sighed. "I should. A theatre stage, I mean. Look," she turned to face him. "I've been thinking about what's happened to Laura, and I've made a bit of a plan. With the emphasis on bit. When we get back, I'll either have to sign up for another season or quit. And I think I should sign up, not because I love the show, but because without it I won't have any clout. Which I'll need if I go into battle with HUAC."

"Tell me why that's a good idea," Russell said. He hadn't seen this coming.

"Because it's time someone told the truth?"

"There's no denying that, but these days telling the truth has a cost."

"Why would it cost me? I've never been a member of any Communist Party, so I have no names to give them. What excuse could they have for putting me on a blacklist?"

"I think the word is 'uncooperative.'"

"Well, if they do they do. Really, I'm happy to be Mrs. Luddwitz for another season, and I'm sure we could use the money. But we don't need it, and I'm just as happy to tell her goodbye. I feel like a fight. People like Laura have too much to lose, but people who don't, like me, well, it's up to us. What do you think?"

"I think I love you."

"Well, that's good to know, but what do you think of my plan?"

"It needs work. If you have nothing they want, how will you persuade HUAC to give you a platform?"

"I haven't worked that out yet. I thought you might help— you've always been good at selling untruths. Always on the side of the angels, of course."

"Of course."

Another hour later, when Effi was asleep, and Russell could see a desert moon rising through the crack between window frame and blind, his thoughts turned back to Holleman.

"Stop it," he told himself. Like HUAC, Holleman could wait. They were both going home, Effi in triumph, him excited by the prospect of seeing his son and his friends.

But not without a frisson of trepidation. There had been two stories about Berlin in the *Times* that week, the first claiming that 4,000 East Germans had crossed the intracity border in a single day with no intention of returning, the second that the Soviet occupation forces were handing back control to their civilian counterparts. Assuming both were true, Russell saw trouble ahead—if things were that bad in the Eastern sector, it didn't seem a good time for the Soviets to be loosening their grip.

Replacing the Wiring

They all slept well on the first night of the journey, so well that they almost missed breakfast. Much of the day was spent in the observation lounge, Effi reading magazines, Russell his book, and Rosa—for once not drawing—just sat by her window watching the parched Southwest pass by. They stretched their legs on the platform at Albuquerque, snoozed away the afternoon in their rooms, and watched the sun go down behind the distant Rockies over a splendid dinner.

A day to savour, Russell told himself, so why was he finding it so hard to do just that? Why did his brain keep dragging him back to Greer Holleman?

He told himself for the umpteenth time that whatever the man had hoped to find out by having him followed, the fact that he'd called off the tails suggested he must have found it. And then done nothing, because whatever his fears had been, he had come to realise that they were groundless.

The hole in this argument was that only a couple of days had passed between the surveillance ending and their departure. Holleman hadn't really had time to do anything.

Anyway, getting out of LA had to be good. Not that Berlin would be offering any guarantee of safety. But he didn't have to worry about Beria and the Soviets until their plane touched down at Tempelhof. In the meantime he got to cross America by train and the Atlantic by luxury liner, to visit friends in New York and a son in London.

Be thankful, he told himself. Worrying about things in advance was rarely helpful, and usually ended up spoiling things for everyone. So live in the present.

Which was easier said than done. That night he dreamt he was walking through the half-flooded maze of trenches he'd known at Ypres, looking for something but not knowing what, tripping over corpses, slapping off the rats that tried to climb his legs. He woke with the usual gasp, his nose full of shit and decaying flesh.

Effi stirred but didn't wake, and he lay there for several minutes, willing the real world back into focus. Knowing he wouldn't get back to sleep in a hurry, Russell put on a pair of trousers and quietly let himself out of the room. The train was slowing down, the occasional lights of a sleeping town giving way to the yellow glow of a yard and station. Newton was the name on the side of the station building; the clock on the platform said 2:45. A handful of tired-looking people were waiting to get on.

He climbed down to the platform, only to be shooed back aboard: "We only stop for a minute."

As the train pulled out, a smallish-looking town swam briefly into view on either side of the tracks, but soon they were back in open country, starlit fields stretching into the distance. He hadn't had a dream like that for a while but knew he would keep on having them for the rest of his life. Some things you didn't get over. An abusive parent, the death of a child. In his case a year in a human abattoir that returned in nightmares and reawakened memories. Which was bad enough in itself, but not the whole story. The flashbacks came and went, but the person transformed by those experiences was ever-present—it was who he was.

THE *SUPER CHIEF* WAS FIFTEEN minutes late drawing in to Chicago's Union Station, but that still gave Russell more than two hours for the meeting he'd arranged with Jack Slaney. While Effi and Rosa took the chance to walk down to the lake-shore, he headed for the station bar, pausing only briefly at the newsstand when he noticed the headlines proclaiming Everest's conquest.

In the bar he found Slaney already ensconced with a large glass of beer. The two had known each other since 1936, when Slaney arrived in Berlin to cover Hitler's Olympics. A colleague's illness had resulted in his staying on as the *Post's* correspondent, and over the next five years they had shared numerous journalistic assign-ments, poker games, and thoroughly cynical conversations. In 1941 Slaney had been thrown out of Germany for comparing Operation Barbarossa to the Charge of the Light Brigade, but over the succeeding years he and Russell had made a habit of run-ning into each other, sometimes deliberately, sometimes not. Slaney was now over sixty and retired from journalism but claimed to be writing a book on the 1936 Olympics in Berlin and their impact on both Germany and the US.

"You look like you need a beer," was Slaney's first comment.

One was duly ordered. After taking a sip, Russell looked in vain for a briefcase or bag. "Did you bring the stuff you wanted me to check in Berlin?" he asked.

"Ah. You're off the hook there. I've decided that the book I had in mind would probably take a damn sight longer than I have. And definitely longer than I care to spend on the goddamn Nazis."

Russell could empathise with that. "I thought the book was supposed to ease the transition from work to complete idleness."

"So now I'm writing a different one—my memoirs. You know the great thing about memoirs—they don't need any research. You just write down what you remember and settle a few scores along the way."

"Sounds great. But I'm sorry about the one you've aban-doned—I was looking forward to reading it."

"And I hate wasting research, so maybe I'll turn out a couple of articles."

"Good. It's a story that needs telling."

"It does, but by someone else. You could do it."

"I'm already doing my own. And getting nowhere fast with it. Would you believe I've been told to cease and desist?"

"I should think you'd be used to that by now."

Russell laughed. "Yeah. I don't suppose you've heard of Greer Holleman?"

"Republican candidate in the special election. One of the swanky LA districts—I can't remember which. He inherited the Lettson Corporation from his wife when she died young, correct?"

"Correct."

"And Lettson did very well out of the war. Legally, as far as I know, which probably isn't that far. What's *your* interest in Holleman?"

Russell explained about the series he was writing on the special election, and how, after doing an apparently innocuous interview with Holleman, he had found himself under almost constant surveillance for more than two weeks. "Holleman's campaign paid the agency who did it, and I'd like to know why. Preferably before I get back from Europe, so I don't come home to an ambush. I was hoping you might know who to ask."

"He's from the South, right?"

"Little Rock, according to the official bio. Do you know anyone down there?"

"Not any longer, but once upon a time . . . In the twenties I had a couple of jobs in the South—being younger and a lot less cynical, I thought an American journalist should spend some time outside the big cities. So I worked a few months for a paper in Montgomery, and more than a year for another in Memphis. That was definitely enough. There were good people down there, people who weren't so set on keeping things the way they were, but they lived on the sufferance of those who were. It was the same for journalists: you quickly got to know what lines you couldn't cross, and the best ones I met just spent their careers trying to move that line another quarter inch towards decency. All those years abroad, I didn't keep in touch, but maybe one or two are still alive. I'll do some digging."

"Thanks." Russell tore a sheet from his notebook, wrote out Thomas's Dahlem address, and handed it across. "That's where I'll be if you come across something you think I should know. Otherwise I'll see you here on the way back."

Slaney folded the sheet and slipped it into his shirt pocket. "So how have you been finding LA? Or the US, come to that?"

Russell winced. "It's hard to say," he began. "The way you just talked about the South, I found myself thinking that's how I feel about the whole country. There are good people here, but they're not the ones in charge, and the place seems haunted by its past. Slavery's gone, but the ghosts are everywhere. The same with the Indians. A country built on death, that knows no other way of life than violence." Seeing the look on Slaney's face, he paused. "Sorry, I'm probably exaggerating. And I am an outsider. I'm not seeing the whole picture."

"Outsiders are sometimes the only ones who can see the whole picture," Slaney said, surprising him. "Not to blow my own trumpet, but when I arrived in Germany in '36 it didn't take me long to work out where that country was headed. Whereas most of the decent Germans I met didn't have a clue."

EARLY JUNE IN MOSCOW WAS a huge improvement on early March. The temperature was in the high sixties, the bright sun doing justice to the pastel-shaded elegance of the city centre streets and boulevards. The myriad small parks seemed full of flowers and blossoming trees, and even the people looked less down-at-heel than their DDR counterparts. Not a high bar admittedly, but somehow surprising all the same.

But the SED delegation was not there to enjoy the weather, or indeed anything else, as their construction site of a hotel had already made clear. They were there because the CPSU had received yet another dire catalogue of its German satellite's woes and were intent on reading the riot act.

The summons was to the same Kremlin conference room as last time, the gratuitous wait even longer. Eventually the same ten people found themselves facing each other across the same polished table, and Gerhard Ströhm found himself staring at what he couldn't quite believe was the same gently shimmering cobweb. Bonhomie was in short supply.

Watching and listening, Ströhm noticed two substantial differences between this meeting and the last. The first was that the Soviets had finally lost patience and were not in the least interested in what their supposed comrades had to say. The SED *would* call a halt to forced collectivisation, *would* relax judicial controls, *would* shift resources from heavy industry to the production of consumer goods. And not in a month or a year—this dramatic change of course *must* be announced within a fortnight. When Ulbricht protested that this was not possible, he was simply told to be quiet, and sat there looking for all the world like a little boy who'd just been slapped.

The other change was less noticeable but probably more important, at least in the long run. The five Soviet leaders on the other side of the table were all singing from the same hymn sheet when it came to the DDR, but in every other respect they seemed ill at ease with each other. They might be trying hard not to show it, but there were too many half-rolled eyes, too many malicious glances. These men were all too busy distrusting each other to create a stable collective leadership.

Talking to his Soviet friend Oleg Mironov on a bench in the

Alexandra Gardens an hour later, Ströhm had his guesses more or less confirmed. The struggle was not yet out in the open but was definitely underway. "A week ago I would have bet on Beria and Malenkov," Mironov told him, "but the word this week is that they've fallen out. So who knows?"

What Mironov wanted from Ströhm was his opinion of how the SED Central Committee would react to Moscow's latest fiat.

"Some will be in shock, some will be relieved," he answered. "Like I am. There might even be enough of us to bring down Ulbricht, but would that be allowed?"

"I've no idea," Mironov said, "but it's a very good question."

THEIR TRAIN PULLED INTO NEW York's Penn Station early on Tuesday afternoon. Ali was waiting at the exit to hug them in turn, looking more like a chic young New Yorker than the fugitive orphan Effi had lived with in war-time Berlin.

When Effi and Russell had first met her, Ali had been Thomas's seventeen-year-old bookkeeper at the Schade factory in Treptow. Being Jewish, she had been required to quickly change into a cleaner's clothes whenever the Nazi authorities came to visit. Even in 1941, it had still been legal to employ Jews, but only in the most menial of capacities.

At that time, Russell had been trying to keep track of what was happening to Berlin's battered Jewish community, and Ali's family had swiftly transitioned from journalistic sources to friends in need of help. Unlike her parents, who had followed orders and died in Treblinka, Ali had gone underground rather than board a train to "the East." Effi had done the same following Russell's escape from the Reich, and six months later, when the two women ran into each at the Uhland Eck café on Ku'damm, they had decided to see out the war together, living as aunt and niece. Eventually they had joined a group smuggling Jews abroad which was run from the Swedish Embassy.

During that time Ali had met Fritz, the fellow Jewish "U-boat" who was now her husband. They had left for the States in 1947, when Fritz had got a teaching job at a black university in Alabama. Their experience there had been more interesting than enjoyable, and when, two years later, he had been offered a teaching post in Brooklyn they had gladly accepted it. A second reason for welcoming the move to New York had been the better chance it offered for Ali to find rewarding work, and early in 1951 she had met a fellow German Jewish survivor in Prospect Park, who wanted to start a music publishing company but claimed she had "no head for business." Two years later, the two of them had an office in Broadway's Brill Building.

The couple's social life had also expanded by leaps and bounds. As whites working with blacks in Alabama, they hadn't been fully trusted by anyone, and often felt stranded in a social version of no man's land. In Brooklyn by contrast, as Ali triumphantly mentioned in one of her letters, they had friends of "every conceivable colour."

They lived in a divided brownstone on South Slope. "It's a very mixed area," Ali said as their taxi crossed the Brooklyn Bridge. "There are lots of Jewish families, but it's not a Jewish neighbourhood. We wanted to mix, especially after Alabama."

The sidewalks felt busy after Melrose Avenue, but then most sidewalks would. Their apartment was quite spacious, but already filling up with books and knickknacks. For reasons she couldn't quite put her finger on, Effi found it touchingly reminiscent of the Blumenthal home in Berlin. To Rosa's delight there was a gramophone and several wooden crates of records, one of which held Fritz's blues recordings.

"I can't believe you and John are only staying one night," Ali told Effi in the kitchen. "More on the way back, I hope."

"So do I," Effi replied. "But everything's up in the air with the show. I still don't know if or when they want me back." She'd just noticed the framed photographs on the wall, one of Ali's parents, whom she'd known, and one of Fritz's, whom she hadn't. All had suffered the same fate. Effi had a vivid recollection of Martin and Leonore twelve years earlier, sitting in the apartment on Oranien-burger Strasse, him intent on hoping for the best, she not wanting to burst his balloon.

Fritz got home from the college soon after six, and the five of them spent the rest of the evening sitting round the dinner table, eating, drinking, and talking. The memories of time spent together in Berlin perhaps loomed largest, but there were also Hollywood and HUAC, race and education, Israel and the new diaspora, the past and future of American music. The adults didn't agree on everything, but Effi was struck by how in tune they all were when it came to the things that really mattered.

And the thing she found most wonderful was Rosa's obvious delight in being there. Her daughter was basking in the joy of an extended family, Effi thought, and in all the many miracles needed to bring these five people back together, healthy, sane, and prosperous, so far away from the city which had been their home.

Later, as she and Ali made up the guest beds, they talked about Rosa. The girl seemed so grown-up to Ali that Effi felt the need to add a word of caution. "She can seem so worldly, then act like a real innocent. I tell myself I shouldn't worry, that one thing she isn't is reckless, but I can't help myself."

"We'll take good care of her," Ali insisted.

"She wants to visit record stores in Harlem," Effi told her.

"Then we'll all go together. You're not to worry."

"Okay, I won't. Not too much, anyway. Tell me to mind my own business, but do you and Fritz want children?"

"Yes. We do. In the next few years, I think." Ali paused. "I don't really understand why, but after, you know—it didn't seem the right time. There were Jews we knew going on about how important it was to start replacing all those who'd been lost, and we both thought no, that's no reason to have children. But now, yes, I think it's time. Or soon will be. I'll be thirty in December."

"Plenty of time."

"Do you regret not having children with John?" Ali asked, seeing the sadness in her friend's eyes.

Effi exhaled. "I never wanted children until I had one," she said. "And by then it felt too late to have one with John. But he has Paul, and we both have Rosa. For a while at least."

"For keeps, I'd say."

Effi smiled. "It's so good to see you."

Lying in bed with a sleeping John, she thought about the time she and Ali had spent on Bismarckstrasse. It had been an extraordinary time, terrifying and somehow wonderful at the same time. She had never felt more alive, or more useful, than she had in those two years, and when they were over she'd told herself not to forget that, not to fall back into thinking that acting was anything more than a job. An enjoyable one, a challenging one, sometimes even an important one, but a job was a job. If she never trod another theatre or sound stage she would be sad, but not diminished. Her life was more than her work.

AN ATLANTIC CROSSING IN JUNE was relaxing in more ways than one. The sea was mostly calm, sunshine and blue skies so much the norm than an hour of rain felt almost insulting. Spending six days in mid-ocean, out of contact and obliged to embrace inaction, proved, after a brief transitional period, a wonderful way to shrug off anxiety about everything but one's weight. And for the latter there was always the deck walk, with so many circuits required to work off each meal.

There were plenty of physical activities on offer if you were that way inclined, but Russell wasn't. Playing deck quoits might be preferable to jumping overboard, but not by much. The indoor entertainment was more appealing, the shows in the theatre to a decent standard, the music salons even better.

Not many of their fellow passengers were to Russell's taste, but then he'd always had trouble liking the rich. Watching a group in the bar one day he found himself wondering how Rosa would have drawn them. George Grosz's cartoons came to mind.

The number of well-to-do tourists was down on prewar days, but there were enough Americans doing their 1950s version of the Grand Tour to irritate him. Most were going to London or Paris, a few to Switzerland; the few people travelling to the ex-enemy countries were either American administrators and businessmen charged with rescuing local capitalism from the Soviets or German relations of GI brides returning from a visit.

There were few celebrities: some B-list British and American actors, a couple of British writers Russell had never heard of who were returning from book tours, and a Russian ballerina who never took her fur coat off. She was, she told Russell, pining for home, and praying that Mother Russia would take her back now that the principal ogre was dead.

Effi was recognised by several crew members, but by only a few of their fellow passengers—*Please, Dad* was probably not their sort of show.

The one English couple he engaged in conversation—they were placed together at dinner—offered a grudging acceptance that the postwar Labour government hadn't done too much damage. And "now things are back to normal," the man had continued, entitlement oozing from every pore.

And they were, Russell supposed. In America too. After the shocks of depression and war, the old order was reestablishing itself. Business was back at the helm, the Republicans and Democrats looking more and more like two sides of the same coin.

And then there was race. There were only three black couples on the ship, and two of them turned out to be African. The

Americans, a professor and his wife from Atlanta, were seated a couple of feet away from Russell and Effi at dinner one evening, and their obvious surprise at being engaged in ordinary conversation by two white people was only slightly alleviated when they discovered that this pair were not American. He worked at an all-black college, she in all-black hospital, and the city, he said, was fully committed to an all-black police force for the all-black districts. "And they consider that progressive," he added with a sad shake of the head.

They were going to Lancashire, where his all-black unit had been stationed for almost a year before D-Day, and then on to Paris, where he'd first seen black civilians treated like normal human beings. "Maybe it was just the war," he said, "but it felt so different."

ONCE THE LEADERS HAD RETURNED from Berlin, the SED Central Committee spent a long weekend debating Moscow's instruction to halt their construction of socialism. Though "debate" was hardly the word. As Ulbricht and Co laid out the new line, their attempts to claim the credit for this "bold new initiative" seemed ludicrously at odds with their past statements and sullen demeanour. Their old guard friends thought they should have stood up to Moscow, and those who welcomed the grandly named New Course thought that more enthusiastic adherents were needed to oversee its introduction. Ulbricht and Grotewöhl's position was weak and getting weaker, and the two of them knew it. Which perhaps explained their insistence on retaining the unpopular work norm increases. With all this kowtowing to Moscow, they had to flex muscles at someone.

Would it save them? The rumour that Moscow was considering Zaisser and Herrnstadt as replacements for Ulbricht and Grotewöhl seemed omnipresent that week, despite butter-wouldn't-melt denials from the two men in question. Herrnstadt confided to Ströhm that he wouldn't accept such a poison chalice, but the gleam in his eye told a different story. And the DDR could do worse, Ströhm reckoned. Herrnstadt might have spent the war in Moscow but he still had a functioning brain.

At the end of the five-day meeting, Ulbricht formally announced the Party's adoption of the New Course, having somehow jettisoned the petulant voice and furious looks which had informed most of his earlier contributions. The reception in the chamber was mixed, some loudly applauding, others sadly shaking their heads. Most just looked apprehensive, which, Ströhm thought, was a pretty sane reaction.

He had more to be worried about later that afternoon. Dropping by his office to pick up some papers, Ströhm sensed that something was different. The chair by the fireplace had been moved, he finally realised. He could now see the telephone socket.

"Has anyone been in my office today?" he asked his secretary Hannelore.

"No," she said instinctively. "Oh, yes," she corrected herself. "The telephone engineer. They came to replace some old wiring."

Once she was gone, Ströhm started looking. It took him five minutes to find the bug. Or one of them. He left it where it was, and sat down on the sofa. Was this now standard procedure, or had he been selected for special treatment?

ENGLAND LOOKED GREEN FROM THE train, green and quietly prosperous, at least until they reached London, where the war's destructive legacy was still visible in the occasional buddleia-colonised bomb-site. Paul was waiting at the barrier, and Russell, catching sight of his son before he saw them, was struck by the earnest expression. Paul had always been a serious boy, and Russell felt a pang of regret for not giving his son a more carefree childhood.

Still, Paul's pleasure at seeing them both was clear enough, and the happy smile remained on his face as he carried most of their luggage through to the Waterloo taxi rank. A few minutes later, as the cab drove past a line of red double-deckers on Westminster Bridge, Russell remembered his son writing that he was feeling more British than German. "Except when I need something organised, and then I wonder how the British ever won the war."

With American money and Russian blood, Russell thought sourly as they drove up Victoria Street. And by bankrupting their empire.

Effi was asking Paul how Marisa was doing.

"She's fine. She was sick in the mornings, of course, but that seems over now, and the doctor can't find anything to worry about."

"When's the baby due?" Russell asked.

"The end of October."

Marisa was waiting for them at the Maida Vale flat. Paul's wife had arrived in England early in 1945, having spent several months travelling on foot through the still-contested Balkans to the newly liberated Greece. Her parents, visiting family in Transylvania when Hungary entered the war in 1941, had long since perished in a Romanian pogrom, but it was only after meeting fellow escapees in Athens that Marisa discovered their fate. The one distant relative she knew of in London was Russell's long-time literary agent Solly Bernstein, who arranged her passage to England and gave her a job. It was there that she met Paul, after Solly had taken him on as a favour to Russell.

She certainly looked healthier than the waif-like refugee he'd first met, Russell thought on seeing her now. And if, in the first few hours, she appeared over-anxious to make a good impression, by evening she seemed quite at ease. She and Paul were clearly not just besotted with each other—they were a happily functioning partnership. Rather like him and Effi, Russell thought, pleased to put something on the plus side of his legacy as a father.

Marisa's English was as good as Paul's now, and with even less of an accent. According to the latter, his half-German ancestry had caused no problems with their neighbours. "If anything, they feel sorry for me," Paul said with a laugh. "Until I lived here I never really understood how unbelievably proud the English are of being English. How did you escape that?" he asked his father.

"I'm glad you think I did. Having an American mother must have helped. That and the First War. Not our finest hour."

WHEN PAUL AND MARISA LEFT for work at eight on Wednesday morning, Russell and Effi went in with them on the 176 bus. Even with all the rush hour traffic, the journey took only forty minutes, which, as Paul pointed out, might be slower than the tube but was certainly more enjoyable. Effi was hoping to meet potential British agents that morning, and after arranging to meet her for lunch at the Lyons Corner House on Strand, Russell walked up Shaftesbury Avenue with Paul and Marisa to the Bernstein Agency offices. Looking up at the first- and second-floor windows, everything seemed familiar, but the steam laundry which had once occupied the ground floor was now a swanky-looking Italian restaurant.

"Is it any good?" he asked them.

"Very," was Paul's answer. "Expensive, though."

"Why don't we eat there tonight? Our treat."

This agreed, Russell walked back to Charing Cross Road, and ambled his way south past the many bookshops. After checking that the Corner House was where he thought it was, he walked down to the river. There seemed fewer boats than he remembered, and the new Festival Hall looked surprisingly lonely on its otherwise empty stretch of the southern bank.

Walking past Cleopatra's Needle he found himself under the windows of the Savoy Hotel, where he, Zarah, and Lothar had stayed in 1939. Convinced that her four-year-old son was slow on the uptake—not a condition one willingly advertised in eugenics-obsessed Nazi Germany—Zarah had persuaded Russell to accompany them on a trip to London, where Lothar could see a Harley Street doctor. It turned out that Lothar was basically fine but a little strange, a description which, in Russell's opinion, still fitted the boy quite well.

Effi's morning, he discovered on reaching the Corner House, had not gone very well—everyone she'd been to see had been either out or fully engaged. But she had secured two appointments on Friday.

The food did nothing to lift her spirits. "I guess everything tasted better in 1945."

Russell told her about the Italian restaurant.

"Ah, now you're talking."

They went their separate ways again, she to "further frustrations," he to visit Solly at his home in Hampstead.

"So this is where all my agents' fees went," Russell said, once he'd been taken through to the large back garden by Solly's resident carer.

"You should consider paying agents' fees a measure of your success," was his old agent's instant response. "The higher they are, the more you've earned."

Russell laughed and took the other deck chair. Solly looked much frailer than the last time he'd seen him, but there was still a wicked glint in his eyes. He had celebrated his seventy-second birthday that April, but Paul had seen a birth certificate, and the man was actually eighty-one.

"I'm glad I stuck with you," Solly observed. "If I hadn't, I wouldn't have the pleasure of watching your son run my business."

"Glad to know I've been of some use."

"John, you were never one of my highest earners, but you were a lot more fun than most of them were. And I'm serious about

Paul—he and Marisa run the agency a hell of a lot more efficiently than I ever did. Your boy's a natural. He's smart and he gets on with almost anyone—not as common a combination as you might think."

"True. And I assume he'll have to impress whoever takes over. Not that you won't live forever, of course."

"Another year will be a miracle. But don't worry on Paul's account—I'm leaving him the business. Him and Marisa. All signed and sealed."

"That's wonderful."

"But don't tell your boy. He might get cocky."

Russell laughed. If there was one thing he'd never associated with his son, it was cockiness.

"I'm saving the announcement for a birthday present," Solly added. "The baby's."

THAT EVENING AT THE RESTAURANT Russell was still basking in his secret knowledge of Paul's good fortune when his son announced less welcome news. "I don't want to spoil our dinner," he announced when they were all seated, "but I think you should know at once. A letter was on the mat when we arrived this morning." He said, passing his father the envelope. "It was addressed to me, but it's actually for you."

Russell took out the single sheet of paper. *Dear John and Effi,* he read. *I need to see you both before you fly to Berlin. I suggest the Freemasons Arms on Downshire Hill at 6pm tomorrow (Thursday). I shall be there, so please ring me on HAM3678 if you will not be, so that we can set a time on Friday which is acceptable you. I am sorry to make such demands, but this is very important. Yours, Natasha Shchepkina.*

Russell had last seen Natasha five years ago, soon after he and her father had clinched the deal with Beria which allowed her and mother to leave the Soviet Union. Since then, as far as Russell knew, the two women had been living in England, though where and in what capacity he had no idea. Up until now they had shown no interest in reestablishing contact with Yevgeny's partner in espionage.

He passed the letter to Effi and watched her read it.

"Do you know what it's about?" Paul asked his father.

Russell shook his head. "But I doubt it's anything good."

"How does she know we're here?" Effi asked, echoing the question already occupying her husband. "And how does she know we're flying to Berlin?"

"We can ask her when we see her," Russell said, a lot more lightly than he felt. "In the meantime, we might as well enjoy our meal. Yes?"

Quonset Hut

June 11 was a difficult day for Gerhard Ströhm. That morning the SED's "New Course" was brought to the attention of the East German public via the pages of the Party paper *Neues Deutschland*. The abandonment of the much-lauded collectivisation programme, a halt to the anti-religious campaigns, less pressure on private businesses, and a rise in the production of consumer goods—so many U-turns at once came as a real shock, to both the lower reaches of the Party and the people as a whole. Knowing that the main beneficiaries of these changes would be farmers and business owners was deeply upsetting to those who believed they were building a worker's state; the fact that the increased work norms remained in place merely added insult to injury.

Could anything good come out of this? Could it really be a new beginning? Ström wanted to think so, but the voice in his head kept saying that it was too little, too late.

At Party HQ almost everyone seemed confused. Were they pausing for breath, changing their minds, just giving up? What in God's name did those at the top think they were doing? Ulbricht's vision of the future might have been too ambitious, but at least it had been clear. They had known where they were supposed to be going.

Now everything seemed up in the air. Which of course was dangerous, because no one knew what might now be permissible. And because the Party looked weak.

It wasn't Ströhm's job to reassure the faithful or show a confident face to the masses, and for that he was grateful, fearing that his performance would be less than convincing. His job was to assess how well the New Course was being received, and Mironov would not be expecting his provisional judgement until at least a week had passed.

Visiting the canteen for lunch and idly roaming the building thereafter, Ströhm didn't like what he found. Rather than the sense of excitement a new beginning might evoke, there was irritation, anger, and an undercurrent of fear. Here, in its own HQ, it felt like the SED was under siege.

Back in his office, Ströhm spent much of the afternoon wondering what he should say to Annaliese. She and the children were leaving next morning for a long weekend in the Western sector, staying three days in Spandau with her late first husband's parents and then two at the Schade house in Dahlem, where Effi and John Russell were about to arrive.

He reached home just before her and the children. "How about a trip to the park?" he suggested.

"I really need to pack," was her tired response.

He got paper and pencil, wrote down *we really need to talk*, and showed it to her.

"But you're right," she said. "It's a lovely evening, and the packing can wait."

Once outside, she asked him what he needed to tell her.

"Wait till we're in the park," he cautioned.

She gave him a look but said no more. Crossing Leninallee opposite her place of work, they made their way past the hospital extension site and on to Friedrichshain Park and its brightly coloured new playground for infants.

"There's trouble coming," Ströhm began, once Isla and Markus were happily occupied. "Everyone's on edge, and even after admitting so many mistakes, the Party is still refusing to cancel the increase in norms. The construction workers are furious."

"The ones at the hospital site were working slow today," Annaliese told him.

"They won't be the last. If nothing is done—and I don't think it will be—things could turn very nasty very quickly."

"I can see that. But I don't see . . ."

He told her about the bug he'd found in his office.

"And you think our apartment is bugged as well."

"Quite possibly. But it may not be personal. They may have decided to bug the offices and homes of all Central Committee members—our new Stasi are certainly keen."

"But that's appalling."

"Yes, of course, but it's where we are." He sighed.

"So you wanted to warn me about speaking my mind at home?"

"Not only. The trouble ahead—there's no way of knowing how things will go. I could get promoted next week. I could be in prison."

"It's that bad?"

"Yes, I think so."

They sat there in silence, watching the children, for a long moment.

"Do you not want me to go away this weekend? I . . ."

"On the contrary. But you may have to stay away for longer than you planned. Until things have settled down again."

"And if they don't?"

"Then I'll come and join you."

"If you're not in prison."

"If I'm not in prison," he agreed.

Another silence, this one longer.

"We'll have to abandon everything," Annaliese said eventually.

"There's nothing we can't buy in the West," Ströhm said. He couldn't believe they were having this conversation.

"No," she said. "I didn't mean our things. You know me better than that. I meant our work, what we've achieved."

"You can do what you do—and just as wonderfully—anywhere in the world."

"Perhaps. But you can't. And this was your dream."

"Once upon a time."

She took an arm in hers, and snuggled up to his shoulder. "I'm sorry."

"Me too. Look, when you're in Spandau, and after that in Dahlem, we'll talk each day on the telephone. We'll have normal conversations about the kids, and if I ask you to bring me back some . . . oh, I don't know, some real coffee, that means I want you to stay in the West. At which point you'll tell me that you've had a very bad stomach and are staying a few days longer."

"And what will you be doing?"

"God only knows. Putting out fires, probably. Ones I'm not even sure I want extinguished."

TAKING A WALK ROUND THE local streets on Thursday morning, Russell and Effi came across Little Venice, an area he had heard of but never visited. It wasn't much like its bigger brothers in Italy and Los Angeles.

That afternoon they set out early, intending to take a long walk on Hampstead Heath before their meeting with Natasha. Russell found himself hoping against hope that what seemed important to her would not be important to Effi and himself, that she needed some sort of help from them that had nothing to with the power struggle which seemed to be convulsing the Kremlin. Wishful thinking, probably, like him and Effi imagining they could do a lot of walking two days in a row. In the event they spent most of their time on benches, lamenting their aching legs and feet. "I'm surprised that more Angelenos don't lose the use of their legs," Russell said at one point, provoking a rare laugh from Effi. Like him, she was not looking forward to whatever it was Natasha had to tell them.

Still, the Heath worked its magic, as it had during their six-month stay in 1945. "England's green and pleasant land," Russell had said back then, impressing Effi until he'd admitted he was quoting William Blake. "The satanic mills are all up north," he'd added, and had to explain that too.

Eventually they found an empty bench on the prow of Parliament Hill and sat there looking at the city and its smoky shroud.

"We're so lucky," Effi said out of the blue, and he couldn't disagree. Whatever their problems, whatever new crisis Natasha might be about to unleash, they had so much.

Far below them, a toy-like electric train was heading west on the North London Line.

"Remember that day we went to Kew Gardens?" Effi said. "All of us went—Zarah and Lothar, Paul and Rosa, you and me. And we were all talking German in the tearoom, and that woman went and got the police, thinking . . . well, I don't know what she was thinking. But the constable was very nice."

"He liked your smile."

"I think he was more taken with Zarah's breasts."

"Maybe both."

Effi laughed. "I hate to say it, but it's time we went to meet Natasha."

They started down the slope. Walking through the trees, and down the path between the ponds that led to East Heath Road, Russell asked himself for the umpteenth time why Natasha Shchepkin wanted to see them now. In his brief acquaintance with her and her mother, they hadn't struck him as the kind of people who would read about Effi's success and ask for money, but he rather hoped he was wrong, because, try as he did, he couldn't think of another reason that boded in any way well.

The pub Natasha had chosen for their meeting was only a few

hundred yards from the Heath, and the large outdoor patio was presumably one of her reasons for choosing it, in that any potential eavesdroppers would have trouble concealing their presence. After leading Effi to a suitably peripheral table, Russell carefully checked its underside for a mike. "Old habits," he murmured in response to Effi's look. "And down the rabbit hole we go."

Natasha was fifteen minutes late. Winding her way through the tables towards them, she looked attractive and well turned-out; up close, it was hard to see past the worried expression. "My mother is not well," she said in English, "but she sends her regards."

"Your English is good," Russell said, relieved. He had expected to be translating everything for Effi.

Natasha shrugged. "It has to be, living here."

After taking her and Effi's orders, Russell went in to get the drinks. Since their first meeting eight years before, Natasha had clearly grown a protective skin. He supposed she had needed to. She'd only been nineteen then, which meant she was now about twenty-six.

When he got back to their table, she was telling Effi about her translation work, and how she was applying for a job with the BBC's Russian service. "The way things are going in the world, they will need people like me."

What would Shchepkin have thought? Russell wondered. His daughter working for the enemy. Then again, by the time he died, enemies were all he had.

"And you. You are both well?" Natasha asked politely.

They said they were.

"Good." Natasha sighed. "You are not going to be happy about what I have to tell you." She looked at them both, as if seeking permission to continue.

"So tell us," Effi said.

"Very well. You know what the GRU is?"

"Soviet military intelligence," Russell replied, his heart preparing to sink.

"They came to see me and my mother. Here in London, in Somers Town where we live. They asked us—ordered us—to approach you. Both of you."

This was alarming on so many levels, Russell thought. "How did they know we were coming to London?" he asked.

Another shrug. "I do not know. But they did, and they gave us the address of the agency where your son works—they didn't know you gave it to us five years ago—and said we must tell him to tell you that we want a meeting. And that it's about the film."

Russell's heart duly sank.

"The one my father told us he had hidden, but not where. He never told us what it was, or what was on it, but he did say that he and the two of you were the only people who had watched it."

The only living people, Russell thought, remembering the young Soviet soldier who had discovered it in the Karlshorst office of the MGB security police. And now there was just him and Effi. "But how do they know we saw it?" he asked. "Did you tell them?"

"No. They already knew you were my father's partner in this, and they found the studio in Berlin where the copies were made. A young man who worked there identified Effi from a publicity photograph."

"And they say you can't have too much," Effi murmured.

Russell was wondering if he could trust Natasha and remembering often asking himself the same about her father. Did it matter if he didn't?

"What do they actually want?" Effi asked.

"They want signed affidavits—it is the same word in Russian—from both of you, in which you describe in detail the contents of this film. I get the impression they are especially keen to get one from Effi, but I don't know why this is. And they say the matter is urgent."

"Good for them," Russell said, thinking fast. The GRU and their Politburo allies—whoever they might be—wanted to use the film against Beria, and in the absence of the real thing, were gambling that legal-looking hearsay would prove sufficient. Which seemed like a splendid outcome, if it actually came to pass. But what if Beria survived? Wouldn't his and Effi's insurance be gone? "Why," he asked Natasha, "do they think we'll agree to this?"

"They didn't say. They say that they'll ruin our lives if you don't, but why would you care about that? Perhaps they think you feel indebted to my father, but I can't see why you would."

Russell could see one good reason for acceding to the GRU's request, and that was the possibility of some sort of justice for Beria's millions of victims. But he doubted that was on the GRU's list of priorities. He could see several reasons for refusing, starting with the possibility that it could all go wrong, and ending with the certainty that even if it all went right, and Beria received the bullet in the back of the neck he'd ordered for so many others, his and Effi's careers might both be unsalvageable.

"How do I contact them?" he asked Natasha, playing for time.

"You'll do it?"

"I don't know," he said honestly. "We'll have to talk about it," he added, glancing at Effi for confirmation.

"We do."

"I understand," Natasha said, abruptly getting to her feet. "You have my number, yes? Maybe next time you are here we can meet again, in more pleasant circumstances."

"I hope so," Effi told her.

She and Russell waited until Natasha was gone, then slowly made their way to Hampstead Heath Station.

"What do we say to Paul and Marisa?" Effi asked as they waited on the platform.

"Good question."

"You never told Paul about the film?"

"No, of course not. We agreed that Shchepkin would tell Irina and Natasha of the film's existence, and that it was a valuable piece of anti-Soviet propaganda. But no details and no mention of Beria. And nobody else should even know that much."

"We have to tell Paul and Marisa something. The same as Shchepkin told Irina and Natasha?"

"I suppose we must," Russell said. He didn't want Paul involved, but it wasn't fair to leave him and Marisa in ignorance. "And we'll have to name Beria," he added, "or the film's current relevance won't make any sense."

Back at the Maida Vale flat, a bottle of Chianti was waiting to be drunk, and by the time their glasses were empty Russell had told the story of how they had come by a film that could end Beria's career, and how they had used it to free themselves and Shchepkin's family from the Soviet embrace.

"And you watched this film," Paul said, as if he couldn't quite believe it.

"With Shchepkin."

"What's on it?" Paul wanted to know.

"You're better off not knowing," Russell insisted. "Have you been following Soviet politics at all?" Russell asked the two of them, expecting a negative answer.

"A little," Marisa said, surprising him. "Are you saying that the anti-Beria faction in the Kremlin want this film to discredit him?"

"I can't think of any other reason."

"It's probably a stupid question," Paul interjected, "but why should we care what happens to a killer like Beria?"

"We don't," Marisa said quietly. She seemed less shocked than Paul by the whole business. "But I think your father is worried that there's no way of knowing how things will turn out."

"I am," Russell agreed. "'Opening a can of worms' is the English phrase. Doing what Natasha's Soviet visitors want could result in our part of this—mine and Effi's—coming out. The GRU might want to know what's on the film for a private confrontation with Beria or some sort of secret trial, but once they have our written testimonies who's to say what use they might make of them?"

"And people on our side will wonder why it took you five years to come forward," Paul said thoughtfully.

"If we had, we would probably have both been killed."

"Of course, but many won't see it like that."

Russell sighed. "No, they won't," he conceded. "And some will want chapter and verse on how we got to see it in the first place. I was supposedly working for American intelligence at the time, and I didn't tell my bosses. Because I knew damn well they would have happily sacrificed us for a huge propaganda coup."

"Perhaps you could drive some sort of bargain," Paul suggested. "The Soviets get their affidavits but only on condition they keep them secret. I mean, surely no one in the Kremlin wants this out in the open—Beria has been one of their top dogs for almost twenty years."

"Maybe," Russell admitted. "But what sort of guarantee could we get that would actually bind them? Once Beria was gone, what would stop them putting a new price on nondisclosure? More comradely cooperation. I'd be back where I was in 1948. No, like I said—a can of worms. One best not opened."

"And Natasha?" Effi said.

"I feel sorry for her," Russell said, "but the threats against her are probably empty. If we say no the GRU, punishing her won't help them."

"There's always spite," Effi said.

"They might make her life more difficult, but I can't see them killing her, whereas . . . If Beria and his people find out what we're offering to do, they might well try to kill us."

"But I thought that would trigger the release of Shchepkin's copy."

"It will. But if Beria thinks we're about to testify to the contents, he'll be desperate. He might decide that seizing power at once is his only chance, that once he's in full control, he can brazen the whole thing out, say the film's been faked, that some enemy of the people has used a double to frame him. The story will be all over the Western press, but at home he can claim it's just propaganda."

"And if the GRU succeed in using the film to get rid of Beria, then where do you stand?" Paul asked.

"In a slightly better place. Once Stalin's succession is settled, I'm hoping that whoever wins will decide that letting us live is a price worth paying to keep the film buried. But there's so many unknowns. We don't know who'll end up in charge, whether one man or several, and what their priorities are. We don't know what havoc living with Stalin has wrought on the sanity of these men. They might be sharing each other's relief that he's gone; they might all be quietly plotting to fill his boots. It could go off in any direction."

"Which is why your best bet is just to stay out of it," Paul said.

"If we can," Russell agreed, remembering how many times in the last twenty years he'd harboured such hopes in vain.

FRIDAY WAS THEIR FINAL FULL day in London. Effi had prospective agents to see, and Russell decided on impulse to visit the town where he'd grown up. Boarding the train at Waterloo, he found himself scanning the coach for Slavic faces, and realised how much he'd scared himself the previous evening.

It was a hot day, and most of the windows on the Portsmouth train had been left part or wholly open by sweltering inbound commuters. These days the trip took around forty minutes, and thirty of those were spent getting free of London's sprawl. After alighting at Guildford, he first made his way to the cobbled High Street, then up the familiar hill to the home where he'd grown up.

It looked much the same as it had nearly forty years earlier, but now had a blue Ford Poplar parked where half their front garden had been. There were clearly people at home, but for reasons he couldn't explain, the thought of seeing the inside again was not an inviting one.

He walked on, and out onto Pewley Down, where the view of the Chantries ridge and distant hills was almost eerily unchanged. This was the countryside that he and his friends had used as their playground before the First War. Most of them had died before it ended, and the faces he could picture were all alarmingly innocent.

He walked back down to the centre of town and ate a sandwich for lunch in the castle grounds. There was nothing for him here, he thought, and probably nothing in England, apart from Paul and Marisa and his unborn grandchild. There were things to like about the place, he supposed. The soothing sound of Test cricket pouring out of windows, the absurdist humour he remembered from the trenches, a police force that didn't need guns. It wasn't just nostalgia. The new NHS—created by Labour and, so far at least, accepted by the Tories—spoke well of the British people, as did the current widespread support for abandoning the death penalty.

But the streets were still littered with the flotsam of last week's coronation, and who could take a country with a hereditary monarchy seriously?

Back at the station he watched a small steam engine chuffing towards him from the roundhouse-style shed beyond the road bridge, and just for that moment it felt as though he'd been whisked back into his childhood. But then a green electric train slid out of the tunnel under the Downs and pulled him back to the present. He'd been away too long, he thought. England was where he'd grown of age, but it wasn't his home anymore.

THAT FRIDAY ALL THE TALK at the increasingly ill-named House of Unity was of yesterday's protest at Brandenburg. Six transport workers had met outside the local prison to protest their current work and conditions, and five thousand comrades had turned up to express their support. Five thousand! The DDR's well of discontent seemed to be deepening by the day.

At least Annaliese and the children were safe in the western sector. She'd called from Spandau when she arrived, and related, with apparent enthusiasm, how thoroughly their papers and personal belongings had been checked at the border. "It's good to know that all those people so keen to enjoy a capitalist life won't have a penny to spend once they get here," she told her husband and whoever was listening in.

Ströhm was about to go down to the canteen for lunch when his secretary announced a visitor. Egon Hupka was a candidate member of the Central Committee. Ströhm barely knew the man but had heard good things about him from people he respected: that Hupka was hard-working, efficient, and less inclined to dogmatism and self-promotion than some of his colleagues.

Today, though, the man seemed remarkably unsure of himself. "I was hoping for a chat," he began awkwardly. "About the situation in the south. With the Soviets," he added, in a nod to Ströhm's position.

"Of course," Ströhm said. There was, as far as he knew, no such situation, so getting Hupka out of his office seemed like a good idea. "Have you had lunch? How about a bratwurst from Siggi's?"

"What a good idea!"

Luxemburg Platz was only a two-minute walk away, and at noon the queue at Siggi's van was still a short one. Having bought and dressed their bratwurst rolls, the two men retired to an empty bench in the small nearby park. After enjoying a first mouthful, Ströhm took a look round, and wondered if he or Hupka would one day come to regret lunching with the other. Since finding the

bug in his office, he had begun to imagine such devices everywhere.

Out in the open, Hupka seemed more sure of himself. "I have
a brother," he said, "a foreman on one of the Stalinallee construction sites. A Party member, but not a very active one. He always
says having one of those in the family is quite enough."

"Yes?"

"He's worried. Really worried. He says he's never seen the men
so angry or determined. He says they won't accept the increased
norms."

"What will they do?"

"The big question. My brother doesn't know. Some want to
push for talks, some to work slow, some—most, he thinks—
believe that downing tools is the only way they'll get a proper
hearing."

"Strikes."

"Yes, of course. But the important thing, the thing that's different, is the level of coordination. People are going from site to site,
making plans, agreeing times and dates. Party members, most of
them," Hupka added. Something that obviously didn't surprise
him.

"So why have you come to me with this?" Ströhm asked, in as
neutral a tone as he could manage.

Hupka took a deep breath. "Forgive me if I'm wrong, but I
have gathered the impression over the last few years that you—
how I shall I put this?—that you think our way of doing things in
the DDR has become too top-down, that in a worker's state the
workers should be more than passive recipients."

"I do believe that. We all do, or say we do. At least in theory."

Hupka shook his head. "You're right, the people at the top still
say they do. But the workers no longer believe it, and someone
has to tell these people that they're leading us to disaster."

"Me?"

"You must talk to them all the time. I couldn't even get a meeting."

Ströhm forbore from telling him that the Soviets had already told Ulbricht as much, with less than total success. "There have been discussions at the highest level," he said. "Lots of them. People have said what you have just said, but the votes have always gone against them. The people at the top have heard your warnings and have chosen to ignore them. At their own peril, perhaps."

Maybe it was the tone Ströhm had used to utter that last phrase, but Hupka suddenly seemed more animated. "Are you saying that our only hope lies in their fucking up so badly that someone removes them?"

I probably am, Ströhm thought. "The Politburo and the Central Committee are both divided. Around sixty-forty in Ulbricht's favour, I should guess. A disaster would probably reverse those figures."

"Would the Soviets accept a change?"

"Hard to say. They have their own interests, but I don't see how a crippled DDR could be one them."

"So we wait for the dice to roll themselves?"

A nice image, Ströhm thought. "I can't see any alternative, can you?"

WALKING WITH PAUL TO THE local grocer's on Saturday morning, Russell asked his son whether he ever thought about going back to Germany.

"Never," Paul said flatly. "Even if I wanted to—which I don't— Marisa would never agree. And Berlin was my home, not Germany. I think London's a bit the same. It's not really England."

"I know what you mean."

"Are you going to stay in LA?" Paul asked him.

"If Effi and Rosa want to. I can't say I'm mad about the place, but there's nowhere else I really want to be."

"Not even Berlin?"

"I'll tell you in three weeks. I do miss Thomas and Hanna."

"So do I. Could you come back here?"

Russell didn't want to upset his son. "Maybe," he said non-committally. His family seemed destined to live worlds apart, so he supposed he should be grateful they could afford to visit each other. "I think I'd like to end up by the sea," he volunteered. "No place in particular. Rügen Island or Malibu Beach, the Sussex Coast. When I'm really old, that is. Assuming I get there." He hadn't told Paul about Greer Holleman, and he didn't intend to. The GRU was enough for his son to worry about.

And he was worrying. "Are you sure it's a good idea, going back to Berlin?" Paul asked.

"Not completely. But I wouldn't miss Effi's triumph, let alone ask her to. We'll be careful. All the festival venues are in the western sector so we won't be setting foot in the east."

His son looked unconvinced, so Russell tried not to.

THAT AFTERNOON THEIR LANDING AT Tempelhof was surprisingly smooth. A good omen for their visit, Russell thought hopefully.

He was soon disillusioned. At passport control Effi was hurried through to a bouquet-bearing festival official while he was ordered to wait. Several requests for an explanation were ignored by the British official, and Russell was beginning to lose his temper when Effi appeared at his side. "What's going on?" she asked.

"God only knows. Look, there's no point you hanging around. I'll meet you at Thomas's."

"No, I'll wait," she said firmly. "And kick up a hell of a fuss with the festival people if they keep you too long," she added in a loud voice.

He was smiling when a hand took his arm. "This way, Mr. Russell," another Brit said, ushering him gently towards a door.

Outside the sun was shining, and the terminal building roof which he and Paul had frequented in the thirties was crowded with a new generation of plane-spotters. Berlin, he thought, was a map of memories, good and bad. And he was looking forward to visiting some of the better ones.

They were heading towards one of the larger Quonset huts, which he soon discovered had been neatly partitioned into more than a dozen well-lit offices. According to the sign on the door, the one he was ushered into belonged to a Major Stapleton, but the man behind the desk wasn't wearing a uniform, unless the buzz-cut counted as such. An Allied colleague from the US Berlin Operations Base, if Russell wasn't mistaken. He had worked for BOB himself in 1947 and '48, and knew the type only too well. "And here I was, thinking this was the British sector," he said pointedly.

"Travis Henley," the American introduced himself curtly without getting up. "Take a seat, Mr. Russell."

"If I must."

Henley looked up. "As a former BOB employee, you know how important the work we do is. I assume you're aware of how difficult our current situation is?"

"More or less," Russell replied. It sometimes paid to be polite.

"We currently have over five thousand people—men, women, and children—crossing the city's intersector border each and every day. A number that seems certain to rise as the situation in the east deteriorates further. And the political allegiances of all these people must be checked before we can send them on to West Germany proper. I wouldn't want you repeating this, but we don't have the manpower to do exhaustive checks, so experience has to make up for the lack of thoroughness." He gave Russell an ingratiating look. "And you have that experience."

"Are you offering me a job?" Russell asked. He couldn't believe it.

"Not exactly. We're requesting your assistance for a short time. Monday to Friday, for a fortnight. It doesn't seem a lot to ask."

"Out of the question."

Henley sighed and twirled his pencil. "I know your wife is waiting, so I won't waste time trying to persuade you."

"Good."

"I shall just outline the consequences of refusal." He looked Russell in the eye. "I can't say I'm happy with this," he said almost smugly, "but I have my orders. You should know that we will revoke your current visa and block any attempt you make to get another. I think persona non grata is the diplomatic phrase."

Russell knew that throwing the man's desk at him would achieve precisely nothing and only let the impulse linger because it felt so good. Simply put, saying no was not a feasible option. They had the power, and they wouldn't hesitate to use it. Hell had no fury like a spymaster scorned.

He could cope without America, but he also had to think of his wife and daughter. He didn't think Effi would be heartbroken on her own account, but he suspected she might be on Rosa's.

"Is there a carrot?" he asked.

"What?"

"Your people usually offer a carrot to go with the stick. It must be in the manual."

Henley looked pissed off for the first time. "A chance to prove your loyalty to your new home. To wipe the slate clean, as it were. Is that carrot enough for you?"

"It might be if I believed a word of it. By the way, I won't go into the Soviet sector."

"And why would that be?"

"Hazard a guess."

Henley smiled. "Actually, none of our people do these days. We use Germans for all the cross-border work."

"Hmm. Do I at least get paid?"

"Of course," Henley said rummaging through a drawer, apparently in vain. "There's a paper I need you to sign," he said, getting up. "Just wait here," he added, and left the cubicle.

Russell waited. This turn of was events was definitely annoying—another "revoltin' development" as Riley would say—but maybe no more than that. If the job was all that Henley said it was, it might not be so bad. Interesting even, in a nostalgic sort of way.

But was it on the level? This sudden recruitment felt odd. He supposed some bright spark at BOB might have recognised his name on the incoming passenger list and wondered how to make use of his presence in Berlin. But still. Threatening to kick him out of the US seemed a pretty extreme method of securing his services. Surely they couldn't be that short-staffed. And if they didn't trust him to live in America, why would they trust him to identify German communists?

Henley returned, flourishing a form.

Russell checked that he wasn't signing his whole life away, and grudgingly put pen to paper.

"You don't look that happy at getting the chance to help us protect our freedoms," Henley observed.

"What would make me happy is a life without borders, and people just getting on with each other. But you'd probably call that socialism."

"Yeah, right. It sure doesn't sound like the world we live in."

"True," Russell conceded. What harm could a fortnight in Dahlem with BOB do him? There couldn't be many places on earth where Beria would find it harder to reach him. At least he hoped so.

"You report in on Monday morning," Henley told him.

"Föhrenweg at eight A.M. I assume you remember how to get there."

"It's engraved on my heart," Russell assured him.

Back in the terminal building, an anxious-looking Effi was waiting with her festival greeter.

"Just some old friends wanting a chat," he told her. "Sorry to keep you waiting," he said to the festival official.

"No problem," the man said in English. "The car is waiting outside."

It was a one of the new Mercedes. As he opened the door to get in, Russell's eye was caught by the familiar red light atop the distant Funkturm. Welcome or warning, he wondered. It was most likely both.

BOB's Your Uncle

Russell sat at the kitchen table with the last of his coffee, waiting for Thomas to finish whatever he was doing upstairs. Through the window he could see Hanna and Effi laughing and talking as they fed the chicken who'd provided their breakfast eggs.

It was so good to see Thomas and Hanna. The previous evening the four of them had sat around the dinner table for several hours, bringing each other up to date with their far apart lives, and happily reliving joys they'd shared over the last twenty years. Russell wasn't sure how consciously they'd all sought to avoid politics and all its depressing ramifications, but for just the one evening it had certainly felt like a blessed release. His own secondment to BOB had been mentioned, and blithely passed over as no more than "a pain the arse."

The black Labrador lying next to the stove began thumping his tail as Thomas came down the stairs. He'd been named Groucho by the GI who found him injured in the ruins and taken on by Thomas when the soldier was hurriedly called home by a death in his family. Two years without word had passed since then, and Groucho was now part of the family. Hanna had even named the hens Chico and Harpo to make him feel more at home. All they needed now, Russell thought, was a budgie named Zeppo.

It was a five-minute walk to Finkenpark. "So how does it feel being back?" Thomas asked as Groucho paused to sniff his first tree. "And about working for the Americans again?"

"Too soon to tell," Russell replied.

"Are you worried the Russians will come calling as well?"

"No. Not yet anyway. The Americans . . . this doesn't feel like the way people behave. Even intelligence people. I mean, imagine the conversation—we want this guy's help for a couple of weeks, so let's use the threat of deportation to get him on board. Talk about motivational."

"You've always told me that intelligence services attract people who lack any sort of empathy."

"True, but . . ." Russell decided to change the subject. "How's Lotte doing?" he asked. Thomas's daughter had hardly been mentioned the previous evening.

"Well, I think."

The tone said more than the words. "Have you had a falling out?" Russell asked, hoping the answer was no. The Schades had lost their son, Joachim, in the war, and Russell knew how much Lotte meant to Thomas.

"No, nothing as . . . as straightforward as that. She hasn't been to see us for over a month, which is unusual. But she calls us every week—the telephone system still works, most of the time, anyway—and she doesn't actually *say* anything that would make us worry. Perhaps that's it—because worrying us has sometimes felt like her project for life. I think she sounds more guarded than usual; Hanna says she hears a hysterical edge. We just don't know."

"You told me she had a new boyfriend. Werner, yes? Have you met him?"

Thomas frowned. "No, but I did ask Gerhard to find out what he can about the boy. According to one of Werner's work colleagues, he keeps himself and his politics pretty much to himself. Which could be good news, could be suspicious. If he's as idealistic and committed as Lotte claims, you'd think he'd be more outspoken. Unless of course . . ."

"He knows what he wants to say would get him arrested," Russell completed the sentence. "How does Lotte think things are going in the DDR?"

They were in the park now, and Thomas steered them towards an empty bench. "I'll let him off the lead for a while," he added, freeing Groucho. "We haven't talked about that lately," he said, resuming their conversation. "Which is also unusual. The last time we did, she was making the usual case—you know, a work in progress, Western provocations and propaganda, prioritising freedoms from over freedoms to. There are enough grains of truth there to keep the believers happy, but I can't help thinking that the numbers now opting to leave must be sowing some serious doubts."

"In Lotte?"

"Who knows? These days she doesn't want to talk about it. At first I thought she was just tired of the arguments, but now . . . I don't know."

"How about Gerhard?" Russell asked.

"Still in the same job last time we saw him, but God only knows what he's thinking. He was hoping to get across one evening while Annaliese and the kids are with us, but we haven't heard anything more. She should be here before lunch, and maybe she'll have news."

Groucho was almost fifty yards away, but a call from Thomas brought him gambolling back.

"Whatever happened to Hitler's Blondi?" Russell wondered out loud.

"Which one?"

Russell laughed. "The dog."

"The bastard used her to test the suicide pulls Himmler sent over."

"Ah."

"And another interesting fact you probably don't know—one of Eva Braun's two terriers was named Stasi, like the DDR's new intelligence service."

"What was the other one called?"

"Negus."

"It doesn't have the same ring, does it?

"Not really."

The two of them sat in silence for a moment, watching Groucho and enjoying their friendship.

"We met up with Natasha Shchepkin in London," Russell said eventually. "At her request," he added.

"What did she want?" Thomas asked. "Was it something to do with the film?"

Russell remembered telling Thomas about the film when he and Hanna had come out to LA the year before. He had taken Thomas to a game at Gilmore Field and told him the story over a beer during the seventh-inning stretch. Everything, of course, but the details of what had been filmed, which he and Shchepkin had agreed would be safer kept secret.

Now, as they both watched Groucho chase a whirling leaf, Russell recounted how Natasha had been approached by the GRU, and what she as a consequence now wanted from him and Effi.

"Why didn't they approach you directly?"

Russell shrugged. "I guess they knew we'd just say no."

"Haven't you anyway?"

"We said we'd think about it. And we have. We discussed the whole business with Paul and Marisa, who thought we'd be mad to say yes while Beria is still breathing. I'm just hoping his Soviet enemies manage to finish him off without any help from us, and then we can all forget about the damn film."

"I imagine your American employers would be happier to see it reach the light of day," Thomas observed.

"Wouldn't they just? But they'd also want to know why we kept such a juicy bit of propaganda to ourselves all these years."

"I suppose they would."

WHEN EFFI WELCOMED ANNALIESE AND the two children at the Schades' front door the men were still out. Markus had her blond hair and blue eyes, Isla the darker looks of her father. Both were clutching colouring books that their adoptive grandparents had bought for them, and an obviously tired Annaliese was happy to let them set themselves up on the dining room table.

"Oh, it's so good to see you," she told Hanna and Effi. "I do love Berta and Kurt, but their idea of child-care is winding the children up like a clockwork toy, and then just standing back and watching. It's exhausting."

While Effi made a pot of coffee for the adults, Annaliese asked Hanna if they could stay for a few extra days. "I know it's a cheek, but I'm hoping Gerhard will be able to take a couple of days off, and . . ."

"Of course," Hanna said. "You know how big this house is. We had thirteen people living here straight after the war, and honestly, it rarely felt crowded."

"That's great," Effi said. "A couple of days did seem grossly inadequate."

"Why don't we sit in the garden for a bit," Hanna suggested. "I've got fifteen minutes before I start cooking."

Out in the sunlight, Annaliese looked even more tired to Effi. "You look like you need a few days' holiday," she said. "You're not pregnant again, are you?" she asked in her usual forthright manner.

Annaliese laughed. "God, no. At least I hope not. No, it's just life that's grinding me down," she said wryly. "Work is hard. Good, but hard. And Gerhard's having a hell of a time. We're both so busy we hardly see each other Monday to Friday. Or the kids, for that matter."

The dog came tearing round the corner of the house, followed, at a more sedate pace, by his walkers.

After exchanging hugs, Russell asked Annaliese if Gerhard was coming.

"Not today," she told him.

"She was just saying how busy she and Gerhard are," Effi interjected.

"It's not been a good few months," Annaliese said. "It sounds ridiculous, but everything seems to be falling apart. It's all so fraught, and Gerhard doesn't seem to know whether this New Course they've just announced will make things better or worse. And if he doesn't know . . ."

"Then no one will," Russell completed her thought.

THAT SUNDAY LUNCH WAS A splendid affair. Hanna's vegetable garden was having a very productive year, and visits to several markets had provided a wealth of other ingredients for the traditional feast. It all reminded Russell of prewar times, when the children had been Joachim, Lotte, and Paul, and the adults had all looked a great deal younger. Thomas's hair was now a uniform iron grey, and Hanna's was headed in the same direction. As for himself, he was learning to stay away from mirrors.

The women did most of the talking, with both Hanna and Annaliese keen to hear stories of an actor's Hollywood life, and Effi eager to catch up on all the people they'd left behind in Berlin.

It was early in the evening, and Effi was reading bedtime stories to the children, when Annaliese found Russell alone in the garden. "I've been wondering why Gerhard didn't come with me on Friday," she said without preamble, "and the answer that came to mind was him fearing that a whole family might be stopped at the border. Whereas a married woman and two young children—they would be coming back."

"He didn't say anything?"

"He said I should stay in the west until he tells me different."

"He's thinking of defecting?" Russell was both shocked and not.

"Gerhard wouldn't like that word."

"No." Defecting implied betrayal, and Ströhm would think it was German socialism that had been betrayed.

"But the answer to your question is yes. He is thinking about it."

"And how do you feel?"

"Conflicted. As he is. And ready to make the best of things, whichever way they go. There are hospitals everywhere, but only one Germany supposedly building socialism. It has to be his decision."

"Any idea what it'll be?"

She shook her head. "There's a real crisis coming, and if things go badly, I think he might decide to finally call it a day. But if there's still a chance of a good outcome, well, you know him, he hates to give up."

THE AMERICAN BERLIN OPERATIONS BASE worked out of a high-gabled two-storey building on Föhrenweg, which sat in its own small wooded park and had several subterranean levels. BOB had started life as an offshoot of the war-born OSS, but these days formed part of the new CIA's global empire. As far as Russell was concerned its HQ was much too close for comfort, a mere five-minute walk separating the sanity of family and friends from the familiar cesspit of dead-eyed young men with buzzcuts and meaningless smiles.

After a quick frisk-down at the entrance, one of two Rita Hayworth lookalikes at reception checked his papers, dug out a preprepared nametag and sent him on down to the middle basement, where only the faces seemed to have changed in the last five years. Passing one open doorway, Russell recognised the room where the Soviet defector Konstantin Merzhanov had first mentioned the Beria film.

Back then, the cavernous waiting room had been full of Slavic faces—walking through it now, they all looked German. In the section head's office beyond, the man in charge was surprised to see him, but eventually found the requisite notification in his bulging in-tray. "A volunteer, eh," he said straight-faced.

Russell smiled at that but didn't argue.

"Well, let's get you working."

And work he did, for the next five hours, as part of a two-man interview team sifting its way through the roomful of Soviet sector refugees. His partner Chad Brickell was in his thirties, a policeman's son from Salinas who'd fought in the Pacific, and used the GI Bill to attend university before eventually joining the fledgling CIA. He was pleasant enough as a work companion, and seemed to have good instincts when it came to deciding which refugees merited further investigation.

It was, by necessity, a speedy process. The interviews only lasted around twenty minutes, which didn't seem like much time for the man or woman concerned to shake off any suspicions and earn a green light to the West. They were asked about their backgrounds, work, and any postwar allegiances, but not, to Russell's surprise, about their lives before 1945—these days being an ex-Nazi was clearly a lot more acceptable than being a card-carrying communist.

Assessing the applicants brought before them, Russell saw no obvious signs of either. These men and women had just had enough of life in the DDR. They didn't expect a new one in the West to be a bed of roses, but all assumed it would be better than the one they were leaving behind.

Russell and his partner processed thirteen applicants that morning, and saying yes to each and every one of them left him feeling more satisfied than he'd expected. He'd made some people happy, earned a few marks, and no one had offered him a secret recording of Ulbricht torturing kittens. Berlin was still full of surprises.

THAT SAME MONDAY MORNING EFFI stepped aboard a northbound tram on the renamed Clay Allee. The Berlin she saw through the window as it rumbled towards the British sector looked in much better shape than the one they had left three years before. The craters and broken walls were still in evidence, but now vastly outnumbered by new buildings and busy construction sites.

The Berlinale HQ was in a freshly refurbished block on the Ku'damm which, if memory served her well, had once housed a secretarial college. With the festival not opening until Thursday, the only person on duty was a woman in her twenties. After initially failing to recognise Effi, she apologised profusely and went off to find someone more senior.

While she was gone, Effi studied the festival programme. There were two German films in the competition, both directed by men she knew, albeit not well. Of the other twelve entries, six were from Europe, two each from Japan and Brazil, and one from Africa's Gold Coast. The one American film was directed by the famous Elia Kazan, who had so divided Hollywood opinion when he'd agreed to cooperate with HUAC.

As far as Effi knew Kazan wasn't coming to Berlin, but one American who definitely would be was Gary Cooper, who had a new film being premiered outside the competition at the outdoor Waldbühne. His recent success *High Noon* had been seen by many as a condemnation of HUAC and the moral decadence it represented. She might have come six thousand miles, Effi thought, but she still couldn't get away from the wretched committee.

The secretary returned with one of the festival organisers, who asked Effi to join him for coffee in the "hospitality suite." Helmut, as he insisted she call him, proved both nice and knowledgeable, and after listening to the obligatory kind words about her own career, she asked him about the health of the current German film industry.

It was doing quite well, he thought, though the subject matter still seemed quite limited. "Hospital dramas and village romances," he said wryly. "Nothing to upset the powers-that-be." But this was the third Berlinale in three years, and the first two had offered ample proof that many Germans had an appetite for challenging cinema. And sooner or later the mainstream would reflect that. Because upsetting people in a creative way was what cinema should be about. "Another five years of remorse," he said. "Maybe ten. And then we can get back to where we were in the 1920s."

Ten years, Effi thought. A bit too many for her.

Walking down the Ku'damm afterwards, she was recognised and stopped by several passersby in want of an autograph. There was more in the shops than she'd expected, and the people on the sidewalk looked better dressed and healthier than they had three years before. Berlin really did seem to be rising again, as the post-war song had promised it would.

She could come back, but she probably wouldn't, if only for Rosa's sake. In 1945 Ali and Fritz had wanted to stay, despite all that had happened to their fellow Jews, and when they'd eventually left Effi had asked Ali why. Was it the job Fritz had been offered, or had he sought the job because they finally wanted out?

"A bit of both," Ali had replied. "The job looked more exciting than a future in Berlin." She had paused to marshal her thought. "I know how many Germans disapproved of the persecution, let alone the death camps. I know there were many who actually died trying to help us. But there were also the ones who sat on their hands, and the ones who loaded the trains and herded us into the chambers. And the problem was, I went to the shops or a film or a party, and I didn't know which of these people I was talking to. Do you know what I mean?"

"I think so," Effi had said at the time. Rosa would feel the same, she thought now, watching the innocent-looking faces pass her by.

STRÖHM HAD COME TO WORK early—with Annaliese and the kids away the flat seemed almost eerily empty—and lunch was his second canteen meal of the day. The meat had been tough but tasty enough, and the cake had been moister than usual, so the privileged few had little reason to complain. Their culinary fare might be less than exceptional, but it was presumably better than anyone else's outside of Karlshorst.

He was lingering over his coffee because he'd spotted Lotte Schade on the other side of the canteen. Ströhm knew Thomas was worried about his daughter, and was hoping for a private chat on his friend's behalf, but ever since he'd caught sight of her she'd been deep in conversation with a young man.

They were, he realised, arguing about something, and a few seconds later the man abruptly got up and walked out.

"Werner," she called after him, more exasperated than angry, but he didn't look back.

She looked more frustrated than angry, and Ströhm took his chance, swiftly wending his way to her table before she decided to leave. "Lotte," he said, "do you mind if I join you?"

"No, of course not," she said. The words were polite enough, the tone not exactly welcoming.

"My wife and children are staying at your parents' house this week. I expect you know that John and Effi are visiting."

"Oh. Yes. I knew they were coming but I'd forgotten when. Effi has a thing at the film festival."

"She does. But how are you? I don't imagine this is the easiest time to be working at *Neues Deutschland*."

She gave him a look, as if she was wondering how loaded the question might be. "Oh, I'm only a copy editor," she said. "And everyone seems to be behind the New Course," she added almost breezily. The last time they'd met—several months ago in Dahlem—she'd been defending the old one, and close to accusing him of being a Yugoslav-style heretic. "But I'm sure you know better than me how things are going," she said with a hint of provocation.

"Maybe," Ströhm said. "But then again, maybe not. I used to think I had a pretty good idea of what is actually possible, but these days I'm not so sure."

Lotte looked surprised. "Can I ask you a question?" she asked, almost in a whisper. Looking, Ströhm thought, more like her truculent younger self.

"Of course."

"The meetings on Stalinallee and the other construction sites—are they the beginning of something?"

"Something good? I hope so, but I really don't know. What do you think?"

She didn't answer him directly. "I remember an argument I had with Uncle John and my dad several years ago, about whether it was possible to build islands of German socialism in a Soviet sea."

Ströhm smiled. "A fanciful thought, one I've had myself. What was the verdict?"

"I think we all agreed it was impossible but drew different conclusions from that as to what we should do."

"I can imagine."

"What's your opinion, comrade?" she asked him, challenge in her eyes.

"I always thought of socialism as a way of life that would increase individual freedom," he said carefully. "As Marx believed it would. But it seems to be having the opposite effect, at least in the short run."

"So even members of the Central Committee have their doubts," Lotte said, shaking her head.

"I think the only time I had none was when we were fighting the Nazis," Ströhm said. "But what about you? What conclusion did you draw when you realised that a separate German road to socialism was off the table?"

"Then? That we'd just have to bide our time."

"And now?"

"That perhaps we can't afford to wait." Lotte got to her feet. "It's been nice talking to you, comrade," she said.

Ströhm considered going after her, and insisting she be careful, but knew there wasn't any point. He just watched her walk out, the dark brown ponytail swinging from side to side. He'd wanted to lessen Thomas's fears, but this conversation had been the opposite of reassuring.

IT WAS THE LAST REFUGEE of the day that interested Russell. Gregor Kubina was Paul's age and had brought along genuine-looking documents to prove he'd been a minor functionary at the DDR's housing ministry. He answered all of their questions without hesitation, prompting Russell to ask himself whether Gregor had already known what they'd be. This was not in itself suspicious—a friend or relative might have gone through this process at any time over the last six months—but it was worth noting.

Gregor flatly denied having any political affiliations, but his "they're all the same, aren't they?" sounded too rehearsed. He said that his parents also wanted to leave but couldn't bear the thought of leaving all their possessions behind.

"What did you do in the war?" Russell asked, departing from their usual script with a brief glance at his partner.

Brickell gave him the slightest of nods.

"I was called up in April '44 and sent to France. I was captured in July, spent over a year in a POW camp, and got back to Berlin in October. I was lucky," he added.

"Where in Berlin?" Russell asked.

"Wedding," Gregor said after the slightest of hesitations.

"Ah. I used to live in Wedding. Back in the thirties. Did you know it then?"

Gregor gave him a look. "Not really," he said.

A DDR plant or a disillusioned comrade? Russell wondered. Did he care? He probably did. "How do you feel about capitalism?" he asked.

"What do you mean?"

"The free-enterprise system. What we have in the West."

"It seems to work," Gregor said, without a great deal of enthusiasm.

"Better than socialism?"

"Better than Ulbricht's version. That's why I'm here."

Russell had his answer. And as far as he was concerned the Federal Republic could only benefit from an influx of socialists who had grown to hate the DDR. The people upstairs might be horrified, but they themselves were employing former Nazis, and someone had to even the playing field. "Approved?" he asked Brickell and received an indifferent nod in return.

Once the surprised-looking Gregor had shaken hands and left the room, Russell and Brickell just sat there for a minute, savouring the end of their workday. "How about a beer?" the American asked eventually. "The kitchen upstairs has a full refrigerator," he added, "and they've put some tables out back. Nothing fancy," he added. "It's like a decompression chamber after a day full of hard luck stories. You ever do any diving?"

Russell had to admit that he hadn't.

After grabbing their cold beers, the two men went out to the impromptu patio, where a couple of Brickell's friends involved in monitoring the Eastern sector were full of the latest news. "The construction workers are downing tools all over the place," one said smugly. His friend had heard from another section that the Soviets were recalling troops to Berlin from their summer training camps.

Russell found himself thinking that this tiny beer garden would be a great place to hide some listening devices, and even ran a hand under their table to check.

Back at the house on Vogelsangstrasse an hour later, he found Thomas listening to the American station RIAS on the wireless.

"So what's happening?" Russell asked.

"Hard to tell," was Thomas's measured answer. "Since Ulbricht and Co can't make up their minds whether or not to persist with the work norm hike, the workers can't make up theirs about whether or not to strike. Which sounds like it should be quite easy to resolve, but you can never underestimate human stupidity in situations like this. It certainly sounds like a mess, and I'm sure the Americans are rubbing their hands. The way RIAS is reporting it, you'd think there was a revolution underway."

The cynic in Russell wondered whether the Western powers were doing more than just rubbing their hands, but after what he'd heard at BOB, he was inclined to believe that, on this occasion at least, the SED and the Soviets could rely on each other to royally fuck things up without any foreign assistance.

IN THE FLAT ON TILSITER Strasse Ströhm was also listening to RIAS. Ordinary citizens of the DDR were merely advised against listening to the American station, because proscription would be hard to enforce and much too reminiscent of the Nazi era. The Party elite, however, were actively encouraged to listen, as part of their continuing duty to know the enemy.

On this particular evening it wasn't that enemy Ströhm was concerned with. His unsettling talk with Lotte Schade, the fact that his phone was probably tapped, the growing worker unrest which so excited RIAS—these had nothing to do with the West, everything to do with the DDR, what it was and where it was going. Until a few weeks ago he had thought that a better future might be worked out around tables in Moscow and Karlshorst, but now he feared it would die on the streets.

He put his jacket back on and left the flat. It was a warm summer evening, a bit close beneath the blanket of cloud, but pleasant enough for a stroll. He walked down past the cemetery, turning left onto Auer Strasse as he headed for Stalinallee. There he turned left again, following the widened thoroughfare towards the old centre of the now-divided city.

When he reached the Block 40 construction site around ten minutes later, workers were heading off in all directions, and he realised that a mass meeting must have just broken up. He also noticed that many of the men seemed to have a spring in their step, as if they'd just received good news.

The married men would mostly be heading home, but many of the single ones would be seeking a drink, and the popular beer garden on Schillingstrasse seemed like a good bet. Walking up the street in question he experienced a moment of doubt—what sort of reception could a member of the Central Committee expect from workers so angry about their leaders? They had no way of knowing that he was angry as they were.

Then again, if he was afraid to face workers in what was supposed to be a worker's state, then what in God's name was the point?

He kept walking until he reached the beer garden, which was as expected doing good business. After working his way to the bar, he bought himself a stein of beer and went back outside in search of a face he knew. There were none, though some seemed to recognise his, if the cold looks were any guide.

He found a table with only one seat and sat himself down. A few feet away a party of seven were listening to one of their number reading from yesterday's *Neues Deutschland*. "Listen to this," the man said: "'The Norms department is sadly mistaken if it imagines that it can act with impunity against the interests of the building workers for long.' And that's the lead article!"

"Yes, yes," an older worker said. "But there's two other articles in the same paper saying the exact opposite."

"But they're criticising their own people at the sites," a third man declared. "That must mean we're pushing at an open door."

God I hope so, Ströhm thought, just as someone pulled up a chair and sat down beside him. It was Berndt Escheback, a member of the local Party committee whom he'd met on several occasions.

"I hope you're not here in an official capacity," Escheback said with a smile.

"God no. The wife's away, and I fancied a drink. But what's all the excitement?" he asked innocently.

Escheback hesitated, but only for a moment. "Well, it's no secret. We just had a block meeting. It was called by the union to approve an official thank you for the New Course. Everyone agreed, but then someone suggested an amendment reinstating the old norms. Which was also approved. And then someone must have phoned union HQ, because a message arrived saying we should wait until one of the high-ups got the chance to explain things more fully. At which point the men said fuck that and elected two men to deliver our resolution in person."

"Who to?"

"Ulbricht and Grotewöhl. Who else?"

Ströhm felt a shiver down his spine. "So what exactly was in the resolution?" he asked, as casually as he could.

"Like I said, we're refusing to accept any raise in the norms.

And we want their agreement by noon tomorrow. Or else we stop work."

"Was the threat to strike in the message?"

"No, but it didn't have to be. What other power do we have? And there's enough informers on the site to keep them in the picture." He raised his empty glass. "You want another?"

"No. Thanks. I've had enough." Ströhm got to his feet. "I hope it goes well tomorrow," he added before turning away.

Walking home, he realised he still had to call Annaliese. What should he tell her?

Speaker Vans

Tuesday morning Ströhm woke early, the dream he'd been having slipping out of reach before he could reel it in. He just lay there for several minutes, reluctant to get up, before eventually forcing himself out of bed and into the bathroom, where a stranger's face was waiting to greet him.

In the kitchen he put on the water for coffee and walked through to the living room window while he waited for it to boil. People were going into work as normal, male and female staff walking up Tilsiter Strasse towards the hospital, construction workers heading down to the sites on Stalinallee. But many of the latter were carrying placards, which certainly wasn't usual.

He made his coffee and sat there with it, bracing himself for the day to come. The previous night he had called Annaliese from the public phone in the hospital foyer, rather than risk using their own, but the queue which had quickly formed behind him had prevented any real conversation. When she'd told him what RIAS was reporting, and asked how bad things really were, all he could say was "It's not good" in a tone that cried out understatement.

So how bad was it? He decided he would go down to Stalinallee and see for himself, and then take the U-Bahn into the centre.

Outside, the weather was poor for early summer, warm enough for a light jacket but grey and decidedly humid. This time he reached Stalinallee to find workers converging from all directions on the agreed meeting place. At 8 A.M. Strausberger Platz was already full of men talking and waiting, most looking more excited than nervous, and as he worked his way slowly through the throng towards the U-Bahn entrance, Ströhm tried to gauge the mood. There were many copies of that morning's *Tribune* being read and angrily waved, and buying a copy told him why—there was a prominent article explaining how important it was to retain the work norm hike.

Was the leadership—or some elements thereof—actually trying to make the workers angrier? Why would they do that, unless it was some ludicrous plan to flush out the ringleaders and have them all arrested? No, Ströhm told himself, this was just more evidence of how utterly out of touch the so-called worker's leaders were. When in doubt, an old comrade had once told him, always plump for cock-up over conspiracy.

The crowd was getting bigger, hundreds reaching towards thousands, and the wide road was now effectively blocked to traffic. All the placards Ströhm could see carried slogans demanding a reduction in the norms. One was a relic from a state-sponsored demo in which words welcoming the rise had been heavily crossed out.

Despite the groups of men still arriving from other sites, despite the lack of obvious stewards or organisers, the crowd was beginning to move, funnelling into a column and slowly heading east towards the city centre. Its predictable destination, confirmed in conversations Ströhm overheard, was the enormous House of Ministries complex on Leipziger Strasse, built in the thirties for Goering's Aviation Ministry and now the home of the DDR government.

How would the leadership react? he wondered. How would the Soviets? Today was the day he could expect a call from Mironov.

Ströhm stood by the U-Bahn entrance for several minutes, a

mass of confused emotions. He would have loved to join the march but knew that such a brazen statement would put paid to any influence he might still exert over the course of developments. It would be an indulgence, nothing more.

He went downstairs to catch a train, emerging again ten minutes later in a strangely quiet Alexanderplatz. There was no sign of increased activity outside the Alex police HQ, or on Prenzlauer Strasse. There were the two usual cops standing sentry outside the House of Unity, and they were ready with their usual tight-lipped smiles. If precautions were being taken against a major public disturbance, Ströhm could see no sign of them.

He went straight down to the canteen, partly for breakfast, mostly for gossip. Copies of *Tribune* were much in evidence, though here at Party HQ the number defending the norm rise as an example of "necessary firmness" seemed roughly equivalent to those rolling their eyes at the idiocy of persisting with a policy that both Moscow and its own workers wanted scrapped. Tray loaded, Ströhm carried it over to a table where Arkady, one of his old comrades from the resistance, was sitting alone.

"So what do you think?" Ströhm asked him, nodding at the open *Tribune*.

Arkady smiled at him. "I think it's hard to tell which way the wind is blowing," he said.

"But it is blowing."

"No doubt about that." Arkady leaned forward. "It's Tuesday, so the Politburo will be meeting this morning. And it seems that Ulbricht's majority is hanging by a thread, so I'm expecting an announcement this afternoon that the increase has been postponed."

"Ah. I wonder whether that will be enough to satisfy the construction workers."

"It's what they're asking for, isn't it? And anyway, Ulbricht's more worried about Herrnstadt and Zaisser than the Stalinallee situation. When someone brought that up, he said that once it started raining, the demonstrators would all go home."

Ströhm didn't think the men he'd seen in Strausberger Platz would be deterred by the prospect of getting wet, but decided not to say so.

Up in his own office, he found several new files in his in-tray demanding attention. Though most only involved minor infractions by DDR-based Soviet personnel, a couple had longer-term significance. Increasing integration of the Soviet Bloc economies was one thing requiring careful handling; while such an objective clearly made sense, it had to be well-presented as a coming together, and not, in Mironov's words, as "the wolf integrating his prey." The other issue was the teaching of Russian in DDR schools, which the Soviets were insisting should be compulsory. Many older German educators were less than enthusiastic about this, and could, for the moment, rely on the fact that there weren't enough Russian-speaking teachers to make it a reality. It might be only a matter of time, but diplomacy would still be needed to bridge the gap.

None of which seemed particularly relevant when your country was perched by a precipice, and Ströhm found concentrating on any of it next to impossible.

Instead he spent increasing stretches of time by the window overlooking Prenzlauer Tor, watching the slow and steady thickening of a crowd below. It was still only about a hundred strong, and no one was actually demonstrating, although a stack of placards was leaning up against a wall in waiting. There were a few more police in evidence, but no attempt was being made to disperse the crowd.

Why not? Ströhm wondered. The longer they left it, the bigger the crowd, and the harder it would be. Was someone waiting for the Politburo meeting to end, and for one of them to make the decision?

The incompetence angered him, which he knew was ridiculous, because at this point it served his own interest. What he wanted were demonstrations big and powerful enough to rid the SED leadership of Ulbricht and cronies, yet not so powerful that the Soviets would feel obliged to come to Ulbricht's rescue in the interests of bloc stability. A fine line to walk, with a long drop either side. He wasn't feeling optimistic.

By half-past twelve the crowd below had doubled and doubled again, yet still seemed more like football spectators peacefully awaiting the start of a match than proletarians come to storm a Winter Palace. Was anything more dramatic happening outside the House of Ministries, a couple of kilometres to the southwest?

He picked up his phone and asked the switchboard to connect him to a friend who worked there. Siggy Fremlich was an old railway colleague, a thoroughly decent man whom Ströhm had helped secure a relatively lowly job in the Ministry of Transport. He was enough of a conformist that Ströhm had no fears he would say anything a potential Stasi eavesdropper might take exception to.

Fremlich's "hello" sounded overly anxious, but when he heard it was Ströhm he managed to calm down a little.

"I was just wondering how things were going over there," Ströhm said. "And I remembered you had a window overlooking Leipziger Strasse. A front seat, so to speak."

"Oh, you wouldn't believe it," Fremlich said. "There must be about ten thousand people out there."

"What are they doing? They haven't tried to get inside?"

"No, not yet anyway. No, it's been extraordinary. They tried to deliver a message, but they were turned away at the door. Then the crowd started shouting in unison for Comrades Ulbricht and Grotewöhl to come out, and there were lots of rude remarks about them hiding in the cellar. But they aren't here, so a couple of junior ministers were given the job instead. A table was taken out for them to stand on, but they weren't allowed to speak. There were calls of traitor, insulting references to their hands being flabby—it was unbelievable. Eventually one of the workers climbed onto the table and said that if Ulbricht and Grotewöhl didn't show up in the next half-hour they'd all march through the city centre and go out on strike tomorrow. A general strike, they said. That was about twenty minutes ago."

"Ulbricht and Grotewöhl are probably still in the Politburo meeting here. They might not even know what's happening, but rumour has it they intend to revoke the norm increase."

"That was only one of the demands," Fremlich told him. "They also want reduced prices and immunity from punishment for their spokesmen. Where's this all going, Gerhard?"

"Your guess is as good as mine, Siggy. I'll call you again if they storm the House of Unity."

Five minutes later he was in the canteen, waiting like everyone else to hear what decisions had been made upstairs. Soon after one o'clock some news finally arrived—the norms were being revoked, presumably not over Ulbricht's dead body.

So far so good, Ströhm thought. If the workers accepted this grudging gift and asked for no more . . .

BOB'S CANTEEN THAT LUNCHTIME WAS a sea of smiles, with punches in the air and whoops of delight whenever fresh news of the DDR's troubles came in. It felt more like a football match than a social and political crisis, and Russell suspected that the only thing which might have excited his colleagues more was the sound of distant gunfire.

It wouldn't be a game to his old friend Ströhm, or to Thomas's daughter, Lotte, who would both be smack in the middle of whatever came to pass in the next few days.

And then there was the film festival, which was scheduled to open on Thursday. This year the venues were all in the western sector, but thousands of tickets had been sold in the east. Would the border be closed if the situation deteriorated? Would the festival be cancelled if it was? It was a small matter in the grand scheme of things, but Russell would hate to see Effi lose her day of acclamation.

He was just about to leave for the afternoon shift when a breathless young operative arrived to announce that the SED had given in to the workers' demand that the increase in work norms should be cancelled. He clearly saw this as victory, but the facial expressions of his audience were decidedly mixed. Many, Russell realised, were afraid that this was how Ulbricht and his Soviet masters would dig their way out of the hole they were in.

WITH HIS OFFICE WINDOW OPEN, Ströhm could hear but not see the approaching marchers. They were moving eastward on Wilhelm-Pieck Strasse, having now walked more than three-quarters of their promised circular tour of the city centre. The House of Unity was the one remaining political landmark on the marchers' way back to Strausberger Platz, and most of the people in the building were presumably praying they wouldn't stop for a visit.

It must have felt like this in the Winter Palace, he thought wryly. The Tsar hadn't been at home in 1917, and Ströhm found himself wondering whether Ulbricht was still in the building.

Several minutes ago, two speaker vans had set off down Wilhelm-Pieck, and he could now hear an amplified voice in the distance. It was presumably spreading the glad tidings of the norm increase's cancellation, and Ströhm was waiting for the sound of cheers when the other speaker van suddenly reappeared, reversing at what seemed a ridiculous speed and scattering pedestrians out of its path. It looked like someone had tried—figuratively at least—to shoot the messenger.

He waited in vain for the van's now silent partner to reappear.

The leading marchers, meanwhile, were filtering into the circular Tor below, and many workers were pausing to stare at the wide facade of the Party headquarters. Ströhm guessed there'd be faces at every window, and the looks they were getting from down in the street were not overflowing with loyalty, love, or even fear. Many of his comrades would be outraged; some, like him, would feel shame at bringing the Party to such a pass.

And then the other speaker van appeared, workers on its roof and clinging to the sides, looking for all the world like the spearhead of an army of liberation. Its new driver did a half-turn on the far side of the Tor intersection, and almost immediately a voice rang out. It was loud and distorted, but the message could not have been clearer.

The increased norms were not mentioned—their cancellation had already been banked, and the new demands were for so much more. They wanted the government's resignation, and free all-Germany elections. They wanted the release of each and every political prisoner; they wanted less guns and more butter. They wanted what a free worker's state should have already given them, and the general strike beginning tomorrow would see that they finally got it.

Only they wouldn't, Ströhm thought with a dreadful pang of sadness. Because neither the Soviets nor the DDR could give them what they wanted without risking everything.

Having put their demands on record, the marchers began moving on. Unlike the Winter Palace, they seemed to be saying, the House of Unity was not even worth an invasion. The SED had become an irrelevance, the operatives staring down at them like specimens of some long-extinct species preserved behind sheets of glass.

AT BOB, RUSSELL'S AFTERNOON SEEMED vaguely unreal, as he listened to another dozen refugees denouncing the regime that some of his and Brickell's colleagues thought would be gone in a matter of days. Personally, he doubted it. The younger Americans were letting their hopes obscure reality— whatever the DDR's workers wanted, the Soviets were not going anywhere.

When the last refugee had smiled his thanks for their blessing, Russell and Brickell cemented their ritual of an after-work drink. Since the evening before, someone had fixed up an outside speaker in the impromptu beer garden, so people on a break could follow the DDR's collapse on RIAS. But its presentation of the crisis was surprisingly cautious, and so, it transpired, had been its actions. Three DDR workers had arrived at the station wanting to broadcast to the Soviet zone, but their request had been refused. RIAS seemed happy to report what was happening, but wary of becoming an active participant, which suggested to Russell that either the high-ups at BOB or their distant bosses in Washington were getting concerned over where this might all end up.

Today at least was a wrap. The march was now over, having concluded its triumphal tour of Berlin's city centre. There had been no reports of violence, either by the workers or the strangely dormant East German police, and no real response from the government. Russell found the latter particularly puzzling. Had the regime decided that after the norm revocation they could just sit back and let the workers walk off their anger? It seemed like a gamble, but maybe there were no other options. Certainly the most obvious explanation for the regime's inaction was that Ulbricht and Co had run out of ideas for saving themselves, and were now sat like rabbits in the middle of a road transfixed by oncoming headlights.

SOON AFTER 5 P.M., STRÖHM was told that a mass Party meeting would be held in the Friedrichstadt-Palast at seven.

Every off-duty cadre in Berlin was expected to attend this special event, at which the leadership would be presenting its latest assessment of the DDR's programme for the construction of socialism.

The news from Strausberger Platz was that the march had dispersed, the marchers having promised to reconvene in support of a general strike on the following morning. Outside the Alex a couple of cops had arrested two workers and taken them inside, but when the march refused to move on the two men had been released. Reports were coming in of clashes elsewhere in the city, mostly between groups of young workers and local police, but so far at least these didn't seem serious.

A fleet of taxis had been arranged to take the House of Unity workers to the Friedrichstadt-Palast, but Ströhm decided he wanted to walk. The fitful rain seemed to have finally stopped, and it was only a couple of kilometres. On the way he noticed an unusual number of cyclists on the major streets, and after a while guessed the reason why—a general strike had to be general, and the Stalinallee workers were sending out emissaries to every industrial concern in the Soviet sector.

He reached the Friedrichstadt-Palast a quarter-hour early, and stood by the Spree admiring the building. After hosting a market hall and a circus, it had been artistically rebuilt as a theatre immediately after World War I, complete with a stupendous ceiling boasting hundreds of large plaster stalactites. Considering the latter "degenerate art," the Nazis had torn them down, but as Ströhm knew from previous gatherings, the building's interior was still quite striking.

There were about three thousand seats, and all would be full that evening. Ströhm took one in the block reserved for Central Committee members and gazed up at the still-empty row where the Politburo would sit. What were they going to say tonight? What could they say and still save face?

Looking around, he spotted many dour expressions and very few smiles. And when the members of the Politburo arrived en masse to take their seats, a thin ripple of applause quickly faded to nothing.

The "special event" went on for a couple of hours. The only people to speak were those on the podium, and no matter their private differences, they had clearly come to speak as one. Mistakes had been made, albeit in good faith. Some had shown excessive enthusiasm, others excessive trust in the people, though none admitted to an excessive belief in themselves. What mattered was that lessons had been learned, and that adopting the New Course should give them all faith in their future.

The day's worrying disturbances were not, however, solely—or even significantly—the result of the aforementioned mistakes. The main factor here was foreign interference: the Western media in Berlin had been actively inciting the opposition and many foreign agents were playing a major role in provoking incidents between the people and their police.

Hearing this, Ströhm took time to study the faces of the delegates in his vicinity. Were any of them buying this nonsense? He had no doubt that the Americans were delighted, and that some West Berliners—whether curious, idealistic, or simply out for trouble—would have come across to join the marchers. But to pretend that such people were responsible for the construction workers' disaffection was an insult, not least to the workers themselves. And it was blatantly untrue, as every member of the audience not wearing blinkers knew only too well.

The Party's mistakes were the source of its problems, and since it was willing to admit they'd been made, why not go the whole hog and just tell the truth? Why not use the moment of Soviet indecision brought on by Stalin's death to change course? To listen to what the people—what the workers—were saying, and act accordingly. To set an example to the Soviets and the other

East European parties of what was possible if dogmatic preconceptions were abandoned and basic socialist values allowed to guide a real change of direction.

A five percent chance of success? Probably. But Ulbricht's way offered none at all.

When the meeting broke up, and Ströhm filed out through the door reserved for the Central Committee, he found a grim-faced Oleg Mironov in wait.

"A chat," the Russian said. It wasn't a question.

They walked down to the Schiffbauerdamm, and crossed over to the walkway by the Spree.

"How worried should we be?" Mironov asked without preamble.

"I don't know is the honest answer. You heard what I heard."

"People with their heads in the sand."

Ströhm shook his head. "Yes and no. They may be idiots, but they're also used to more guidance. Look, I wasn't invited to any of the top-level meetings today, so I really don't know what they're thinking. If I were you, I'd talk to Herrnstadt or Zaisser tomorrow."

"Tomorrow may be too late."

Ströhm caught the tone. "Are your troops on standby?"

"As a precaution. They haven't been ordered into the city," Mironov added evasively.

"But they could be?"

"What do you think?"

"I think if you're not careful, the DDR will become a millstone around your neck."

AT THE HOUSE IN DAHLEM the wireless was on all evening. Once the children were in bed, the five adults sat in the living room, drinking Thomas's favourite Riesling and listening to events unfold.

RIAS had already admitted that three delegates from the Eastern sector demonstrators were camped out in its studio, and soon after seven the men in question were finally allowed to broadcast their demands. There were four on the list: the norms to stay the same, immediate help for ordinary families, immunity for strikers and their spokesmen, and free and fair elections.

They were followed by the station director, who congratulated the East Berlin construction workers on already forcing a government climb-down on the first of these demands and urged everyone in the DDR to support the campaign to secure the other three. His sole caveat was that they only "demand what is reasonable."

"Which begs every question in the book," Thomas noted. "One man's 'reasonable' is another man's 'out of the question.' Still, one down and three to go."

"They might manage two and three," Russell said, "but free elections? The leaders might as well go back into exile. Always assuming Moscow would have them."

"What do you think, Annaliese?" Effi asked. Her friend was looking more anxious as the hours went by.

"I don't know. Gerhard's been hoping that shaking things up will make them better, but I have a horrible feeling they'll just get worse. He was trying to sound positive when we spoke, but I could tell he was feeling the opposite. I'm just praying that he'll be all right."

IT WAS DARK BY THE time Ströhm got home. After his conversation with Annaliese on the hospital foyer phone, all he had really wanted to do was go to her and the children, but here he was back in their flat. Spending this particular night in the west would not have gone down well, and as long he harboured any hopes of a better future for the DDR that had to concern him. He still wasn't ready to simply leave.

Maybe the Soviets would see sense, would ditch Ulbricht, put someone more palatable in his place, and get whoever that was to promise the people a real change of direction.

"It's not too late," he told the empty room.

"Oh, yes it is," he heard himself reply.

Getaway Limousines

Ströhm woke up around five, after barely four hours' sleep. His mouth was dry, the result of one too many schnapps the night before. It was already light and outside the birds were singing. Sunday was midsummer's day, though in political hours today seemed likely to be the longest.

He used the bathroom, got himself dressed and downed a large glass of water. Was he going into work as if it was a normal day? Liaising with the Soviets and helping to crush this new revolution?

Not yet. First he would walk down to Strausberger Platz and see what the mood was. His as well as theirs.

Outside it was raining much harder than the day before, but on Stalinallee no one seemed aware that they were getting drenched. At least it was warm—nobody would die of pneumonia.

It wasn't yet six and already the crowd was bigger than yesterday's. And these were almost all construction workers—thousands of workers from Berlin's other industries would be gathering at different locations before heading into the centre.

The overall mood astonished Ströhm. Nearly everyone seemed to be smiling, as if they were waiting to leave on a holiday outing, not challenge a frightened but well-armed government. And it wasn't because they expected an easy victory—or indeed one of any complexion—it was because for one day at least they had broken free. Their minds and bodies were their own to direct.

Were his? Should he join them, become again a simple soldier of the revolution? There was every reason to believe that the day would end with the Soviets in control—there was simply too much elemental force they could bring to bear. So if he wasn't shot down in the street, he might well be arrested, and any high-ranking Party member caught abetting the enemy would be foolish to expect any mercy.

Even if he didn't have Annaliese and the kids to think of, what would be the point?

He was a serving member of the Central Committee, someone with influence. The Soviets could take back the streets, but as the last two days had proved, no government could be effective without at least a modicum of consent from those it tried to govern. Moscow would be keen to make the job easier, and surely retaining Ulbricht and Co would only make it more difficult. People like Herrnstadt and Zaisser, people like himself, would be their best chance of putting the cork back in the bottle. This crowd felt like home, but his place was at Party HQ.

Somewhat to his surprise the U-Bahn was still running; the transport workers had obviously decided that moving strikers around Berlin was more important than getting the transport workers out on the streets. As on the previous day, Ströhm got off at Alexanderplatz and walked up Prenzlauer Strasse to the House of Unity, which now had a much-enhanced police presence to protect it.

Once inside the building, he walked straight through to the rear entrance and out into the parking lot. And there they were, nine shiny limousines parked in a row. The leaders were already here, and these, he thought, were their getaway cars.

Down in the canteen, he received confirmation that the Politburo was already in session upstairs. Deciding what? Ströhm wondered. Surely all the important decisions were now being taken in Karlshorst or Moscow.

He took the long way up to his office, gathering news and information from comrades he met on the stairs and in corridors, and ones whose doorways happened to be open. It often amazed him how many he knew by name after thirty years in the Party.

He learned that thousands of steelworkers were on their way in from Hennigsdorf, along with hundreds of electrical engineers from Treptow, and workers from smaller concerns all over the city. Even the tax collectors had declared their support for the Stalinallee workers. And it wasn't just Berlin—reports were coming in from across the DDR of marches and strikes. One might say that the country was up in arms, except that the only weapons the workers had were voices and fists.

On the other side of the city centre the House of Ministries was again besieged, but there was no sign of protesters underneath Ströhm's window. Which was, he thought, a mistake on the workers' part, because here and in Karlshorst was where the real power lay. Maybe they would turn their attention this way, but he wouldn't want to bet on it. There was no real organisation behind the uprising, which was both its glory and its probable downfall. No one was telling these thousands of workers where to go for maximum impact, or what they should do when they got there.

He called Fremlich for the news from Leipziger Strasse and was shocked by how panicky his old friend sounded. Around a hundred workers had forced their way into the House of Ministries, and though they'd since been persuaded to leave, Ströhm got the impression that most of the civil servants were still hiding in cupboards or under their desks.

He went back to his own window. The Tor was still clear, but as he looked down one of the limousines emerged from the car lot and took a left turn onto Wilhelm-Pieck. Another one followed, and another, until all nine had been driven away towards Karlshorst and safety.

It looked very much like his superiors were consigning the DDR's people to Moscow's tender mercies.

Wanting to be sure, Ströhm put in a call to Mironov. His liaison partner was in a meeting and could not be interrupted. The meeting might last several hours.

Which told him what he needed to know. The Soviets had decided to take back the streets and would only decide who they wanted to run the DDR once they had done so. He might as well go to Annaliese and the children while the border was still open. He could always come back if and when Moscow decided to abandon Ulbricht.

So what he was waiting for? What did he need to take with him? He slipped the photograph of Annaliese and the children out of its frame, and took two others from a drawer, the only one he had of Ryfka, his first real love, whom the Nazis had killed, and his mother and father, whose death more than forty years ago had brought him back to Germany. All the dead people who had loved him.

He was putting on his jacket when the phone started ringing, and after a short debate with himself over whether or not to answer, he reluctantly picked it up.

"Gerhard, this is Thomas."

"Thomas," Ströhm echoed. They might be only ten kilometres apart, but today that felt like worlds.

"I've just had a call from Lotte."

Ströhm thought about stopping his friend, but then remembered warning him that the line was bugged. This had to be important.

"She sounded awful," Thomas was saying. "She told us not to worry if we didn't hear from her in the next few days, which of course had the opposite effect, and then the line went dead. At her end—I checked."

"What do you want me to do?" Ströhm asked, now feeling guilty that he hadn't tried to reach Lotte during the last two turbulent days.

"If you have the time, could you try and call her? And if you can't get an answer, go round to her flat. It's not far from where you are."

"Of course. Give me the number and the address," he said, reaching for a pencil. "I'll do what I can," he promised, after writing them down. "Things here are . . ."

"I know. I wouldn't ask, but . . ."

Ströhm knew that Lotte and her parents hadn't always—or even often—seen eye to eye, but he was also aware of how much she meant to them. "I'll call you back as soon as I have any news."

"Thank you, Gerhard," Thomas said.

Ströhm put the phone down and ran a hand through his hair. It looked like he wouldn't be leaving until the afternoon.

A few hours shouldn't make any difference, but just to be sure he called an old friend at the Ministry of Transport, who told him that as of that moment the cross-sector trams and trains were still running as usual, and that the road crossings were still open to cars and pedestrians.

He had some time.

The next call was to Lotte's flat, where the phone just kept ringing. Phoning her place of work, he was told that she hadn't come in that day, and that no one knew why. Who else could he try? He hadn't spoken to any old comrades who worked at the Alex for months, but what other options did he have?

He decided Stefan Heitzer was his best bet. Heitzer had worked in the political department since the war, but hadn't, like many of his colleagues, switched to the recently established Stasi.

Heitzer was surprised to hear from him, but agreed to check the day's arrest sheets for Charlotte Schade and talk to a couple of Stasi friends who might know something.

"As quickly as you can," Ströhm pleaded, pushing his luck.

"I've got nothing else to do," Heitzer told him. "The Soviets have all but told us to stay at our desks."

"They haven't locked you in?"

"Not yet."

Ströhm laughed and broke the connection. All he could do now was wait and hope. A quarter-hour went by, and then another. He was standing by the window when he heard a single burst of machine gun fire. It was coming from the south, probably a couple of kilometres away.

Another followed from the same direction, and then there was silence.

Not wanting to leave his phone, he put his head round the door and asked his secretary to find out what was going on.

His secretary Hannelore was gone for ten minutes, and when she came back there were tears on her cheeks. "There have been large demonstrations in Leipziger Strasse, Potsdamer Platz, and Marx-Engels Platz," she told him. "Troops—Soviet troops—have been ordered to disperse the protesters."

So the gunfire was coming from Marx-Engels Platz. Or the Lustgarten, as ninety-nine percent of Berliners still called it. "God help us," he murmured to himself.

"And there's something else," Hannelore said, wiping a cheek, "I was talking to other Central Committee secretaries and their bosses have been advised to make their way to Karlshorst in shared taxis. We haven't received the same message, and I'm assuming that's because the Soviets may want you here in the city, but I just thought I'd mention it."

"You're probably right," he told her. "I think you might as well go home. There won't be any more normal work today."

Once she had gone, he found himself remembering Herrnstadt's advice to at least give the impression of being part of the team. Was not being invited to join the exodus to Karlshorst something he should actually be worried about? Had he already crossed a line that he shouldn't have? In his thoughts he certainly had, but not, as far as he knew, in word or deed.

It was almost noon when Heitzer called him back. "Bad news, I'm afraid. She's not here, but she's on the list of people the Stasi plan to pick up once the Soviet troops move in. No one will tell me whether or not they've done so already, and I think I've used up any good will I had left with the comrades in Lichtenberg."

"What do they want her for?" Ströhm asked.

"Sedition. Her group was planning to print and distribute copies of Alexandra Kollontai's old Workers' Opposition pamphlet. The one demanding more power to the workers and less to the party bureaucrats. Which, needless to say, enraged the latter. Lenin had it banned."

"Oh shit," Ströhm thought. "I owe you," he told Heitzer, aware that it might prove a difficult debt to repay.

Hoping he wouldn't arouse suspicion, he called his friend at Transport again, and found that all tram and train traffic across the city sector border had now been halted, but that cars and pedestrians were still being allowed through.

He knew he should visit Lotte's flat. Although there was next to no hope that she would be there, a neighbour might have witnessed her arrest. If the border slammed shut in the meantime, he would just have to wait until it opened again.

Metzer Strasse was only a five-minute walk to the north, her flat on the fourth floor of a modern five-storey block. It might have been luck that the lift was working, or maybe the probability that half the tenants were Party officials, but Ströhm was grateful regardless. His heart sank when he saw that the door to Flat 14 had been jimmied open but rose again when a young female neighbour told him the plain-clothed police had left without her. "I heard her in there this morning, so she must have gone out just before they turned up."

Or saw them coming, Ströhm thought, imagining her by a window as she spoke to her dad on the phone.

He made his way back to the House of Unity and took the lift up to his office. As far as he could see, there was nothing more he could do with the information he had. Lotte was out there somewhere, but he had no idea where. She might even be in the west by now, in which case Thomas would eventually call and tell him.

But until he knew, he couldn't just leave. Lotte looked like she'd be needing powerful friends, and he doubted she had any more powerful than him. That line of fleeing limousine had convinced him it was time to leave the DDR, most likely for good, though miracles sometimes happened. But now that he had crossed that mental Rubicon, the urgency had somehow slipped away. He would leave tomorrow, or the day after that, or whenever he could. The Soviets might shut the border for several days, but they would have to reopen it eventually—the city sector economies were still too interdependent.

There was a booming noise in the distance, which he recognised as tank-fire, a sound they'd all got used to in the final days of the war. From the Marx-Engels Platz, he guessed, though there was no rising smoke to prove him right. Looking down at the street, he saw a plain black car perform a fast and illegal U-turn before pulling up in front of his building. Two men got out, one in a leather coat. "They even dress like the Gestapo," as one of his oldest comrades had disdainfully remarked a few months ago.

The Stasi had come for him. He had no evidence to back up that sudden realisation, but somehow he knew.

They were already inside the building. Ströhm reached for the phone and called reception. "This is Gerhard Ströhm," he told the woman who answered. "I'm expecting visitors. Could you let me know when they arrive?"

"Oh, they're already on their way up."

For several seconds the abruptness of it all left him paralysed, but then the survival instinct kicked in.

Grabbing the photographs from his desk and slipping them into a pocket, he took a last look round his office of three years and headed out the door. Finding a blissfully empty corridor, he hurried to the staircase by the lift shaft. A lift was on its way up, so he started down the stairs, going as fast as seemed safe. As he half-tumbled down the eight flights he asked himself where he was going. To the West, of course, and as fast as he could—the relaxed defection that had seemed so possible ten minutes earlier was now out of the question. If he didn't get out today, he might spend the next twenty years in Hohenschönhausen prison. Assuming they didn't execute him.

The Bernauer Strasse crossing point seemed his best bet. It wasn't that far to walk, was one of the less frequented, and usually manned accordingly. It would take the Stasi some time to alert every possible crossing point, and until they did there seemed no reason why his papers and rank wouldn't see him safely through.

The guards on the rear entrance who watched him leave would soon be telling the Stasi which way he'd gone, so he took the eastern Prenzlauer Allee exit and walked a few hundred metres north before turning west through mostly empty back streets to the busier Fehrbelliner Strasse. Despite telling himself that he should still be well ahead of the pursuit, each passing vehicle seemed to raise his heartbeat another notch.

Meanwhile his mind was trying to take in what had happened. The fact that he was now on the run certainly felt astonishing, but also strangely akin to donning a well-worn coat. He had, after all, spent many more years of his life in hiding than he had in government. The only real surprise was that this time the hunters were from his own side.

Bernauer Strasse was up ahead, the U-Bahn station bearing its name on this side of the border, the street itself in the old French sector. The barrier was down, but a queue of would-be crossers seemed to be offering up their papers and getting permission to do so.

Ströhm hung back in the U-Bahn station entrance. Was this wise? What if they already had his name? That would be that.

As he watched, one of the guards stepped into their hut and put a telephone to his ear. After speaking a few words and writing something down he re-merged to update his two partners. They didn't look surprised, as surely they should have if his name had been mentioned. Or was he inflating his own importance?

It was too risky, but how else was he going to get across? He walked back down towards Anklamer Strasse, wondering what to do.

AT THE FESTIVAL OFFICES JUST off Ku'damm you could hear rifle shots, staccato machine-gun bursts, and the occasional heavy thump of a tank firing on the other side of the sector border. It was extraordinary, appalling, a terrible shock, and yet hardly surprising.

Effi had arrived early for a newspaper interview and been talking to the chief press officer when the news came in that Gary Cooper had no intention of cancelling his visit because of the Soviet sector disturbances, and would be flying into Tempelhof the next morning, presumably from London or Paris. A few of the lesser celebrities had called to opt out, but those biding their time would hopefully follow Gary's example. The trouble was bound to cast a pall over the festival, but the western half of the city was still deemed a safe place to visit.

Whether it was in good taste to celebrate movies and movie stars while people were dying within earshot for demanding a decent wage was another question, and one to which Effi still had no answer. Calling the whole thing off would appear to help no one, but then again . . .

The journalist arrived. Franz Illner was from one of Berlin's less serious papers, and not much more than half her age. He began, predictably enough, by asking her about the occasionally audible disturbances across the sector border.

"What can I say?" she said, remembering Calvin Sikorsky and his request that she shouldn't give any comfort to the enemy. This had to be a wet dream for him, the Soviets behaving badly with movie celebrities peering over the fence. "I gather the construction workers have a good case," she said. "But it would be naive to expect that the Soviets would stay out of it. We are on the front line of the Cold War."

"So you're condoning their actions?"

"Not at all. To explain is not to excuse," she added, using one of John's favourite lines. "And I'm an actor," she went on, "here to talk about film and the Berlinale. Do you have any questions about those?"

Reluctantly, he did. About the German films in the competition, neither of which she had seen yet, about her careers in Nazi Germany, postwar Berlin, and America. He was actually more knowledgeable than she had first thought—her expectations of journalists had clearly taken a beating in Hollywood—but couldn't resist a final return to politics. Given the circumstances, did she think the festival should still go ahead?

"I'm glad that's not my decision to make," she told him.

He smiled. "Gary Cooper is arriving tomorrow. Maybe he'll sort the Russians out."

"Maybe," she agreed, a picture forming in her mind of *High Noon*'s Marshal Will Kane striding down a deserted Stalinallee towards Ulbricht and his sneering cronies.

MAYBE IT WAS WALKING PAST the Catholic cemetery that gave him the idea of going under rather than through the border. Ströhm had worked on Berlin's railways for most of his adult life, and one of the projects he'd been involved with was the North-South tunnel which the Nazi government had built for the S-Bahn. Opened on the eve of the war to provide a cross-city link, it had ended up as a home for hospital trains and then been partially flooded. He remembered that John Russell had used it in the final days of the war to cross the city undetected.

A few years after the war the tunnel had been reopened, but only in the Soviet zone, the trains from north of the city all stopping at Potsdamer Platz. Beyond that point the tunnel had been bricked up. But—and here was the hope—between Potsdamer Platz and the next station north on Unter den Linden, the line ran along the edge of the Tiergarten, right beneath the sector border. Ströhm distinctly remembered that some of the access shafts were on the western side. These might have been blocked in the last three years, but with no real restrictions on movement between the sectors, it wouldn't have been a priority.

It was worth a shot. Almost literally, in his case.

He walked round the neighbouring Protestant cemetery and onto Invalidenstrasse. The old Stettin Station was a few hundred metres away, and a crowd of strikers was gathered in front of it, listening to someone on a loudspeaker. Fortunately the underground S-Bahn station was closer, and as he clattered down the steps Ströhm felt more than a little relieved to be off the street. Now all he needed was for the trains to be still running.

They were, but at rather long intervals, as a morose official informed him. In the event he only had to wait twenty minutes. The train when it came was virtually empty, and there was no sign of any police. It was only when he reached the Potsdamer Platz terminus ten minutes later that he realised he needed a torch. He should have bought one on Fehrbelliner Strasse, though looking back he couldn't remember any shops being open. He could go up aboveground and search for one in

Potsdamer Platz, but for all he knew several thousand demonstrators were up there doing battle with the Red Army. As if to
confirm that probability, three men came down the stairs to the
platform, where two of them helped the blooded third into
the train that Ströhm had arrived on.

He would make do without a torch.

The train sat there with no apparent desire to depart. Ströhm
stood in the shadows, willing it do so.

"We're leaving," the guard eventually shouted at him.

"I'm waiting for someone," he yelled back, causing all the few
onboard passengers to turn their heads his way.

The guard raised a hand in acknowledgement and closed the
doors; the driver set the train in motion. As it slid into the tunnel,
Ströhm was quickly striding in the same direction, eager to be out
of sight before any more would-be passengers came down the
steps. At the end of the platform he clambered down to the track
bed, stepped carefully across the electrified third rail, and started
walking north in the wake of the still-visible train.

The tunnel was tight in width and height, no larger overall
than those on the U-Bahn, but with no trains behind him he was
safe on the northbound track. After a couple of minutes the train
he was following disappeared round the curve into Unter den
Linden, but the light from the station he'd left was still good
enough to see by. As his eyes grew accustomed to the gloom, he
realised that some extra illumination was seeping through the
tunnel roof. War damage, he assumed, which one of his old colleagues at the Hallesches Ufer railway offices had decided was
insufficiently serious to merit immediate repair.

He was counting out his paces, and after reaching 250, reckoned he must be under Ebertstrasse, with the old government
district up to his right, the Tiergarten up to his left. Needless to
say, the first access shaft he reached was on the right, and with
no train audible or visible he crossed the southbound tracks to

investigate. Looking up the iron ladder and detecting no hint of light, his spirits dropped a notch. Of course the lid might just push off, but there was no point in climbing this particular shaft to find out.

Walking on, he was starting to worry that all the exits on the western side had indeed been bricked up when he finally found one open. At almost the same moment, an arc of light swept across the tunnel ahead—a train was approaching. Knowing he had only seconds before the driver caught sight of him, he stepped too quickly across the third rail, almost losing his balance and missing a probably fatal contact by not much more than a centimetre. Heart thumping, he huddled in the shaft between ladder and wall as the tunnel brightened and the train eventually rattled past, thinking what a stupid way that would have been to die.

The shaft above looked dark and uninviting. He started up the ladder, feeling the rust flake off in his hands, but not encountering any cobwebs. There was no life here, he thought, until something painfully raked across his face. An animal? No, it was a drooping limb of bramble.

There was hope. If bramble could get in, maybe he could get out. Ströhm gingerly pushed his way up through the sharp-threads, one hand feeling for the ceiling he couldn't see, and finally his fingers felt concrete. Finding and following an edge, he established that it was a circular manhole. There was an iron handhold in the centre for pulling it down, and presumably one on the other side for pulling it up.

Arranging himself on the ladder for maximum thrust, expecting, dreading, that the cover would refuse to budge, he took a deep breath and pushed as hard as he could. Much to his surprise, the concrete disc almost flew out of the hole, letting in a rich smell of rotting vegetation. There was light above, but no more than you'd see through a dense forest canopy.

Raising his eyes above the rim of the hole, he saw that he was deep in a large clump of bramble-infested bushes. Exiting the shaft involved squirming himself into a tent-like space studded with thorny stems that supported an even thornier roof a foot or so above the ground. And if getting himself out and horizontal wasn't painful enough, reversing his body to replace the concrete cover was even more so. Another eye-watering turn and he was able to begin snaking his way towards the open ground he could just about discern through the undergrowth. Finally, pausing within reach of the open air a thousand scratches later, he could make out a group of boys playing football in the distance, but no one any closer.

Another few feet and he was rolling onto his back in the grass and staring up at the light grey sky. He was out. For the moment at least, he was out.

AT BOB THE EVENTS ACROSS the border were preoccupying those who had recently crossed it. Some of Russell and Brickell's interviewees that day were worried about the people they'd left behind, some felt guilty for not staying to join the rebellion. A couple even volunteered to join any liberation army the Americans put together.

Among the CIA staff, yesterday's triumphalism had turned into vague apprehension—where, the faces said, might all this lead? Nowhere, if the higher echelons had their way—they were clearly intent on not giving the Soviets any excuse to use them as scapegoats and cut off West Berlin. But it seemed as if no one had told RIAS, whose newsreaders and commentators were still cheering on the strikers from the sidelines.

Russell doubted the conflict would spread. The Soviets would slam down the lid, and that would be that. Though he supposed a lot would depend on what was happening in Moscow. If two factions in the Kremlin were fighting a war for Stalin's crown, this would become one of the crucial battlefields, with consequences for both the DDR and the Soviet Union that were almost impossible for an outsider to foresee.

As the afternoon wore on, and reports started coming in of trouble all across the DDR, he revised his estimate somewhat, but only in terms of how long it might take for the Soviets to take back control. They would do so eventually because they couldn't afford not to.

After the obligatory beer on BOB's patio, he walked back through the building and called himself a cab. The walk was short, but after finding out he'd been taking it alone, Effi had put her foot down. They had agreed, she reminded him, that the Soviets would try to make contact once they reached Berlin, and that though there was no way of stopping a phone call, there was a lot they could do to avoid abduction for an unfriendly chat. Like taking cabs everywhere rather than walking.

And like carrying a gun, Russell had decided later. He had expected BOB HQ to be concerned about allowing such weaponry on the premises, but a single day's observation had convinced him that anyone with an appropriate nametag could probably smuggle in a howitzer, and he was now wearing Thomas's war-issue Luger at the back of his waist.

The cab arrived and carried him back to Vogelsangstrasse. So far all he'd seen of Berlin was Thomas's house, the BOB HQ, and a few suburban streets, which was hardly the homecoming he'd looked forward to. At least the cab was quick, and the fare, when compared to New York, almost reasonable.

Once inside, his pleasure at seeing Gerhard Ströhm at the kitchen table was quickly dispelled by the expressions on all the faces. Thomas, Hanna, Annaliese, and the new arrival—they all looked distraught. Ströhm looked like his face had taken on an angry cat and lost. "What happened?" Russell asked.

The two men took turns telling the story, Thomas recounting

his call and the reasons for it, Ströhm his discovery of Lotte's predicament, and his own sudden need to escape.

"So you're out for good?" was Russell's first question.

"I don't know," Ströhm told him. "I'm safe for now. We need to get Charlotte out."

"We don't even know where she is," Hanna lamented.

"She'll call again," Thomas insisted. "If she's still free."

"We've no reason to think she isn't."

Hanna had been crying, Russell realised. He had never seen Thomas look so grim, while Ströhm and Annaliese both seemed exhausted. In the kitchen RIAS was on the wireless, as if intent on providing a political context for their family crisis.

"I hear you're working for the CIA," Ströhm said, managing not to sound accusative.

"Not voluntarily. They insisted—believe me, saying no was not an option—that I help them screen refugees from your side of the border for a couple of weeks. I still don't know why, unless it's just because they could."

Ströhm shook his head and smiled. "I think you just enrage them."

"Few people better to enrage. So when Lotte calls, what are we going to tell her?"

"I think that'll depend on what she tells us," Thomas said.

"It's always good to think ahead," Russell insisted. "Let's assume she says she's safe where she is, at least for the moment."

"Tell her to lay low until things calm down," Ströhm suggested.

"She couldn't use the same route you did?"

"I wouldn't recommend it."

"Neither would I," Russell agreed, remembering his own trip down that tunnel eight years before. He could still smell the blood.

It suddenly occurred to Russell that if the GRU had Lotte they could use her as a bargaining chip to force him and Effi to write the affidavits they wanted so badly. But that, he knew, was very unlikely—if anyone had her, it would surely be the Stasi or the local police. No, there was probably nothing to worry about there.

"Things will quiet down," Ströhm said, "but not for a few days."

In the kitchen RIAS was announcing that the sector border had just been closed.

"SO THIS IS IT," ANNALIESE said as they got ready for bed. "The children and I have about four changes of clothes, and you have just the one."

Ströhm sighed. "Thomas said he'll lend me some. We're about the same size. And there's still a chance we'll be going back."

Annaliese just looked at him.

"Things can change."

"You've been telling me that for the last five years. They haven't and they won't, not enough anyway." She turned to face him. "Gerhard, you tried—God knows, you did—but that life is gone, and we have to make a new one."

He was silent for several moments. "You wouldn't go back," he said eventually, as if the possibility had only just occurred to him.

"I would if I thought that things might get better. But I can't imagine a world in which that's going to happen."

Ströhm took that in, wondering if he could. "Then I guess we start again," he said. It sounded forced, even to him.

"You've got to let it go. For the children, for us, for yourself. Even for socialism's sake. The DDR has become a stain on the whole idea."

"I know. You're right. And there's another decision I have to make. I doubt that the Party will announce my defection, and at the moment they're probably hoping I'm still on their side of the border. But it will come out eventually, and then the Americans will come looking. And when they find me and take me into custody, what will I tell them? They'll want to know everything. They'll want a traitor who won't stop talking."

Annaliese looked aghast for only a moment. "You'll do what's right," she said.

"Whatever that might be. For the moment I plan on staying indoors—at least until Lotte is safe or . . ."

"Beyond our reach."

"Yes."

High Noon in Berlin

Next morning, while checking through the identity papers of their latest bunch of refugees, it occurred to Russell that any attempt to rescue Lotte would require false ones for her and the rescuer. So when he went to file the morning's batch, he took time to remove a small sheaf of IDs previously surrendered by females who were roughly the same age as Lotte. Using such papers to cross the border might be too risky, but they should survive a spot-check on a Soviet sector street.

Back in their interview room, he transferred the sheaf to his outdoor jacket and then made his way to the canteen. There the mood was subdued, with most conversations featuring the word "bastards" in a variety of tones. The Soviets were still mopping up.

Returning home after work he found a glum-looking Thomas and Ströhm drinking beer at the kitchen table. "No call?" he asked, just to be certain.

"Not yet," Thomas replied.

Russell took a seat. "And we haven't a clue where she might have gone?"

"No. If she knew the whole group was about to be arrested, she wouldn't have gone to one of them. If. We're assuming her boyfriend was in the group, but maybe he wasn't and she's hiding at his place, wherever that might be. She may have been picked up today—we just don't know." Thomas gave Russell a despairing look. "So we wait. Why don't you get yourself a beer and bring a couple more for me and Gerhard."

Russell did as he was told and was on his way back when the telephone rang in the hall. Thomas almost knocked him over in his rush to answer.

He returned looking disconsolate. "It's for you," he told Russell. "A Russian, I think."

It was indeed. "Ah, Mr. Russell. I am Pavel Patolichev, Soviet official here in Berlin. And first I assure you this line secure."

"Good to know."

"I believe Comrade Shchepkin's daughter approach you in London."

"She did."

"And she pass on what we want from you and your lovely wife."

"She did. And she tried very hard to convince us. But I am sure you will understand why we have to refuse."

"No, no, I no understand. Please explain."

"It's quite simple. You want to use what's on the film against . . . well, you know who I'm talking about. But you're not interested in showing the world what a murderous piece of crap the man is—you just want the film for a weapon in your power struggle." Russell paused. Patolichev's GRU had given no sign that they knew about Shchepkin's copy, or the fact that the Russian had made sure it would be released into the public domain should any of the people on the list they had submitted five years earlier meet an unnatural death. If the GRU had been aware of that, they would surely have kept killing likely suspects until the film popped out of its unknown hiding place.

Then again, they must have wondered what other threat could have stayed Beria's hand for all these years.

Trying to think through all the ramifications had always given

Russell a headache, and he hoped the same had been true for the GRU. For now, it seemed easier to keep things simple. "If we give you what you want and Beria wins, then our hold on him is gone, and they'll be nothing to stop the man killing us."

"But we will win."

"If you were that confident, you wouldn't be so desperate for dirt on your enemy," Russell observed. "But look," he added, keen to not to close the door completely. As long as the GRU thought he might come round voluntarily, they should be more reluctant to force the issue. In an ideal world, at least. "I would like to see you win. Perhaps you could come up with a plan that guarantees our safety. One that my wife and I are happy with. I will talk to her again."

"Forty-eight hours," Patolichev said.

"For what?"

"You doing what we want. Guarantees maybe, but forty-eight hours. Okay?"

"Okay."

Forty-eight was better than twenty-four. Or zero. One thing was clear, though—the East German police might have Lotte, but the GRU clearly did not. If they had, then Patolichev would have suggested a deal.

In the kitchen Hanna and Annaliese had just returned from their walk with the children and dog, and while the latter three played in the garden, the adults went back to their vigil. A quarter-hour later, as Hanna got up to start making dinner, the phone rang again. She and Thomas hurried to answer it, and the relief in their voices told the others it was Lotte.

It was a short call. "She was calling from a street phone," Thomas explained. "She thinks she's safe for the moment. She's hiding in the flat of an old Party friend who she knew was away on a fortnight's course, and who always leaves her key under the mat. Out in Luisenstadt, almost next door to St. Michael's

Church. So as long as she doesn't go out, she should be all right. There's some food so she won't starve. But she's really upset that her boyfriend's been arrested, and she doesn't know what to do. I told her to stay put, at least for the weekend."

"What has Werner been charged with?" Ströhm asked quietly.

"Sedition, she thinks."

"Thinks?"

"On her way to where she is now, she saw all their pictures in a frame outside the local police station. 'Wanted for Sedition' was the heading."

"So this has nothing to with the current troubles," Ströhm observed. "The Stasi must have already had them under surveillance."

And now they'd be perfect scapegoats, Russell realised but managed not to say—Thomas and Hanna were depressed enough already. He found himself wondering whether the situation really was desperate enough to countenance a deal with the GRU. The problem was he didn't know who was thick with whom, and putting their trust in Patolichev felt like something a four-year-old would know enough to shy away from. No, that whole idea felt far too dangerous.

There was only one other option. "We'll have to go in and get her," Russell told the rest of them. "*I'll* have to," he corrected himself. "Gerhard's obviously out of the question, and since Thomas stood in the last election half the city knows his face."

"I could go," Annaliese spoke up. "No one's looking for me."

"No," her husband said. "Whoever goes will have to use the tunnel, and that's just too dangerous for someone who's never had to walk along electrified tracks. It has to be John or me."

"It can't be you," Russell insisted, deciding not to mention that when he'd used the tunnel to cross the war-ravaged city in April 1945 the power had been turned off. "You'll need to show me the entrance, and maybe wait at the bottom of the shaft. As long as the trains are running okay, I should be back with Lotte in a couple of hours. And another thing," he said, suddenly remembering. He took the papers from his jacket pocket and laid them on the table. "In case we're stopped."

Thomas wasn't convinced. "They know your face too."

"And Effi won't want you to do it," Annaliese added.

"Look," Thomas said. "We appreciate the offer, but I don't want you to do it either. Seriously. At least not until we've tried everything else. If the Soviets catch you, they will *kill* you."

Russell remembered telling the man in the Quonset hut that he wouldn't consider crossing the sector border. He didn't want to. And Effi, Paul, and Rosa apart, there was no one other than Thomas and Hanna whom he'd ever consider doing it for. "I have a horrible feeling that there'll be no other way," he said, "but as long as Lotte's safe there's no point rushing into it."

"After the weekend will probably be safer," Ströhm interjected. "I imagine things will be pretty much back to normal on Monday."

"Okay," Russell agreed. "And of course I must talk to Effi." He looked at his watch. "I'm supposed to be meeting her in under an hour for the opening ceremony at the Gloria-Palast."

With Hanna making supper, Thomas insisted on driving him to Ku'damm. He needed to get out of the house, he told Russell, and give his mind something else to think about.

The sun was still high as they motored north on Pacelliallee, the warm summer breeze on their faces. The sidewalks were busy, the shops and restaurants doing a brisk trade—this part of Berlin was almost back to normal. Whatever that might be where Germany's hub was concerned.

His brother-in-law seemed disinclined to talk, but not, Russell thought, because of any hunger for silence. "We'll get her out," he said, as they swung onto Mecklenburgische Strasse. Soon they'd be passing the street where Paul had lived with his mother Ilse before the war.

"I love Lotte," Thomas said. "Of course I do. But she's always had this ability to drive me up the wall. Right now, while I'm terrified of what might happen to her, part of me is thinking, 'What has my crazy daughter gone and done now? How could she do this to her mother?' All the clichés. While another part is feeling so proud of her. She followed what looked like a dream, and when it turned out to be something else, she had the sense and the guts to walk away. Which of course in her case meant going to the opposite extreme."

"All true," Russell agreed. "I still think we'll get her out. One way or another." He wasn't ready to mention the possibility of swapping Lotte for the film, because he still wasn't clear how high the cost might be.

"One day at a time," Thomas said. "Another cliché."

Ten minutes later he pulled the car over beside the red-carpeted sidewalk outside the Gloria-Palast. The opening ceremony was presumably well underway by this time, and any crowd had long since dispersed. "Here's your moment," Thomas said to Russell with a hint of the old mischievous smile.

"Thanks," Russell said wryly, stepping out onto the carpet and being promptly shooed off it by an over-dressed doorman. He explained that he was late, and that his wife, Effi Koenen, had probably left the invitation at the box office.

"You're Effi Koenen's husband?" the official almost scoffed.

"I'm usually better-looking," Russell said, pulling out his wallet with its family photo.

That did the trick, and within a few minutes he was working his way past disgruntled sitters to the empty seat beside a shimmering Effi. Onstage someone was calling Berlin "a beacon of cinema."

"Sorry I'm late," he whispered. "You look amazing," he added.

"Thank you. You haven't missed anything."

"One never does at an opening ceremony."

"How true. Has Lotte called?"

"Yes. She's safe," he said. "I'll tell you later," he added as the number of "sssshs" escalated.

The trailers for the films in competition were more interesting than the speeches, but soon gave way to more of the latter, and Russell felt nothing but relief when the ceremony ended.

"I could do with a drink of some sort," Effi said after obliging the handful of autograph-hunters on their way out. "Or should we go straight back?"

"A half-hour won't make any difference," Russell told her. "There's nothing we can do or decide tonight."

The Café Kranzler was a short walk away. Russell had heard it was open again, but the temporary building left a lot to be desired in the elegance stakes. As they sipped the still-excellent coffee he told Effi about the call from Patolichev.

"What happens after forty-eight hours?" she asked.

"He didn't say, but my guess would be nothing. I think he's bluffing. Killing us wouldn't help them, and neither would abducting us and forcing us to sign their wretched affidavits. If they're not given voluntarily, they're not worth having." Unless, of course, they were used to bluff Beria, a depressing thought he kept to himself. "Anyway, forty-eight hours is forty-eight hours. We'll just have to keep being careful."

"Mmm," Effi said, clearly less than convinced. "And what about Lotte?"

"I'll have to go and get her," Russell said.

"You're kidding me!"

"I wish." He explained why only he could do it, and how he felt he had to. "You know how I feel about Thomas. He's lost one child, and I'm damned if he's going to lose the other."

"And what if you're caught?"

"Strange as it may sound, I think I'd be okay. Beria wouldn't dare kill me, and his minions have no reason to. And the CIA would want me back before I spilled all their precious beans, so they'd probably swap me for someone the Soviets want returned."

"Really? This is me you're talking to."

"Well, I'm almost convincing myself. The odds are pretty good."

"They'd better be."

SHORTLY BEFORE FRIDAY'S LUNCH BREAK, Russell got a message he was wanted upstairs. A room was specified, but no reason given, which didn't bode well. Had they already missed the DDR identity papers, or had some human sniffer dog discovered the gun in his locker?

No and no, as it turned out. What waited for him in room 208 was his old friend Travis Henley from the Quonset hut.

"It's your lucky day," Henley told him as he took the proffered seat.

"Someone shot McCarthy?"

Henley stared at him for a second, then apparently saw the funny side. "Not that I'm aware of. No, my good news is that now the border's closed we'll only need your services for a few more days. But not here. One of our men out at Neukölln has taken ill, and we need you to take his place for a few days. Doing the same job, of course."

Neukölln was close to the sector border, Russell thought, but why should that worry someone who was planning to cross it?

"Once the backlog is cleared, you'll be free to leave," Henley was saying, as if he was doing Russell a favour. "The outpost isn't far from the new terminus at Köllnische Heide terminus, and today I'll get someone to drive you up to the station at Wilmersdorf."

And that was that. A GI with a jeep was waiting outside when he finished lunch, and ten minutes later he was back on a Ring-bahn platform for the first time in three years. Back in the thirties, when he'd mostly seen Paul on weekends, the two of them had often spent an afternoon doing the orbital tour.

The old KPD stronghold of Neukölln also had its memories, most of them much darker. It was there that he'd escaped a Nazi raid by the skin of his teeth in 1933, there that the woman whose name he couldn't remember had hidden her supposedly backward daughter from the Nazi eugenicists. It was there that the Fat Silesian had had his studio, providing everything from wedding pictures to artfully doctored papers.

Looking down from the train, Russell felt a wave of absurd nostalgia for a world that he knew was far better gone.

Just beyond Neukölln station the Ringbahn curved round to the north, but with the border closed his train took a short east-bound spur before coming to a halt in Köllnische Heide station, a mere two hundred metres from the Soviet sector. The CIA "out-post" was about a half-kilometre to the north, and after passing a closed horticultural school Russell could see the sequestered house at the end of a lime tree–lined drive, in the centre of what must once have been a private park. The name at the gate was familiar, and maybe that was why the place looked vaguely dis-turbing—this, he remembered, had been one of the gathering points for Jews being shipped to the East.

Now the building seemed too big for its current purpose. The three CIA screeners—four with himself—had their offices on the ground floor, and the basement housed those still waiting their turn to be processed. A rotating pair of guards took individuals up and down during the day and locked the whole lot in at night.

Here, for some reason, the workday went on until six, and this would probably make him late for his pre-film dinner with Effi, which was annoying. Much as he liked Hanna's cooking, he'd missed eating out in Berlin.

His new partner was a burly, balding Atlanta native about ten years younger than Russell. His clothes didn't fit him that well, and he had no social graces, rarely offering a reply to anything Russell said. But he obviously enjoyed the work and seemed both clever and heartless enough to do it well. He was, Russell thought, an obnoxious young man, and when offered the chance to leave early—the American was probably afraid to let him loose on the paperwork—Russell took it willingly.

The other two screeners had already left for some reason, so he headed off alone down the densely shadowed avenue of lime trees. The sky had clouded over while he was inside, and away to the west a distant thunderstorm was throwing tiny flashes of light into a reddish sky. He was listening out for an accompanying rumble of thunder when something shifted in the surrounding shadows, and the side of his head caught fire.

THE LIMOUSINE PURRED ITS WAY through Berlin's west end. On her way to watch one of the films in competition, Effi was finding it hard to forget that the other side of her city— and if RIAS was to be believed, much of the DDR—was still a virtual war zone. No one knew how many had died in the last three days, but she was sure it was more than the Soviets were claiming, and in circumstances like this, attending a Japanese film about medieval-era love triangles seemed singularly inappropriate. She had wanted the festival to go on, but not as if nothing had happened.

They were halfway down Ku'damm, and in the distance she could see a crowded sidewalk in front of the Marmorhaus cinema. There was another limousine ahead of them, and as it pulled up alongside the entrance, the crowd spilled out around it, like hands reaching out to gather in a ball.

"Pull up here," Effi told her festival chauffeur, not wanting to turn the red carpet even redder.

He did as she asked.

"Let's wait until whoever it is . . ."

"It's Gary Cooper," the driver said excitedly, as the familiar figure emerged, and screams of adulation reached their ears.

Effi was surprised by her sudden upsurge of disgust but knew she shouldn't be. Annaliese and Gerhard had lost everything, the Stasi were looking for Lotte, and many Germans were still dying while their compatriots here were screaming their hearts out for a Hollywood film star. An average actor at best, in Effi's less-than-humble opinion, but that was beside the point. It wasn't belief in the man's acting prowess that was fuelling such worship. It was looks, fame, money. Celebrity status.

Effi had a sudden desire to be home, wherever that was these days. Back with John and Rosa. In a life that felt real.

"Miss Koenen?" the chauffeur interrupted her thoughts.

"It's Mrs.," she almost snapped. Up ahead the star and his family had disappeared into the throng, and their limo was pulling away. "Sorry," she told the driver. "I was having a bad moment."

He said nothing.

"So let's go," she said. For more than twenty years agents and studios had been telling her how she needed to play the game, and her minor rebellions had always stopped short of outright refusal. Now she found herself wondering how many people went to their deathbeds wishing they hadn't been so accommodating.

They were outside the cinema, the chauffeur opening the door. As Effi stepped out onto the pavement a few cheers went up, and the hands reached out with their autograph books. She smiled sweetly, putting her acting skills to work.

RUSSELL CAME TO IN WHAT he quickly realised was a hospital bed. The hovering nurse was one clue, the rock-hard mattress and institutional décor a couple more. "Where am I?" he asked, feeling like someone in a badly scripted movie.

"The Urban," the nurse replied.

The Urban was an old hospital in Kreuzberg, which he thought had been destroyed in the war. He remembered the SA storming the place in 1933 to beat up its Jewish directors. But why was he here? The moving shadow in the park, he thought. His hand went up to the side of his head, and the gentlest touch made him wince. "How did I get here?" he asked. Another ridiculous question.

"In an ambulance would be my guess," the nurse said drily. "There's someone outside waiting to talk to you. I expect he'll know."

It was a young American in civilian clothes whom Russell recognised from BOB HQ. "Luke Smith," he introduced himself. "How are you?"

"Alive, apparently. What the hell happened?"

"Someone tried to shoot you dead but didn't quite manage it. You've got a new groove in the side of your head. And a serious bump on the top that we think you got when your head hit the ground."

Which didn't make sense. "So why didn't whoever it was finish the job?"

"Because he was dead himself. You're either a very good shot or lucky as hell. One bullet, straight to the heart. Do you really not remember any of it?"

"No. I really shot someone dead!?" He had no memory of it, no memory of anything after the blow to his head. How had he managed to pull out the Luger, let alone use it?

"The gun was in your hand, and had recently been fired," Smith was saying. "I expect it'll all come back eventually," he added blithely.

Russell wasn't at all sure he wanted it to.

"Your assailant was Russian," Smith continued. "He was carrying a Tokarev machine pistol, so probably MGB."

"I see," Russell said, though he really didn't.

"So how come you were packing a gun?" Smith asked with what felt like exaggerated casualness.

The American's tone was making Russell's suspicious, so he told himself to be careful. "I borrowed it from my brother-in-law. This is not the safest town in the world."

"No."

"Where is the gun?"

"The German police have it. They got there first, and we didn't want to raise any suspicions by demanding it back."

Russell still felt shocked, but he was beginning to feel more compos mentis. "Do my family know I'm here?"

"Yep. I spoke to Thomas Schade—that's the brother-in-law, right?—about half an hour ago. He should be here soon. I don't suppose you have any idea why this Russian wanted to kill you."

"None whatsoever, unless it's where I was working. I assume the Soviets know about that place."

"I would think so. But in case it was personal, we're leaving someone here overnight."

"They're keeping me in?"

"They say it would be foolish not to. Bangs on the head, et cetera."

"Okay." He had to admit he didn't feel so good.

WHEN HE WOKE UP AGAIN he felt a bit better. And there was someone else in the chair.

"So who's been using you for target practice?" Thomas asked. "This family seems to have a death wish at the moment," he added wearily.

"No news of Lotte?" Russell asked.

"None. Who shot you?"

"Someone I've never seen before. A Russian, according to the BOB guy who was here. He shot me and I shot him. I was leaving work out in Neukölln, and all I remember is movement in the shadows and a moment of excruciating pain in the side of my head."

"Well, you didn't imagine that," Thomas said, looking at the wound.

"No, and I suppose I must have killed the bastard, because I can't think what else would have stopped him from killing me."

"Maybe he walked over to do just that, and you were still conscious enough to use the Luger."

"Maybe," Russell said. "It doesn't feel right, not remembering."

"The main thing is you're alive. Do you think this man was sent by you-know-who?"

"Why would he?" Unless Beria had been told that the GRU was about to learn what was on the missing film and had decided he might as well go for broke.

"The GRU then."

"Why would they, when they've given us forty-eight hours to give them what they want? That doesn't make sense either."

"Well, thank God you're still with us."

"Effi will be wondering why I didn't turn up at the Marmorhaus."

"Annaliese went to fetch her when we heard. They should be here before long, and then I'll head back home. Just in case."

"Of course," Russell agreed. "I must look like hell."

"A bit worse than that."

"I'm afraid the German police have your Luger."

Thomas shrugged. "I'm just glad you had it."

Russell had another thought. "Could you ring Paul in London? Tell him to be extra careful until we know what's happening."

"Will do."

Effi and Annaliese arrived a few moments later, and duly

grimaced at the state of Russell's head. After Annaliese had cast a nurse's eye over the bullet wound and pronounced it "better than it looked," she and Thomas set off back to Dahlem in the car.

"Good film?" Russell asked, after running through what had happened and what he's learnt from Luke Smith.

"Not bad," Effi said, "but hardly what we should be talking about. That bullet was only an inch away from killing you."

"You could see it like that," Russell admitted, "or you could say it was only an inch away from missing me altogether."

"Fool."

"A lucky one, though."

"Hmm. I'm staying the night in case someone else comes to finish you off."

"That would be nice, but I think I already have a guardian angel outside."

"He looked sleepy to me, and in any case," she added, lowering her voice to a whisper, "are you sure you know which side BOB is on? It was them who sent you out there."

"You have a point."

THEY SURVIVED THE NIGHT. WHEN morning came Russell's head still throbbed if he moved it, but his mind felt clear enough, and the attending doctor agreed he could go home, provided he took it easy for the next few days and came back if anything changed for the worst. When their CIA guard offered them both a lift home Russell allowed himself only a moment or two of paranoid hesitation before accepting.

"I assume I won't be expected at work on Monday," he said when they finally drew up outside the house on Vogelsangstrasse.

"I'll tell them," Smith replied. "I think getting shot in the line of duty warrants a few days off. You might even get a purple heart." Watching the car drive off towards Föhrenweg Russell realised he couldn't tell whether or not the man was being serious.

Later, sitting in the sunlit garden, he found himself wondering what sort of investigation into the shooting would be underway. He had killed a man after all, albeit apparently in self-defence. Had the Americans temporarily adopted him as one of their own, and closed ranks against any local interference? Or would the German police have more to say in the matter?

More to the point, why had this Russian tried to kill him? And would whoever had sent him hire a replacement?

He would have to be on his guard. In the meantime, he had promised to rescue Lotte, and was now in no position to do so. He supposed the wound would look less obvious in a few days, but at present it was depressingly livid, and invited attention. And a bandage, given the current situation across the city border, would mark him out as someone who had challenged the police or the military. Crossing over would be far too risky. For him and Lotte.

They hadn't heard from her since Thursday, which hopefully meant she was still safe at her friend's flat. She was supposed to ring tomorrow. As far as they could judge from the reports on RIAS, the situation in Berlin was more or less back to normal, at least in terms of how people were behaving. What they were thinking and feeling was another matter. Outside the capital snuffing out the embers of resistance was clearly still a work of progress, but in Berlin at least the expectation was that everyone would turn up for work on Monday morning.

An ideal day for someone who looked half-normal to sneak in and out of the closed Eastern sector, Russell thought. It was a shame he no longer fit the bill.

THE WALDBÜHNE WAS A GIANT amphitheatre in Charlottenburg which had been built for Hitler's Olympics. With more than twenty thousand seats, it was now mostly used as an entertainment venue. The huge arcs of outdoor seats and sunken stage overlooked by tree-covered slopes made it look like Berlin's version of the Hollywood Bowl.

That Saturday evening it was hosting a Berlinale extravaganza. A well-known dance orchestra essayed a selection of film themes with help from a few famous singers, then celebrity guests were introduced to the crowd. Everyone was invited to light matchstick fireworks, including Gary Cooper, who was sitting four rows in front of Effi and Annaliese, flanked by his wife and daughter.

After all that, the chosen film seemed disappointing. Otto Preminger had made two versions of *Die Jungfrau auf dem Dach* simultaneously, one in English and one in German, with two different but overlapping casts. As far as Effi was concerned one would have been too many. The script was risqué for the times, but the irritating characters and silly story soon had Effi's thoughts turning elsewhere, to Lotte and the business of getting her out.

There was no way John could go. Even if Annaliese had been convinced that he was fully over the concussion—which she wasn't—there was no way he could play the Scarlet Pimpernel in East Berlin looking like a war casualty. Someone else would have to rescue Lotte, and the only real candidate was herself. The prospect didn't faze her—she'd spent the last two years of the war doing much the same job, escorting wanted people across Berlin for Erik Aslund's escape network. But in wartime people had different expectations, and she realised that persuading the others wouldn't be easy. No matter how sane and intelligent men might seem, most of them were still trapped in ridiculous notions of what women could or should do.

John was different, but he still wouldn't want her to go. He wouldn't doubt her ability, just be terrified of her having bad luck. He would feel the way she would if he were the one going.

Would being famous help or harm her if she was caught? That, she thought, could go either way. As a German she surely couldn't be shot as a foreign spy.

Coming back, two women would look less suspicious. And with her makeup training she could do a much better job of altering Lotte's appearance than John could.

She had to admit that she didn't look forward to Gerhard's tunnel.

"The film's over," Annaliese told her. "You can wake up now."

"I wasn't asleep, I was thinking."

"About what?"

Effi told her.

Annaliese wasn't surprised. During and after the war the two of them had shared some adventures, including one particularly scary confrontation with penicillin smugglers. "I could come with you," Annaliese suggested. "I know the area."

"So do I," Effi retorted. "I had an aunt who lived in Luisenstadt. And you have two young children who need you. Plus, if a plus was needed, you're a citizen of the DDR. Helping someone accused of sedition evade capture would probably count as treason."

"True, but they won't be charging you with trespassing."

"I know, but who else can go? Don't mention this to Gerhard," she added. "I'm going to give myself twenty-four hours to think it through before I make any decision."

RUSSELL HAD SPENT THE DAY recuperating and wondering what to do. A combination of hat, scarf, and makeup might hide his wound, but anyone wrapped up that well on a warm summer evening would be bound to attract attention. There was no way he could cross the border in the next few days.

Which meant the other option had to be considered, or at least kept open. Patolichev's forty-eight hours were up that evening, and the Russian would surely be calling again. Indeed, he had only just finished coaching Thomas—"Ask for more time, tell him I'm flat out in bed with something"—when the telephone rang downstairs.

A few minutes later Thomas returned to relay Patolichev's message. The matter was indeed very urgent, but the Russian was willing to wait another two days. "He didn't sound surprised that you were out of commission," Thomas added. "And he didn't ask why."

"He already knew," Russell thought out loud. Which raised any number of questions.

Mrs. Luddwitz Visits the DDR

Effi went into town on Sunday, first to have lunch with an old theatre friend, and then to attend a matinee showing at one of the festival venues. She arrived home just before five and took Russell up to their bedroom to win his support for her going in to bring Lotte out. Laying out her plan, she watched his face go through the expected gamut, shock giving way to concern, and that to resigned acceptance. "You don't have to like it," she told him. "I don't like it. But you have to back me up or Thomas and Hanna won't agree."

"Okay," he said with a sigh, taking her hand.

"Lotte's supposed to be ringing between eight and nine, so we should talk to everyone now."

They went down to gather the others.

Effi was all business, and Russell realised that this was the first time he'd actually seen the wartime resistance organiser of his imagination. Once Thomas and Hanna's flat rejection had been gradually whittled away, Ströhm was able to offer further encouragement.

"When we were thinking of John going in, I imagined he'd use the same route as I did, but there were hardly any trains running that day, and everyone had their eyes on what was happening up in the open. Things will have changed since then, and stepping off a platform unobserved may be impossible. But there may be an alternative." He explained about the first shaft he'd come to, the one on the other side of the sector border which he hadn't bothered to check. "If that one opens too, and isn't overseen, then you'd only have a hundred-metre walk along the tunnel."

"The shorter the better," Effi agreed.

"So what I suggest," Ströhm continued, "is a recce tonight. If Thomas will drive me up the Tiergarten, I'll go and check the other shaft. Any problem, and I'll be back in the park before anyone can catch me," he added, looking at Annaliese.

"But I'll go in tomorrow," Effi said. "Up the shaft on the eastern side if that's possible, using the station if it isn't. When would be the best time?" she asked Ströhm.

He thought about it. "We need to get you out of the tunnel around ten, when it's almost dark. A five-minute walk to Potsdamer Platz, fifteen on the U-Bahn to Schönhauser Platz, then a five-minute walk to the flat. Allow a ten-minute wait for the train and you should be there in under forty minutes. Ten minutes getting Lotte ready, and you should be back at the shaft before eleven-thirty."

"Sounds good," Effi said, looking round the table. None of the others looked like they shared her assessment.

LOTTE RANG SOON AFTER EIGHT. "She couldn't believe it when I told her the plan," Thomas reported back, "and she doesn't want Effi to put herself in danger. But I managed to convince her," he said, with an apologetic glance at Effi. "She gave me some details to help you find the flat, and said she'll be ready to go whenever you get there."

TWO HOURS LATER, THOMAS PULLED the car over on Tiergartenstrasse, a few metres short of Kemperplatz and the border. After letting an excited Groucho out of the back, he and Ströhm walked into the wooded park and headed east towards the shaft in the bushes. The sun was down, but it was still quite light and there were a few other walkers visible in the distance.

It was good to be out in the world, Ströhm thought, after days of not leaving the house, though this would not have been the place he would have chosen to enjoy an hour of freedom. This time he had brought gardening gloves to hold off the brambles, and a blackout-adapted torch for tunnelling through the undergrowth and climbing the unexplored shaft on the other side of the tracks. Leaving Thomas on a bench and Groucho sniffing his heart out, he managed to pinpoint his previous point of egress, and worked his way painfully through the thicket until his hand was on the concrete cover.

Pushing the lid aside he manoeuvred himself into a face-down position with his lower legs above the shaft, then levered himself backwards and down until his feet found the ladder. After a short pause to catch his breath he started the descent, pausing when he heard an approaching train to watch the light from its passing windows flicker beneath him. It was heading north, which meant the nearside track would be clear for several minutes.

Reaching the bottom and sticking his head out of the refuge, he could see red rail lights moving through the station and into the siding beyond, where the driver would walk back through the train before drawing it into the opposite platform. Confident he had enough time, Ströhm walked briskly south down the centre of the northbound track, looking for the shaft on the eastern side. When it hove into view he carefully stepped his way across the live and dead rails and started climbing the ladder, taking out his torch around halfway up and pointing its thin beam at the cover above. Once within reach of the latter, he tried a gentle push.

The cover moved. Bracing himself with his elbow against both sides of the shaft he pushed it upwards with both hands until he could move it sideways. The stars were now visible, which at least meant he hadn't come up underneath a Soviet tank. Lifting his eyes above the rim of the hole, he found himself only twenty metres away from the once-busy Ebertstrasse, now forlorn and empty under dim and widely spaced streetlights. In the opposite direction, the wasteland that had once housed Hitler's old and new Chancelleries stretched away into blackness, the silhouette of the old propaganda ministry on the other side of Wilhelmstrasse barely visible against the cloudy night sky. There was neither person nor vehicle in sight, and only a slightly brighter glow above Potsdamer Platz a few hundred metres to the south offered any proof that the DDR was still alive. Which could hardly have been better. As far as he could see, Effi's only potential problems were being spotted coming out of the shaft and a chance encounter with police. With care, the first was avoidable; the second would be mostly a matter of luck.

Ströhm pulled the cover back into place, descended the ladder, and checked the tunnel. The train he had watched arrive was now moving towards him, and as he waited for it to go by, he realised that there was nothing to stop him bringing Effi this far.

As the noise and lights of the train receded into the distance, he walked briskly back to the other shaft. Another climb, another crawl through brambles, and he was back with Thomas and Groucho in the rapidly darkening park.

"Better than I hoped," he said in response to Thomas's enquiring look.

"That's good," Thomas said. "Groucho and I had a minor set-to with a schnauzer."

MONDAY MORNING, EFFI VISITED THE festival office in search of German actresses, and eventually found one who knew where a decent theatrical shop could be found. A cab took to the Fehrbelliner Strasse location, and she spent twenty minutes choosing and buying the makeup she needed to convincingly age herself and turn Lotte into a closer approximation of the face on Russell's stolen identity paper.

She was nervous about the evening ahead, but that, as she knew from wartime experience, was only par for the course. Once she was over the border, nerves would be the least of her worries.

NOT LONG AFTER EFFI HAD set off for the shops, a jeep screeched to a halt outside the house and its GI driver hurried to the front door with a letter for Russell. "My dad knows Jack Slaney," the soldier explained, "and Jack thought the army post would be quicker." Refusing a cup of something hot, he almost bounced his way back to the jeep on spring-heeled feet, reminding Russell what it was like to be young.

He took the envelope up to their bedroom and slit it open.

"Dear John," Slaney wrote, "I've been doing what you asked, looking into Greer Holleman. Here's what I've found out, mostly from official records and contacts. Some of it you doubtless know already, but I thought it was safer not to assume too much.

"The man was born in Little Rock, Arkansas, in 1905. His father, Jake, walked out when the boy was two, and it doesn't look like he ever came back. His mother, Florence, never remarried or had another child, and everything points to them doting on each other. When he eventually moved to LA he took her along and cared for her until she died. As far as I can tell, he never had a bad word to say about her.

"Anyway. Florence ran an upmarket boardinghouse in downtown Little Rock, and she made enough money to eventually send Greer to the state university and then law school. After passing the bar in 1930, he was taken on by a local practice. If you want to know how successful he was, and what sort of cases he handled, you'll need to seek out an old colleague.

"More relevant to your inquiry, I think, a German exchange student named Rudolfe Ehler was a resident at the boardinghouse from September 1932 to the following July, and it seems that he and Greer became good friends. Rudolfe's sister Heidi joined him there for the last few weeks.

"Greer spent the next two summers at their house in Berlin. Whether as Rudolfe's friend, Heidi's boyfriend, or both, I have no idea. I assume these were just vacations, but who knows? He was on the ship back from the second trip when he met Beckett Lettson and his daughter Gwen, whom he married a year or so later. I can't find any record of Holleman meeting either Rudolfe or Heidi again, but he did visit Berlin twice more, in 1938 and 1940, apparently on business. The second trip seems to have been all about a preemptive severing of the company's ties to the Nazi state. He could have seen Rudolfe or Heidi while he was there, but there's no reason to think he did.

"Rudolfe died in Russian captivity, probably in 1947, but as far I know Heidi's still alive. I imagine that seeking her out will be easier from Berlin than from here. The same goes for any official traces of what Greer was actually doing in those two summers he spent with the Ehlers. Last but not least, if you have a strong stomach, the local press in Little Rock might have some useful stuff on file. Maybe a stopover on your way back to La-La-Land.

"Say hi to Berlin for me.

"All the best, Jack."

REALISING THAT A PARTY OF four adults roaming this end of the park at nightfall might raise suspicion, Effi and Ströhm left Thomas and Russell in the car on Lennéstrasse and strolled arm in arm across the wet grass towards her illicit entrance to the DDR. As far as Effi could see the recent shower had sent any late walkers home and cleared the Tiergarten out for the night.

At the edge of the bushes Effi put on the stiff theatrical mask she'd bought that day, thinking it would protect her face from suspicious-looking scratches. A wise move, she told herself, as she began crawling along through the wet undergrowth in Ströhm's wake. She had never enjoyed much of a relationship with the plant world, and this, she decided as the thicket grew ever thicker, was probably why.

Eventually they emerged into the slightly more open space which Ströhm had thought to create with Hanna's secateurs on his last visit, and Effi took off the mask. As she contorted her body to follow him down the shaft, she had her first real misgivings—had she grown too old for this sort of caper?

It was too late to worry about that now. The tunnel below proved brighter than she'd expected, lit by the warm glow of the Potsdamer Platz platform lights away to their right. The live electrified rails were frightening, but as they patiently waited for the departing train to pass, she told herself sternly that it was simply a matter of stepping across them. There was no reason to trip and fall.

And she didn't. The train having passed, Effi followed Ströhm along the centre of that track, and then across the remaining rails to the bottom of the other shaft. Near the top of the iron ladder, she hung there in the darkness as Ströhm carefully moved the cover away, thinking "Mrs. Luddwitz Visits the DDR" might make a good future episode.

"All clear," he said softly, and clambered out.

She climbed out behind him into the twilight. The scene was just as Ströhm had described it earlier, a wide stretch of no-man's-land between the fence and road that formed the border and a row of war-ruined buildings that were still awaiting reconstruction eight years on. An area that was walked through rather than lived in.

"I'll wait for you down below," Ströhm reaffirmed. "And don't forget to replace the cover." After lowering himself back into the shaft he offered a smile, which she assumed was meant to be encouraging, but felt more like "Why the hell are we letting you do this?"

After dragging the cover back into place, she took another quick look around and started walking. The darkness to her left offered concealment, but walking over broken ground would probably be treacherous, and almost certainly slower. She set off down the obviously little-used pavement, hoping to reach Potsdamer Platz without meeting anyone. So far, she thought, the only crime she'd committed was illegal entry. With any luck they'd just kick her out again.

Voss Strasse was now just a flatter ribbon of the wasteland, but as she crossed it, more lights swam into view far away to the east. Potsdamer Platz was now in sight, a few figures moving in the square that had once pulsed with life. Now it looked utterly forlorn, still bedecked with war's ruins, an abandoned corner of the Soviet sector. The one relic of the past was the odour of grilling bratwurst wafting from a mobile kitchen, which almost overwhelmed her with nostalgia.

There were probably about twenty people in a space which had usually hosted hundreds, and the only uniforms she could see belonged to a pair of policemen on the farther side, chatting away beneath the arched façade of the wrecked Potsdam Station. She walked briskly towards the subway entrance, and hurried down the steps to the U-Bahn booking hall, where, after a mercifully brief moment of confusion as to which coins were which—why hadn't she asked Gerhard to talk her through the recent changes?—she managed to purchase a ticket. Another flight of steps brought her to the platform and a train that was primed to leave, the signal turning green as she reached the rear carriage.

The doors swished shut behind her, causing a fellow passenger to remark, "Just in time." She returned his smile and slowly walked down to the other end of the carriage, hoping her aging makeup wasn't looking too obvious under the lights. There were no uniforms on view, just two more lone men, both reading newspapers, and a young couple who only had eyes for each other. Five days had passed since the events of the previous Wednesday, and at first sight it looked as if things were more or less back to normal. Only the lovers looked happy with life, but at least there wasn't any blood on the carriage floor.

So far, so good, she thought. Even if a posse of police swarmed aboard at the next stop, she should be all right. Her papers weren't hers, but they were genuine.

No one got on at Kaiserhof, which she saw had been renamed Thälmannplatz after the old KPD leader. Four more stops and eight more minutes and she'd be back aboveground. She knew the streets were no safer than the U-Bahn, but it felt like they were.

If she was stopped, the papers wouldn't betray her, but there was always the chance that she'd give herself away. That was the way it had usually happened to others in the war, a slip of the tongue or the wrong look in the eyes.

If they found out she wasn't who the papers said she was, she'd really be in trouble. She could hardly claim to have come across when the border was still open and been stranded on the wrong side ever since. Not with her picture in the West Berlin papers attending various festival events during the days in question. So how had she crossed the closed border? And even more to the point—why? She had played dumb curiosity often enough in her early career, but no one would buy it from her now.

The answer, of course, was not to get caught.

Spittelmarkt came and went; her stop was the next one. Then she would have a ten-minute walk through darkened streets to Lotte's building. She might have exaggerated a little when she said she knew the area—an actress friend had lived near St. Michael's Church, but that had been in the early thirties, and if any city's geography had been utterly transformed in the last twenty years it was surely Berlin's.

At Märkisches Museum she was one of only three people

leaving the train. Reaching the street above, she realised the relief she felt at being back out in the open had no factual basis—the streets would be at least as well-patrolled as the U-Bahn.

She had memorised her walking route as a succession of street names, relying on her proficiency at learning scripts over her lack of such when it came to reading maps.

Emerging onto Wallstrasse, she almost walked into a uniformed cop standing close to the station entrance. "Sorry," she murmured, and got a smile in reply. Now he would recognise her when she came back.

Assuming she did. Effi took a few deep breaths to calm herself as she started down Wallstrasse, noting how seedy the once-prosperous buildings looked. After a minute or so she turned right onto the equally shabby Inselstrasse. A car went by in the opposite direction, but there were no pedestrians on either sidewalk. Had they mistimed things? They'd hoped for sparsely populated streets, not completely empty ones, where anyone keen to check papers had only her to pick on.

As she walked on, it was only the street names that offered any guide. The first few streets, with their seemingly random mixture of new apartment blocks, untouched ruins, and old buildings in various states of repair, looked completely unfamiliar, but after a while she began to have flashes of recognition. Neanderstrasse looked much like she had remembered it, with several bars doing good business, and myriad lights in the apartments above. On this busier sidewalk she took greater care with aging her walk, just to be on the safe side. Her face had been well enough known by the cinema-going public before the war, and fans had a distressing habit of popping up when you least wanted them to.

Turning south on Schmidstrasse, she could see the dome of St. Michael's church tower, one of the few that had survived the bombing. Lotte's street was this side of the church and its grounds, a turn to the left and a turn to the right.

The bustle of Neanderstrasse was gone, the street she turned into deserted, save for a young man lighting a cigarette while his dog fouled the pavement. He gave her a cursory look and wrote her off as old.

Josephstrasse—the street where Lotte was staying—was next. Effi was mere metres away from the intersection when the sound of an approaching car behind her set off inner alarm bells and forced a change of plan—rather than turning up the street she stood waiting at the corner as if intending to cross. As the black vehicle swept round the corner and across her line of sight, she saw several heads silhouetted inside, one of them turned her way.

The car moved up Lotte's street towards what felt like its inevitable destination—the furthest block on the right-hand side where Lotte's friend had her apartment. As the car squealed to a halt out front, two men almost jumped from its doors and hurried inside.

What should she do? The young man and dog were almost at Schmidstrasse and turned the corner as she watched. Halfway up Lotte's street a bombsite full of bushes offered a better vantage point, but the risk of being spotted by the man or men still in the car was too great, so she stayed at her corner, knowing that might also look suspicious to any Ulbricht devotee staring out of a window.

In the event she didn't have long to wait. The two men suddenly reappeared with a woman in tow, and even from this far away Effi could recognise Lotte. She'd arrived a few minutes too late, she thought, and could almost hear John reply that if she'd come two minutes earlier the Stasi would have got her too.

In any case, there was not a thing she could do, and standing there in shock was liable to get her arrested.

She started walking briskly back the way she had come, thinking about the Stasi and the Gestapo. The DDR's secret police employed many former employees of Hitler's, if the Western newspapers could be believed. She wondered how a man like Gerhard Ströhm could serve a regime that used torture. Perhaps the fact that he'd left was her answer.

On the busier Neanderstrasse she brought the older woman's gait back into use. A man outside a bar wolf-whistled at her nevertheless, making her wonder how many steins it took before age became irrelevant.

She was approaching Märkisches Museum station when she remembered the smiling cop. Would he find it odd that she'd turn up again at this time of night? Should she seek out a different station? Getting lost was the worst thing she could do.

Seeing the cop was still there, she hesitated, but then took the cover offered by a man headed in the same direction, walking close enough that the cop might assume they were together. The man gave her a strange look, but by then they were on their way down the steps, and a "what the hell do you want?" look simply left him shaking his head.

His train came almost immediately, while the wait for hers seemed interminable. Only two got on and two got off when it arrived—the DDR's Berlin clearly went early to bed. Judging by what she'd seen it was probably the most exciting place to be.

The journey back to Potsdamer Platz was uneventful, giving her plenty of time to dwell on the cost of failure. Lotte would almost certainly end up in prison and might even face something worse. How would she cope? How would Thomas and Hanna?

Back aboveground, her intention of leaving the still-populated square as quickly as possible was thwarted by the sight of two men in uniform heading in the same direction. A regular patrol or just two mates heading home? Maybe two men seeking sex in the ruins of Hitler's old garden. Whatever it was, she couldn't afford to follow them too closely.

But with the bratwurst man pulling down his shutter her last excuse for staying in the emptying square was gone, so she started walking anyway, hoping the two men wouldn't slow down or stop. In the event they turned right onto the remains of Voss Strasse, and she was able to increase her pace towards the shaft and safety. Too much so, in fact, because the few lights on Ebert-strasse were no longer burning, and she walked right past her way out in the darkness. Only a loudly whispered "Effi" stopped her in her tracks.

It was Ströhm, his head sticking out of the shaft like some unsprung jack-in-the-box. "I thought it must be you," he said as she walked back towards him.

She wondered what he'd have done if she'd been someone else.

"No Charlotte," he said, stating the obvious.

"I watched her being taken away," she said, taking one last look at the forbidden half of a city she'd lived and worked in for twenty-five years. "Let's get out of here."

An Expendable Girl

As he and Effi waited for the others at the kitchen table, Russell was thinking that the hours he and Thomas had spent on Lennéstrasse that evening had been some of the strangest of his life. They had sat there in the front seats talking about everything except what was actually happening. They had trawled through almost thirty years of sharing their experiences as husbands and fathers and citizens, as football fans, drinkers, and lovers of books. At one point they had laughed so hard the car seemed to shake, but they had not talked about the danger that Effi and Lotte were in, or losses that might turn their lives upside-down.

He had never felt closer to Thomas, and the wave of relief which swept through his body when he saw Effi returning with Ströhm was swiftly succeeded by the pang of sorrow which accompanied Lotte's absence.

Now they had to decide what to do. Thomas and an understandably distraught Hanna had needed some time with each other, and Ströhm's children, no doubt aware that something was wrong, had needed the reassurance of a bedtime story.

The other four adults arrived together, Thomas looking grim, Hanna still mopping up tears. Ströhm was also clearly upset. He was probably feeling responsible on his regime's behalf, Russell thought, which was as absurd as it was understandable—until recently, Lotte had been a much less ambivalent supporter of the DDR than he had.

"Effi and I have been talking," Russell began, intent on making it clear that he was speaking for them both. "We do have another way of getting Lotte out. I was hoping we wouldn't have to use it, but beggars can't be choosers. The two of us have something some people on the other side want very badly, and I think there's a good chance that they'd be willing to do an exchange. It won't be straightforward, because it's probably the Stasi who have Lotte, and it's definitely Soviet Military Intelligence—the GRU—who want what we have, but I'm assuming that the Soviets will be willing and able to pull rank."

"You can count on that," Ströhm said. "But what are you talking about? What do you have?"

"We have a film. Or, more precisely, a knowledge of what's on it—we don't know where the actual film itself is hidden away. It's the one the GRU tried to get from us five years ago," he told Ströhm, "the night they nearly killed Effi, Rosa, and me, the night you saved us."

"But you burned that with the car."

"There were two copies." Russell paused. "For this to make sense to everyone here, I need to go back to the beginning." He smiled. "Once upon a time, I was spending New Year's Eve at a hotel in Danzig—now there's a name from the past. 1939 was about an hour old when a Russian named Yevgeny Shchepkin knocked on the door of my room, and I made the mistake of letting him in. He worked for one of the Soviet security services—I was never sure which, either then or later—and he had an innocent-sounding proposition, one which would earn me some much-needed money and should upset the Nazis, which were both things I wanted to do. I managed to convince myself that it was just one piece of work, but of course it wasn't. Still, the various jobs I did for them over the next few years didn't trouble my conscience—in Europe at least, the Communists were offering the only serious challenge to the Nazis. And it was the comrades who got me out of Germany in 1941, and probably saved me from the ax.

"I was free of the Soviets for the next three years, but then I got re-entangled—I won't bore you with the details of my subsequent dealings but suffice it to say that by 1948 Shchepkin and I had managed to create a situation where both Moscow and Washington believed that we were their double agents. And I was supposedly sifting through defectors for the Americans down on Föhrenweg that autumn when one of them told me about a film in his possession that compromised Stalin's police chief Lavrenti Beria. I managed to keep this from my American bosses, and eventually got hold of the film, which Shchepkin and I then used to blackmail Beria. We threatened him with exposure if he wouldn't let us walk away. We told him that if anyone on the list we gave him—which included all our families—was to die in suspicious circumstances, then the film would be automatically released into the public domain, but that if we were left alone, it would remain forever hidden. When Beria agreed to those terms, it meant the end of our working for the Soviets, which in turn made us useless to the Americans. Shchepkin was already terminally ill, but he'd got his wife and daughter out. And I was free of the lot of them.

"That deal has lasted five years, but Beria's enemies in the Soviet leadership, who have always known of the film's existence but not what's actually on it, have now decided that it might help them bring him down."

"You still haven't told us what's actually on the film," Thomas said.

Russell took a deep breath, remembering the horror which he, Effi, and Shchepkin had seen projected onto the living room wall in Carmerstrasse. "Do you remember Sonja Strehl?" he asked.

"The actress who killed herself," Annaliese answered.

"Yes. She had a fifteen-year-old sister named Nina. Beria had the two of them brought to his rooms at Karlshorst, where he raped them both and murdered Nina. Sonja was spared for some reason but killed herself soon after."

"And the rapes and murder were all filmed?" Thomas exclaimed. "Why, for God's sake?"

"Someone forgot to turn the hidden cameras off, and one young Russian technician—the one I met sifting defectors—realised that the film could buy a much better life in the West for him and his Czech girlfriend. It didn't—Beria's men caught up with them—but by then Shchepkin and I had got hold of it."

"And this is the man I hoped would soften the Soviet line," Ströhm said bitterly.

"Maybe he means to," Russell said. "Being a psychopathic shit doesn't blind you to what needs changing. But for us, here, Lotte has to matter more than who gets to strut around in the Kremlin."

"Of course," Ströhm agreed.

"If you no longer have the film, what exactly do the GRU want?" Thomas interjected.

"Signed affidavits from Effi and me testifying to the contents. Effi particularly, because she's a public figure with no obvious political ax to grind. They presumably think that finding out what Beria did—and the knowledge that somewhere out there proof of his crime still exists—will be enough to swing the leadership contest the way they want."

"There must be some real risk attached to this," Thomas observed, "or you and Effi wouldn't have opted for this evening's rescue mission."

"There is. If we give the GRU what they want, and they somehow fuck things up and Beria comes out on top, we'll all be in danger. Once he's in sole control, it won't much matter to him if the film comes out. He'll swear blind it's a fake, and there'll be no one in any position of power to say that isn't so. After which he can take his time coming after the people who dared to blackmail him, and everyone we put on the list.

"If the GRU *doesn't* fuck up, and Beria loses the succession struggle, I imagine they'll kill him. But even that might not be the end of our troubles, because they still won't want the film in the public domain. Beria was Stalin's right-hand man for almost twenty years, and having a rapist and child-murderer on the Red Square podium is not a good look. So, in their ideal world, we and the film would cease to exist. As things stand, the fear of triggering its release should deter them from coming after us, but people do stupid things."

There was a silence lasting almost a minute.

"So do we take the risk?" Thomas asked. "Obviously I would and Hanna would, but . . ."

"I think we should," Effi spoke up. "The threat to Lotte seems more real and more urgent than the threat to the rest of us."

"I agree," Russell said. "And I'm sure Paul will too." He turned to Ströhm. "Gerhard, you have no stake in this, but I'd value your opinion."

Ströhm thought about his answer. "It's a sad thing to say, but now that the Stasi have her, the Soviets are our only hope."

"Agreed?" Russell asked everyone.

"Agreed," was the unanimous answer.

UP IN THEIR BEDROOM, RUSSELL asked Effi if she was okay.

"I think so," she said. "It was like old times in a way, but a gentler version, if you know what I mean. Back then, you knew that the Gestapo would want you to suffer before they killed you, and that made the whole business both terrifying and absurdly exhilarating. Tonight . . . honestly, stepping across the live rails was what frightened me most." She sighed. "I just wish I'd gotten to Lotte an hour earlier."

"We'll get her out. Meanwhile . . ." He handed her Jack Slaney's letter. "It came this morning."

She read it through, her frown deepening as she did so. "We still don't know why he's so interested in us," she said on finishing, "but if it's all about the German connection, presumably Heidi will know."

"If she's still alive, and willing to talk. But Lotte first, and I'm going back down to write out what I remember of the wretched film. If Patolichev's willing to deal, I want to be ready."

"I should help."

"You should sleep."

FIRST THING TUESDAY MORNING, WHILE Thomas phoned his solicitor friend and Effi anxiously waited, Russell walked down to the phone kiosks at Dahlem-Dorf U-Bahn station and dialled the number which Patolichev had given him during their last conversation. The fact that the all-city telephone system was still operational was something of a gift, and one he had no wish to squander by using a private phone which might be monitored.

Russell's Russian had grown rusty through lack of use, but his name was all he needed to get himself put through to Patolichev. A good sign, he thought. They were still eager. Desperate, even.

If so, Patolichev was not going to admit it. "Mr. John Russell," he said. "This is surprise," he went on in English. "No more hospital, yes. You discharge."

"I do. And I am willing to give you what you want," he added in Russian.

"Mmm. I hear noises. You are on a public telephone?"

"I am."

"That is good. A secure line, always."

"Most definitely."

"And you have what I asked for—affidavits with witnessed signatures? Yours and your wife's?"

"I will have them later today. But first there is the matter of what I want from you."

"I did not agree to give you anything."

"No, but you will. My friend's daughter Charlotte Schade was arrested last night in East Berlin. At an apartment in Joseph Strasse. By State Security, we think, but perhaps another DDR apparat. I will only give you the affidavits in exchange for her."

The ensuing silence lasted quite a long time, but Russell waited it out.

"What was she arrested for?" Patolichev eventually asked.

"Sedition, I think."

"Oh, Mr. Russell, this is not good."

"She's young and idealistic, and she hasn't killed anybody."

Another silence.

"This is the price," Russell patiently said.

A disapproving grunt from Patolichev. "I will see what is possible."

"I will call you again at two o'clock," Russell told him and hung up. The fish was on the hook, he thought. Lotte could have castrated Ulbricht for all Patolichev cared.

"THE TWO OF YOU HAVE an appointment in half an hour," Thomas told him when he got back. "His name's Wilhelm Dartsch, and I've known him since school. A bit old-fashioned, but a stickler for the rules—I'm sure as I can be that he won't betray a client's confidence."

"Where's his office?"

"On Hohenzollerndamm. You can take the car."

With Russell driving, Effi had time to read his account of the events caught on film, and the accompanying explanation of how the film had come into their possession. "I don't think you missed anything," she eventually said in a strained voice. "I still find it hard to accept that anyone could do such a thing," she added more calmly a few seconds later.

"I've never liked the idea of a person being intrinsically evil," Russell said, "but men like Beria make you wonder."

After parking the car in a side street, they walked round to Wilhelm Dartsch's office, where the solicitor was waiting with a friendly smile. "Thomas has often spoken of you," he told Russell, "and of course I know you by reputation," he said to Effi. "Now where is this document?"

Russell passed it over and watched the solicitor's face turn grimmer as he read it.

After he was done, Dartsch lowered the papers carefully onto his desk. "I don't know what to say," was his initial reaction. "I mean, I remember Sonja Strehl. I didn't know her personally of course, but . . ."

"It's a shocking thing," Effi told him. "We were shocked when we first saw the film."

"We just need you to witness our signatures," Russell pointed out gently.

"Of course, but a crime has been committed."

"Indeed. And these documents should ensure that the perpetrator is punished."

"Are you certain of that?"

"As certain as I can be. Herr Dartsch, these documents do not constitute proof of a crime. The only proof has been locked away in a secret location by someone who's been dead for five years. So taking this to our police here in West Berlin would be utterly pointless."

"And you and your wife could always claim that you had made the whole story up," Dartsch said with the faintest of smiles.

"I wish we had," Russell told him.

Dartsch reached for his pen. "I don't know you, but I do know Thomas. I will not go to the police."

WHEN RUSSELL CALLED THE GRU again at two, Patolichev wasted no time humming and hawing. "As a gesture of respect to a fraternal party, the SED has agreed to release Charlotte Schade," he announced.

Or perhaps because they've been told to, Russell resisted retorting.

"Do you have what we want?" Patolichev ploughed on.

"I do."

"That is good. Please be in the buffet at Zoo Station at seven o'clock. A pretty young woman will come up to you and say she's afraid you'll miss the beginning of the film."

"How will she know me?"

"From studying the many photographs in your file, Mr. Russell."

"Ah."

"She will bring you to the exchange."

"I'll be there."

This time it was Patolichev who cut the connection. Russell walked slowly back to Vogelsangstrasse, knowing that Thomas would be upset not to be coming with him. He also wondered where the GRU were planning to make the exchange. Somewhere discreet, he hoped, because he didn't want BOB to be watching.

Where else could it be but one of the border crossings? Keeping them all under round-the-clock observation would surely not be possible, and the Soviets would pick their spot accordingly. They wouldn't want Russell arrested and questioned.

Still, it paid to imagine the worst. If the Americans witnessed the exchange, how was he going to explain it? No one would believe that Lotte's release was a random act of Soviet kindness, so what had he given her captors in return?

THE GIRL WAS MORE THAN pretty, but she hid it well with straggly hair and no makeup, mismatched clothes and a marked reluctance to smile. There was a hint of perfume though, when she leaned across to give him a peck on the cheek and deliver the prearranged line. "Who is this?" she whispered, looking past Russell at Thomas, who had insisted on coming.

"The girl's father," Russell explained.

"What girl?"

"The one we are exchanging for these," he said, letting her see the envelope in his inside pocket.

"I was told only one."

"I only come if he does," Russell insisted, hoping she didn't call his bluff.

She might not have known about Lotte, but the quickness with which she gave in suggested her bosses had made sure she knew how important the documents were. "Okay," she said. "But you must keep your distance," she told Thomas. "Two men and one woman will attract attention."

"I will," Thomas agreed.

Two minutes later they were all on the eastbound U-Bahn platform, Thomas five metres away from the others. A city checkpoint, Russell assumed from the direction of travel, rather than one of the more isolated crossings between West Berlin and the rest of the DDR.

Changing at Gleisdreieck narrowed the options still further, to somewhere southeast of the old city centre, and when they stayed on the train to the end of the truncated line, he knew it had to be either the Uberbaumbrücke over the Spree or the next crossing south at the Landwehrkanal.

It was the former. The girl—she couldn't have been more than eighteen—took Russell's arm and guided him out of the station and across the wide and deserted Schlesischestrasse, another major artery rendered minor by the city's division. On the far side a small alley of derelict workshops ran beneath the viaduct approach to the bridge, and just before they reached the river the girl took a quick look round before ushering Russell and Thomas through a rickety door.

It was dark inside, but the girl's torch illuminated another door. This one was sturdy and boasted a shiny new padlock to which she had the key. Once they were through and the lock reengaged, she led them to the foot of a long iron staircase which Russell presumed led up to the tracks.

It did. The sky was still light, and off to their right the rails on the bridge's upper deck stretched out across the dark river beneath the war-decapitated towers, the sector border now marked by nothing more solid than a concertina steel fence. Up here they couldn't be seen from the deck beneath, which carried the road and boasted a fully manned checkpoint. Patolichev had chosen a good spot for an exchange, and Russell could only hope that the Russian had nothing else in mind.

There were figures coming towards them. Three men and one woman, all dressed in what looked like anonymous workers' clothes.

"We stay here," the girl told Thomas. "You go," she ordered Russell.

Thomas nodded his acquiescence, and Russell walked on towards the makeshift barrier, wondering again whether not coming armed had been wise. There was some reassurance in knowing how useless the affidavits would be if his corpse ended up in the Spree, but not nearly enough.

The woman was Lotte. Two men each had an arm, holding her back as the third man came forward.

"Colonel Patolichev," the latter introduced himself. He was younger than Russell expected, probably still in his thirties. The smile was less real than the worry in his eyes.

Lotte was not smiling and hadn't yet given any sign that she recognised him. Had she been drugged?

"She is fine," Patolichev said, seeing the look on Russell's face. "She just needs a good sleep. You have the affidavits?"

Russell pulled them from his pocket but ignored the hand reaching over the barrier.

"Charlotte first," he said.

Patolichev nodded and gestured his men to bring her forward. Their being armed was hardly surprising, but the gun butts in the cut-back holsters still seemed to glint with menace.

As the fence was pulled back, Lotte gave him a look of recognition that assuaged his fears, but once the guards had ushered her through the gap, she ignored the arm he offered.

"Your dad's back there," he told her.

"The affidavits," Patolichev said impatiently, his tone a notch shriller.

Russell handed them over. "As you will see when you read the account, a copy of the film still exists."

"The traitor Shchepkin's copy," the Russian said, scanning the document. "Which no one can find."

They'd obviously tried. "My guess would be a Swiss bank," Russell said helpfully, "but it is just a guess. Whoever has it also has the list that was given to Comrade Beria, of all those people whose unnatural death would trigger the film's release."

"We thought it was something like that," Patolichev admitted. It seemed like the weight of the world had been hoisted from his shoulders.

But you no more want the world to know than Beria does, Russell thought. He and his family would remain off-limits because the reputation of the Soviet Union had to be protected. "So, happy reading," he told Patolichev by means of farewell. "I hope you bring the bastard down."

"I'm sure you do," the Russian said with a sigh. He also knew what failure would mean for them both.

Russell turned and walked back towards Thomas, Lotte, and

their young guide. Patolichev had obviously thought the girl expendable, because there was nothing to stop Thomas and himself from manhandling her to the nearest police station. Nothing except a heartfelt desire to stay out of their wretched games. And the unlikely possibility that she had a black belt in judo.

As the girl led them back to the narrow staircase he took a last look round from their high vantage point, and noticed a depressingly large number of unlit windows on this side of the river from which they could have been observed. And if they had been . . .

Time would tell. Back at street level, the girl refastened the padlock, pocketed the key, and said that they should leave first, as if daring them to question that she was still in charge. Thomas characteristically thanked her for her help, and soon the three of them were back on the U-Bahn, Lotte looking like she'd been hit by a psychological train, her father like the happiest man in the world.

EFFI WAS ALREADY BACK ON Vogelsangstrasse, having despaired and walked out of the German film she was watching. The story—in which an idle man cynically marries a dying heiress, only to fall in love and spend all the money trying to cure her—would have challenged any director and had run right over this one. Effi doubted that anyone would believe her claim to be unwell but had decided that life was too short to care.

Taking a cab back home, she had only just walked through the door when Hanna announced that Rosa was on the telephone. As they had agreed to write rather than phone, Effi's first thought was that something bad must have happened to Ali or Fritz, but her relief at finding this wasn't soon turned into sadness. Rosa's friend Juan had written to say that his uncle Cesar had passed away in the family home, that the head injuries he'd sustained that night in the Ravine had after all proved fatal. And that the city coroner had ascribed his death to natural causes.

Rosa seemed more angry than upset, which Effi thought was

understandable. "I didn't really know him," Rosa said, "but I know he didn't deserve this."

Otherwise, her daughter seemed to be having a wonderful time. Life in New York City was proving even better than she expected; the three of them had spent the previous Sunday at the beach, and yesterday she had attended one of Fritz's lectures. Today she'd accompanied Ali to a recording session and had drawn most of the musicians.

Once the call was over, Effi found herself wondering whether New York might be their future.

AS THEY MADE THEIR WAY home, Russell observed Lotte's mental numbness soon giving way to some seriously mixed emotions, with confusion, dismay, and anger prominent among them. In answer to Thomas's anxious enquiries, she insisted she hadn't been badly treated during her twenty-four-hour confinement. There'd only been one brief interrogation, and no physical mistreatment. It was the waiting and uncertainty before her arrest that she'd found most difficult, and particularly not knowing what had happened to her friends. Once in custody it had seemed quite unreal, she told them, like a bad dream from which she would soon wake up.

Now she had, only to find that the life she'd been living had been comprehensively consigned to the past, her friends gone forever. The resulting anger was incoherent and ill-focused, encompassing the DDR in general and the Stasi in particular, not to mention herself, her comrades in sedition, and even those who had rescued her, buying her back like "a piece of meat" and condemning her to permanent exile in the West.

Russell felt sorry for Thomas, but also for Lotte. When your whole world collapsed in a matter of days it was hard to think straight or make much sense of what you were feeling. Things that for everyone's sake she needed to do before the night was out.

Once back at the house, Russell gave the family only a few minutes to enjoy their reunion before taking Thomas aside. "We all need to talk, including Lotte. Because everyone needs to realise that this isn't over. If the Americans know of the exchange, they could be here at any moment."

Thomas's face fell. "How could they know?"

"First off, they could have watched it. If you were BOB wouldn't you be keeping an eye on all the crossing points? Second, they have lots of German informants in the East, and no doubt some of them work for the GRU."

"Okay, but what will the Americans want from her? She hasn't done anything illegal, not here in the West at least."

Russell gave him a look. "You know better than that."

Thomas managed a half-laugh. "I do, don't I. All right, I'll go and prise her away from her mother."

"I'll get the others."

Five minutes later all but Markus and Insa were seated around the kitchen table. Lotte looked more like her normal self than she had earlier, which might, Russell thought, not be the best news—telling people only what they wanted to hear was definitely not her forte, and the Americans would accept nothing less.

Everyone was looking at him. "I know we're all feeling relieved that Lotte's back," he began, "and I'm sorry to rain on the parade, but we aren't out of the woods yet. It's possible that the authorities here in West Berlin are unaware of the deal we just did with the Soviets, or that there are now five escapees from the DDR living in this house. If so, the rest of us have nothing to worry about, and the escapees will be able to choose how and when they report their arrival. Unfortunately it's also quite possible that the Americans or one of their informers witnessed the exchange on the Oberbaumbrücke from one of their watching posts. If so, they'll be here before too long, because the Soviets aren't famous for handing out free gifts, and the Americans will assume they got some sort of payment for Lotte."

"You told me it was information," Lotte said. "But you didn't say what about. Or who will suffer as a result."

"Hopefully only a man who richly deserves to," Russell told her, "but I can't tell you any more than that. I know it's a lot to ask, but you'll just have to take it on trust—the information we passed across cannot be safely shared, not even among us few. And certainly not with the Americans. Telling them the truth would open a Pandora's box of consequences for everyone here." He looked around the table. "So when they ask the question, which they certainly will, we need a fiction that fits all the facts. One agreed between us now, before we're questioned in separate rooms."

"Okay," Thomas said. "So what can we tell them we gave to the Russians?"

"I have an idea," Russell said. "But first I need Gerhard's agreement."

The Doting Sister

The Americans arrived in the middle of breakfast, and Russell barely had time to wish Effi good luck with her big day before he and Lotte were bundled into separate jeeps and driven the short distance to Föhrenweg, where the "interview" rooms on the lowest basement level awaited them. He'd had time with Lotte and Ströhm to synchronise a story and could only hope that Thomas's daughter was sufficiently together to follow his script.

His main worry was that whoever had sent him out to be killed the previous Friday would now try and finish the job, and he was relieved to find a new face in charge of his interrogation. The man's name was Ransome, but he didn't look the sort to write children's books.

"John Russell," he began, with the air of a disappointed father or teacher. "What were you doing on the Oberbaumbrücke at 7:42 P.M. yesterday evening?"

Not wearing a watch, Russell was tempted to say, but managed not to. Someone had been observing, but from how far away? The fact that Thomas hadn't been brought in suggested he'd not been spotted. "I was accepting delivery of my friend's daughter from the Soviets," he said.

"Charlotte Schade."

"Who's probably in the next room."

"She is. According to our information she is a long-time

communist who chose to live in the east and who works for the Communist Party newspaper. Why would a person like that defect?"

"Over the last year she's grown increasingly disillusioned, and rather than simply cross the border, she joined a group pushing for change. With all the recent troubles the regime decided on a crackdown, and all the group's members were arrested over the last ten days."

"Including her."

"Correct."

"So why did they let her go?"

Russell shrugged. "Perhaps expulsion is cheaper than imprisonment."

Ransome smiled and pulled a grainy photograph out of the folder in front of him. "It had nothing to do with these papers changing hands?"

Russell examined the picture with care. The cameraman must have been at least a hundred metres away, but there was no mistaking his own profile or the hand reaching out. "The technology really is improving at a phenomenal rate," he said admiringly, as he mentally pulled back to his second line of defence.

"You wouldn't believe what we can do these days," Ransome agreed. "So what did you give them in exchange for Charlotte? Papers from here?"

"Certainly not," Russell said indignantly, as if the very idea was too awful to contemplate. "Have you heard of Gerhard Ströhm?"

"He's on the SED Central Committee, their liaison man with the Soviets. What's he got to do with this?"

"He's also in West Berlin with his family. Also disillusioned, also defecting. The papers I gave the Soviets were ones he'd brought with him, full of stuff that would have kept you busy for months."

Ransome looked confused. "But you just said you swapped them for a young woman."

"It's hardly a crime to give East German documents back to their owners," Russell said, somewhat optimistically. "And it's no skin off BOB's nose. Ströhm knows what was in them, and a whole lot more. He'll tell you it all in exchange for a life in the West. I think 'intelligence goldmine' is the phrase you're looking for."

"Where the hell is he staying?"

"At Thomas Schade's house. He wanted a few days with his wife and children before you started debriefing him."

"Well he's had them," Ransome said, reaching for his phone.

"I think he was going shopping this morning, and planning on turning up here this afternoon," Russell announced. "I take it I can go," he added. "It's my wife's big day at the Berlinale, and I'm sure you wouldn't want me to miss it. Not after I served up such a catch for you and BOB."

Ransome looked like he wanted to say no but couldn't think of a good enough reason.

"One last thing," Russell said from the doorway. "You should send Charlotte home to her mother and father. She won't be going anywhere, and you'll get more out of her once she's realised this is permanent. I've known her all her life, and she's never responded well to a head-on challenge. If she won't cooperate, then do what you have to, but give her a chance, and you might learn a lot about the way things are going over there."

"I'll bear that in mind."

Which was the most he could hope for, Russell thought, as he rode up in the familiar elevator.

YOU COULD HAVE TOO MUCH of a good thing, Effi thought, after watching herself for almost five hours. She'd been glad of the lights turned down low, because the audience might have found her facial expressions more intriguing than the stuff on the screen. Everything she'd ever felt about her work—from pride and satisfaction to a nagging sense of underachievement and an occasional wince of real embarrassment—had come roaring back to her as the clips, whole films, and TV shows, paraded past. But at least she knew the difference between what she'd done well and what she hadn't. She'd known enough actors who didn't.

The DEFA films she'd made between 1945 and 1948 were her favourites, and the way the Soviets had swapped their sophistication for propaganda when the Cold War intensified still felt like a lost opportunity, for German cinema if not for her. It had been understandable but self-defeatingly stupid—a sign of the times, if ever there was one.

Scheduling the two episodes of *Please, Dad* at the end of the programme was chronologically correct, but the show was only a career high in the financial sense, and Effi found herself realising that she'd hate to be mostly remembered for Mrs. Luddwitz. That said, the audience did find the housekeeper funny.

The first question she faced on stage mirrored her thoughts. Didn't television feel like a comedown, one bearded young man asked, after all the years of film and theatre?

"I have two answers to that," Effi said. "First, I want to earn a living as an actor, and film parts for a woman my age are few and far between. Second, any genre in any art form can be done well or done badly, even a Hollywood sitcom. I like the challenge of making people real. Even Mrs. Luddwitz."

"When you were making films for DEFA," a young woman in a beret asked, "did you not worry that you were making propaganda for the Russians?"

"No, or I wouldn't have made those films. The only good propaganda the Soviets got out of DEFA came from their willingness to encourage German filmmaking. There was nothing pro-Soviet about the five films I made with them, and when they offered me one that *was* mostly propaganda I turned it down."

"What was the film?"

"I'm not going to say, because another actress took the part, and she's not here to give you her reasons. Most of us have lines we won't cross, and hers were obviously not the same as mine. But getting back to your question—my working for DEFA was no more an endorsement of the Soviet Union than working on *Please, Dad* is an endorsement of the United States." As she took a sip from the glass of water, Effi found herself wondering if either half of that statement was true.

The next questioner wanted to know what she thought of Joseph McCarthy and HUAC.

"I think he's wrong. As simple as that. I don't believe communists or communism pose any threat to the United States."

"So why are HUAC so keen to go after them?"

"A good question. What do you think?"

The questioner had a ready reply. "Because a campaign like that makes people afraid to express any leftish criticism of the establishment."

"A good answer," Effi said with a smile.

The next question was harder: Did she regret working for Goebbels's film industry in the 1930s?

It was the same thing Beth has asked her a couple of months before. "It was the only work on offer in Germany, and all my ties were here. But yes, I do regret my involvement in certain projects. All I can say—and as an explanation, not an excuse—is that the ones I now most regret seemed so risible at the time that I failed to appreciate that people would actually take them seriously."

"Are you saying audiences were more stupid than you thought?"

Effi thought about that. "Yes, I think I am. Some of them, at least. It wasn't intelligence that filled the rallies and had people cheering our troops off to fight for Hitler. We were fooled, and we need to admit it, to ourselves if no one else."

The last few questions concerned films she'd made and people she'd worked with, which was something of a relief.

"How was I?" she asked Russell when she found him in the hospitality suite, waiting with a glass in either hand.

"Superb."

"When did you arrive?"

"In time for *Please, Dad* and your interview session. Once BOB let me go, Thomas and I spent a couple of hours tracking down Heidi Ehler. I have seen all your movies," he reminded her.

"Did you find Heidi?"

"We did. She wasn't in the telephone book, but Thomas managed to get an address from a friend in the tax office. I'll be paying a visit tomorrow."

"I wonder if she'll see you."

"We can but hope."

Others came over to congratulate Effi, and it wasn't until they were on their way home in a cab that she thought again about what she'd said about working for Goebbels, and whether the same was true when it came to working in Hollywood, at least on a show like *Please, Dad*. Wasn't the show's ultimate message—that white middle-class family life in a flag-draped bubble was not only the best thing going, but all that anyone should ask for—a form of propaganda?

HILDEGARDSTRASSE WAS A BLOCK SOUTH of the Volkspark, where Russell had often played football with Paul in the early thirties. The modern apartment blocks looked prosperous and relatively undamaged, ideal companions for the several newish-looking Mercedes and BMW cars parked out front. Heidi Ehler's block stood next to a police station at the street's eastern end, and her ground-floor apartment was at the back.

A trim-looking woman in her early forties answered his knock on the door. "Are you Heidi Ehler?" Russell asked.

"I am."

"I was hoping I could talk to you about Greer Holleman," he said. A less direct approach might have stood more chance of success, but he hadn't been able to think of one, and was counting on pure curiosity to get himself invited inside.

It worked. After looking him up and down, and deciding he wasn't a rapist or robber, she ushered him in. "I never say no to the past," she said cryptically, as she led him through to a living room, whose open French windows framed a brightly flowering garden. "My passion," she said, as if to explain the lack of others.

He knew from Thomas's research that her husband had died at Kursk a fortnight after the wedding, and that she hadn't married again. She was still extremely attractive, so that probably wasn't for lack of offers. Though there was something about her affect that said she would not be an easy match.

Coffee was offered and accepted, and Russell used her time making it to study the two framed photographs on the mantelpiece. One was obviously of her family before the First War: the parents looked stuffy and rich, and she, around four or five years old, was holding the hand of a smiling older brother. Rudolfe—it had to be him—was the sole subject of the other picture, which had been taken about thirty years later. There was intelligence there, Russell thought, and a decidedly outgoing smile.

"Your brother?" he asked, as she came back with the coffee.

"Yes, that is Rudolfe. He and Greer were friends for several years." She paused and gave him a shrewd look. "But before I reveal any family secrets—I don't believe you've told me the reason for your interest in Greer Holleman."

"I'm writing a book about Germany and America, how the two countries have related to each other over the last hundred years. A lot of enmity, but also friendships like your brother and

Greer. And they became friends at a particularly difficult time, so I'm interested in what pulled them together, and finally pushed them apart. Your brother was also a lawyer, yes?"

She nodded. "Yes, they met as students, when Rudi spent a year in America. In Little Rock, Arkansas. Greer and his mother lived there, in the boardinghouse she owned and ran."

"Did you meet Greer there?"

"Yes. I spent a month in Little Rock at the end of Rudi's college year. And Greer came to Berlin a couple of times."

"Was he your friend too?" Russell risked asking.

A slight smile. "For a while. But he would never have left his mother . . ."

"You could have gone there."

She looked shocked. "And leave Rudi behind at such a moment in our nation's history? No, of course not."

"Why did Rudi choose to study there?"

"To understand their race laws. That was when we were preparing to formulate our own, and Rudi went to learn what parts of American practice could be replicated in our new Reich."

"The Jim Crow laws."

"Not so much, no," she said, irritated by his ignorance. "Those are mostly to do with segregation. Miscegenation law was Rudi's speciality, and Greer's too. When Rudi got back he became an important voice in the discussions, and he was at the first meeting called to formulate our new laws."

"The Nuremberg Laws. When was that meeting?"

"In 1934, June or July, I think."

There would be a record of it, Russell knew. "Was Greer with you that summer?"

"Yes, he was a great help to Rudi. Greer had lived in the South all his life, so he knew the different ways their laws could be interpreted, how they worked in practice, what worked and what didn't. The three of us used to stay up half the night talking about it. American law is much more flexible than ours, and simply replicating their race laws would not have worked."

Russell refrained from asking how the Nazi laws had "worked." "They were not thought severe enough?"

"No, no. On the contrary. The problem was that the American laws were too severe. Once you believe that a single drop of the wrong blood corrupts the whole body, then complete segregation is the only thing that suffices. But that was not possible here in Germany. There were too many Jews in important jobs for them to become a segregated underclass."

"You should have been a lawyer yourself."

She grimaced. "My father was not a believer in female education."

Neither was Hitler, Russell thought but refrained from saying. "But you have studied these matters nevertheless."

"I have read my brother's book many times."

A book, he thought. "Did Greer and your brother have a disagreement, or was it just that they lived so far apart?"

"I was never sure. Greer helped Rudi a lot in 1934. He even wrote part of the presentation, under Rudi's supervision of course. And when he came back the following summer he helped Rudi with the book. They wrote to each other for several years after that, and I remember Rudi saying how disappointed he was that when Greer came back in 1938 he seemed less enthusiastic about their politics than he had before. But they didn't have a big falling out or anything like that. If that rich woman on the boat hadn't turned his head . . ."

"I don't suppose you have a spare copy of your brother's book?"

"No, and I'm sorry, but I wouldn't lend mine to anyone."

"I'm sure I can find one to buy," Russell assured her. "And thank you for the coffee and your time."

On the way out one more question occurred to him: Had Greer Holleman actually attended that meeting in 1934?

"He was there in the building, but not at the table," Heidi told him. "Rudi used to slip out and see him when he needed more information."

And that, Russell told himself, as he walked back towards the tram stop on Mecklenburgische Strasse, was what Holleman had needed kept secret.

HE SPENT THE REST OF the day being careful. If the GRU had started passing copies of the affidavits around Moscow the previous day, then Beria would know about them by now, and would be planning a response. Russell hoped the man would be too busy fighting off his enemies in the Politburo to take revenge on a few insignificant foreigners.

With Effi spending most of her afternoon and evening in the relative safety of the public eye, he decided to ensure his own by keeping on the move. He'd spent most of his time back in Berlin holed up in either BOB's basement or Thomas's house, which wasn't how he'd imagined the homecoming. A nostalgic cab tour would both keep him safe and make up the deficit.

Quite a chunk of the city was now out of bounds, and some bits that weren't, like his journalistic home on Kochstrasse, were so close to the border that they'd lost their original raison d'être and turned into virtual cul-de-sacs. The block on Neuenburger Strasse where he'd lived in the late thirties was gone completely, but his home before that in working-class Wedding was still standing. He got the cab driver to park across the street and sat there remembering the day he'd come down those steps with a wanted Communist fugitive, only to find the Nazi block warden standing in their way.

That had been twenty years ago, a call so close it could easily have killed them both. He would never have got to see Paul grow up, never have met and fallen in love with Effi.

From Wedding he directed the driver to the house on

Bismarckstrasse where he'd found her in 1945, and then south to Carmerstrasse and the flat she still owned where they'd first lived together. Ku'damm, where they'd eaten so many meals and enjoyed so much entertainment, was just to the south. And though noticeably fuller of life than it had been three years before, Berlin's showplace still seemed a shadow of its former self.

The way things were, Russell thought, this half of his city was on its way to becoming the world's most vibrant backwater. There might be worse fates than that, but there were certainly better ones.

He arrived home to find Thomas had stopped by the book shop he part-owned and picked up a gift.

"I have these boxes full of books which were published under the Nazis," Thomas explained, "and I found this among them."

It was Rudolfe Ehler's tome on American race law and its relevance to the new Reich. Turning to the acknowledgements, Russell found: "Many thanks to my friend Greer Holleman."

"Well, now I'm glad I kept all those Nazi books," Thomas said. "I thought about burning the lot, but that seemed—I don't know—almost too respectful. People only burn books when they're afraid of them. Then again, I can't say I want to keep the damn things. I suppose I could donate them all to some institution or other."

"A Hitler Memorial Library?" Russell suggested.

"Perhaps not."

ON THE FOLLOWING MORNING, THOMAS called Russell to the phone. "It's your favourite Russian," he said, passing on the earpiece.

Patolichev proved an unexpected bearer of good tidings. "This is not yet common knowledge," the Russian said, speaking his own language for once, "but it will be announced in a week or so. Comrade Beria has been arrested, and there is absolutely no likelihood of his regaining his previous influence."

"Are you calling to say thanks?" Russell asked. "Is there an Order of Lenin in the post?" he added facetiously.

"No, but there may be something else if you breathe a word about the film. We know that one day it will probably be released, but we will take no action to hasten that moment—you understand what I am saying?—and in return we expect you to show the same restraint. No newspaper articles, no sensational revelations. The new leadership wishes to be judged on what it does from this day forward, not on the depraved behaviour of one man, no matter how prominent a position he once held. Mr. Russell, there are things you know about us, but there are also things we know about you. You mentioned the Order of Lenin . . . well, what if we gave you one for helping to steal those German atomic secrets in 1945? Those papers were far more important than anything Julius Rosenberg gave us and look what happened to him."

A shiver went up Russell's spine. "You've made your point," he told Patolichev. "And no one in my family will say or write anything. You have my word on it."

The Russian laughed. "The word of a serial traitor? I believe you, but only because you know what the consequences of breaking it will be. Farewell, Mr. Russell."

The line went dead. Russell hung up his phone, and sat on the chair beside it, taking in the news. Beria was arrested, as good as dead if past experience was any guide—there was no way his Politburo colleagues could ever rest easy if they let him live. Was that some sort of justice for Nina and Sonja, and all the man's myriad other victims? No, it was merely revenge, which should feel less satisfying than it did.

But this had to be the end of it, as far as he and his family were concerned. He got up and went in search of the others. Russell wasn't sure how real it had all seemed to Thomas and Hanna, but both seemed extremely relieved that Beria was gone. Ströhm of course saw things from a more political angle. "After hearing what was on that film, it's impossible to regret the bastard going down, but I can't say I feel like cheering. Weeping, more like, though weeping for what I'm not sure. For a lost revolution, I suppose. You realise, this will be Ulbricht's salvation. Herrnstadt and Zaisser gambled on Beria coming out on top, so the Soviets will have no choice but to keep Uncle Walter in place. On a tight rein, no doubt—they won't let him take any risks, and they won't take any either. They'll keep the DDR afloat, but only because letting it sink would reflect so badly on them."

"But what about you?" Russell asked. "What are you and Annaliese going to do?"

Ströhm smiled. "Take it as it comes. Annaliese has already applied for a job at her old hospital and found several schools where Markus could start in September. As for me . . . I suspect the Americans will be reluctant to set me free any time soon, mostly because they refuse to believe I'm giving them all I can give them. I try to explain how things work over there, but they just don't get it. Why would I have information about military and intelligence matters?—I wasn't involved in either. But they seem to think I must know the names of every Stasi agent in the West. I have been giving them my impressions of all the leading figures in East Berlin and Moscow, and the mechanics of how the relationships work between the two parties, which I would think should be useful. But mostly they just seemed bored by it all. I have to throw in an imaginary sexual peccadillo every now and then to wake them up, because anything else seems to bore them. Since these people don't even realise that they're thrusting their own ideology down the world's throat, they can't conceive of a country in which conscious ideological imperatives play any significant role. So when I tell them that studying ideological differences in the Kremlin would help them understand what the Soviets are doing elsewhere, they look at me like I've just arrived from Mars. Which I suppose I have." Ströhm smiled. "Three years ago you told me you'd given up on politics, and I said I hadn't. I think I've caught up. But I have no idea what else I might want to do."

"Have you thought about America? You were born there, so wouldn't they have to let you in?"

"With my political history? I imagine they'd look long and hard for a way to keep me out."

"Maybe. My own situation in that regard isn't what I'd call secure. But I expect they'd let you visit. And we'd love to see you all in LA."

Ströhm looked serious. "You know, it's been over forty years since my parents were killed in California, and I've often thought I should like to visit their graves. I've no idea why, but I would."

"Well, come then."

Ströhm shook his head, looking bemused. "Remember those nights we watched the Jewish transports leaving for the east— well, I can't say I thought I'd be looking you up in Hollywood twelve years later."

"Me neither. I thought we'd both be lucky to survive another year."

GIVEN THE POSSIBILITY OF ANOTHER attempt on Russell's life, he and Effi decided to forgo the last two days of the Berlinale and leave the next day. They were in their bedroom making a start with the packing when Thomas called up the stairs that Russell had a visitor.

"A Kriminalinspektor from the local police," he added quietly when Russell came down. "I've put him in the front room."

Russell walked through and found a tall detective with greying hair looking out of the window. "How are you?" the detective asked. "My name is Wentker, by the way. I'm the Kriminalinspektor looking into your case."

"I didn't know I had one," Russell said. "And I'm fine, or will be soon. It looks worse than it feels."

"May I sit?"

"Of course." Russell took the armchair opposite, wondering how the German police had become involved.

"Your superiors have taken a particular view of the shootings," Wentker began. "Yours and your antagonist's . . ."

"They're not really my superiors," Russell interrupted. "I'm not a member of any intelligence organisation. I did work for these people five years ago, and when I arrived with my wife for the Berlinale . . ."

"I know who she is."

"Well, they asked me to help out with the refugee screening for a couple of weeks."

Wentker looked up. "Out of the blue? Were you surprised?"

"Unpleasantly so."

"But you agreed."

"We are living in America at the moment, and they suggested I show some gratitude."

"Ah, I understand. To go back, your American employers have satisfied themselves as to what happened on Friday evening."

"But not you?"

Wentker allowed himself a quick smile. "They have concluded that a Soviet agent tried to assassinate you as you left their 'outpost,' as they call it, like something from one of their Western movies. They have not decided whether the attacker was targeting you in particular or just an American intelligence officer, and neither do they seem that concerned to find out. It would not be easy of course—the man is dead, so they can't ask him. But the fact that they initially put a guard on this house suggests to me that they think it probable you were the target."

"They also advised me to leave Berlin."

"Did they indeed? Why didn't you do so?"

"We are going tomorrow," Russell said. "Why exactly are you here?" he asked Wentker.

The detective blew off steam and offered his brief smile again. "I am here because your employers' version of what happened is undoubtedly false, and I thought you should know that. And because I am curious. Did you recognise the man who attacked you?"

"I never saw him."

"Does the name Caleb Shapell mean anything to you?

"No. Was that his name? Wasn't he a Russian?"

"The Americans assumed he was, or so they told us. And they did have their reasons—his gun and clothes were Russian, and who else would be likely to attack an American agent a few hundred metres from the sector border?"

"So what was he?" Russell asked. He couldn't tell whether he should be alarmed or relieved by this turn of events.

"The body was eventually given to us, and someone noticed the man's underwear was American. More importantly, our pathologist noticed the dental work was too. So we checked our fingerprint files, and there he was. An American who'd arrived here in 1945 as part of the occupation bureaucracy and chosen to stay after his discharge. Shapell had a very nice flat in Charlottenburg, and a lot of money in the bank, despite having no obvious source of income. We found a three-week-old telegram from 'N' in a jacket pocket announcing that the money was 'on the way,' and his bank has admitted that two thousand US dollars were recently transferred into Shapell's account from an American source. So if you're sure you've never seen the man before, it seems probable he was hired to kill you by another American. One who wanted it to look like you'd been killed by a Russian. One whose name begins with N."

Holleman's campaign manager, Nick Hayden, Russell guessed, doing his best to appear confused.

"A provocation perhaps by your CIA colleagues," Wentker suggested. "Have you done anything to seriously upset them?"

"Any number of things, but I can't see them hiring someone to kill me. They're too stingy for a start—why pay someone to do something when they could do it themselves for free?"

"You can't think of anyone who'd want to kill you?"

Two candidates sprang to mind, but there wasn't any point in telling Wentker their names, not when one was probably in the Lubyanka, and the other—whose name began with N—lived in distant Los Angeles. "Not a soul," Russell told the German. "Can you tell me what the 'American source' was? Whose account the money came out of?"

Wentker shook his head. "The bank here has not been very cooperative. Whether out of habit or because someone's leant on them is hard to say. But pressure is being applied."

"I would appreciate being told whatever you find out. We'll be gone tomorrow or the next day, but my brother-in-law would forward a message."

"Of course. In the meantime I would keep your guard up— there's someone still out there who wants you dead." Reaching inside his coat he pulled out a small package wrapped in oilskin. "And you might be needing your gun again," he added, getting to his feet and handing it over.

"I might," Russell agreed.

Once he had shown the detective out, Russell confirmed with his eyes what his hands had already guessed—that the gun in the oilskin wasn't Thomas's Luger.

Two shocks, two revelations.

If this gun had killed the man he now knew was American, then it hadn't been Russell who shot him. There had been someone else on the scene, someone who had saved him from his attacker. And not, Russell was willing to bet, for altruistic reasons. A GRU shadow seemed the most likely candidate. Knowing they needed him alive to sign the affidavit, they had probably provided a guardian angel. Which of course explained how they knew he'd been shot, and why they'd been willing to give him more time.

And then there was the other revelation. Whoever had hired Caleb Shapell had wanted Russell's murder to look like it had everything to do with Berlin, the Soviets, and his intelligence past, and nothing to do with Los Angeles and his journalistic present. Who else could that be but Greer Holleman?

But how could Shapell have known Russell would be working that afternoon at the house in Neukölln? He could only have found that out from someone at BOB. Russell remembered that day in his Hollywood study, thinking that the "Cabal" which ran Los Angeles would have useful contacts in politics, the police, and the military, and in intelligence organisations like the CIA. A contact like the Georgian, who had contrived to send him down that path alone. A contact like Henley, who had organised his forced recruitment on arrival in Berlin and then had him transferred to a vulnerable outpost. Or maybe the contacts were these men's superiors, and they themselves just innocent conduits for the transmission of orders.

Orders given as a favour to old pals in Los Angeles.

Russell had expected trouble from Holleman, but not an attempted murder thousands of miles from LA. He'd been naive, he realised, in assuming that people like Holleman and his friends would balk at murder to hide his secrets and protect their political interests. All they would care about was getting caught, and killing him in Berlin with a Tokarev machine pistol would put enough distance between them and their victim to more or less ensure impunity.

After recounting Wentker's news to a surprised Thomas, Russell phoned his son in London and told him that there was no need for him and Marisa to worry—the enemy they'd discussed in London was no longer a threat and had not been responsible for the previous week's attack.

"Then who was?" Paul asked, sounding exasperated. "Who else wants you dead?"

"The man in LA who had us followed," Russell told him calmly. "I'll tell you more when we see you tomorrow."

Paul sounded less than satisfied with the answer but allowed his father to shift the subject to the upcoming baby.

Russell wasn't expecting to hear from Wentker again, but later that evening the detective called with good news. Shapell's Berlin bank had generously decided that confidentiality might be waived where dead would-be assassins were involved. The two thousand dollars had come from an account opened a few months earlier at the Beverly Trust Bank on Sunset Boulevard, in the name of Greer Holleman's election campaign.

No Time Like the Past

Russell's eagerness to leave Berlin for the sake of his and Effi's safety didn't make parting with Thomas and Hanna any easier, but once aboard the plane there was no denying the sense of relief. Given their situation, the city they loved and thought of as home was too full of people who saw inflicting violence as an exhilarating hobby.

The flight itself was uneventful, and the coach ride into London from the city's huge new airport didn't take as long as Russell had expected. By late afternoon he and Effi were ensconced around Paul and Marisa's parlour table, recounting their adventures of the past two weeks.

That evening he took time out to call Natasha Shchepkin and tell her that the GRU would probably not be paying her any more visits. He was assuming that the latter would keep their side of the bargain, if only because doing nothing required less effort than something vindictive.

She did sound relieved that he and Effi had done what the GRU had asked, and almost excited by his news that Beria had been arrested, quite possibly as a consequence. "Maybe my dad had the last word after all," she said almost proudly.

"Maybe," Russell agreed. "But there's been no official announcement," he cautioned her, "so I wouldn't start spreading the word just yet."

"I did live there for twenty-five years," she calmly retorted, sounding just like her father.

THERE WERE STILL FOUR DAYS until the *Queen Mary* sailed, and with Paul and Marisa both at work Russell was left with plenty of time to think. Holleman must know that Shapell had died on the job, so what was he planning now? A second attempt presumably, because none of the reasons for the first had changed. He'd missed the chance to try again in Berlin, but there was still London and the boat, New York and the train.

Would Holleman be in any hurry? Unless Heidi had written or telegraphed him, he had no reason to think that Russell had uncovered anything incriminating, let alone knew he'd hired the shooter. Would he not wait to finish the business on home ground, where his friends in the LAPD would be only an emergency phone call away?

On the other hand, in the unlikely event that Heidi had alerted her former boyfriend, the American would not want to waste any time. It occurred to Russell that a simple telegram—"Heidi told me, and I've told twenty friends"—would ensure his and Effi's safety, because killing them after that would be utterly pointless. But he was reluctant to send such a message, because that would be the end of Holleman's candidacy—if the man didn't take himself out of the race, the sponsors would do it for him, then find another suitable face and carry on as if nothing had changed.

No, Russell thought, it would be better to hold his fire, and hope he could bring down the lot of them.

And instinct told him he needed more. The acknowledgement in Ehler's book *should* be enough to end Holleman's political career, but for all Russell knew the man had seen the error of his ways in 1935 and spent the last eighteen years writing checks to Jewish charities. What could be proved? That an American named Caleb Shapell had tried to kill him in Berlin, and that the German police, investigating this, had uncovered a payment of two thousand dollars from Holleman's campaign in the would-be-assassin's Berlin bank account. But there was no invoice "for murderous services rendered," nothing to legally tie the money to the act, or indeed to Holleman as an individual.

Russell still wasn't sure he had enough to wreck Holleman's candidacy without risking an expensive suit for slander, and as things stood he had next to no chance of forcing a criminal conviction. He needed more evidence, but where would he find it?

Wentker was a possibility, one that he should have thought of earlier. He would need a copy of the bank transfer document, and maybe Thomas could persuade the detective that justice would be served if he agreed to provide one. There had to be links between Hayden, Shapell, and one or more people at BOB, and maybe Slaney's intelligence contacts could help him find them. Any such evidence, albeit only circumstantial, would make a newspaper exposé both more convincing and less vulnerable to litigation.

And then there was Little Rock. Some nice background, maybe some old newspaper photographs—the young American lawyer with his Nazi friend. One of those pictures that really were worth a thousand words. He decided he would go straight there from New York and learn all he could. Once he had all his ducks in a row, he could decide exactly what to do.

"It's a plan," Effi agreed when he outlined his thoughts. "What about Rosa and me?"

"If you catch the train for LA a couple of days after I leave for Little Rock, we should arrive back in Hollywood at roughly the same time. But I think a hotel would be safer than home, just till we know how things are turning out."

"How about the Beverly Hills Hotel? I've always wanted to stay there."

"Okay." At the moment LA seemed a long way away.

LEAVING HIS SON WAS THE usual emotional wrench for
Russell, this one tempered by a promise of returning early next
year to meet his first grandchild. As he and Effi watched the
Lizard Lighthouse recede from the *Queen Mary's* starboard deck
he wondered how many more times he'd be crossing this ocean by
ship. The British had pioneered jet passenger flight with the de
Havilland Comet the previous year, and though the plane had
since been grounded by serious problems, the future was not hard
to discern. Soon they'd be crossing the Atlantic in a winged metal
tube, stuck in their seats for up to twelve hours like railway commuters in an endless rush hour.

On the second day at sea, Russell took Rudolfe Ehler's opus on
American race law out to a deck chair and reluctantly started to
read it. He had removed the dust jacket, not wishing to upset his
fellow passengers with its fanciful juxtaposition of swastika and
star-spangled banner.

The contents were equally challenging, despite being presented
in mostly dry legalistic tones. American Negroes, Ehler wrote,
could never be given real political equality because that would
make sexual separation of the races impossible—any sexual min-
gling was, of course, instinctively offensive to racially sensitive
white Anglo-Saxons. But since most white Americans prided
themselves on their supposed commitment to that equality—all
men were created equal, et cetera, et cetera—a rigged judicial
system was needed to deprive Negroes and other coloured minor-
ities of the rights they were supposed to have. Ehler considered
this problematic, but not because it entrenched white supremacy.
What disappointed Holleman's German buddy was white America's refusal to resolve the contradiction by openly following its
racist impulses. Germany, he hoped, would not be so timid.

"How bad is it?" Effi asked when she joined him just before
lunch.

"It's depressing, because the man's far from stupid, and his picture of America is hard to dispute. He, of course, doesn't dislike what he sees. One of his heroes is Thomas Jefferson, who apparently said"—Russell consulted the notes he'd made—"'It is certain that the two races, equally free, cannot live in the same government.' He also admires Abraham Lincoln, who was still arguing halfway through the Civil War that America's only real hope was resettling all the Negroes somewhere else. In Ehler's reading, the Gettysburg Address was just window dressing, because Lincoln knew only too well that freeing the slaves meant a new kind of servitude. Hence Jim Crow."

Effi grimaced. "That is a bit surprising, even to someone who knows as little about history as I do."

"It is," Russell agreed, closing the book. "But it does make sense of the America we know."

"I suppose so. I see what you mean by depressing."

THE SHIP DOCKED AT CUNARD'S Hudson pier early on Tuesday. Ali and Rosa were there as they came off the gangplank, and soon all four of them were heading for Brooklyn in a yellow taxi. As Rosa and Effi delighted in reunion, Russell kept an eye on the streets behind them, hoping not to notice a permanent shadow. The fact that he still hadn't seen one when they reached the brownstone in south Park Slope was nice in itself but no reason for complacency.

As he planned to leave next day, Russell lost no time explaining the latest developments to Rosa, Ali, and Fritz, and the latter was then dispatched via the building's back door to a nearby travel agency, returning an hour later with an American Airlines ticket to Little Rock via Washington, DC. Departure from LaGuardia was at 12:30 P.M., arrival at Little Rock almost seven hours later.

That settled, they could enjoy the evening. Rosa was as full of New York as Effi had feared, having been to more plays, movies, and galleries than seemed possible in little more than a fortnight. She and Fritz had also bought records at a famous store in Harlem, and the three of them had eaten Nathan's hot dogs and ridden the Cyclone down at Coney Island. To Russell, it all sounded a lot more interesting than sifting defectors for BOB and getting shot in the head.

One thing he did want to hear, in the light of reading Ehler's book, were more of Fritz's and Ali's impressions of the American South. "How was it for you?" he asked them. "I mean, as white people teaching black people, how did the local whites treat you?"

Ali looked at Fritz, inviting him to answer. "We didn't meet that many," he said eventually. "And maybe that was as much our fault as theirs—I don't know. Some people made it very clear we weren't welcome, which didn't encourage any effort on our part. We lived on campus and the people we worked with were mostly such good company that we didn't feel any real need to seek out white friends. The segregation did feel weird, though, and some-times it was scary. One local white woman who taught at the college had her house burnt down. Not when she was in it, thank God, but still . . . That was around the time I got the job offer here, and I must admit it played a part in our decision to leave. After the Nazis . . . well, you know what I mean. We didn't want to be always looking over our shoulders, not again. And unlike our students, we had somewhere to go where we knew we would be accepted. Leaving didn't feel right—it still doesn't—but we knew we had to do it."

IT WAS PROBABLY COMPLETELY UNNECESSARY, but soon after ten the next morning Fritz escorted Russell out of the building's back door and through a maze of passages that led to the street behind. From there they walked to Prospect Avenue, where empty cabs were cruising to and fro like sharks in search of prey. Reaching La Guardia more than an hour early, Russell had time to down a second coffee while he read the *New York Times*. There was still no mention of Beria, and he was beginning to wonder why. Had the comrades killed him already, or had the bastard deposited his own form of life insurance—damning evidence of his fellow leaders' sexual practices, for example—in a place beyond their reach? A Swiss bank, perhaps. Russell hated the thought that he and Shchepkin might have given Beria the idea.

The flight, or flights—there were twenty-minute stops in Washington, Knoxville, Nashville, and Memphis—seemed to last forever, and he had to keep reminding himself that the train would have taken three times as long. Surveying the earth from above was interesting, but not for hours on end. The bland lunch served on the first leg, and the cursory snack on the last, at least broke the monotony for a little while. As did the child across the aisle who screamed about the pain in his ears whenever the plane descended.

The latter, as the brochure in his seat pocket proudly boasted, was a DC6B, the "future of aviation." So Russell found it somewhat ironic that Little Rock's Adams Field airport was still holding on to the past. On his way to the cab stand he noticed signs for Colored Waiting and Rest Rooms, and a restaurant with an all-white clientele.

The cab drivers were white as well. His was friendly enough, and happy to suggest a suitable hotel in the centre of town. Its name was the Riverview, and for once the name was appropriate, at least for those on the third or fourth floor. Russell's room was on the former, with an excellent view of the wide Arkansas River and two of its bridges, the one to his right full of cars heading in and out of the city across five big spans, the other to his left a heavier girder affair for trains, now starkly silhouetted against the orange sky.

After a day spent mostly sitting down, he needed a walk. He knew from crossing it earlier that the city's Main Street was only a few blocks away, and after turning north and sauntering up to the river he walked back to a bar that had looked inviting. It was a warm evening, and several ceiling fans were doing their best to cool things down for the numerous patrons.

"You don't sound like you're from around here," the bartender opined as he poured out a beer, and Russell agreed that he wasn't. "I'm from England," he admitted quietly. "Just travelling," he added, hoping to forestall any further questions.

The bartender nodded and left him to it, sipping his ice-cold beer and listening to the soft Southern drawls filling the air.

IT WAS EARLY EVENING IN New York City, and after coming home from shopping with Rosa, Effi took advantage of the time difference to call up her producer in LA. Her primary motive was just to check in after the weeks in Europe, but her contract was up for renewal at the end of the month, and she also wanted confirmation that no one had changed their minds, that the part was still hers to play.

Dick Furness was the producer she had the most time for, which was perhaps why he was given the phone. He sounded evasive from the start, and after answering a string of increasingly vapid questions about her summer travels she finally lost patience. "What are you trying not to tell me, Dick? Am I leaving the show?"

"No, no, not at all. It's just . . . well, there's a new clause to the contract, which you're not going to like."

"Which is?"

"It's not just your contract, it's in everyone's."

"What is?"

"Well, I guess you'd call it a loyalty oath."

Effi put the speaker to her chest, took a deep breath, and brought it back to her mouth. "Is there anything else you could call it?"

Furness audibly sighed. "No, not really. After the business with Laura, the sponsors are insisting. We've tried to change their minds—honest to God we have—but no dice. You either sign or you're out."

"Just out of interest, who or what am I swearing loyalty to?"

"The United States, the . . ."

"How could a German agree to that?"

"Well, all you're basically signing is an agreement to respect the Constitution, and not to try and overthrow our government by force. That's the gist of it."

"Nothing about communism."

"Well, as I understand it, communists do want to overthrow our government by force, so yes, you may have to swear that you've never been a communist. But you haven't, have you? I've heard you say so."

"I don't think that's the point," Effi retorted. "Overthrowing the government by force is presumably against the law, and I would expect to suffer the consequences if I set out to do so, but having to promise in advance never to even entertain the idea feels way a bit extreme. How would you lot have gotten rid of the British?"

Another sigh. "I know. It's ridiculous, but that's the world we have to deal with, and I don't think the sponsors will change their mind. Even for Mrs. Luddwitz. Obviously we don't want to lose you, but our hands are tied. Will you think about it? The show won't be the same without you."

Effi took a deep breath. "I'll be back in LA early next week. I'll give you my decision then."

"All right."

She hung up, and sat by the phone for a while, letting her anger ebb away.

Back in the living room she explained the situation to the others. Rosa was as angry as she was, Ali more inclined to sadness.

"How many of us who came here from Germany are feeling like they've seen all this before, and are terrified that things will go the same way?"

Fritz shook his head. "They won't. All the HUAC stuff—it's just politics, all on the surface. And I doubt the committee will be around for much longer. But the economic system and the culture it needs to spawn to stay alive—they'll still be with us long after McCarthy is gone."

RUSSELL SLEPT WELL DESPITE THE humid night air, and after eating a hotel breakfast called the number that Slaney had given him two nights before. Brad Luman, the retired editor whom Slaney had worked for several decades earlier, picked up the phone.

"Hi. My name's John Russell, and . . ."

"Jack called me. I take it you're here in town. Where are you staying?"

"The Riverview."

"Okay. Well, I'd love to talk to you—any excuse to get out of the house. What say we meet at Peggy's Coffee Shop on Main. That's between 6th and 7th. Say half an hour?"

"Sure."

The line went dead, leaving Russell wondering when he'd last had such a willing interviewee.

The coffee shop was easy to find, and the sharp-eyed, silver-haired man at the window table looked like Hollywood's idea of a small-town editor, albeit minus the eyeshade and inky fingers.

While waiting for coffee they talked about Slaney, and how much he'd hated the South. "And for all the right reasons," Luman conceded. "But I was born and raised here, and most folks are sadly inclined to give the place they're used to a freer ride than they should. You follow?"

"I do," Russell said.

"But you're not here to talk about that. Jack said you're doing a piece on Greer Holleman."

"I am. He's standing for Congress this fall, and I'm following the election for my papers in Britain and Germany. Showing them how American democracy works—that sort of thing. Do you remember Holleman well?"

"So-so. I knew him when he was a boy—my son went to the same school, and I was one of several volunteers who helped out with the baseball team. Holleman had a good eye as a batter, but he wasn't that interested, and helping out his mother took a lot of his spare time. You know she ran a boardinghouse?"

"Yes."

"All on her own after her husband skedaddled."

"Did you like the boy?"

"I did. He was quiet and kept to himself, and I got the feeling—particularly later on—that he was quite ambitious. But there was something decent about him. I didn't see much of him once he'd qualified as a lawyer, but I did hear he wouldn't turn people away for lack of money."

"White people."

Luman grinned. "This is Arkansas."

Russell smiled back. "I don't suppose you remember a German friend?"

"Ah. If it's skeletons you're looking for, that would be the place to start. He was another law student, here for a semester or two. I never met him, but I do remember a story the *Echo* ran about him. The Nazi who attended a couple of Klan meetings. I seem to recall he claimed it was just for research, but it did create a bit of a stir. The local Klan probably had visions of welcoming Goebbels as a guest speaker at one of their picnics."

"Interesting," Russell said, trying not to sound too excited. "Do the *Echo* or the local library keep an archive I could search?"

"Both of them do. I can give you a name of someone who

works at the *Echo*, the grandson of a friend of mine, name of Chet
Bailey. In fact, I can use Peggy's phone to tell him you're coming.
Peggy won't mind."

After he'd done so, the two of them chatted for another ten
minutes before saying goodbye. The *Echo* offices were on West
3rd Street only a five-minute walk away, and a young man who
had to be Bailey almost leapt from his desk when Russell came
through the front doors.

"Happy to oblige," he said, when thanked in advance. "You
might get a bit dusty back there, but we still have every issue,
right from the beginning."

"Back there" turned out to be a largish room, lined almost to
the ceiling with boxes and shelves. There were only four of the
latter for each of the paper's early years, but by 1932 each box
held a month's worth of issues. Mercifully for Russell, each year
boasted an index, albeit handwritten and covered in corrections.

"The new boys get to do them," Bailey explained. "They're told
it's a vital skill to learn, but really it's just a horrible job, and no
one else wants it. Anyway, let me know if you need anything. I
won't be going out this morning."

Left alone, Russell checked through the index for 1932, and
drew a blank on Ehler or Germany. There was, however, a single
entry for Florence Holleman. Digging out the relevant issue and
page, he discovered that Greer's mother had been appointed secretary of a cemetery renovation programme.

The 1933 index proved more fruitful. Searching Ehler elicited
two references, both in the month of March, the second of which
was also listed under Holleman, Greer. The first referred to an
interview the young German had given the paper, in which he
offered his opinions on where things were headed back home, in
the aftermath of the Reichstag Fire. The second, two weeks later,
concerned his meeting with local Klan leaders at a rally. Both he
and the Klansmen were quoted at length, both lamenting the

threat to white, Aryan civilisation and stressing their resolve to deal with its enemies. And—wonder of wonders—alongside the columns of text, a photograph of the happy event. There they were, smiling at the camera: three unhooded Klansmen, Rudolfe Ehler, and Greer Holleman, all named in the caption.

Russell laboriously copied out the text of each article. When he'd finished, he stared at the photograph, wishing he'd thought to steal a spy camera during his time at BOB. Ripping out the page and taking it with him seemed a poor return on the welcome he'd been given, but what was the alternative? He was stealing himself to commit the act when he realised there might also be a photo archive, and a search of the shelves soon proved him right. These boxes weren't indexed, and it took him the best part of an hour, but he eventually found the original, which he proceeded to stuff up inside his shirt. Once he'd had a copy made in LA, he would mail the original back, and no damage would have been done.

After thanking Bailey, he walked back to his hotel and transferred the photo to his suitcase, before taking a cab out to the airport and booking his flight the next day. Back in town, he lunched in a diner he'd spotted earlier, then sought out the address of the former Holleman boardinghouse at the town library. The man behind the desk had never heard of it, but after calling his mother was able to offer Russell both the address and the establishment's new name.

It was a ten-minute walk to the south, between Main and the Mt. Holly Cemetery mentioned in the *Echo*, a large three-storey corner house set amid trees on a sizeable chunk of land. Almost twenty years on from the Hollemans, it looked in need of some care, rather like the middle-aged man in a vest who answered Russell's knock.

He said he didn't remember the previous owners, but the woman who owned the drugstore opposite was about a hundred years old, and probably did.

Russell walked across to find a young man at the counter, and after explaining his mission, was taken through to the shaded yard at the back, where a woman of around seventy, grey frizzy-haired and considerably overweight, was sitting in a dilapidated armchair.

She introduced herself as Queenie. "Of course I remember Florence Holleman," she said, after Russell had explained the reason for his visit. "She and her boy went West," Queenie added, somehow making it sound like they'd gone to the moon. "How is she?"

"I'm afraid she died. Before the war."

"Oh. Poor Florence."

"But her son's still alive and doing well. He married a business-man's daughter, and now he owns a big business."

"Hmm. He was always a smart one. A nice boy, though. Always took care of his ma. She ran a good house, unlike that lot over there now."

"Do you remember the German boy that Greer met at college?"

Queenie thought for a moment, and then her face lit up. "You know, I do. They were thick as thieves, those two. He seemed nice enough for a German, a bit full of himself maybe. His English wasn't so good, and I think he took Greer around with him to help him with the talking."

"Do you remember a sister?"

"Oh yes. A pretty thing, she was, and her English was better. She couldn't get enough of the soda fountain. Greer used to bring her over, and I think he was a bit smitten. Truth be told, I think both of them turned his head a little. He was always a bit of a mother's boy, and he hadn't been anywhere, except maybe Texas, and they were like a window on the world for him. I seem to remember he even went to Germany to visit."

"He did."

"And you say he's now a big businessman."

"One of the biggest. And he's standing for Congress this fall."

"Hmm. Is he married?"

"He was. His wife died young. He has a son though, and the two of them seem to be close."

"Like Greer and Florence."

"Yes," Russell agreed, somewhat reluctantly. He didn't like feeling sympathy for a man who'd tried to have him killed.

The Boy on the Mountain

Next morning, Russell was out at Adams Field by 9:30. Having coffee in the restaurant room prior to boarding his first flight, he solved the mystery of the apparently all-white clientele—the small screened-off section reserved for black folks in the far corner was not visible from the concourse.

His connecting service to Dallas was delayed by an overlong stop at Texarkana, and the DC4 only landed a few minutes ahead of the Convairliner that would take him on to LA. This plane was quite crowded, but a much more comfortable affair than the DC4. The only scheduled stop was in El Paso, where hot dinners were due to be ferried aboard, and three hours after that they'd be touching down at LA International.

He watched East Texas roll away beneath him. Yellow-brown with touches of green, small, parched-looking towns, an occasional arrow-like highway or railroad line. Comanche country, he seemed to remember. Where had they ended up?

Hitler had been fond of comparing Germany's need for "living space" in the East with the conquest of the American West, and had offered a similar vision of forts, reservations, and enormous farms and ranches. The one big difference was an expectation that the conquered would be turned into slaves. America already had enough of those.

Which led Russell back to Greer Holleman, and how he should

deal with the man. The acknowledgements in Ehler's book and the photograph from the *Echo* should render him unelectable, particularly in a Congressional district with so many Jewish people. The Klan hated them as much as they hated black people.

He would make sure the man lost his shot at political stardom, but was that enough? If not, what would be? Implicating the men who'd sponsored him, at least in print if not in court? But what would that achieve? These people had too much influence, too little shame.

He told himself exposing such corruption was always worth it, that not being able to bring down the system was no reason to give its beneficiaries a free ride. That argument sounded less convincing than it had when he was thirty, but being jaded was not much of an excuse.

There was no point in being a Don Quixote, no honour in just looking away. Somewhere between those two extremes he had to find something he could live with. Which was easier said than done.

El Paso came and went, the smell of the dinners suffused the cabin, and Russell managed a few more chapters of the new John Wyndham he'd acquired in London before falling asleep for a couple of hours. *The Kraken Wakes* was better than *The Day of the Triffids*, which was saying something. He had gotten it for Rosa, but having started the book on the *Queen Mary*, was now intent on finishing before he handed it over.

He was woken by the announcement that the plane would soon be landing, and not much more than a half-hour later was walking out through the terminal doors and into LA's usual golden sunset. He had seen nothing that looked like a welcoming committee inside, and no one seemed to be following him now, which rather surprised him until he saw the evening paper headline—HOLLEMAN PULLS OUT OF CONGRESSIONAL RACE.

The bastards had beaten him to it. After buying a copy and

reading the relevant piece in the back seat of his cab, he didn't know much more. The new candidate's name was Kyle Myerson, another forty-ish LA businessman; the reason given for Holleman's withdrawal were his "family obligations." The explanation—implied but not actually stated—was the candidate's realisation that while he knew he could both serve the people and care for his boy, he was far from sure he could do both well.

So Russell could still tell his story, but only Holleman would suffer. By acting when they had, the sponsors had put clear water between themselves and any scandal. Look how quickly we dumped him, they would say. The minute we knew, we told him he was done.

Which at least meant they had no reason to come after him, Russell thought. On the contrary. They would stay as far away from him and his story as they could.

"Change of plan," he told the cab driver. "Take me to Melrose and Gower." He would still check in to the Beverly Hills Hotel, but having the Frazer with him while he was there would save a fortune in fares.

Having his car keys on him, he didn't even bother going into the house, just got himself and his suitcase into the car and drove to Beverly Hills. It was dark by the time he got there, and after having his things sent up to the room he sat in the bar with the paper and went through the piece again, looking for anything he might have missed. There was nothing else in that particular story, but as he skimmed through the inside pages another headline leapt out at him—SOVIET POLICE CHIEF ARRESTED.

It was official, in *Pravda*. Beria was finished, as good as dead. Russell resisted the temptation to order champagne, settling instead for a good single malt, which he silently lifted in memory of all the man's victims.

As he put the glass down, he was shocked by how strong the

wave of relief was. Five years, he told himself, five years the threat had been there at the back of his mind, the threat to himself and his family. No wonder it felt like a weight had been lifted.

RUSSELL WAS TAKING HIS TIME over breakfast, wondering what, if anything, he ought to do next, when the bellboy approached his table. By his reckoning Effi and Rosa were currently crossing Kansas on the *Super Chief* and thinking that they were the only ones who knew where he was, the news that he had a call was somewhat surprising.

He walked through to the lobby, picked up the phone, and found himself listening to Nick Hayden.

"Mr. Russell. You remember me? Greer Holleman's campaign manager."

"I remember. It seems you're out of a job."

"For the moment, yes. Mr. Russell, I was hoping we could meet today. There are some things I would like to discuss with you, some matters I would like to set straight. Would that be possible?"

Russell supposed it would be. Hearing what Hayden had to say might help him decide what course he should take. "How about here?" he suggested—the Beverly Hills Hotel was as far away from a dark alley as it was possible to get. "Say eleven in the Polo Lounge."

"I'll be there."

Russell hung up the phone and took the elevator up to his room. The only thing Hayden could want was for him to refrain from broadcasting Holleman's story, presumably because his people feared that some of the mud would stick, however undeservedly, to their new boy. Would it be carrots, sticks, or both, Russell wondered, not that either would deter him.

An hour or so later he watched the man climb out of his Cadillac, leave his companion—the obligatory muscle, if Russell wasn't

mistaken—and walk towards the entrance. Hayden looked casually dapper, like someone intending to lunch at his golf club.
There was something annoyingly cocksure about the man's face
and walk—his failure to save his first candidate from imminent
exposure clearly hadn't left him burdened with self-doubt.

In the Polo Lounge they shook hands, ensconced themselves in
wicker chairs and ordered coffee.

"We know that you know about Greer Holleman's Nazi connection," Hayden announced without preamble.

"Who's we?" Russell asked politely.

"The campaign committee."

"Now renamed?"

"Of course. We couldn't possibly go to the electorate with such
a compromised candidate. Mr. Russell, I can't tell you how
shocked and saddened we all were when Greer finally told us his
guilty secrets. I wasn't present at your first interview with him,
but Martha—the woman who helps look after Luke—she told
me that Greer was upset by your German connections and
blamed me for arranging the interview. When I asked him about
this, he said she was exaggerating, that he was annoyed because
you would be reopening the issue of the firm's dealings with the
Nazis, when those had already been thoroughly investigated. I
didn't believe him—I could see he was shaken—so the campaign
committee took the decision to investigate you, and hopefully
reassure ourselves that you posed no threat to the candidacy. You
may have noticed you were being followed?"

"Uh-huh."

"At great expense. And, as it turned out, most ineffectively. The
people we employed concluded that you were only rechecking the
old investigation into the Lettson Corporation's wartime activities
for your book, and since we knew that there was nothing new to
find there, we decided you weren't a threat. So you can imagine
my surprise when Greer came to me a few days ago and admitted

to helping the Nazis codify their race laws. He told me that you had been to see his old girlfriend in Berlin, and then talked to people he had known in Little Rock when he first became friends with this young German lawyer. That you knew everything, and that he had no choice but to withdraw his candidacy. And we of course had no choice but to accept his decision. He claimed it was youthful folly, that he's not like that now and deeply regrets his involvement, and I believe him. He's a decent man—you only have to look at the way he cares for his son."

Russell was having trouble believing a word of Hayden's presentation, but reckoned it was wiser not to say so, or at least not until he heard the final pitch. "Could you not tell the electorate that?" he asked straight-faced.

"We would have been fools to try. Much as I respect him, as a candidate Greer was dead in the water. People who know politics tell me there's every chance that anyone stepping into his shoes, no matter how squeaky-clean, will probably get sucked in right after him. Mr. Russell, I'm hoping that you haven't yet shared this story professionally?"

"No, but . . ."

"So just with family and friends?"

"There's quite a few of them."

"Okay. But people you can rely on to remain silent, yes? The story can still be kept out of the public domain?"

"Give me a reason not to write it."

"I'll give you several. Greer Holleman is a good man at heart, and I think losing his political future is punishment enough for a mistake he made twenty years ago. If all this comes out he will be ostracised, his firm and his employees will suffer, his son will have a diminished father. On the other hand, if you agree to drop the story, leave the past in the past, then we will write a large check for any charity you choose, Jewish orphans, whatever. And of course compensate you for any lost earnings. Just name a figure."

"I'm tempted," Russell lied. "But what if I decide to go ahead? This may not be the story of a lifetime, but it's not far off. It's not just about Holleman, is it? The Nazis finding Southern race laws too harsh, that'll make a hell of a splash, don't you think?"

"Probably less than you might think. Plus, you could always tell that story, but leave Holleman out of it."

"First law of journalism," Russell said, "give wider issues a personal focus. The story would lose all its resonance without Holleman." He looked Hayden in the eye, as if daring him to make a threat.

Hayden smiled back. "We would of course try to protect Greer," he admitted. "He was, is, a friend and colleague. And given the evidence I assume you have amassed, I suspect we would have to discredit you. And indeed your wife. You are both foreigners with dubious links to this country's current enemies, whereas Greer's ill-advised connections were at least with an enemy who longer exists."

"Neatly put," Russell told him. "I shall consider your offer most carefully, and let you know what I decide."

Hayden looked disappointed but shrugged his acceptance. They shook hands again, and Russell watched his would-be killer wend his way through the tables to the exit. A drink, he thought, as the bar caught his eye.

There were several stools available, and the French sauvignon blanc was as good as he thought it would be.

What had he learned? That Hayden was a fluent liar who knew how to fashion a convincing argument. It had sounded rehearsed, and probably had been. All of which was as expected.

If he'd learned anything useful, it was that Hayden had no idea that Russell knew about Shapell and the bank transfer. As far as Hayden was concerned, this was all about Holleman's past, not the drastic way the two of them had tried to cover that up. Every word the erstwhile campaign manager had uttered had been coated in phony reluctance or regret.

What had Hayden learned from their conversation? Only what Russell had wanted him to, that Holleman's secret was now known to lots of people and could no longer be suppressed by a simple killing or two.

Knowing that Hayden had paid for the murder attempt, Russell was inclined to think that Holleman had been the sole driving force behind what came before. It seemed more likely that he had gone to Hayden with his worries and asked his No.2 to do whatever he considered necessary to make them go away. Holleman might not even know that Hayden had opted for the simple, lasting solution.

Which was something to ask Holleman, he thought. Before he nailed the man to a journalistic mast, he needed to hear his side of the story.

First, though, he wanted to talk the whole business through with Effi, and she wouldn't be back until the next morning. He could take the afternoon and evening off, call Holleman after he'd talked it over with Effi, and fix a meeting for Monday.

After a lunch that more than lived up to his expectations, he took the Frazer out for a drive. It was a beautiful blue-sky day, sunny but not too hot, and the mountain roads were full of people who'd had the same idea. After climbing Coldwater Canyon, he took Mulholland Drive all the way to Woodland Hills before driving back. Still enjoying the ride, he continued on to Laurel before turning south, and was halfway to Hollywood when he spotted a turn he'd never noticed before. Over the last couple of years he and Rosa had enjoyed tracking down many of the locations in *The Big Sleep*, a film they had both seen several times. They had visited the rare bookstore, the Lido Pier where the chauffeur died and numerous other spots, but there was one which they'd never managed to find, and here it was in front of him. It looked so different in the full light of day but was still unmistakably Geiger's House. He couldn't wait to show his daughter.

Back at the hotel that evening, a call to Jack Slaney improved his mood still further. It turned out that Nick Hayden, Caleb Shapell, and his Quonset hut friend Travis Henley had all been members of the same OSS unit in 1945.

Over a nightcap in the bar, Russell went back over his dealings with Henley, looking in vain for signs he had missed. The man had handled the temporary assignment to BOB and sent him off to be murdered with icy aplomb but had shown the sense not to visit him in hospital. Thinking that Russell had killed his friend Shapell, Henley had probably realised that a further meeting might overstretch his acting skills.

RUSSELL WAS UP AT SIX on Monday, and had time for two coffees at Union Station before the hour-late *Super Chief* pulled in. "Fritz told me that Holleman backed out" was the first thing Effi said after they embraced. "Does that mean it's safe to go home?"

"It is," Russell agreed, "but we're staying at your dream hotel anyway," he added, lighting up her smile. "If we get a move on, they'll still be serving breakfast."

"So the business with Greer Holleman—it's all over?" Rosa asked once they were on the road.

"The dangerous bit is. Now we get to learn, yet again, that the pen is nowhere near as mighty as the wretched sword."

"Yet still we keep writing," Effi said cheerfully.

"We do. And I found Geiger's house," he told Rosa.

"How? Where is it?"

"Completely by accident and off Laurel Canyon. We can go this afternoon if you like."

"Maybe. I have to see Juan, and tell him and his family how sorry I am about Cesar."

"We can do that too."

"Oh. Okay."

After breakfast, once Rosa had disappeared with her drawing pad to explore the hotel and grounds, Russell and Effi took chairs on the plant-strewn patio and brought each other up to date.

"Stopping him from standing has to be worth something," Effi said, once Russell had told her the different explanations offered for Holleman's withdrawal by Hayden and the newspapers.

"Maybe it is, but a few percentage points off their victory margin in November doesn't feel like adequate punishment for attempted murder. And they'll still have their stooge in Congress."

"So what are you going to do?"

"Kick up a stink, and maybe put someone in jail. Wentker came through, with a copy of the money transfer Shapell received, and Thomas has put it in the post."

"How much was Shapell paid?—you never said."

"Two thousand dollars. I like to think it was only a down payment."

"Of course you do."

Russell grinned. "And last night Jack Slaney told me that Hayden, Shapell, and Henley—the guy who sent me to the BOB outstation—were all OSS buddies. They were the means, and the stuff I dug up from Holleman's past provide a pretty good motive. All circumstantial, but it should make a decent case, at least in the so-called court of public opinion."

"But not a real one?"

"Who knows? These people have the most expensive lawyers known to man, but if we get people in front of a jury . . . I think we should get Hayden, but that might be all."

"Worth a shot, surely."

"Oh yes. He came to see me yesterday—we had coffee together in the Polo Lounge, while his bodyguard waited outside."

"What was Hayden like?"

"Smooth, cold, about as human as a dollar bill. He obviously wanted to know if I'd kept the story to myself and was therefore still worth silencing. When he found out my far-flung family were all in the know, he fell back on a well-prepared tissue of lies. According to him, Holleman was the one behind everything, and Hayden only found out about his candidate's past once the attempted cover-up had failed. Not that he wanted me to go after Holleman—he thought his former boss had suffered enough, and that dragging up his past would hurt the son and employees without helping anyone else. If I really wanted to help the Jews that Holleman and Ehler had had a hand in persecuting, I'd be better off accepting a large check for an appropriate charity."

"He had it all worked out, didn't he?"

"I tell you, after listening to the man for twenty minutes, I found myself almost believing that Holleman was innocent. Hoping so even, though God knows why."

Effi shook her head. "But Holleman must have set the whole business in motion, because only he knew about Ehler and their dealings with the Nazis."

"He was involved, all right—we just don't know how much. I need to talk to him."

"When will you do that?"

"Tomorrow I think. One thing I didn't tell you—Hayden couldn't resist a few vague threats to go with the bribe. If I defied them and wrote the story, he and his business friends would have to 'protect themselves,' mostly by smearing us as foreign communist sympathisers. And they'd probably succeed. HUAC for you, Immigration for me."

"They might have to join a queue," Effi said. "Before we left New York I got a call from my producer. The sponsors have taken fright, and there's a loyalty oath waiting for my signature at the studio."

"That's unfortunate. Are you going to oblige them?"

"My initial instinct was to tell them where they could put it, but then sensible Effi kicked in and thought she should read it first. I mean, I think I am willing to rule out personally using force to overthrow the American government. While of course pointing out what an absurd thing that is to ask of anyone with my lack of interest in politics."

"Okay. If you get kicked out of the country, I think I'll come with you."

"You may not have a choice."

"True."

"And in any case, we may get kicked out of here before that. Rosa's down by the pool drawing the rich in their natural habitat, and somebody's probably complained by now."

"Oh."

"They say it's a free country."

"It is for them."

REACHING THE STUDIO SOON AFTER ten the next morning, Effi was shown straight in to Dick Furness's office. The producer was around the same age as she was, and always seemed to be stroking his head, as if to check how much hair he had left. Not much was the answer, but the extravagant sideburns and moustache were doing their best to provide compensation.

Effi had never really disliked the man, but she found it hard to forgive the way he anticipated the sponsors' every possible complaint or desire, whether or not they had worked out what these should be. Today he was all smiles, at least until she spoke.

"I'm not going to sign it," she said, as he tried to pass her the sheet of paper.

"Oh. I'm surprised. Almost everyone else has. Don't you even want to read it?"

"No. You said 'almost'?"

"Beth quit, but I think she was planning to anyway."

"Ah." Effi smiled. "You won't find it easy to replace her."

"Oh, I don't know."

"She was the one who brought the stories to earth. Which is what makes a show like ours special. You'll miss her."

"I think we'll miss you more."

"No, you won't. For a good character, Mrs. Luddwitz is pretty easy to play. I don't think you'll have any trouble finding someone else."

Furness looked unhappy. "Is it just the oath? Has someone else offered you more money, because if that's . . ."

"It isn't."

The producer spread his hands. "Okay then. You do realise we will have to tell the press why you're leaving?"

"I'll be doing the same. No, I won't be blaming you or anyone else," she added, seeing the look on his face.

"Once people know you refused to sign, you won't find any work in Hollywood."

"I'm sure I won't, but I think my bank manager will find that more upsetting than I do."

"So what will you do?" Furness asked in a kinder voice.

"I don't know," she said, getting up. "Enjoy being a wife and mother. Work in Europe. Write my memoirs."

They shook hands, and Effi walked back through the familiar stages to her car. After opening the door she stood there for a moment, taking in the familiar surroundings. "And goodbye to you," she told the lot in Mrs. Luddwitz's voice, before driving out onto Highland.

AS HE DROVE EAST ALONG Melrose, Russell wondered what kind of reception he would get from Holleman. When he'd phoned the evening before to ask for a meeting, the ex-candidate had agreed to a time and place with all the emotional intensity of someone arranging a conversation with an accountant. There had been no edge in his voice, none of the angry resentment that Russell had expected as payback for torpedoing the political career Holleman had ostensibly wanted. He had sounded beaten.

Which, Russell supposed, was at least appropriate. Holleman *was* beaten, and once his story hit the newsstands his life would never be the same again. However he was judged—as Klan ambassador or Nazi dupe—he would always be remembered as a rancid exemplar of international cooperation, a representative of one racist cesspit happily offering help to another.

It had been ten weeks since Russell's first visit to the house on Normandie Avenue, but the Holleman who answered the door looked ten years older. He ushered Russell into the house without a word, and led the way through to the lounge where Luke was playing with his model railroad. This time it was a freight train circling the track, with several box cars and a red caboose behind the sort of steam locomotive that always appeared in Westerns.

After taking in the visitor, and offering up the usual bright smile, Luke turned back to his train.

"Coffee?" Holleman asked.

"No, thanks," Russell said, feeling suddenly anxious to get started.

"Then I'll just get Martha, and we can talk in the garden."

The latter was unchanged, save for the grass being browner. Taking the same canvas chair, Russell had the sense of coming full circle.

"I was surprised to get your call," Holleman said, seating himself in the other. "I assumed you had the whole story, and I'd be reading it in the press."

"I have all I need to know about you and Rudolfe Ehler," Russell agreed. "But I'm missing a few details when it comes to this summer."

Holleman offered a wintry smile. "Like what?"

"Like whose idea it was to have me killed in Berlin."

Holleman's head jerked up. He was either shocked or an excellent actor. "Did somebody try? I didn't know that. Maybe I should have, but . . ."

"That doesn't sound like a declaration of total innocence," Russell said.

"It isn't, but . . ."

"I think you need to tell me the whole story, starting with the last time I came here. Something I said must have spooked you."

Holleman managed a brief smile. "You could say that. After finding out you wrote for a German paper—something Nick hadn't thought to tell me—I asked him to run a quick check on you just in case. And what he came back with was pretty alarming. You were a leftie who had lived and worked in Germany for decades, with all the journalistic connections that implied, and if you *were* intent on exploring my past you were very well placed to discover my dealings with the Nazis." Holleman paused and pulled a pack from his shirt pocket. "And then I made what was probably a huge mistake. I told Hayden about Ehler and the Nazi race law meetings and asked his advice about what to do. He said he'd have you properly investigated and find out whether you were coming after me." He offered the pack to Russell, who declined.

"And those were the weeks when I couldn't go anywhere without a PI in close attendance."

"I suppose so. The only things Nick told me about the investigation were how much it cost and what it uncovered."

"So what did he find out?"

"That you were writing a book about American businesses which collaborated with the Nazis, and that you were about to visit Germany. Either of which might mean you were looking into my past or might have nothing to do with me. The Lettson Corporation had been cleared of any such dealings, and the timing of your visit seemed to have more to do with your wife and the film festival. I got the feeling Nick was more worried than he let on, but he denied it. He said if a problem arose, he'd deal with it, and at the time I assumed that meant he would follow the usual practice and buy you off. When he joked that his old wartime buddies in Berlin could probably get you handed over to the Russians, I didn't take him seriously. I should have done, because—as I found out several weeks later—he really did try to do just that."

"He actually told you so? Did he say how they intended handing me over? Did he name the 'wartime buddies'?"

"They were going to lure you across the border, or close enough for a Russian snatch squad. No names were mentioned, and there were no other details. He did say that the only thing that stopped them was the city border closing when all the trouble broke out in East Berlin."

"Which I presume is when he decided to simply have me killed."

"You're telling me he did. Have you any actual proof that he tried to have you killed?"

"The old wartime buddy who took the job had just received two thousand dollars from America, and it came out of your Campaign Fund."

Holleman was silent for several moments. "I had no knowledge of that," he finally said, "but maybe I should have guessed. The other thing Nick wanted to know was whether there was anyone left in Berlin who knew about my connection to Ehler. He had found out Rudolfe was dead, and up until then I hadn't told him about Heidi. She was never involved in the politics, and I had no idea where she was or whether she was married with a family. And—I don't know—maybe I just didn't want her involved. But I did tell Nick about her that day, and last Friday he told me that one of his buddies had managed to track her down. You'd already been to see her, and presumably found out all about Rudi and me."

"And his book, with its thanks for your help."

"That was when they told me I was being dropped," Holleman said. "My secret was out and couldn't be reburied. He said you'd even gone down to Little Rock. What did you dig up there?"

"A photograph of you and Ehler socialising with the local Klan."

"Perfect," Holleman said drily. "So I guess you have it all."

"Where you and Ehler are concerned," Russell agreed. The murder attempt in Berlin was another matter. It hadn't been hard to imagine Holleman resorting to desperate measures when his reputation and future were both at stake. But Hayden? Why would a mere campaign manager risk arranging a murder?

Because he thought no risk was involved, Russell realised. Not with sponsors like his, and a network of buddies in positions of power. There was no one to hold him back. To people like these, war business was war. Laws and the values they supposedly upheld were just obstacles to work around, and anyone who really got in their way—as he had—would be pried or forced aside by whatever means proved necessary.

Hayden being solely responsible made more sense to Russell than Holleman being so, but there was still the possibility that the pair of them had done everything in concert. "There's one thing I want to ask you," Russell went on. "When I talked to Heidi, she said that you and Ehler continued writing to each other, but that the intervals got longer and longer, and that when you finally came back in 1938 you made excuses not to meet up with him. Was there a reason for that?"

Holleman smiled sadly. "When I went back to Germany in 1938 I ran into someone I'd met in 1934, and he told me about their plans to kill off all the retarded children—'unworthy to live' was the phrase he used. And by then I had Luke." He looked at Russell. "When someone you love is deemed unworthy to live because of something he cannot help, you find yourself thinking about all the others who are in the same boat. Like the Negroes, like the Jews. And I knew this wasn't something that Rudi would ever understand, so I just cut him out of my life. When I went back again in 1940 to close our German operation down, I didn't try to get in touch."

This had the ring of truth, Russell thought, and inclined him towards giving Holleman the benefit of the doubt where the rest was concerned. "What you did in the thirties and what you did or didn't do this summer are two different matters," Russell said, as much to himself as to Holleman. "I am going to write the thirties story because it says something important about this country, and if you get crucified in the process, then that's too bad. Actually, I doubt you will be. Fraternising with the Klan and recommending Jim Crow to the Nazis might have cost you a Congressional seat in LA, but it won't do you any harm in most of the South or Midwest."

Holleman grimaced. "I won't deny anything," he said. "Not about that."

"And having me killed to bury the story?"

"I did want the story buried. I'd like to believe I would never have agreed to having you killed, but leaving everything to Nick, I suppose might as well have. I have no real excuse."

"You could go to prison," Russell said, a new idea taking shape in his head. "With the evidence I have," he went on, exaggerating more than a little, "someone from the campaign will probably end up inside, and I think we can guess who your former backers will want that to be."

Holleman looked shocked, as if he'd expected self-disgust would be his only punishment. "For how many years?" he asked. "I wouldn't care for myself, but Luke won't understand what's happened."

"I've no idea," Russell said almost absent-mindedly, as another thought occurred to him. "There is an alternative."

"Which is?"

"We lay the blame where it belongs, on Hayden and your business backers."

Holleman's expression mixed doubt with hope. "And how would we do that?"

"I believe it's called a frame-up. In return for your help in nailing them, I will lie to keep you out of prison. We'll go to the police together, and you'll say that when Hayden told you about his plan to murder me you were appalled and sent me a warning. I'll confirm that I received one and add that it saved my life. We'll need to get the details straight, but I can't see any reason why it wouldn't work. And you'd be off the hook."

Holleman looked confused. "Why would you do that for me? You have your big story, and you've only my word for it that I wasn't involved in what happened to you in Berlin. Are you that determined to get Nick Hayden?"

"I do take exception to people who try to have me killed, but that's not my only reason."

"You won't get the people behind him, but you might make them angry enough to come after you."

"Maybe. And there's another reason I'd like to keep you out of prison," Russell said, realising it for the first time. "Nothing to do with politics. A need for atonement, perhaps."

"Atonement for what?"

"For failing someone who needed my help." He might as well tell the story, Russell thought, see how it played out on Holleman's face. "During the war my wife worked in the German resistance to Hitler, smuggling Jews out of Berlin, and a couple of weeks before the war ended, she was given a young Jewish girl to look after. Her mother was dead and her father missing for years, so we were able to adopt the child—in those days the formalities were a lot less strict. But Effi, my wife, she couldn't shake the fear that the father would turn up and take back the child, so when we went back to Berlin at the end of that year we started looking for him. We tracked down several men with the right name, none of whom were Rosa's father, and then found another who was already on his way to Italy, hoping to catch a boat to Palestine. I went after him, travelling with another column of emigrants, and we were high in the mountains close to the Italian border when we ran into a middle-aged man and his young son, who also claimed to be Jews on their way to the promised land."

Holleman fidgeted in his chair. "Why are you telling me all this?"

"You'll see," Russell said, remembering how Effi had once accused him of an obsessive need to explain things. "Anyway, I knew who this man was—an SS officer named Hirth who had blackmailed me into doing an intelligence job for him back in 1939. But none of the Jews recognised him, and he begged me not to give him away, not for his own sake but for the boy's, whose mother had recently died in the bombing. Or so he claimed. And I agreed, because it felt like the price of bringing the father to justice was much too high for his son."

"I do see," Holleman said quietly. "So these two survived."

"No. I said nothing, but after someone noticed the boy had a foreskin, they forcibly checked the father. Of course he had one too, and a search of his clothing turned up a dagger with SS runes engraved on the hilt. The Jews shot him, and when the son refused to let them take him out of the mountains, they— and I—chose to leave him there. When we left he was scooping out a grave by hand, and I've never been able to forget the heart-break in that boy's face. Or forgiven myself for abandoning him."

"You're doing this for Luke."

"I'm doing it so I can live with myself."

Holleman studied his face. "I can understand that. Well, I'm game. What are our chances, do you think?"

"Of kicking up a stink? Pretty good. Of bringing down your cabal—absolutely none."

Once back in his car, Russell drove a few hundred yards down the road and then pulled over. Everything he'd said about the Hirth boy was true, but he had used the story to manipulate Holleman, because his chances of nailing anyone else were close to zero without the other man's help.

It was morally messy, but then most things were.

Fragments

A week after he and Holleman had agreed on their plan of action, Russell was shopping at the local drugstore when he noticed Lavrenti Beria staring back at him from the cover of *Time* magazine. The words "Enemy of the People" sat beneath the portrait, whose artist had given Beria an arrogant self-confidence which rendered his current imprisonment somewhat ironic. The story inside listed Moscow's usual litany of crimes—"criminal anti-party and anti-state actions, intended to undermine the Soviet State in the interest of foreign capital," et cetera—but no mention was made of personal idiosyncrasies, like the rape and murder of young women. Sonja and Nina Strehl would never know that their killer had eventually run out of victims and luck.

Knowing that Beria was, for all intents and purposes, a dead man walking certainly made Russell's summer more relaxed than would otherwise have been the case. So did Effi joining the ranks of the unemployed, and Rosa enjoying the usual interminable American school break. There were lots of drives into the mountains, lots of days at the beach and afternoon matinees. They went to gape at the world's largest wisteria and walked in the Palo Verde hills.

It was not all simple pleasure. One afternoon Russell and Rosa drove down to Dolphin's, partly to buy records, partly to make a point. They took company—his journalist friend Cal Tierney, the lawyer Don Cheveley, who had helped with Cesar, and an eager young photographer named Chip. The cops on duty did not disappoint, and neither did LA's premium papers, all of whom refused to print either the telling photographs of their gratuitous harassment or Tierney's explanatory article.

Russell couldn't say he was surprised. Racism, it seemed, was as American as apple pie, and nothing he had seen in the last few months suggested real change anytime soon. Baseball and the military had been desegregated, but despite a slowly rising clamour, not much else seemed on the cards. If better civil rights were guaranteed to black people, some other way would be found to keep most of them down. Ehler had been right about that—White America couldn't cope with political or economic racial equality.

Of course there were "good Americans," just as there'd been "good Germans," but as far as Russell could see the former were little more inclined to lift their heads over the parapet than the latter had been.

That same week in August, Congress had passed legislation "detribalising" descendants of many of the country's original inhabitants—henceforth there would be no assistance for the tribes, and each individual native American would be left to sink or swim. Adding insult to injury, its framers named it the Termination Bill, apparently oblivious to the echoes of "final solutions" in their own country's murderous past. Calling it the "Wounded Knee Consolidation Bill" would not have been inaccurate.

Most of the Americans Russell met had little understanding of their country's history, and very little interest in any events which hadn't ended in a violent triumph. Which wasn't perhaps surprising, given the size of the lies which had taken root over the last two centuries, starting with the so-called Revolution which had replaced one bunch of wealthy men in wigs with their home-grown equivalents, and continuing on with the Civil War and

Emancipation that had successfully turned slaves into segregated serfs. And then there was winning world wars for democracy, the communist threat to life on earth, and the rarely challenged mantra that this was the greatest country on earth. Small wonder that Hollywood had become the world's most successful purveyor of fantasy.

"American exceptionalism" was what they called it, with a hubris that was far from original. The Romans, the Chinese, the British—the list was long, and kept on lengthening. Hitler and his Nazis had also believed themselves crowns of creation, but the only exceptional thing about them had turned out to be a willingness to kill millions of people in cold blood. Russell remained hopeful that America would prove less homicidal in the long run, even when the fate of the country's original inhabitants, the still-infected wound of slavery, and a never-ending love affair with righteous violence—still winning child converts with each new TV Western—all suggested otherwise.

And maybe that wasn't the worst of it. What really got to Russell was the emotional shallowness and ludicrous profligacy. For all their friendliness and apparent openness, most Americans seemed determined to deny themselves any sense of responsibility for their fellow citizens or the world around them. Real love was reserved for family, friendship, or romance; a shriller, more abstract version for country, God, or sports teams. But in between, in the social realm, the lack of love and kindness poisoned everything. With a justice system that imprisoned too many, and a health-care system that served too few, a pervasive sense of insecurity was all but guaranteed. Deeply divided by wealth and race, Americans might put their trust in God, but outside the home they couldn't trust each other.

And this was the way of life which Uncle Sam was now successfully exporting to the rest of the world—not so much a beacon as a blight. Military power, economic power, cultural power—all reinforcing one another in support of the two big lies which defined the fabled American dream, that anyone could make it when clearly everyone couldn't, and that any personal and social handicaps a person was born with or into could invariably be overcome by sheer hard work and determination.

AFTER KEEPING HAYDEN HANGING FOR almost a month, Russell and Holleman took their concocted narrative to the FBI around the middle of August, when most of the men in the syndicate were making use of their yachts in one sea or another. The feds might have been more reluctant to listen if Russell's written account hadn't been simultaneously splashed across several big newspapers—that, and the fact that Holleman, despite his newly revealed mistakes, still possessed some residual clout, ensured they at least got a listen. And, for a short while at least, Russell was able to relish the sense of rattling people who really weren't used to being challenged.

It didn't last. Within days, the cabal's lawyers were erecting barriers to truth with an efficiency that Stalin and Beria would have envied. Nick Hayden was, of course, shown the door, but with enough in the way of financial and legal support to keep justice so far at bay that a criminal conviction was unlikely in Rosa's lifetime, let alone Russell's.

He had done all he could, and Holleman, rather to Russell's surprise, had come through in spades. And keeping Luke with his father felt some small atonement for leaving Hirth's son on the mountain.

BACK IN BERLIN, LOTTE AND Ströhm had both been "released" by BOB. Lotte had proved more sensible than Russell had expected, mostly thanks to Ströhm, whose status as a former comrade made him worth listening to. According to Thomas, Gerhard had advised her to profess ignorance when it came to anyone she wished to protect, but otherwise tell the truth. Confessing to the failures of the DDR would not be an endorsement of capitalism.

What most troubled Lotte was the fate of her friends in their ill-starred group, many of whom had been given twenty-year sentences. Werner was among them. "It's not that I was still in love with him," she'd told Effi over the phone in late July. "We'd more or less broken up before it happened. But I knew him, and the others, and for the next twenty years I'm going to wake up knowing they're all still in prison. How am I going to live with that?"

"Not easily," Effi had sympathised. "But we all wake up each day to so much injustice, and we either live with that knowledge or lie to ourselves. And hopefully on those rare occasions when it looks like something can be done, we manage to get out there and do it."

As the summer had turned to fall Lotte had seemed more accepting of her new situation, without making any obvious effort to find a new life for herself. She helped in the bookshop but otherwise mostly stayed home, reading or helping her mother in the kitchen and garden. Finding a new purpose in life would and should take time, Russell thought, hoping that whatever it was proved less all-consuming than the previous two. Her father was praying it wouldn't be religion.

The Ströhms, by contrast, were adapting faster than Russell had expected. Annaliese was enjoying being back at the Elisabeth Hospital, the children, after a short time grieving lost friends, happy enough at their new school. Gerhard, having turned down an offer from BOB to join "freedom's team," was busy redecorating Effi's old flat in Cramerstrasse, which had unexpectedly become available at just the right time. He was still slightly concerned that the Stasi might seek some sort of revenge for his defection, but everything he knew about his former comrades suggested they would rather forget his existence than put him back in the headlines. A preference he had hoped to reinforce by politely refusing all Western offers to really dish the dirt on Ulbricht and the others.

On the other hand, an account of his time in the anti-Nazi resistance would provoke a lot less paranoia in the East, and might even, according to Russell's publisher son, Paul, make Ströhm some money. If, by some miracle, BOB finally came through with the promised new passports, the world could still be his and his family's oyster. Giving up his dream had been a mighty wrench, but several months on he was in no doubt—he preferred this new life to the old one.

IN LATE SEPTEMBER EFFI WAS summoned to testify before a locally convened HUAC committee. The hearing in early October was public, which allowed Russell to attend, and to see for himself how Effi delivered the script they had cowritten in anticipation of the usual questions. And what a performance it was.

"Are you, or have you ever been, a member of the Communist Party?" the chairman asked.

"No."

"Have you ever associated with members of the Communist Party?"

"That would depend on what you mean by 'associated.'"

"Your husband was a member, I believe."

"He left the Party seven years before I started 'associating' with him," Effi replied to general laughter.

"Let me put it another way. Have you ever knowingly worked with Communists?"

"In theatre, cinema, and television we rarely have time for political discussions. In the anti-Hitler resistance I expect I did meet a few, but I couldn't be sure. Again, when you have real work to do"—Effi ran her gaze along the row of committee faces—"you don't sit around wondering who's a Communist and who isn't. You judge people by what they do, not by what books they might have read or whose company they kept ten years earlier. I might remind you that in Germany, under the Nazis, it was Communists who offered the most effective resistance. They were fighting Hitler in 1933, eight years before a Japanese attack forced the United States to take up arms against him."

"You have friends who are Communists?"

"That depends on what you mean by communists. If you mean supporters of the Soviet Union, then no, I haven't. If you mean people who believe in regulating private enterprise for the common good—like, say, Theodore Roosevelt or FDR—then yes, I do."

"Would you please name these individuals?"

"No, I will not. The names of my friends are none of your damn business. Would you name all your friends in government and business, so we can see who you've been bought by, and who you really serve? Because it certainly isn't the ordinary people of this or any other state."

"That's enough, Madame. I . . ."

"I think you represent the worst of America, sir. People who call themselves Christians, yet never show any Christian kindness, because their one true God is money. People who prattle on about freedom, but only because they can use it to exploit their fellow man. People who cling to a system of racial discrimination and oppression that most civilised countries would shrink from. People who . . ."

At that point her mike cut out, and the cameras started flashing.

"I assume that was my last Hollywood performance," she told the waiting press outside, "and I wanted it to be a good one."

THREE WEEKS LATER THE MAN who'd been chosen as Holleman's replacement won the special election, and business as usual—a phrase that seemed to Russell more ominous with each passing year—could be resumed. Money had spoken and money had answered—why rock such a well-stocked boat? Even so, the majority was significantly down, and Russell could only hope that the glimpse he and Holleman had offered of how things actually worked in LA had played a part in reducing it. A few crumbs of comfort were better than none.

There were few to be had where Chavez Ravine was concerned. Poulson's mayoral victory had killed off the idea of using the confiscated land for public housing, but the new mayor couldn't stop the city council from decreeing that the area be reserved for public use, which effectively saw off those developers interested in building luxury private estates. So, as Russell saw it, Holleman's old sponsors would be spending the next few years desperately seeking a definition of "public use" that would allow them to make a lot of money. A new major league baseball stadium was already being mooted, although how that met a public need was a moot point in itself. "Try asking women that question" as Rosa succinctly put it.

In the meantime a few of Cesar's neighbours were still refusing to leave, and the bully-boys who'd killed him were waiting to see who their next employers would be.

The news from abroad was no better. The new Beria-less Soviet leadership seemed cautiously inclined to reform, which Russell suspected was akin to tugging on a stray woollen thread in a sweater—soon the whole damn thing would unravel. In East Germany, according to Ströhm, the prospect of any progressive changes had receded since the uprising, and the numbers heading West through the reopened city border were rising rather than falling. Ströhm thought Ulbricht would need to either dig a moat or build a wall if he wanted to keep his workforce.

Outside the Soviets' new and rapidly coagulating empire,

America increasingly held sway. In August, with a little help from their British equivalents, the CIA had ejected the democratically elected Mossadegh government of Iran, after the latter had cheekily laid claim to its own oilfields. The old Shah's exiled son had since been brought in as a stooge-cum-figurehead and looked about as stable as the new rabble in the Kremlin.

The Korean War had ended in July, but without any settlement, and a wider conflict seemed on the cards in Indochina, where the French, with increasing American help, were still trying to preserve their colonial rule against a Communist-led liberation army. That fall they had, for reasons best known to their general staff, dropped their elite paratrooper units into an isolated provincial capital named Dien Bien Phu. On reading that the town's surrounding hills were now occupied by the Communist Vietminh, Russell found himself remembering John Steinbeck's observation on the German occupation of Norway, that "the fly had conquered the flypaper."

Meanwhile, America's favourite new ally Israel seemed determined to cast itself as a pariah, proving the old saw that those abused were inclined to ape their abusers. In October an officially sanctioned raid into Jordan did to the Arab village of Qibya what the Nazis had done to so many Jewish hamlets in Poland and Russia.

There were, of course, some better tidings. The French had shut down the notorious Devil's Island, albeit before Russell got round to offering Paris a list of those he wanted sent there. A young Cuban named Fidel Castro had led a quixotic attack on a government barracks and made his mark in court with a suitably defiant speech. Even the new Soviet hydrogen bomb could qualify as welcome news, since nuclear equality bred mutual deterrence and made another world war less likely. That it would also probably encourage a proliferation of small ones was admittedly unfortunate, but nothing was ever perfect.

IN DECEMBER, RUSSELL, EFFI, AND Rosa moved to New York City, exchanging Hollywood's eternal summer for the snows of a northern winter. Effi had won a good part in an off-Broadway show, and Rosa was more than willing to give the city a try before she chose her art school for the following fall. Zarah was upset but resigned, and relieved it wasn't Berlin or London. Ali was delighted.

Another good reason for the move was the serendipitous retirement of the New York–based American correspondent of Russell's existing German employers, and their offering him the job. Who, he asked himself, could want more than the chance to share one's knowledge and opinions with people who lacked the time, experience, or education to work the world out for themselves? And get paid for doing it!

New York City was also growing on him. The constant buzz sometimes brought back memories of Berlin in the twenties, which he hoped was not an omen. The racial diversity was certainly different, and if racism here was still rampant, the city still seemed torn between segregation and the melting pot. Violently so at times, creatively so at others. Russell found himself increasingly drawn to new music, and when Effi was working and Rosa out with friends he would often spend the evening listening to jazz on Fifty-Second Street or the increasingly politicised folk music down in the Village.

To say he was happy might be stretching things a tad. The older one got, the fact that life led only to death was bound to get depressing. And anyone shackled, as Russell was, to a gut sense of injustice was doomed to spend much of his time pissed off. Nor did throwing truth at a wall of lies and having it just bounce back offer much in the way of job satisfaction, but you had to do it anyway. He as a journalist, Effi as an actor, Rosa as a visual artist—they were all fighting the same battles.

There was a line in Eliot's *Waste Land* which had always spoken to him—"These fragments I have shored against my ruins." He could only guess at Eliot's meaning, but he knew how the line applied to him. In a world that seemed sicker by the decade, there was still a gorgeous sunrise, a last-minute winner, a piece of music that took your breath away. There was laughter with friends, a son who would soon be a father, a love and life shared with someone quite wonderful. These were Russell's fragments, shoring him up as he approached old age. And standing in the gently falling snow on Rockefeller Plaza that Christmas Eve with Effi and Rosa he felt as happy as anyone had a right to be.

Looking at the huge, brightly lit conifer, he remembered the pathetic little tree someone had brought into their trench in 1917, and how they had all huddled around it, trying to warm themselves up with some dreadful hot drink and their own appalling singing. Many of his companions that night hadn't lived to see the peace. They would never get to hear about Stalin or Beria or experience a Great Depression, never hear the word "Nazi," or suffer through another war only to find that their hard-won freedom had McCarthy and a reborn Klan lying in wait for them. "Strange Fruit" indeed.

More to the point they would never know lasting love, never get the chance to realise whatever potential they had. Whereas he . . .

He was the luckiest of men, Russell thought, leaning his head into Effi's hair and gently squeezing her shoulder.

Acknowledgments

Many thanks to everyone at Soho Press, particularly my editors Juliet Grames, Nick Whitney and Rachel Kowal.